The Side Project

by

Laurel Osterkamp

Chrissy,
 HeRe's to
finding ouR HEAs!
♡
J Osterkamp

Dedication

"I believe that what we become depends on what our fathers teach us at odd moments, when they aren't trying to teach us. We are formed by little scraps of wisdom."

— Umberto Eco

For my father. Thank you for your huge generosity and the little scraps of wisdom. I miss you every day.

Chapter 1

Rylee

I sniff the cuff off my dad's old flannel shirt, hoping for a hint of his ivory soap and pine scent. But who am I kidding? He's been gone for over ten years. Instead, I get a whiff of my orange spice hand cream as the classroom behind me comes to life.

In a parallel universe, my dad would teach this graduate-level fiction writing course.

No. In a parallel universe, my not-dead dad would have moved to California and won a Booker for his next Great American Novel. Instead, he's left me to achieve that dream. And I will, even if my path has more twists and bumps than I want it to.

Glancing around the room, I try to calm those first day-of-school jitters. My eyes are drawn to the window, and outside the sun on the lake is so bright and beautiful that it hurts to look. I focus on my professor instead.

Professor Aldrich stands behind the lectern, her tall, thin frame balancing on a stool as she clutches the edges of the wood with her ringed fingers. She clears her throat.

"Welcome, everyone. I'm Professor Aldrich. In this class, you will learn how to write fiction."

I smile at her, eager for more. And yet, I'm not a novice at fiction writing. Still, here I am, in my familiar alma mater in the small Northern Minnesota town I've lived in all my life and where flannel is always in fashion.

"Let's start by discussing what makes a piece of fiction stand out," Professor Aldrich says. "Anyone can tell a story, but what makes that story unique and interesting? Is it the plot, characters, and dialogue? Or is something else at play?"

A couple of my classmates respond. Professor Aldrich dives into the importance of vivid language and strong author tone and point of view. As she speaks, she tucks a few stray strands of gray hair back into her bun. She pauses. The ambitious students are already taking notes.

"Here's the shocking thing about fiction writing," Professor Aldrich adds. "You must be willing to expose your innermost thoughts and feelings, take risks, and make yourself vulnerable."

Suddenly, her finger snags on one of her long gold dangling earrings. She pulls, and it becomes entangled with the scarf around her neck. Panicked, Professor Aldrich tries to free it.

Everyone freezes. Is this part of the lesson? Maybe she's showing how something small can escalate. How every action has an equal and opposite reaction.

A calm, deep voice from the back echoes, as if coming from a much larger space than this classroom affords. "Don't move!"

Before I can place why I recognize the voice, a young man bounds up to Professor Aldrich. And I may as well scrape my jaw off the floor. It's none other than Carson Meyers coming to her rescue.

"Let me help," he says. "I don't want you ripping your earlobe in two."

He gently but firmly pulls the scarf away, freeing the

earring. A collective gasp of relief passes through the room of around twenty students.

"Oh my gosh, thank you!" Professor Aldrich beams at him. "You're a hero."

Carson's cheeks go pink. He says, "No problem," before returning to his seat. Class goes on. Except my heart has stopped.

Back in high school, Carson had it all: looks, charm, compassion, and intelligence. He'd even been accepted into Harvard. But that fell through, and now he's a science teacher at Bemidji High. My mind races with questions like it's a game show host on speed. How is he here today? Shouldn't he be lecturing bored teenagers about mitochondria? And why didn't Mel, my best friend and Carson's younger sister, say that he enrolled in my grad program?

I shouldn't care, but I had a huge crush on Carson Meyers a million years ago (okay, more like ten). I thought he'd be my happily-ever-after.

And how's this for irony? Because my father died so young, I don't even believe in Happily Ever Afters.

They only exist between the pages of romance novels. Trust me—I'm an expert: I've read hundreds, I wrote three, and I'm working on my fourth. But I learned the difference between truth and fiction a long time ago.

And while the heroines I craft are fearless, clever, and wise, never succumbing to cringeworthy moments or bad hair days, that's not me. I dye my mousy brown locks every four weeks (shade IN1, dark intense indigo). Oh, and I'm scared to admit I'm a romance author because if I ever make it to graduate school in California, all my peers and writers of legit literary fiction will laugh me out of the MFA program. That's why I use a pen name.

Professor Aldrich has recovered from her earlobe trauma and is back to addressing the class.

"What do you all say? Which element of fiction is most important when crafting a new piece?"

I guess Carson's invigorated by his heroic act because he speaks up first. "Setting," he states with confidence. "It's for sure setting."

"Setting?" Professor Aldrich tilts her head in question. "That's an unusual response. Tell me more."

He drums his pencil against his desk, tapping out a gentle melody as he elaborates on his thoughts. "Place informs everything about who we are and what we need. It defines character and conflict."

Professor Aldrich scans the room, locking eyes with anyone who meets her gaze. "I see. Do others share this opinion?"

"Not at all." I push back my shoulders and speak louder than I intend to.

"Really?" Professor Aldrich claps her hands. "Wonderful. Our first debate! Go on," she says to me.

"Okay," I respond, giving Carson a contrary glance. "I mean no disrespect, but it depends on the author. Like Ernest Hemingway. His stories could take place anywhere. It's the characters and conversations that drive the story forward."

Carson nods, perhaps to concede my point. "Are you a big Hemingway fan, Rylee?"

My cheeks burn. Back in high school, Carson and I often ran into each other in the media center because we're both book nerds. He never judged me for checking out historical romances, and I never asked how a guy who planned to attend Harvard had time for so many science fiction novels.

And never once did either of us check out anything by Hemingway.

I scan my brain for a deft response. To be honest, I find Hemingway's work way too alpha male. "He's okay."

Carson's large glasses slid down his nose, so he pushes them back up. "Just okay? Why are you using him to prove your point?"

"I wasn't trying to prove a point. I have no point."

"Yeah, you do."

"No, I don't!"

A girl sitting next to Carson bats her comically long false eyelashes at him. Then she addresses me. "Maybe your point is that when novels rely on setting and use lots of descriptions and adjectives, they aren't as good as books with a *less is more* vibe." She shifts back to Carson, the corners of her lips pulling into a satisfied smirk. "Right?"

Carson answers her with a raised eyebrow, and they totally share a moment, which totally makes me want to puke.

"Wait, hang on. Don't put words in my mouth." I'd bet major cash that my cheeks have turned pink, and I'm nervous to meet Carson's gaze. But I do it anyway.

He wears his benevolence like a badge of honor, and his voice fills the room. "Sorry. I didn't mean to offend you. It's just… I remember the sort of books you used to read."

Studying his expression, I search for a hint of sarcasm. "Books I used to read? Like what?"

Like books with a certain look about them. Bright covers, shiny with the author's name in purple cursive.

The title in red letters on a white background, evoking a sense of romance, a promise of passionate love that will last forever.

With a shrug, Carson replies, "Like with lots of detailed descriptions and all that."

Should I be grateful he didn't say more, or annoyed he put me in this position? None too soon, Professor Aldrich breaks in.

"How about this? Forget about labels for books and writing. Focus instead on the power of using words to bridge gaps and bring people together." She takes a steadying breath. "Call me a romantic, but I believe that the written word has the power to heal, connect, and push us forward. Writing fiction is like starting a new relationship. We'll achieve more by taking risks and laying ourselves bare."

For some weird reason, my chest tightens as Professor Aldrich speaks. I fixate on the desk in front of me, determined not to look at Carson.

"That said," Professor Aldrich continues, "in this class, you will work in pairs and beta-read for each other. If there's someone with whom you'd like to partner up, let me know. Otherwise, I'll assign you." She scans the room for questions, but there are none. "Let's review the syllabus."

After the rest of the first day nuances, class ends, and I pack up my stuff, sliding my laptop into my backpack.

"Hey," I hear from behind me.

I turn and find Carson standing about six inches away. His glasses, his tufty hair sticking out, and the gray Henley over his white V-neck T-shirt (he still wears those T-shirts) give him a lumberjack/geek-chic look that I wish wasn't so appealing.

I stop short of smiling. "Hi."

"How are you, Rylee?"

He grins, his eyes crinkling in that trademark way that made him his graduating class superstar.

We've exchanged a few words, and already it's like my lungs are squeezing together. There was a time when a conversation between Carson and me didn't compare to a tooth extraction, but that was before the B.A.I. (That's what I call it in my mind: *The Big Awful Incident*.)

Ten long years and we've barely spoken, besides generic pleasantries. Still, I bet he doesn't remember that day as I do—like a living nightmare. So, I shrug and say, "I'm good. How are you?"

False Eyelash Girl stands nearby. Her mouth is half-open. I assume she's waiting for a chance to talk to Carson, eager to ask him if he'll pair up with her.

"I'm doing great," Carson answers. "Hey, I have a question for you."

"Cool. Maybe I'll have an answer."

Carson's gaze darts to the side like he senses False Eyelash Girl is ready to pounce, and I wonder if he even heard me. "Would you like to be partners?"

I wait for the punch line, but it doesn't come. Glancing down at his ring finger, I see it's bare. Mel told me he and Dana split up. While my bestie never mentioned that Carson enrolled in my fiction writing program, she has kept me up to date about her brother getting married and now filing for divorce.

Forming words right now is rough. I say, "You want to work with me?" He peers at me with his deep brown eyes, as if that action alone will answer my question.

"Why?"

Carson takes a step closer, near enough that his subtle cologne lingers in the air. He lets out a soft laugh and shuffles his feet. It's almost like he's shy, but come on. He's no blushing flower. "Because Mel says you're a talented writer." Sheepish, he scratches the back of his neck as he confesses. "And um…you'd challenge me."

Then the revelation dawns—he talked about me with Mel?! When did that happen? Before I can blink twice, my already racing heart pounds against my ribcage. I meet his eyes again, this time unwavering.

"You're damn right I'll challenge you."

"Is that a yes?"

I consider my options. If I say no, he'll for sure think I still harbor feelings for him, that I never got over my schoolgirl crush. Besides, who else am I going to work with? Carson is smart, and he's always been a conscientious student, good enough to get into Harvard, even if he never went.

I could do a lot worse than Carson Meyers as a writing partner.

"Fine," I respond. "Let's tell Professor Aldrich."

False Eyelash Girl's face sags, but in the next instant she adopts a pinched expression and glares at me.

"Great." Carson glances at his watch. "I need to get to school. Do you mind telling her for both of us? I'll email later to confirm."

"Yeah, of course."

"Great, thank you." He slings his messenger bag over his shoulder. "See you soon."

Carson moves through the classroom door.

"He's getting a divorce, and he also has a kid," I say to False Eyelash Girl. "I'd stay away if I were you."

She scowls and stomps off. And, after telling Professor Aldrich that Carson and I want to work together, I head out, as well.

Chapter 2

Carson

I'm standing in the grade school parking lot, eyes riveted to the entrance. Above the door hangs an enormous sign: *Welcome Back, Dragons!* Their friendly, non-fire-breathing mascot is painted on the sign, waving and welcoming new students. That makes me even more impatient to see my son.

Today has been like riding a roller coaster at a snail's pace. The slow climbs and plunges irritate my stomach more than they should. Plus, there was the shock of seeing Rylee Lynch again. Back in high school, her huge ocean-blue eyes sort of freaked me out. And yet, her '90s-era pixie-grunge style drew me in, with her shiny black hair, narrow shoulders always squared, and those tiny wrists adorned with rows and rows of bracelets.

Now, I clench my jaw and kick the pavement. Christ. Is Eddie's school holding the kids hostage? Just when I'm convinced I'll have to storm the building like some badass action hero, the doors open, and there's Eddie, strolling out, wearing a wide grin and an oversized backpack.

I wave, and Eddie runs over to me, giving me a hug and a kiss on the cheek.

"Hey, Dad!" he says, beaming.

"Hey there, buddy!" It's like that belt clenched

around my heart loosens three notches. "How was your first day of school?"

"Good! Miss McCormick is nice, and I have recess with Noah and Mason."

"That's great. Should we go get ice cream and celebrate?"

"Yeah! Let's go!"

I open the door of my hand-me-down Jeep, helping my son in and buckling him into the booster seat he resents still needing. As we drive off, heading out toward Ice Cream Heaven, I glance back, taking a second to admire him in the rearview mirror. Eddie has been my true north since the moment he was born. And right now, he's happy and healthy, despite what Dana and I are going through. Plus, the sun is shining, and the air is gentle and sweet as we drive.

"Can we have pizza tonight for dinner?" Eddie asks.

"You're having dinner with your mom," I answer. "I have the High School Open House tonight, remember?"

"Oh. But this morning, Mom said you were feeding me dinner."

Great, I seethe to myself. *Dana forgot.*

"What's wrong, Dad?"

"Nothing. Everything's fine."

When we reach Ice Cream Heaven, we find a spot in the parking lot and hop out. Eddie shivers, and I realize the afternoon has grown chilly.

"Where's your jacket, bud?"

"At home."

I remove my Henley and hand it to Eddie. "Here, put this on."

We enter the ice cream parlor, which is full of

people, but I find a spot at the counter. I order a double scoop of strawberry ice cream, while Eddie opts for a chocolate cone.

"Dad," Eddie says, his voice thoughtful. "What's your favorite reptile?"

"Probably chameleons."

"Chameleons are cool," Eddie says. "But I really like dogs. Dogs are awesome."

I chuckle. "Dogs aren't reptiles."

Eddie licks his ice cream, a brown streak forming on his chin. "*Duh.*" He speaks with exaggerated patience. "I'm just saying I like dogs, and we should get one."

Sly little devil. "I don't know, Eddie." But I *do* already know. If I get him a dog, Eddie will want to stay over at my house as often as possible.

We leave the shop, and somehow I'm content despite my chaotic life. No, I'll never trust another woman enough to fall in love—not after what Dana did to me. And I'm stuck in Bemidji, employed at the high school where I graduated and where my mom is my colleague. Where I can't do online dating without becoming a headline in the local newspaper.

That's how it will be until Eddie goes to college. But that's okay, as long as he and I are together.

As I climb back into my Jeep, Rylee slides her way back into my thoughts. I wonder if her presence is good, bad, or something in between.

Chapter 3

Rylee

I love the ten-minute walk home from campus, with its dazzling view of Lake Bemidji and all the tree leaves transitioning from green to yellow. The sun warms the back of my neck, giving the faint taste of summer. Yet the crisp air promises autumn—my favorite season—with apple cider donuts, sitting outside under blankets, and dogs wearing bandanas.

It's so beautiful out that I resist texting Brandon. Poor kid. Sometimes I'm less like his older sister, and more like a mini-storm cloud that hovers over his head.

I've tried to shelter him from unnecessary pain. Dad's death was this unexpected hurricane sweeping through our lives, leaving nothing untouched. Brandon was eight, still too young to truly understand. For months, his eyes gleamed with hope every time the front door creaked open.

Meanwhile, I grew up fast. That's when I started calling my mother by her first name. "Hey, Summer," I'd say, like we were roommates.

That must have confused Brandon even more.

For him, our mother was Mom, a definitive authority figure, but also that lady who couldn't hold back tears when she tucked him in at night. So rather than her putting him to bed, Brandon and I stayed up late, whispering shared memories of Dad.

I'll admit. I've been a bit extra. But I learned to back off—until Brandon started getting headaches.

At first, Summer and I dug our heads in the sand, determined that it was nothing. We told him to drink more water and take ibuprofen.

The day that changed everything started like a semi-normal Saturday. Summer breezed into the kitchen, her lilting voice tinkling in the same tone as her bangle bracelets. "Ilsa called. She has a stomach bug. I need to take all her clients today."

"Does that mean you'll work until closing? I thought we were spring cleaning."

Summer kissed me on the cheek. "Sorry. But I can count on you to get it done, right?"

"Do I have a choice?"

She laughed like I'd made a joke, even though we both knew I was pissed. "You're my superstar, Rylee." Grabbing her crocheted purse, she traipsed out through the garage door.

"Hey," I said to Brandon. "Do you want to clean the bathroom, kitchen, or garage? Your choice."

He scowled. "None of the above. I have a headache."

"You always have a headache." I figured he was being dramatic, but a couple of hours later, I realized how wrong I was.

We were in the kitchen, me leaning into the refrigerator with a bucket and sponge, wiping down the shelves. I paused, stood up straight, looked at Brandon, and gasped.

"What?" he said.

I inhaled like I was being chased. "Brandon, you're cross-eyed."

Brandon's mouth dropped open, and for a second, I thought he might smile and accuse me of messing with him. But he turned around, rushed to the downstairs bathroom, flicked on the light, and gazed into the vanity mirror.

Brandon took in his wandering left eye and said, "What the fuck?"

I figured I should keep him calm. "Perhaps you're having an allergic reaction to something?"

"But I didn't eat anything weird," he said.

No way was this normal, and I couldn't pretend that it was.

"I'll call the nurse line."

I was on hold, and it took forever for them to put me through, but then I told a nurse about Brandon's symptoms, including the headache, seeing double, and suddenly becoming cross-eyed.

"Go to the emergency room now," the nurse stated. "Don't wait."

I did as told.

"Aren't you going to call Mom?" Brandon asked as we buckled our seat belts.

I thought about how Summer acted after Dad died. How she became fragile, as if a strong Bemidji wind might break her. Perhaps this would turn out to be nothing. "Nah. We'll fill her in later."

We got there around noon, checked in, and answered "no" when asked if this was a life-threatening emergency. As we sat in uncomfortable chairs, time moved like a line at the post office times a jillion, but finally, they called us in. An attending physician looked at Brandon's eyes, listened as he described his symptoms, and said, "Let's get an optometrist to check you out."

"On a Saturday?" I said. "I doubt we can see one before Monday morning."

The balding physician had long limbs and a matching long face, but he sort of shrank into himself. "I'm sorry, but this can't wait. I'm going to make some phone calls." He blinked twice. "How old are you?"

"Me?" My stomach flipped over. "Twenty-three. Why?"

"Where are your parents?"

Brandon answered. "My mom's at work, and my dad...isn't around."

"You should call your mother," the doctor said. "Please tell her to come as soon as she can."

He left the little closet they called an exam room, and I took out my phone. Before I lost my nerve, I punched out a text to Summer.

We're at the emergency room cuz Brandon's cross-eyed. The doctor's calling an optometrist now.

Summer called me back right away, and then she hightailed it to the hospital.

The optometrist arrived and ordered an MRI. A neurosurgeon came to consult. They decided Brandon needed surgery *that night*, or else he could become brain-damaged and/or permanently blind. It seems there was a mass dangerously close to Brandon's optic nerves. But they would not remove the mass yet. Instead, they'd put in a shunt to relieve the pressure.

Brandon spent his summer before senior year at the Mayo Clinic in Rochester, MN, having a second brain surgery to remove the tumor. They signed him up for five weeks of radiation. It was like five weeks of a siren blaring at half-volume. *This is only a test.* Except it was so much more.

However, there must be a merciful God. Because a couple of weeks ago, the doctors said he was cancer-free, which is reason to rejoice. And yet, Brandon's still tired all the time, and the emotional impact of the entire ordeal continues to take its toll. I can't help but worry.

Now, I turn the doorknob and enter my house through the back, but the door nearly swings off its hinges. "This house is falling apart," I mutter to myself, before hearing some soft popping and electronic sound effects.

"Hello? Brandon?"

I walk toward the living room, where the TV is on, and Brandon plays some video game with a guy running through a dilapidated building, shooting at scary-looking men.

"Why are you home and not at school?"

Brandon, my once ray-of-sunshine brother, scowls. "Why are *you* home and not at school?"

I stand in front of the TV and cross my arms over my chest.

"Rye!" Brandon raises his voice. "Get out of the way."

"No. Tell me why you skipped out on the first day!"

Shoulders sagging, he points at his head, which, okay, is a bit like a lumpy, misshaped kiwi. "Everyone will know I'm the freak with cancer."

I move from my spot and plop down on the couch next to my younger brother. "Sorry, Brandon."

He deflates and leans toward me, ever so slightly. "Don't worry, Rye. The first day is lame. We're in advisory for like, seven hours, playing team-building games and rereading the student handbook."

"Yeah, but aren't you excited to see all your friends?"

His face hardens. "Not really."

Is that because he doesn't have any friends? After two brain surgeries and five rounds of radiation the summer before his senior year, I can't help but wonder. Did he get dumped by all the people he used to hang out with because they didn't know what to say? I don't ask—I just pat Brandon's knee. "Okay, I won't tell Summer you were skipping. But promise me you'll go to school tomorrow and that you'll be your best self."

Brandon pivots toward me. "Seriously? My best self?"

"I'm one hundred percent serious."

A puff of breath. "Fine, I promise."

"Good." I pat his knee again and rise from the couch.

"Where are you going?"

"To my room." I stretch, trying to seem casual. "I have a few hours before work and thought I'd start writing."

"Already?" Brandon shakes his head. "Didn't you come from your first day of class?"

"I'm excited to get going."

I'm not lying, not exactly. I *am* excited to get going. So what if my writing isn't for class? It is creative.

At least, some readers would say it is.

Chapter 4

Rylee

I fling my bag onto my bed with its midnight blue satin comforter, a gift from my last birthday. Books—including all the new titles I've collected over the years, plus Dad's collection of old favorites from his shed—line the walls and shelves of my room.

Dad filled his shed with as many books as it could hold. Space heaters and lava lamps were there to stave off the chill, but nothing could combat that drafty air. On Saturday mornings, he'd bundle me in a flannel blanket and Uggs over my pajamas, before we sat together on two rickety wooden stools while eating cherry Pop-Tarts and swigging instant hot cocoa. He'd read me stories from different cultures—Chinese or South American fairy tales, tales of discovery and beauty.

But now I'm here, in my desk chair, pressing the spacebar to wake up my laptop. QKDP is the first thing I see—Quill & Key's Direct Publishing website is bookmarked as a favorite. It's where I keep track of all my self-published titles: *The Duke's Descent*, *Rescuing Lord Inglethorp*, and *A Confirmed Scoundrel*. I have another, *A Viscount for Vivien,* which I plan to release in a few months.

What can I say? Boredom and loneliness set in when my life veered off track. So I escaped to my first love: Regency romance novels.

When I was ten, Dad introduced me to Jane Austen, and that made me believe in happily ever after. Then came Babette Highland and other Regency romance authors, and I discovered whole new worlds of intrigue and romance. Once Dad was no longer with us, I'd spend Saturday mornings hiding under my flannel sheets with a flashlight and a paperback, reading about how love conquered all, and damsels being wooed by men of honor. College brought piles of classic novels and literary fiction, but nothing compared to what those books meant to me. After graduation, when everything fell apart, I returned to my favorite escape. And it hit me.

Hey, I could write this stuff.

My social life was as exciting as junk mail multiplied by losing Wi-Fi. Besides, I had so much time on my hands I considered growing new thumbs, just so I could twiddle them. Instead: three months to write it, two more to revise. I hired a proofreader and a formatter—and boom! I'm a published author, but I write under the pen name.

Shelby Simmons.

Shelby seems like a name for a scandalous Southern debutante—about as different from me as possible. And Simmons…well, it's alliterative and easy to remember. Almost as easy? Writing these romance novels under her name. My fingers press against my computer keyboard, spinning tales of passionate love. I live vicariously through my characters' grand balls, stolen kisses, and dramatic revelations. Each novel is a world of its own, helping me forget my mundane existence, if only for a while.

After spending a couple of hours pounding out the next Chapters of *A Viscount for Vivien,* I wind down because it's my first day at my new job, and I can't be late.

I arrive at Reynolds Resort as the sun sets, and an orangey glow casts itself over the lake. Fall is truly beautiful up here, a special kind of vibrance that makes me want to wear chunky sweaters, attend tailgating parties, and walk through piles of fallen leaves. And the air always smells like some combo of burning firewood and baking bread.

The lit windows of the lodge beckon. I make my way up the cobblestone path and try to subdue the jumping nerves in my stomach. It's only a temporary job in my hometown, but first days always rattle me. Nevertheless, I walk into the lobby and march right up to the front desk.

"Hi," I say to the young woman sporting a *Reynolds Resort* jersey. "I'm starting work here today."

The left side of her mouth creeps into a half-smile that doesn't come close to meeting her eyes. "Are you Rylee?"

"Yes, that's me."

"Right. There's been a change of plans."

"I'm sorry?"

She smiles with her entire mouth now, and somehow, that seems even less sincere than the half-smile she gave me moments ago.

"We're all good here at the front desk. You're not needed."

Something inside me nosedives. I grip the edge of the desk that this girl sits behind.

"I'm fired before I even start?"

Her laughter crinkles like aluminum. "No, silly. They want you in the restaurant."

"Huh?"

"They're short-staffed in the restaurant." She points to her left. "Go that way. Ask for Dana."

Crap.

Mumbling, "Thank you," I turn towards the restaurant. I take one step and then another. Dana Reynolds stands at the counter. She's always been beautiful, and I experience a pang of jealousy. I'm also hit with panic and an existential crisis, but only because she and I have bad blood.

Well, that's probably nothing compared to the bad blood she has with Carson. Talk about baggage and history.

You don't have to do this, my inner voice cries out. And yet, that isn't quite true.

Reynolds Resort pays more than any other service industry gig in town. Between Brandon's medical bills and, hopefully, his college tuition (please God, let him be well enough to go to college), I should make as much money as I can.

I approach where Dana stands. No wonder Carson once gave up everything to be with her.

She has huge aqua eyes the size of sand dollars, long, chestnut hair hanging in a straight silk curtain, and the height and frame of a runway model. I guess their kid was bound to win the genetic lottery. With Carson's intelligence and Dana's determined personality, he'll have looks, smarts, and drive. The complete package.

"Dana?" I feign uncertainty, thinking she won't recognize me. She glances up from her computer screen, which must contain the restaurant's reservation system. Her mouth forms a perfect "O," and I envy her knack at unintentional charm.

"Hi, I'm Rylee. We've met before, but I doubt you remember. I heard you need me in the restaurant?"

Dana's lips slide into the territory between a grin and a frown. "Of course, I remember you, Rylee." She sniffs, and her nostrils flare. "Have you ever hosted before?"

I square my shoulders. "No, but I'm a quick learner."

Dana raises her eyebrows, perhaps in skepticism or maybe in respect. "Alright. I'll show you the ropes." She glances at her watch. "This isn't the best time to train you in, but since it's a weekday, we should be okay. Shadow me, alright?"

"Sure."

We go through the reservation system and the table map, with the four tops and so on. "Each server has their own section," Dana says. "Try not to overload anyone. We want even distribution. Got it?"

"Of course."

A semi-tense, awkward moment passes. "It's your job to light the candles at each table," she says. "You'll also make sure there's a constant supply of silverware wrapped in our napkins. Come on, I'll show you."

She takes me through the dining room, and we make sure each table has a scalloped glass jar with a lit votive candle inside. With the lights dimmed, the vast picture windows offer a view of the marina and the lake, almost like moving paintings.

The dinner rush is fully underway when Carson arrives, an adorably scruffy boy trailing him. Dana looks up and sees her ex with their son in tow.

"Buddy!" she says to the boy. "What a surprise! I thought you were hanging out with Dad tonight."

"He's got work," he replies.

Dana and Carson's son is practically swimming in an oversized shirt, the sleeves flapping down to his ankles. I realize it's the gray Henley that Carson wore this morning to class. Now Carson has on only a white T-shirt and jeans. He must be freezing.

Maybe I can warm him up a little.

The uninvited idea pops into my brain, and I picture rubbing Carson's bare, taut arms, trying to smooth away his gooseflesh and create friction.

I banish the rebellious idea before it spins out of control.

"I told you I have my school open house tonight. You know teachers can't bring their kids," Carson says to Dana. "And I asked you to pick Eddie up by six thirty."

"No…" Dana's voice goes deep as she expands one syllable into several. "You didn't."

"Yes, I did," Carson says through clenched teeth. "But it doesn't matter." He digs his hands into his pants pockets. "I'm late, and I still need to go home and change."

"Do you want your shirt back, Dad?"

Carson crouches down and meets his son's eyes. "No, that's okay. But you and Mom need to pack a jacket next time, okay?"

Dana flexes her fingers like she longs to make a fist. "Everything is always my fault, right? How am I supposed to take care of Eddie while I'm working? You're not the only one with obligations."

Carson stands. "Don't put words in my mouth, Dana. I don't have time for this."

"You'd better make time," Dana says, as she crosses

her arms over her chest.

Sniffing and blinking, Eddie looks back and forth between his mom and dad.

"Hey, how about I watch Eddie?" I try to make eye contact with Carson, but he acts like he doesn't recognize me.

"Great! Thanks so much!" Dana responds. "You can take him in the back and hang out there."

"I don't need a babysitter," Eddie states. "I'm fine by myself."

"Sorry, bud. But the last time you said that, you ran off."

"Mom, I went for a walk."

I speak to this kid who's like a tiny version of my brother. "Hi, Eddie. I'm Rylee. Do you like evening walks? Because I love them, and hey, maybe you can show me around the resort? I'm new here, and I could use an orientation."

Eddie takes me in, trying to assess if I'm legit. After a moment, he says, "I don't know what orient-tion is, but I can show you my favorite spots."

"That'd be wonderful. Thank you!"

"You're welcome." He's still so boyish, yet I can hear the well-mannered man waiting to emerge. "Let's go." He waves to Carson. "Bye, Dad."

Eddie marches away, and I assume I should follow. I glance at Dana and say, "We'll stay on the property, and I'll check back soon. Should I give him dinner? Has he eaten?"

I direct that last question at Carson. He blinks once. "Yeah." His voice is flat. "Eddie's eaten."

Carson's eyes lock with mine, and something stirs behind them, but perhaps it's the perpetual motion of his spinning brain. I shouldn't take such offence, and I'm annoyed that I do.

A couple walks up to the hostess stand and asks Dana for a table. She picks up two thick menus and leads them into the dining room.

Eddie, who must have noticed I wasn't following right behind him, comes charging back. "Are you coming…" Eddie addresses me. "What's your name again?"

"It's Rylee," Carson answers, and my body temp rises.

Is it because he said my name?

"Be good for Rylee, okay, bud?"

Crap. It happened again. I'm heating up like a cup-o'-soup left in the microwave too long, and I might splatter everywhere.

Eddie rushes at Carson and wraps his arms around his waist, squeezing tight. "I love you, Dad."

Carson returns the hug, arching his torso so his chest meets his son's head. "I love you too. And you'll see me tomorrow, okay?"

"But Mom said—"

"Don't worry about what Mom said. Okay?"

"Okay." Eddie tightens his grip.

"Bud, I have to go."

Ever so gently, he pushes Eddie away.

"Eddie," I say, "can you show me the dock?"

Eddie sniffs back some more tears but says, "Yeah. Come on, Rylee."

I follow, but as I walk past Carson, he reaches out and grasps my forearm.

"Thank you," he mouths.

When he looks down at his hand holding my arm,

he lets go like he's touched a hot stove. But for a long time, it's like his fingers are still against my skin.

Chapter 5

Carson

The parent/teacher open house drags on until eight p.m. Right before it's over, my mother enters my classroom. "Hey, sweetheart. I haven't seen you all day, so I thought I'd stop in and say hello." She scans the space, taking in the new posters I hung on the walls. "I like this DNA double helix painting. Where'd you find it?"

Mom's the high school media specialist. She's always on the lookout for new, intellectually stimulating ways to decorate the library, and she's a big fan of visual learning.

"I found it in the science department resource room," I say. "You'd be amazed at all the discarded stuff in there."

"Hmm. Maybe I should explore. Can you let me in tomorrow?"

Dammit. I should have seen this coming. "Mom, there's probably nothing that's right for the media center's walls. Don't you want posters about books and reading?"

Mom scowls, but lets it go. She used to run the media center where Mel and I went to elementary school. Six years ago, she transferred to the high school. That same fall, I was hired as a biology teacher at Bemidji High. It wasn't easy, going to grade school with my mom every day, but it's worse, having her as a co-worker. Sorta hard to establish my own identity with her hovering around, contributing opinions and a can-do spirit that blurs the line between professional advice and maternal interference.

"How was your grad class this morning?" she asks, combing her fingers through her cropped silver hair. "Did it go well?"

Mom doesn't understand why I'm rearranging my schedule to spend time in a classroom as a student instead of as a biology teacher. Why I've agreed to no prep hour and running the after-school homework center on Mondays, all so I can learn how to become a real writer.

"It was good," I say. "Lots of opportunities for creativity."

"You're a scientist. Why do you need to be creative?"

I don't tell her about my dream of becoming a best-selling science fiction novelist, because the odds of that happening are about as high as getting hit by a meteor. But I'm desperate for a change.

"Because, Mom, I'm going for a license in English as well as Science. That will give me more options."

"Okay." She smooths out a crease in her cardigan. "Options are good."

"Yeah." I glance at my watch. Time to go. "Thanks for checking in, Mom. I'm going to head home. See you tomorrow?"

"See you tomorrow." She hugs me, and I lean into it, just for a moment.

On my way out to the parking lot, I ask myself why I lied. I guess after telling her so many colossal lies, little ones are more apt to escape. Truth is, I'm not going home, not yet. Hockey drop-in ends at nine p.m., which gives me enough time. Since high school, skating has been my escape. Tonight, I need it more than ever.

I pull up to the rink in my old Jeep, grabbing my skates from the trunk.

What a day.

Soon my skates carve into the ice, which is like an elixir, numbing my anxiety. Somehow, the last twenty-four hours seem more benign.

Except for what transpired with Rylee.

I lap the rink again and again.

She must think I'm a total asshole after how rude I was to her tonight. But Dana has a temper, and a fierce jealous streak. I can't let her punish Rylee for her connection to me. How the universe keeps bringing Rylee back into my life, I do not understand.

Meanwhile, Dana refuses to acknowledge it's her fault our marriage is over. Sure, technically, I'm the one who left, but she lied from the start. Then she cheated. And then she lied some more.

I could forgive her for all of it though, if it wasn't for her biggest lie of all time. She doesn't realize I'm privy to the truth; Eddie is not my biological son.

The ice beneath my blades is smooth, and my fingers grow numb since I didn't bring gloves. Crisp air stings my cheeks with each breath, but at least that smothered sensation is gone for now.

It started several months ago. When I came home in the middle of the day, I heard Dana with another man behind a closed door. My first instinct was to run, but I needed to assess this guy's genetics and figure out if he could be Eddie's biological dad. As fate would have it,

Eddie, who is dark-haired with a tanned complexion, has features nothing like the blond fellow who was in bed with Dana.

So I took matters into my own hands.

"Get the hell out!" I growled, and the guy moved fast for someone trying to pull his pants on as he ran. Then, I laid myself at Dana's feet like a sacrificial lamb.

"I'm leaving you," I told her. "You can have the house and everything. Just give me joint custody of Eddie."

Only a T-shirt covered her nakedness, and tears streamed down Dana's face as her lips trembled.

"No, Carson. You can't leave me! Please, I'm begging you. Don't!"

All I could do was walk away and let the silence answer her. Even now, I never want to have an honest conversation with Dana about Eddie's paternity. We must go on pretending that Eddie is my son forever.

As I skate, the lights above the ice rink blur into a gray-and-white dreamlike haze. The place is empty except for me, and I'm filled with a sense of peace. It's almost like lately, every decision I make doesn't have life-altering consequences.

I increase my speed and imagine I'm chasing a puck. The rink stretches out before me, and the boards loom tall on each side, creating a narrow corridor. My pretend hockey stick is poised for victory, and the only sound is my skates cutting through the ice.

He shoots! He scores!

I slow down to catch my breath, and I remember:

Tomorrow I should research getting a dog.

Chapter 6

Rylee

Wednesday. I don't return home from my classes until the afternoon. Brandon relaxes on the couch again. His school backpack lies on the floor nearby, and his kicked-off red canvas sneakers keep it company. Concrete evidence that he did not skip today.

"That backdoor needs to be rehung," I say, leaning against an armchair. "I told Summer to call Leo, but maybe I'll do the job myself before a strong wind rips the door off its hinges."

No response.

"How was your second day of school?"

He shrugs, not taking his eyes off the video game he's playing.

I sit next to him on the couch. "Do you like your classes? Do your teachers seem okay?"

"Sure, they're fine."

"Which is fine? The teachers or your classes?"

He gives me a flash of side eye. "Both."

"Anything interesting happen today? Hey. Do you have Mr. Abrams for AP Bio? I remember he made my senior year impossible. But he was an outstanding teacher."

From the TV, there's a muted explosion and then some electronic song of defeat. "Rye, look what you made me do."

"Sorry. But tell me about school."

With a resigned sigh, Brandon drops the video game controller and turns toward me. "Mr. Abrams retired. The new teacher is some young dude who graduated from there, like, a decade ago. Mr. Meyers."

"Oh." My mouth drops open in shock.

"What?"

"Nothing." I pat his knee and stand. "I'll let you get back to your game."

I almost say, *don't you remember, Brandon? You met Carson Meyers on the night Dad died.*

Hours later, I'm sitting with Mel on Bemidji Brewery's patio, sipping hard cider and savoring nachos. Our friendship began with alphabetical seating charts in grade school, but soon, teachers separated us for giggling too much. Even after all these years, she still gets me better than anyone else.

"Why didn't you tell me Carson enrolled in my grad program?"

Confusion clouds Mel's pretty face. She scrunches up her freckled nose. Her blonde waves turn heads, but she's no ditz. Mel earned a naturalist degree from Michigan State and now works at Itasca State Park, running family programs. Still, sometimes I wonder if her mind is so full of river water and geese migrating patterns that she's not always connected to the here and now.

Mel takes a gulp of beer and nods at the same time. "Oh yeah," she croaks out once her throat is clear. "I knew he was back taking classes, but not creative writing. That's weird. I'll have to ask him."

"It's heartwarming how close the two of you are."

"I've tried," she huffs, "but he's been focused on Eddie and Dana; there's little room for the rest of us."

"Sorry." Reaching out, I snag a chip, smothered in cheese and picante sauce, from our shared nacho platter. "It was sort of a surprise, seeing him in class. Very unexpected."

Mel shrugs and stares out at the lake. "Maybe he's all up in his feelings, with his failed marriage and broken dreams."

I chew slowly, allowing the flavors of the melted cheese and spicy sauce to fill my mouth before swallowing. "Right."

The wind picks up, blowing Mel's hair every which way. She tucks it behind her ear before reaching for her beer mug. She's about to take a drink when I blurt out, "What caused him and Dana to split up? Any ideas?"

The beer mug stops inches away from her mouth, frozen as if dipped in liquid nitrogen. Mel sets it down and glares at me. "Rylee, what's your deal? Please, tell me you don't have another crush on my brother."

My cheeks burn. "I don't have another crush on him," I murmur. "He's been everywhere lately. First, in my writing class, then at Reynold's Resort, and now he's Brandon's AP Bio teacher."

Mel cocks her head and scrutinizes me. "Is that going to be a problem for you? Seeing him often?"

"No!" I drag my finger down the side of my cider mug, letting beads of condensation drip at my touch. "Let's talk about something else."

Mel scooches her foot underneath the table towards mine, giving it a nudge. "I'm sorry, Rye. I wasn't trying to be bitchy. It's just, when you ask about Carson, alarm bells go off in my head."

"You don't have to worry. I promise that I've moved on."

"Okay," Mel says. "But what does that mean?"

"It means I have my sights set on a greener pasture—one with the Pacific Ocean, average daily temps above seventy degrees, and the best creative writing grad program in the nation."

"I see." My friend squints like she can see right through me. "And Jack? Does your beachfront pasture include a relationship with him?"

I open my mouth to give her an answer, but when I realize I don't have one, I snap it back shut.

Four years ago, I stood in the English department mixer when I first spotted Jack—a hipster type with sun-kissed skin and wheat-colored hair. He was cute, but out of my league. A few months later, I walked into the first day of my comparative lit class, and there he was—our TA.

On that first day, he asked each of us to share our favorite twentieth-century author. I silently debated whether to mention Babette Highland, a queen of the Regency Romance, but settled on Ava Barlow, citing her witty writing style and connection to fellow author Grace Palardy.

He rubbed his hands together like a magician preparing for a trick. "Barlow. Good choice." And my heart swelled at the modest praise.

He explained how Grace Palardy and her husband, Jacob Durtz, had this famous house in LA during the '70s, where a bunch of Hollywood and literary elite, Ava Barlow included, partied hard and produced art. "If I could time-travel anywhere, it would be to 1970s LA, to hang at the Palardy/Durtz house. Can you imagine anything cooler?"

Shaking my head no, I realized Jack wasn't just a cute hipster boy from the English department mixer.

He was a cute hipster boy from the English department mixer with dreams that mirrored my own.

I would stay after class and visit his office hours as often as possible without seeming like a stalker fangirl. We became friends, and he shared his goal of pursuing a PhD at USC, teaching at Stanford or UCLA, and taking part in that thriving literary community. It was the same dream my dad once had—moving somewhere warm to teach and write, surrounded by other writers.

Soon, Jack and I were a couple, spending nearly every night together, talking and reading or lying side by side in bed. But Jack finished his MFA program that spring and headed for California.

Before he left, I clung to him and sniffled, burying myself into his black turtleneck, which he wore despite the spring weather. But he had to go. And I had to let him.

I moved back home, delivered pizza for extra cash, wrote short fiction, and tried to get published in literary journals. Weeks and months went by, and Jack and I talked less and less. I applied for USC, was wait-listed, and then Brandon got his brain tumor diagnosis. By that point, Jack and I were officially no longer romantically involved. Except sometimes, he calls to bounce around ideas for his current novel.

I try not to get my hopes up it means anything.

Now, I look at my best friend and say, "Mel, Jack and I barely even talk."

Mel tilts her head to the side like a confused puppy. "Okaaay," she says, drawing out the second syllable, "but if you *are* still hung up on Jack, that's better than reigniting your crush on Carson."

"I don't have a crush on Carson. I'm curious why he's taking a writing—"

Mel puts her hand out in the stop gesture. "Rye, I'm telling you, *do not* fall for Carson. He's unavailable. Sure, he seems like this really sweet, wide-eyed guy, but he's got major issues."

"Don't worry, Mel. He asked me to be his writing partner for class, but—"

"He asked you to be his partner?" Mel leans in. "You said no, right?"

The fib slips out like oil on glass. "Of course I said no."

Moments after the lie, the truth sinks in: I need to contact Carson ASAP and tell him that our working together is a secret. But we haven't even exchanged phone numbers or email addresses yet.

Wait. Carson is Brandon's AP Bio teacher. That means I have a surefire way of contacting him and a great excuse for dropping by.

It's time for a visit to my old alma mater, Bemidji High.

Chapter 7

Carson

I stand before my class of AP Biology students, my gaze sweeping past the expectant faces and into the hallway. More kids filter in, some joke or share stories, while others hurry to get a seat. These advanced students want a challenge, and I relish their bright eyes, energy, and enthusiasm.

But there's a tall boy with a baseball cap pulled down low. Alone, head ducked, avoiding eye contact.

Brandon.

I have only had him in class for a few days, but already, the kid stands out. And it's not because he's recovering from a brain tumor. Brandon is clearly exceptional, with how he participates in class discussions and his written response to our icebreaker activity about electron microscopy.

I turn to the class.

"Hello, everyone. Let's get started."

I project the first slide of the day's information, and all the students listen and take notes. But Brandon exudes intensity as he leans forward, clutches his pen, and writes in quick, intense bursts. His brain waves must run at a higher frequency. I pause and look out over the class.

"Let's see how much you remember from yesterday's lesson." Hoping it's okay to single him out, I say, "Brandon, can you explain the difference between a prokaryotic cell and a eukaryotic cell?"

He furrows his brow. "A prokaryotic cell has no membrane-bound organelles, while a eukaryotic cell contains mitochondria, chloroplasts, and a nucleus." Tapping his fingers against his desk, Brandon bites his bottom lip. "Also, a prokaryotic cell has no nucleus or cytoplasmic organelles, just ribosomes and a plasma membrane."

"Very good."

The rest of the period passes quickly, and soon enough, I dismiss them to go to lunch. My eyes follow Brandon as he strides down the hall, alone.

Doesn't he have anyone to eat with?

As for me, I eat lunch at my desk and pull up the Bemidji Animal Shelter website. Each adoptable pet has a photo and a profile like they're on a dating service. After scanning through the available dogs, I spot a two-year-old retriever/mutt mix named Ferris. He looks straight out of a cartoon movie, with black fur, one pointy ear straight up and the other folded over, a huge nose, white muzzle and mouth, and a large pink tongue that must permanently hang outside his mouth. I swallow bites of my turkey sandwich and picture Eddie and me walking Ferris at Lake Bemidji and watching him bound in and out of the water, stick in mouth, tail wagging up a storm.

Hmm…

The Bemidji Animal Shelter is by appointment only. But they have open hours after school today. I call and set something up for four p.m. As soon as I hang up, an email comes through.

It's from Rylee.

Hi, Carson, it's Rylee Lynch. I'm emailing you

about my brother, who you have in class this semester. Can we please meet ASAP? I was hoping I could drop by this afternoon. I'd like to discuss my concerns.

Suddenly, I make the connection: Rylee and Brandon are siblings. That lost little boy who sat on the edge of my bed, refusing to cry after his father died, is now my most promising student.

I rub my forehead. I swig from my water bottle. I email Rylee back.

Of course. How's today at three? I have an appointment at four, but that should give us twenty minutes to talk. I'm in room 104.

Yes, she writes back. *You're in Mr. Abram's old room. He was my toughest teacher, but also my favorite. See you at three.*

My lips twitch into a smile. *Mr. Abrams was my role model. See you soon.*

Usually, meeting with the family of a student is a stressful proposition. But today, I feel the tightly coiled muscles in my neck relax. Just a bit.

Chapter 8

Rylee

The building still smells the same, like pine-scented cleaner and strawberry lip balm, but there are much worse scents for a high school to have. I check in at the little window past the front entrance, where the attendance secretary, Esther, sits. She's the same woman who sat at the window when I went to school here, and she still looks like she's roughly fifty-five. Esther glances at me but doesn't see me.

"Yes?"

"Rylee Lynch, here to see Carson Meyers."

There's no flicker of recognition on Esther's face. She hands me a visitor badge and picks up her phone. After a moment, she speaks into the receiver. "Yeah. Rylee Lynch is here to see you. Uh-huh. Okay." She hangs up and goes back to scrolling through a document. Keeping her eyes on her computer screen, she states, "He said you can head down."

"Okay, thanks."

Esther punches a large button, and the door buzzes open. I step into the high school, kids bustling in every direction, some outside the auditorium, some inside the gym. Taking a left and walking past the main office, I'm almost to my destination when I'm hit with a demented wave of nostalgia: this is where Carson rejected me.

The scene of the B.A.I.

Ten years ago, Carson was one of the few people who didn't seem intimidated by my grief. Perhaps that's because on the night my father died and my mother was in the hospital, Brandon and I stayed at Mel's house. I sat trembling on the edge of her twin bed, when Carson stepped in, wearing a white V-neck T-shirt and green plaid flannel pajama pants, his hair sticking up and a pair of glasses perched on his nose, making him appear different from his popular-guy-at-school persona. He knelt in front of me, his brown eyes compassionate, and took my hand.

"Can I get you anything?" he asked, in a feather-soft voice.

I shook my head no but said, "Where's my little brother?"

"My mom is getting him set up in my room. You'll sleep with Mel." He squeezed my fingers, and somehow, his warm grip gave me strength.

"No. I have to be with Brandon. He needs me."

"Okay," Carson said. "Let's go. I'll take you to him now."

Brandon and I slept in Carson's room while he must have slept on the lumpy basement couch. Afterward, whenever we bumped into each other at the school library, Carson would smile and ask if I had read any good books lately.

Any therapist worth their salt would say that my feelings for Carson were a coping mechanism after my dad's death, but at fourteen, I needed something to cling to. I was so lost.

On the morning of the B.A.I., Dana stopped me here in the hallway of Bemidji High School, where the northernmost piece of the Mississippi River runs directly behind the building. "I know why Carson's been so nice to you."

I felt the blood drain from my cheeks. "What do you mean?"

"C'mon." Dana rolled her eyes. Then she flat-out yelled, "It's obvious you have a huge crush on my boyfriend."

A sudden hush settled over the crowded hallway. I floundered for a response.

"Don't deny it!" Dana spoke so loud, you'd be able to hear her over a concrete drill. But where we stood was dead quiet. "I see you staring at him, like, *all* the time. Does Mel know that you're after her big brother?"

I was pretty sure Mel had no idea. Thankfully, she wasn't around to witness this confrontation. But the rest of the world was, and there was no way to deny it; I thought about Carson day and night. That truth was so painful and distinct. I may as well have chomped on my tongue and drawn blood.

I was ready to bolt when a hand fell on my shoulder like a blanket shielding me from the cold. Carson. He wore his game-day hockey outfit—a navy blue hoodie and athletic pants. Hockey players weren't often known for their finesse, but his aftershave was subtle, with a musky scent that made me feel safe. My heart rate slowed, and my breathing leveled out.

"Is everything okay?" Carson's hand on my shoulder was divine, with the slightest pressure. The corners of his wide mouth turned downward, his magnificent eyebrows furrowed, and his dark brown eyes were glossy.

The first-hour warning bell rang, the noise of other students talking and laughing resumed, and Dana said,

"Hey, babe!" Like everything was cool. Like she hadn't just destroyed me.

Ignoring Dana, Carson looked like he wanted to shelter me from the hurricane that had rampaged my life. "Hey, it's okay."

His words were soothing, but I couldn't respond. Instead, I stood there, head bowed, as tears streamed down my cheeks. Jeez, I was pathetic—like total train wreck, hot mess, ugly cry pathetic. But life had kicked me in the ass a few months before, and this big, scary grief vulture swooped down and scavenged my remains. There was no fight in me. I could only pray that Carson hadn't heard what Dana said. I dug my nails into my palm, willing myself to pull it together.

Putting his arm around me, Carson said nothing, but the warmth of his embrace kept me from falling apart. He lingered for a few seconds before pulling away.

"Let's get you out of here." He took my hand and led me into a side hallway, where we were alone.

"I'm sorry about what happened," Carson said.

I met his gaze. "It's not your fault."

After looking at me for a long moment, he reached out and wiped a tear from my cheek.

My body went hot and cold all at once, and I arched toward his touch. And then, oh God, I thought he was going to kiss me. So, I leaned in, tilted up my phlegmy tear-streaked face, and parted my lips.

He stepped back and let out a sigh.

Not a sigh of longing. Definitely not that. Rather, it was an apologetic sigh, and I wished to evaporate.

"It's going to be okay," he said. "You'll get through this."

Pretending everything was cool, I nodded as if

agreeing with him about something intellectual and important, like the nuances of quantum physics or the complexities of postmodern literature.

Carson squeezed my hand before letting it go. "I'll see you around." He walked away, and I watched as he disappeared around the corner, my heart pulsing in my throat.

Now a decade has passed, but I stand in the same spot where my hopes once melted like an abandoned crayon against hot pavement. Pushing away any self-pity, I brush off the memory and hurry down the deserted hallway.

I reach Carson's room, and his door is slightly ajar, so I give it a light rap as I peek inside. He's wearing a loose-knit tie and a pale blue Oxford with his sleeves rolled up. In front of him lies the same AP Biology book we used in high school.

When he sees me, his mouth curves into an awkward grin.

"Rylee, hello. Come in." He gets up from his desk chair and motions towards a stool, one of several placed around the large tables used for dissecting frogs or injecting caffeine into onion root tips. I'm pinched by nostalgia, recalling how Mel, who always seemed half-asleep during our first period Bio, joked about injecting herself with the caffeine instead.

I go to the same stool where I sat six years ago. "This was my spot."

"Old habits, huh?" Carson sits across from me. "I bet it's happy you're back."

I scoff. "Please. These stools can be so fickle. Besides, hundreds of high school asses have sat here since—I'm sure mine was hardly memorable."

He arches a single eyebrow. "Are you fishing for an ass compliment?"

"No!" I insist, heat rising up my neck.

Carson chuckles. "Because you're underselling your ass. However, I'm still on the clock as an educator, so I shouldn't say anything more."

He thinks I was being flirty! "I wasn't fishing for an ass compliment—or any sort of compliment. I'm here to talk about Brandon."

I glance down. His thick fingers rest on the table between us. Carson has large hands for such a slim guy—his chest is broad but somehow in proportion to the rest of his body, and his biceps strain against his shirt sleeves.

Jeez, Rylee, focus.

"Of course," he responds. "I was only teasing, but you're right. We should talk about your brother."

He almost sounds sad, like he was trying to be funny, and I shot him down. Time to change course. "Hey! I was impressed when you saved Professor Aldrich from ripping her earlobe in two the other day. That was something."

Carson's cheeks grow pink. "I do what I can."

"It must be boring for you here." I gesture to his classroom and tilt my head from side to side. "There's no one to rescue from earring and scarf catastrophes. Or from any catastrophe."

In a fluid motion, almost like he's a piano player, Carson drums those thick fingers against the table. "Are you kidding? My students use highly dangerous materials, like glucose test strips, conductivity testers, and potato peelers. There are endless catastrophic possibilities. But teachers can get in trouble for tapping a kid on the shoulder, which makes heroics difficult…" He holds out his hands in mock defeat. "It's why I'm going back to school."

I squint in confusion. "Because of the 'no touching' rule?"

"Because I can't be a hero."

"Oh." My foot twitches as a series of nerves travel from my core down to my toes. "Sorry to break it to you, but writing programs offer few opportunities for heroism."

"Unless you make them up."

He has the same sort of look that he used to give me when we stood in the high school media center.

Read any good books lately, Rylee?

I lived for those moments, but now I glimpse past Carson's shoulder at the DNA poster on the wall. "Oh." Clearing my throat, I try again to deflect the awkwardness. "Why *are* you taking a fiction writing class?"

Carson watches me for what seems like an eternity, and I worry I offended him. Just when I'm about to apologize, he answers in a voice that's as deep and sure as ever. "It's part of my new program in English education."

The question slips out. "But why? No offense—I majored in English, so I'm one of those people with limited career options and skill sets who might get their MA in English Education. But that's not you."

He tenses and twists a little, like he's about to get something off his chest. "I never planned on becoming a biology teacher, and I started when I was twenty-two. My friends were all out exploring the world while responsibilities held me back in my hometown, providing for a wife and kid. Don't get me wrong—I wouldn't have it any other way—and yet..."

"And yet, you wish there was more time for adventure and self-discovery? I understand."

Carson looks at me with an unspoken question in his eyes, searching for something more than an answer. "Right. That's exactly it," he says. "Plus, I like to write. When things got bad for me...well, that was how I coped. Don't tell anyone, but I wrote a novel."

My heart skips a beat. "Really? Me too." Biting my bottom lip, I stop myself from saying much more. This isn't confession time. "I mean, it was silly and unreadable, but I understand what you mean. During tough times, writing is my coping mechanism."

"I'm sorry you need a coping mechanism."

"I shouldn't complain," I amend. "Things could be a lot worse. It's just that I'd planned to go away for grad school, but I was indecisive, and Brandon got sick, and cancer is expensive. He's doing okay now, but I couldn't leave, not while he still needs me."

Carson's hand creeps towards mine, like he's going to cradle my fingers in his grasp. But he clenches his hand into a fist. Glancing at the clock, he says, "Is Brandon doing okay?"

"Yes. But you heard about his brain tumor?"

"I have," Carson says, weighing his words. "But I didn't make the connection that you are siblings, not until today when you emailed. I'm sorry about that."

"Why are you sorry?"

A soft line of concern sneaks onto his brow. "Well, because..." He reaches back and rubs the base of his neck. "It's such a horrendous thing for him to have gone through, and for you as well. And I still remember when the two of you stayed at our house after your dad—"

He cuts himself off.

"It's okay," I tell him. "You can say it. *After he died.*"

"Yeah." He meets my gaze, and it's disarming. "Sorry, I'm awkward. But what happened with your dad…well, you were both so young and then I made the connection, and I guess I wanted to apologize, even if none of it's my fault."

"Trust me, none of it is your fault."

It isn't your fault now, and it wasn't your fault back when it happened, even though you tried to make my world right, and I took it the wrong way.

I shake off my unspoken thoughts and straighten myself. "The doctors say Brandon's prognosis is excellent, and he's in remission. The surgery and radiation worked, but I still feel powerless, and I'm worried about his health. Also, he might be depressed."

My hand twitches towards his, but I keep it in place as I choke out the words. "I was wondering if you could look out for him. Email me if he acts exhausted all the time or if he's always alone…"

Silence. It stretches out like a rubber band ready to snap.

"Oh," I mumble, turning in my seat to run from the awkwardness. "I've asked for too much. I should go. Sorry to take up your time."

"No, wait!" Carson says, and my eyes shoot to him. "I…do that sometimes."

"Huh?"

He studies his hands. "Taking a long time to respond because I'm having a conversation with myself. It's not like I'm hearing voices; I just overthink and internalize everything."

A laugh bubbles from inside my chest. "I do that too."

"Oh yeah? I've always thought maybe we're alike in that way."

An unnamed emotion swirls inside me. Shock? Joy? Confusion? All three, maybe.

"What do you mean, 'you've always thought'?"

He chuckles and swallows hard. "I'm not sure. But at the restaurant the other day. You must think I'm the biggest asshole ever."

Asshole? Sure, I've cursed his name before. But now, even though he's not asking for forgiveness, it would be such a rush to give it.

"That's okay. I've seen worse behavior."

His tone is soft and deep. "Oh no. You deserve to be treated well."

Wait, now who's being flirty? I toss away my tingling sensation.

"Anyway, about Brandon?"

"Right. Of course, I'll look out for him. Consider it done."

I exhale in relief. "Thank you."

Carson taps my elbow. "Hey, of course. Also, thank you for watching Eddie the other night." Worried, he narrows his eyes. "God, I should have started with that. Was he okay?"

"He was great." I smile. "It was my pleasure."

Grabbing my bag from near the stool, I stand upright again. "I should go." I pause, suddenly remembering that other important thing I need to share. "Oh. By the way, I told Mel that you asked me to be writing partners, and I said no."

Carson looks at me like I sprouted an extra head. "Why?"

"Because she's Mel. She's opinionated. For some reason, she decided we wouldn't work well together, and I wasn't up to arguing."

He glances at the clock again, and now I'm self-conscious, remembering that he has to be somewhere. "Sure." Carson glances back at me. "But Rylee?"

My stomach flips when he says my name. "Yeah?"

"Maybe don't mention to Dana that we're writing partners, either."

I cross my arms over my chest and stand tall. "I barely know Dana, so I doubt I'll say anything. But if she asks me, am I supposed to lie?"

He shrugs half-heartedly and shifts his weight. "I guess. I don't want her to be weird with you. Dana hates me right now. She could easily extend her animosity to anyone who's my ally."

I back myself towards his door, creating distance but still facing him. "I won't say anything to Dana, and you won't say anything to Mel. Deal?"

"That makes us secret writing partners, right?" Carson shoves his hands into his pockets. "I mean, Brandon shouldn't know either, right? Otherwise, he'll grow suspicious if I pay him a lot of attention."

"Good point." I extend my hand so we can shake and formalize our agreement.

Carson removes his right hand from his pocket, grasps mine, and the warmth and strength of his grip makes me breathless. I imagine him pulling me close and crushing his lips against mine.

Of course, nothing like that happens. All we do is shake hands—but wow, why am I so affected by this?

Chapter 9

Carson

Running late, I stuff my bag with papers that need grading and the AP Bio binder that will be my bible for the next nine months. Yet as I walk out to the staff parking lot where the sun warms my shoulders, Rylee dances through my mind. I compare the fourteen-year-old, devastated version of her to the strong, confident woman she is now. The way she meets my gaze like we're in a staring contest, like she's playing to win—well, that's still unnerving. And yet, I enjoy looking at her face.

I drive to pick up Eddie, pushing away all thoughts of Rylee as soon as he climbs into my Jeep. "Guess what?" I tell him. "We're going to see a dog."

I have Ferris's picture up on my phone, and I hand it back to Eddie.

"Dad!" Eddie proclaims the moment he can process what Ferris looks like. "I already love this dog. He's perfect. Can we please adopt him?"

Pulling out of the parking lot, I say, "Maybe. But we need to meet him first. And there might be another dog we like better."

"No." Eddie's voice is low, serious, and unintentionally comical on someone so young. "Ferris is our dog. It's fate, Dad."

I stifle a laugh. "We'll see."

Soon, we pull up to the Bemidji Animal Shelter. When we climb out of my Jeep, the air is thick with the smell of early autumn, and the sun glints off the metal of the building, blinding me for a fraction of a second. I glance at Eddie, who's brimming with anticipation. He hops from foot to foot.

"Ready?" I ask him.

"I'm nervous." Eddie stops his hopping and goes still. "What if Ferris doesn't like me?"

"Let's go see."

Now Eddie's trembling, so I take his hand in mine, and together we approach the shelter entrance. Inside, it's surprisingly quiet, with occasional whines or muted barks coming from the interior. There's a faint smell of disinfectant in the air, but it's cut through with undertones of hay and animal fur. A middle-aged woman whose name tag reads Emily meets us in the lobby.

"Hello. You must be Carson and Eddie?"

"Yes," I reply. "We have a four o'clock appointment."

"We're here to see Ferris!" Eddie blurts out.

Emily smiles. "He's in the back."

We walk in the direction Emily points, past cats, rabbits, guinea pigs, and even a few exotic birds. My heart breaks for each animal that needs a home, but Eddie is on a mission. He appraises every single dog and doesn't stop until he finds one that matches the profile pic of Ferris.

And—oh God—the dog stands on his hind legs with front paws resting against his cage, looking at us with sad, soulful eyes. On the floor, by his feet, is a ratty old teddy bear.

"That's him," Eddie says, pointing.

"Ferris wasn't catfishing us," I remark.

"Huh?"

"Don't worry about it." I look around for Emily and say, "Excuse me?" After a few moments, a different woman in blue scrubs appears with a clipboard in her hand.

"You must be here for Ferris," she says. "He's a sweetheart."

Suddenly, my stomach bubbles with nerves. When Dana finds out about this, she will be beyond pissed. I can already hear her say, "You're making Eddie choose you over me!"

But I inhale, tell myself to pull it together, and ask the shelter worker, "Can we meet him?"

The woman opens the door, motioning for Eddie and me to come inside. "Take your time," she says.

We step into the enclosure and kneel next to the dog.

"Hello," I say, giving the dog's head a soft stroke. Ferris yips with enthusiasm and presses himself into my leg.

Eddie giggles, and I relax enough to give Ferris a once-over. The dog nearly overflows with energy and excitement. It's like he belongs in a cartoon movie, and I wouldn't even be shocked if he broke into song. Eddie bends down to pet him, and Ferris jumps up, licking Eddie's face as if he's been waiting for this his entire life.

"Please, Dad?"

Eddie looks at me with puppy dog eyes that rival Ferris's. Both dog and boy peer up as if telepathically communicating the same thought.

Now that we've found each other, how can you keep us apart?

I open my mouth to answer, but Dana's in my

headspace again, and she may as well be a muzzle. It was ten years ago, on a perfect day in late spring, when Dana said we needed to talk after school.

"Let's drive to our spot," she'd said.

"Our spot" was in Lake Bemidji State Park, the smaller, lesser-known state park that our town offers. There's a dock that floats on waves made by motorboats, and that afternoon, with the promise of summer and barbecues and water skiing and the countdown to a new, post-high school, post-Bemidji life, I followed Dana out onto that dock. Even though she'd tied her auburn hair back, the sun still bounced off it. Her pinched face was pale, yet her skin looked peach-like, soft and delicious.

My worst fear? She'd tell me we needed to break up, that there was no way a long-distance relationship would work.

I was prepared to argue with her.

But all the words I'd rehearsed died on my lips when she said, "I'm pregnant, and I'm keeping it. You can't convince me otherwise."

I couldn't respond. Even as I opened my mouth, no words came out. It never occurred to me to ask: *Are you sure it's mine?* But what type of asshole would pose such a question? I would never suggest that she get an abortion, or even imply she should think about it.

Finally, I said, "Are you sure?"

"Sure about what? That I'm pregnant? Or that I'm keeping it?"

A breeze ruffled my hair like a gentle caress. It was so contrary to how I felt, as if I'd plunged into ice water. I wanted to dive headfirst into the still frigid lake to escape this moment.

"Both," I answered.

"Yes."

I swallowed, and my throat felt like gravel. "Okay. We'll figure it out."

"*We'll* figure it out? You're not abandoning me?"

All I could see was Dana. She was my entire world—perfect and beautiful. "Of course not."

"You'll stay in Bemidji for college?"

I flapped my mouth open and shut like I was one of the carp that swam beneath me.

"Carson," Dana continued. "Actions speak louder than words. Saying you won't abandon me is meaningless if you do actually abandon me."

"You're oversimplifying things."

"I'm not," Dana answered. "If you decide to go to Harvard, I won't try to stop you. But I'll find someone who will stick around for us both, and I'll tell our son or daughter that he's their father. That's how it has to be."

Dana was so unfair. Now I wonder if she already knew I wasn't our baby's dad.

But I won't go down that rabbit hole because I can't regret my decision to stay. It was the only choice I could make. Still, I'll never get over my parents' devastation when I told them I was scrapping Harvard to become an eighteen-year-old husband and father. It's a constant replay in my mind: first, their excited, proud smiles on the day Harvard accepted me, and then, weeks later, their despondence when they realized I was stuck in this town.

And yet, Eddie is my son. Blood relative or not, I can't turn off being a father like it's a switch I can flip. That means I will always be tied to this place—to Eddie, and yes, to Dana. There's no going back.

But there is a way to go forward. That includes doing what's best for Eddie.

"Yes," I tell Eddie now. "We can adopt Ferris."
Dana will have to live with it.

Chapter 10

Rylee

Do you want to meet at my place? Carson asks via text.

My fingers hover over my phone's screen, and I torture out a response. He must get anxious by those little dancing dots, because Carson sends a second text before I complete my first.

It's safer than meeting in public.

He's right. Plus, we're both adults; I can handle this.

Your place is good, I text back.

He replies with his address and a time on Sunday, adding an unexpected question: *Are you okay with dogs?*

A smile tugs at my lips. *Depends. How many dogs are we talking about?*

Just one, he answers, *but he's needy enough for three.*

I laugh to myself. *Can't wait. Needy dogs are my specialty.*

That's not really true, but I adore any creature who lets their vulnerability show—dogs especially, with their undignified sincerity that mirrors my own. That is, when I'm not trying hard to be something else.

On Sunday, I pull up to Carson's house, a gray bungalow with white trim tucked away on the outskirts of town. Gravel crunching beneath my tires, I turn off the engine and get out.

The barking starts as soon as I approach the door. I knock, and the barking intensifies, followed by the sound of a dead bolt unlatched from the other side. The door swings open, and there's Carson, radiating energy like a crackling campfire. His worn flannel shirt hugs his body in all the right places, and his jeans with rips at the knees show his tan skin. His hair is a mess, like he's been running his fingers through it. Stubble covers his cheeks and chin, and I long to touch it.

"Ferris, calm down," Carson says.

Ferris runs at me and sniffs, wildly taking in all my smells.

"Hello, you!" I pet Ferris.

Wow. If Carson was hoping for a guard dog, he's out of luck. Ferris seems like the type to lick a burglar to death.

"Sorry." Carson pulls Ferris back gently and greets me. "How's it going?"

I step inside, and it occurs to me: with Carson's hair all ruffled, he's totally sporting a *Sunday afternoon lying around* look. I imagine the heat of his skin underneath that flannel shirt.

"I'm okay," I tell him, trying to banish my illicit thoughts. "How are you?"

Carson rubs his eyes and then runs his fingers through his hair, making it stand up even more. He uses his other arm to press down on Ferris's back, getting him to sit. "I'm good. But I'm a little bleary-eyed after helping Ferris acclimate to his new home and grading the first round of AP Bio labs all day. But what can you do?"

"Ferris is a recent addition?"

"Yeah. Eddie guilted me into him, but I was an easy sell."

"He's cute. How old is he?"

"A little over a year," Carson replies. "Ferris is very high energy, and they say his first family couldn't manage. So he went to the animal shelter. And that's where Eddie and I found him."

As if Ferris understands we're talking about him and is embarrassed, he uses his mouth to pick up a raggedy old teddy bear, circles around, and settles on a mat underneath the window, where he nuzzles the toy and half-heartedly gnaws its ear.

"That's adorable," I say. "Did he have that toy at the shelter? It looks well loved."

"Yeah." Carson crosses to the window and gives his dog a pat on the head. "He's quite attached to his teddy bear. Anyway, come in."

I step into his living room, which is low-ceilinged and dark. There's a tan couch that appears stolen from someone's 1980s-era basement, its cushions sagging and velour rubbed away in spots. Otherwise, he has both a coffee table and shelves made from bricks and plywood, a folding table and chairs in the dining area, and a TV mounted on a wire shelf. And that's the extent of his furniture.

I try to hide my shock. But Carson senses it.

He stands next to me and takes in his living room as if he's seeing it for the first time. "Dana got the house and our living room set. It was only fair since her parents bought us everything. Now I'm renting this place until I can find something better, and I'm saving up to buy nice furniture. I wouldn't even care, except I want it to be nice for when Eddie stays over."

I search for an honest yet polite response. "It's comfortable—the type of place you can relax and not worry about making a mess. Perfect for a boy and his dog."

Carson laughs. "That's a backward compliment, but I'll take it." He points to the folding table and chairs, upon which his laptop and some papers sit. "I thought we could work here."

"Great." I take a seat and pull my laptop from my bag, opening it up. "Do you have a Wi-Fi password?"

"Yeah, of course." He tells me, and I type it in.

"Thanks." I retrieve all my relevant files, but Carson remains standing, shifting his weight and maybe at a loss for what to do with his hands.

"Are you okay?"

"Yes. Just tired. Do you want anything? Water? Soda? Wine?" He raises his eyebrows in anticipation of my response.

"Wine?"

"You want wine?" He grins like I told a joke. "Isn't that what your boy Hemingway said? Something about writing while drunk?"

"First, Hemingway is not my boy." Narrowing my eyes, I concede, "However, yes, he said that."

"And second?" Carson asks.

I clip my consonants. "Second, Hemingway also said to revise while sober."

Carson shrugs. "Either way, wine is nice."

Despite my nerves, I laugh. "Why not? Yes, please."

He leads me into his small kitchen, with just enough room for the narrow fridge and two-burner stove. He's like a hot, unkempt sommelier as he uncorks the bottle, pouring us each a generous amount of Merlot into Mason jars. "Sorry, I don't have proper wineglasses." Carson offers me a jar, and we sit back at the folding table.

I take a sip. The wine bursts with the flavor of ripe berries, and I'm no expert, but perhaps chocolate undertones? Humming in appreciation, I say, "This is perfect. And don't chic New York restaurants serve wine in Mason jars?"

"I've never been to New York—only Massachusetts to tour Harvard." He sips, and the mood turn solemn. "Sometimes I wish I had never gone. At least I wouldn't know what I'm missing."

"Don't say that." I put my palm down on the table as if reaching for him. "At least you've had a glimpse of what's possible. I've barely been out of Minnesota. God. I would love to see the coast. Or Europe. Or anywhere different from here."

"Yeah, me too." He drums his fingers against the table like he's solving a math equation inside his head. "Hey, I have an idea." Carson stands and goes to his refrigerator. "We can share a charcuterie board. With that and the wine in Mason jars, it's like you're on the East Coast."

"A *what* board?"

"Charcuterie. A fancy word for a plate of cheese and sausage." Carson takes a block of orange cheddar and cuts it into semi-thin slices.

I'm startled when he yelps. "Ow!" He drops his knife and dashes for the sink. Ferris springs to action, yipping and bolting to Carson's feet.

"What happened?" I leap up, step around Ferris and towards Carson as he turns on the faucet and shoves his finger under the running water.

"I sliced my finger."

"Does it hurt?"

"Nah." But Carson sucks in a sharp breath and goes

ashen.

Grabbing a handful of paper towels, I move right next to him. "Here. Let me see."

Ferris whimpers as if it's him in pain. Carson averts his gaze, holding out his finger for me. I'm guessing a few layers of skin were severed off. I wet the paper towels, wrapping them around his finger and applying pressure.

"You're not going to pass out, are you?"

"I'll be fine. Sometimes seeing my own blood makes me squeamish." He avoids looking down at his hand.

"Weren't you going to be a doctor?"

"Yeah. And I'm cool with other people's blood. Just not my own."

"Oh. That totally makes sense."

"Really?" Carson's voice lilts.

"Not even a little."

We stand there, me pressing down on his cut, him taking deep nose inhales, still not looking down at his hand.

After a couple of minutes, I unwrap the paper towels and inspect his finger. "Maybe the bleeding has slowed down, but what do I know? I was an English major. Do you want to look?"

"Nah, that's okay. Would you mind bandaging it up for me? There's gauze and medical tape in the medicine cabinet."

"Sure."

I head to his bathroom and retrieve the gauze and medical tape. When I return, he still stands in the kitchen, clearly dazed. Ferris sits by him, gazing up in concern. Putting my palm against Carson's shoulder blades, I push him toward his table and chairs. "Have a seat. I'll fix you right up."

He sits, and I stand, my feet in between his legs. "Give me your hand."

Carson holds out his injured finger, and I'm ready to take it, but I need both hands to unwrap and cut the gauze and tape. So, I place one foot on the edge of his chair, dangerously close to his crotch, and place his hand so it rests against my knee.

"Don't worry," I murmur. "I'm a very careful person."

His dark brown eyes meet mine. How anyone can be so charming and boyish while also exuding masculinity is a puzzle, but Carson has the formula down.

Ferris is not sure about me, though. He rumbles out a low growl and steps close to Carson, making me lose my balance. I fall into Carson, my hands pressing against his chest, and almost landing on his lap.

"Ferris, sit!" Carson's command is soft yet strong.

Ferris whimpers in protest but does as he's told.

I struggle back up and start wrapping Carson's finger, first with gauze and then with tape. "Tell me if it's too tight," I say, worried he might sense how flustered I am. "I don't want it to bleed again."

"It's fine." Carson sounds husky, and his intense stare makes my stomach flutter. It would be easy to sit in his lap, curl myself into his brawny arms and broad chest, and kiss him—slow and deep—but Ferris exists, and he'd interrupt us.

So I don't.

"There," I say. "All done." I've successfully bandaged Carson's finger.

"Thank you." His hand, the one with no injured

fingers, brushes the small of my back, and warmth tingles through me. "Sorry, I'm such a wimp."

"You're fine." I jerk back because if I don't create space between us right now, there's no telling what I might do. "I'll put these away." Holding up the gauze and tape, I start towards the bathroom and return them to the medicine cabinet. When I close it, I can't help but check my reflection. The flush on my cheeks makes my eyes seem bigger than normal. I look down at my chest. Can Carson tell that my heart is pounding just by looking at the general area of my ribcage? God, I hope not.

I leave the bathroom and find Carson back in the kitchen. He's returned to slicing the cheese.

"You're very brave," I say.

He deftly slides his knife through the block of cheddar. "I love cheese, and neither pain nor bloodshed will keep me from a good snack."

Crossing my arms over my chest, I study him. "Then you're also an inspiration. But can I help?"

"Nah. Don't worry. I won't bleed on the food."

"I'm not worried. My masterful bandaging won't let that happen."

He opens a bag of pepperoni and puts some next to the cheese. Finally, he grabs a box of crackers, and the charcuterie board is complete. I sit down at the table.

"Exactly like you'd get in all the fancy restaurants." Proud, Carson sets it down in front of me.

"I had no idea you were so sophisticated." I place a slice of cheese and pepperoni on a cracker. Of course, when I take a bite, crumbs go everywhere, onto his card table and onto my chest. I'm wearing a white T-shirt underneath a gray belted cardigan, and when I brush the crumbs away, they lodge themselves into the space between my two garments.

Smooth, Rylee.

"Sorry."

"For what?" Carson asks.

"I've made a mess."

"Are you kidding? You're apologizing after I forced you to dress my wound?"

"You didn't force me, and it wasn't much more than applying a Band-Aid."

Carson shoots me a smile. "Whatever. Besides, you don't have to worry about making a mess here. Remember? You said that."

"Well, thanks for the wine and charcuterie. Kind of swanky, right? Drinking wine and discussing Paul Weaver…"

"Yeah." Carson swigs his wine as he sits back in his chair. "What did you think of 'The Alien'?"

"It's a classic."

Carson shakes his head. "Yeah, but what's your opinion?" The way he asks me that, with his velvet tone and his intensity, it's like he cares what I have to say. And that makes me giddy. Then I remember what Mel said. *Carson can be sweet and wide-eyed, but it's all an act.*

Don't get involved.

I focus on the assignment. "It was okay. A little hard to get into, but once Willy hits the nudists' backyard, it's more interesting."

Paul Weaver's "The Alien" is the story of Willy—a delusional man who's convinced that all his neighbors are aliens. He sets out to expose them, only to realize it's him who is truly alienated.

"What did *you* think?" I ask. "Did you like Weaver's

use of setting?"

I recline in my chair as Carson leans forward, his gauze-wrapped finger waving in the air to emphasize his points. "Weaver's use of setting illustrates how a man can deceive himself while existing in a deceitful society. And Willy's epic quest during the neighborhood barbeque should have been a triumph, but he's just a drunk gate-crasher. He has lost everything, but he can't admit it to himself."

I tilt my head to the side. "Are you quoting yourself here? Did you put that in your written response?"

Carson's mouth falls open. "Yes. And I hoped you'd ask me about the setting, so I could impress the shit out of you."

"You're trying to impress me?" My voice sounds foreign and scratchy to my own ears.

A beat passes as Carson's chest rises and falls. "I…umm…"

The air is thick with anticipation, and my pulse jumps. "What is it?"

A beat passes. "I need to say something. Even though I'm sure you're fine, I still worry about—"

"Don't!" I bolt up as Ferris darts awake beside me. "Don't finish what you were going to say."

Carson chews the corner of his bottom lip. "But you don't know what I was going to—"

"I have a *pretty* good idea." I cut him off before he can mention the Big Awful Incident and drag us both into the murky depths of our past. "And if it has anything to do with high school, let's agree that we were different people. I mean that literally. You're the biology whiz, so I don't have to tell you how every seven years, our cells regenerate, and our bodies replace themselves."

Carson rubs his forehead. "Not exactly. Our cerebral cortex neurons, which control our memories, thoughts, and language, are the same from birth to death."

I wave off his comment. "But you get what I'm saying."

"I do. But there's a problem." His forehead creases like he's weighing some moral dilemma. "I really want to kiss you right now. Given our history, it would be wrong without offering an explanation or an apology—"

"Don't worry about it!" My breathing becomes shallow and quick. "I swear it's not a problem."

Carson stands and comes near me. "Are you sure?"

"Yes!"

My vehemence is so forceful that he reels back. "Okay." His gaze travels the length of my body up and down, and then it lands on my mouth. He dips his head. He reaches and entwines my fingers with his. Gentle heat radiates from his skin, coursing through me like a river of hot buttered rum. He brings my hand to rest upon his chest, so I can feel the reckless thump of his heart.

"Carson…"

His eyelids flutter shut. "Please… say my name again."

"Carson." I'm louder and more deliberate this time. His eyes shoot open.

"Rylee," he rasps, and it's like a promise that even after every disappointment and missed chance, something could still change.

I crash into him, our mouths meeting in a desperate kiss. I run my palms up his chest, enjoying the expanse beneath my fingers. His shirt is loose enough that I can slip it off without snagging on his bandaged finger. He stands before me, broad and beautiful, and the desire to strip out of my clothes overpowers me. But there's no need. Carson lifts my shirt and slides the straps of my bra away with ease. They're discarded on the floor, and he takes me in with one bold glance before cupping one breast in his palm, rubbing his thumb over my nipple until I moan in pleasure. "You're gorgeous," he whispers against my lips.

"Bedroom?" I pant between kisses.

Carson's expression stills as his Adam's apple bobs in his throat. An eternity passes between us, way worse than the one during the B.A.I.

At least then, I was wearing a shirt.

"We probably shouldn't," he says, and a shameful heat rushes to my cheeks.

"Right… I should get going." I hurry to gather up my bra, shirt, and sweater, but I'm unable to coordinate my fingers properly, like the basic task of putting on clothes has become more difficult than rock climbing.

"You don't have to go, Rylee," he urges.

But I do.

He's Carson Meyers. I'm his little sister's pathetic best friend.

It doesn't matter that high school was years ago.

Some dynamics don't change.

Chapter 11

Rylee

Carson steps close enough that I can smell the wine on his breath and the muskiness of his skin. And I'm hyper-aware that he's still bare-chested.

"Please don't go," he murmurs.

"I have to."

"Why?"

I rake my fingers through my hair. Inside my brain, there's an avalanche of replies. Self-censorship is not my strong suit, so I take a moment, literally biting my tongue, trying not to say something I'll regret. "Because you think I'm a slut."

Damn. That's not the eloquent response I was going for, but at least I was clear and concise. Carson's cheeks turn pink, and his mouth drops open.

"No. That's not true. Honestly, Rylee." He searches for his shirt, leaning away from me. Once he locates it, he puts it on but doesn't mess with the buttons. Instead, when Carson sees me fumble with the belt of my sweater, he steps back in and ties it around my waist as if he's protecting me.

"Are you okay?"

I nod. "Sure." Because if anyone can survive being rejecting by the same man twice, it's me.

He pauses. "But…?"

My neck warms. I try to look away, but Carson

stands there in his unbuttoned flannel, looking adorable and sexy and rumply.

"But I've never done this before."

His bottom lip tugs between his teeth. "So, this was your first time…doing what—exactly?"

"Oh, God!" I grip my shirt by the collar like I'm about to burst out of it. "Don't worry, Carson. I didn't just ask you to take my virginity. Simon Bateman took care of that during my junior year."

"Simon Bateman? That asshole kid on the hockey team?"

It's true. Simon had a reputation for being a jerk to his teammates. But he was a charmer at keg parties. I shrug. "I suppose."

Carson shakes his head. "That kid was a punk. One time during practice, he deliberately slammed into a ninth grader and knocked him down so hard that he had to be helped off the ice with a sprained knee." His brow wrinkles. "So, you and Simon Bateman…dated?"

Not exactly. What can I say? If Carson thinks I'm a slut, maybe he's right. I could blame it on losing my dad at fourteen or on my mother, who enjoys being mistaken for my sister. Or maybe I've always been looking for a way to feel complete. Still, there's really no excuse.

A puff of air escapes the corner of my mouth. "Dated? No. We hooked up at a party. I'd had a few wine coolers. You know how it goes." I stare at Carson, daring him to challenge me.

But something inside him shuts down. I can tell by the way his chest caves in. "Sure," he says. "But…what did you mean when you said this was your first time?"

I cross my arms over my chest. "Nothing. It's my first time throwing myself at someone and miscalculating the situation completely. That's all." Not knowing what else to do with my arms, I sit back in my folding chair and press the spacebar on my laptop. It lights up the card table in a pale blue glow.

Carson comes and sits across from me, looking like he's trying to swallow down his own confession. "You miscalculated nothing. It's me; I'm screwed up."

I continue pressing my computer's keyboard, pretending to focus on my screen. "No, no. It's not like I've slept with half of Bemidji or anything. But usually, I can read the room."

Carson rubs the back of his neck and leans back in his chair. "Look, if it's any consolation—"

"No consolation necessary." I raise my hand to establish some twisted sense of authority. "If you try to cheer me up, that will only make it worse." Tinging my laugh with chagrin, I say, "I'm embarrassed."

"Rylee." He exhales my name in a satin tone. "You have nothing to be embarrassed about."

"Right, except, there was that time, ten years ago, when I threw myself at you. I guess what just happened was actually my second time, because tonight, I threw myself at you again." I pretend to focus on my computer screen so I don't have to look at him. "That's not embarrassing. Not at all."

"No," Carson states. "You didn't throw yourself at me, not then and not now. Besides, you said we're not allowed to talk about what happened in high school."

"No. I said *you're* not allowed to talk about it. But I give myself full permission."

Ferris must side with me because he gets up, and tail wagging low and slow, nuzzles my thigh.

"Fine," Carson says. "But Rylee, if anyone should

be embarrassed, it's me. I put the moves on you as soon as you got here. I have no excuse, except I've been lonely. And you—you're *so* pretty. Plus, it seems like you understand me, and lately, no one understands me."

All at once, I'm itchy. Is it because I'm scared? Because I want what he said to be true? Because I feel the same? It doesn't matter.

It can't matter.

"Carson, I'm flattered, and, um…I like you a lot. But we should concentrate on this week's assignment."

He blinks, and for a moment it's like he might disagree, but no. "You're right." He stands up. "Let me finish getting dressed, and we'll get to work."

Carson buttons his shirt, and after that, we're all business. It takes a couple of hours to read and discuss the stories that we each wrote in response to "The Alien," and during that time, we drink water, not wine.

At the end of the evening, I pack up my laptop, thank Carson for having me over, and leave. My dignity, if not intact, at least, isn't totally destroyed.

****

The next morning, I skitter to class moments before it starts, hoping to avoid an uncomfortable encounter with Carson. But there he is, waiting outside the door, already dressed in his teacher's wardrobe. Gray slacks, a thin blue pullover with a white T-shirt underneath, and a smile that makes his eyes shine.

"Hi," he says. "How are you today?"

"I'm not sure." I try not to be intimidated by his put-together appearance—the authority figure wardrobe, his courage in the face of awkwardness—compared to my half-hearted attempt at presentability: ripped jeans, Bemidji State hoodie, messy bun, and only mascara and tinted lip balm for makeup. "Why don't you tell me how you are first, and then we can compare."

He shifts his weight. "Okay. I'm doing good."

"You mean, 'I'm doing *well*.' "

"Right. And I suppose you're doing *well* at being a grammar geek?"

I grin despite myself. "We all have our strengths."

"Here," he says. "This is for you." Carson presents me with a takeout coffee from the student union. He has a cup for himself, which is in Carson's other hand, the one with the gauze-wrapped finger.

I've already got my own travel mug of coffee, which means I'll hold a cup in each hand if I take his. But it would be rude to refuse his peace offering. "Thanks. That was considerate of you."

Seeing that I'm now holding two cups, Carson knits his eyebrows together like he's thinking hard. "Maybe you could pour that into your travel mug? Is there room?"

"There will be." I take a large swig of the coffee I brought from home, but the mug is well-insulated. The coffee burns my throat, and I get that weird crampy sensation in my chest from drinking a piping hot beverage.

"Are you okay?" he asks, when I sort of convulse a little.

"Fine," I choke out. "How's your finger?"

"It's okay." He stares at it. "Hey, about last night…"

I bark out a laugh. "Isn't saying that, like, the worst cliche from the '80s?"

Carson tilts his head. "I'm not sure. I was born in the late '90s."

"Almost a millennial baby."

"I'm glad we cleared that up." He shifts his weight, seeming nervous. But that makes no sense. From my perspective, he's got all the power in this situation. "Anyway, I wanted to say that last night was, umm…well, this is embarrassing, but I've never been with anyone but Dana. That's why I froze up."

I take another scalding hot sip of coffee, trying to mask my discomfort. "Is that right?"

"Yeah…" He takes a deep breath. "Look. I was sixteen when I started dating Dana. We got married at eighteen. She's been the only one for me ever since. Until last night."

Seriously? "Carson, I meant it when I said you don't owe me an explanation."

"Too late. I just gave you one."

I nod. "Yes, but I wish you hadn't."

"Fair enough," he says. "You hate me."

"I don't hate you." My response is quick, and already I'm stung by guilt. "I'm trying to wrap my head around what happened. And how I let it happen."

"Yeah, I get it." Carson pauses. "The thing is, I'm in no shape for a relationship right now. But I hope we can stay writing partners and, well, see what happens."

Relief and indignation spar inside me. "One, I'm not looking for a relationship, at least, not with you. Two, we'd better stay writing partners; I won't have my work in this class jeopardized. As for the rest…I can't think that far into the future."

Carson looks like his brain is racing toward an eloquent response. But he's cut off.

"Good morning!" Professor Aldrich approaches, her long scarf floating behind her. "Are we ready to begin?"

Chapter 12

Carson
She thinks I'm an asshole.

I try to pay attention to the class discussion on "The Alien," but it's impossible to focus. Instead, a mantra plays on an endless loop inside my mind. *She thinks I'm an asshole. She thinks I'm an asshole. She thinks I'm an asshole.*

Eventually, it changes to *I* am *an asshole.*

What was I doing, bringing Rylee coffee? The only thing more awkward was last night when I said no one understands me but her. I grasp my cup's cardboard sleeve and take a sip. But what's with this stupid lid and that tiny little drink hole?

That will never do.

I clutch the lid and pull. A bit too hard—I misjudge because of my gauze-wrapped finger—and all at once I'm soaked with hot coffee. Most of it lands on the desk in front of me, spilling onto the floor. But some finds its way to my shirt and pants, steaming and darkening the fabric.

I jump out of my seat and glance around, praying not to be noticed. Yet Professor Aldrich, Rylee, and my other classmates stare. The dripping of coffee from my desk onto the floor breaks the silence. A deep wave of embarrassment washes over me.

"Oh no," Professor Aldrich says. "Are you okay?

Did you burn yourself?"

"No, no…" Attempting self-deprecation, I hold up my bandaged finger. "But I guess it's not my week." I look down at myself and then at my desk. "Are there any paper towels?"

"You'll need to get some from the bathroom," Professor Aldrich says.

"Okay, I'll be right back." I hurry out, wishing I could just not return. It's not that I'm embarrassed. There's something much deeper—the knowledge that once again, things will go wrong no matter how hard I try.

I grab two huge handfuls of paper towels from the men's room and return to class. "Don't mind me," I say, hoping Rylee isn't watching my clumsy attempt at cleaning up my mess.

"Carson," Professor Aldrich says. "Not to put you on the spot, but we haven't heard from you yet. What are your thoughts on 'The Alien?'"

I consider the question as I soak up the coffee with paper towels, creating a soggy brown lump in my hand. "It was an interesting glimpse into how people change as they grow older, how purpose and meaning slowly slip away until all that's left is an empty shell."

Yesterday, when I discussed the story with Rylee, my response was different. But today, I connect with Willy's hopelessness.

Professor Aldrich smiles, but it's the type of smile someone gives at a funeral. "I agree with your eloquent response. But you're so young, Carson, to make such an observation."

Tossing my head, I cross to the wastebasket by the door and throw away the used paper towels. "I'm old for my age."

"That's a shame," she replies. "Youth is fleeting. It's best not to grow old before our time."

Some of us don't have a choice, I say inside my head. Then again, maybe I had a choice. Perhaps I simply made all the wrong choices.

"No, don't sit there," Professor Aldrich says as I'm about to take a seat back at my desk. "There are still damp spots." She points to an empty desk, which is right next to Rylee. "There's a spot for you, Carson."

"Thanks." I shuffle over, trying hard not to look at Rylee. She leans in and asks, "Do you want some coffee? I have an extra cup."

My whispered response is quick. "Thanks, but if I spill again, it will be all over you."

Rylee places the extra coffee cup on my desk. Her voice is a soft hum in my ear. "I like to live dangerously."

Suddenly, a tiny spark of hope flickers in my chest.

Professor Aldrich calls for volunteers to read their stories, and an enthusiastic, older, mustached guy offers to be first. As he reads, my mind drifts off.

How did I even get here?

Ten years ago, I had it all mapped out. But the moment I saw Eddie, my entire world shifted. After witnessing firsthand the fragility of life and understanding the weight of that responsibility, I couldn't imagine trusting myself with the lives of others. What would I do when a parent's child couldn't be saved?

I became a high school biology teacher. It wasn't the perfect solution, but damn if I've ever discovered anything perfect except for Eddie and my love for him.

Now, every morning I wake up dizzy. In the pitch-black dawn, I hit my alarm clock to shut off the blaring classic rock station because the only other choices are classical or country. As I stumble to the shower, the hot water spraying down on me, I wonder how things got so massively screwed up.

Except today, when I woke, there was Ferris's dog breath, hot against my cheek. "You need to go out, boy?" Minutes later, I stood in my unfenced backyard with Ferris on a leash, who sniffed for the best spot to relieve himself, and my mind drifted to today's fiction class. I want feedback on my novel, but there's no one I can ask.

Besides, maybe, Rylee.

How could I blow my chance to have an amazing writing partner and friend? I wish I hadn't put the moves on her. But she's so damn hot, and I've been so damn lonely that I couldn't help myself.

How do I fix this?

Class ends, and like last week, I step up to Rylee before she can exit room 109. "Hey," I say, jumpy with anticipation. "How about we send each other our stories by Thursday and have our feedback ready to go when we meet at my place on Sunday?"

She eyes me skeptically, twirling a lock of hair around her finger. "I guess there isn't anywhere else we could meet. But next time, let's just get down to business, okay?"

"Yes, of course—strictly professional." I start to exit before she calls me back.

"Wait!"

Pivoting, I find her pointing at my lower section. I follow her gaze. Sure enough, the large coffee stain still looms conspicuously near my crotch.

"You're not gonna teach like that, are you?"

Laughter bubbles inside me. And yet, the mantra resumes.

She thinks I'm an asshole.

Chapter 13

Rylee

The restaurant at Reynold's Resort is slow for a Wednesday evening. Only a few customers come in and out, and Dana and I stand around the hostess station, trying to be productive as the clock ticks on.

Dana peers out the window. "At least it's busier than a year ago."

"When the economy tanked?" I ask.

She nods. "It was the worst. We had to let so many people go. Friends, even."

"That's rough." My focus flits to the few scattered patrons sitting on their own and nursing drinks, their murmur a low hum in the dimly lit restaurant. I look back at her. "I'm sorry you had to go through that."

She scans me up and down, her mouth pursing a bit. "What about you? Didn't you just finish college?"

It's like I'm back in high school, and the coolest girl has noticed me. "Kind of," I reply, trying to sound neutral. "From Bemidji State a year and a half ago. I wanted to go to grad school in California, but that fell through."

A half-grin pulls up one side of Dana's mouth. If I tried that expression, I'd look like a weirdo, but Dana's pretty enough to make it work. "What school in California were you going for?" she asks.

My hands need something to do, so I use a capped-dry erase marker like it's an iron, trying to flatten out the laminated table map. "USC, but now, instead, I'm at Bemidji State again for their Creative Writing MFA program."

"Oh yeah?" Dana inches a little closer, her voice a tick warmer. "Carson's taking a writing class there." She pauses. "Do you ever run into him?"

My throat goes dry. "Uh-huh…" I drop the dry-erase maker like it's incriminating evidence, and I am caught in the act. "We're in class together."

Dana flashes a smile that tries to be genuine, but her eyes stay stoic. "You have a class with Carson?"

"Yup." I shrug. "He's also my brother's AP Bio teacher. Funny how small the world is, huh?"

"Yeah." Dana smooths her already pristine auburn hair. "But Bemidji *is* small." She scowls and bites her bottom lip. "Okay, I'm gonna say something, and it might be awkward, but…well, we'll just have to deal with it."

Is she going to bring up that day when she mortified me and committed emotional homicide? Say she's sorry? Though I wouldn't turn down an apology, it's better to pretend like it never happened. "Okay…"

Dana's flinty stare challenges me, her words setting off alarm bells in my head. "I don't know what Carson told you about our relationship status, but we're still married." Her voice has a dull thud of finality. "And we both want to work it out—for Eddie's sake."

It's as if I'm reliving my teenage years all over again. Back then, she could see I was in love with her boyfriend. Now, she must sense that with Carson, my heart wails like a car alarm.

Oh God. Did he tell her about the other night?

No way is a blush of humiliation NOT blooming

across my cheeks, and my toes curl inside my shoes. "I get it, Dana. But you don't have to worry about me. Not that you would, because I'm sure I'm not Carson's type, but even if I was, well, I couldn't date my brother's teacher." I give a nervous laugh, my cheeks burning beneath her gaze. "It'd be kinda weird if he and I dated, right?"

Dana eyeballs at me, her mouth pressing down at the corners. "That's not what I meant."

"Huh?"

"I wasn't telling you to stay away from him or whatever. That's not how it is." She turns to the window that overlooks the parking lot and perks up. "Oh! Sweet baby Jesus—two families of four pulled up! Tonight isn't gonna be a total bust after all." Dana turns back to me, her expression growing serious again. "But yeah— like—it'd be really helpful if you could tell me if he's flirting with anyone? Women can't get enough of his whole 'boyish charm' thing. Lord knows I've been there." She blinks a couple of times, and for a second, I wonder if she'll start crying.

I hesitate. Does she actually want me to do this? "Yeah… I mean, sure," I struggle out. "If he flirts with anybody, I'll tell you."

"Thank you," she rasps. Either it's a trick of shadow skipping her face, or she winks at me. "You're not half-bad, Rylee Lynch."

****

Thursday. Class is done by two thirty. I'm home and should do my assignments, but my fingers can't resist the pull of *A Viscount for Vivien*. The light reflects off my computer screen as I type, the cursor blinking on the page in front of me. An hour max, I promise myself, and then I'll get to my homework: an analysis of Dani Donnovan's short story "Team Building" and writing a fiction piece inspired by it.

What does it say about me, that I'd rather work on my romance novel? My goal has always been to write literary fiction, like my father did. I'm sure he never thought that I'd write romance.

I wonder what he would think, if he could read my novels. Would he be proud? The fact I will never know is like a splinter lodged inside my heart.

My cell phone buzzes as I'm in the thick of the first flirtatious encounter between Vivien and Anton. Ready to reject the call, I catch the caller ID.

It's Jack.

That has to be wrong. I blink at the screen. J-a-c-k flashes in bold white letters against the black background. Emotions blitz through my mind—surprise, confusion, a hint of fear. But I pick up.

"Hi." I try to sound light and unsurprised, like his calling is the most natural thing in the world. "What's up?"

There's static and feedback, but nothing else. "Hello?" I drop my forehead into my hand, defeat blooming in my chest. Jack called me by accident. That's so much worse than if he hadn't called at all. "Jack? You butt-dialed me. I'm hanging up now."

I'm about to tap the little red receiver icon, but then I hear, "Rylee? Are you there?"

I put the phone back to my ear. "Jack? Hi! I thought you'd butt-dialed me."

He laughs. "I did. But my butt must have a direct line to my heart because I've been missing you. It's great to hear your voice."

He's been missing me? The Jack I know would sooner read chick lit than admit that. "It's great to hear your voice, too. What are you doing right now?"

"Walking along Venice Beach. You?"

"I've been writing."

"Oh yeah? What?"

"I'm working on a story for my short fiction class." The lie pops out like it's the truth. And it's almost the truth.

"Tell me more."

He's interested. Fingers crossed, Jack doesn't ask me to read him my draft so far.

"We have to write something inspired by Donovan's 'Team Building Day.' "

It's this absurdist, dark humor story about a group of coworkers who accidentally kill each other off during a team building exercise gone wrong.

"Ah, yeah. Professor Aldrich's class?" He had the same course load before he became a TA. And Jack could transfer straight into the USC PhD program. Small town Bemidji might be cold and dark, but that means more time for writing. "That was when I wrote my jungle story," Jack says. "The one published in *Ink and Angst*?"

Ink and Angst is a selective online journal and a great credit to have on your writer's resume. He'd told me all about it when we first started dating, and I'd gushed, "That's so cool!"

Now I say, "Well, I'm excited about my idea," and I launch into detail—explaining how it will be in the second person with a contemporary Charlotte Brontë and her husband going through genetic counseling. She has to explain her family's deaths, and they get more and more ridiculous as it goes on, like a parallel universe with dark humor and allusions to Charlotte Brontë's work. And her husband keeps calling her Jane by mistake since she's often confused with her most famous protagonist.

"Huh."

I wait for Jack to expand, but he doesn't. My focus strays to a bulletin board hanging on the wall over my desk. There are thumbtacked mementoes, like ticket stubs, birthday cards, and photos. One is of Jack and me, a selfie I later printed out. Pink-cheeked and sporting silly, sloppy grins, we're drinking bourbon by the firepit in Jack's backyard. It was a cool night, and we wrapped ourselves in the same blanket. I'm not really a bourbon fan, but I drank it to keep warm, and I clung to Jack for the same reason. It was early in our relationship, yet already I felt a strong connection.

Does he think of that night? Because I do—all the time. At least, I used to.

"What's wrong with my story idea?"

I hold my breath, waiting for his response. Jack lets out an uncomfortable chuckle. "I said nothing."

"Exactly," I mutter.

His words come out in a whoosh. "Okay, Rye Bread, I'm thinking, Charlotte Brontë, really? Aren't there already a million reimaginings of *Pride and Prejudice*? It's overdone."

My mouth pops open in silent shock. First, I've told him before not to call me "Rye Bread." More importantly, for God's sake, he's getting his PhD in literature. He's aware that Jane Austen wrote *Pride and Prejudice*.

Since he has to be baiting me, I don't respond. "How's your book coming?" I ask instead.

Jack sighs before launching into an explanation of his book—which is also his thesis project—about a high school kid in suburban Minneapolis who's dealing with the usual coming-of-age anxiety, his parents' infidelities, and the nuclear family's fragility. His publisher has requested restructuring the opening scene and including more exposition around the mother's character arc.

"If you found out your husband was cheating on you with one of his college students," he says, "how would you respond?"

I search my mind for a response that won't involve playing his game. "Umm...can you give me a bit more context?"

Jack launches into an explanation, and I close out my document of *A Viscount for Vivien*. This could take a while.

Chapter 14

Rylee

The late afternoon sun bouncing off my windshield is almost blinding as I pull up to Carson's house, dread and excitement ripping through me in a dangerous game of tug-of-war. But it doesn't matter how determinedly excitement yanks on the rope—dread will always win. There's no chance I'll risk further humiliation by throwing myself at him again, not now that he and Dana are working on their marriage.

I steel myself and step out of my car, determined to keep things businesslike today. The sight of Carson outside raking leaves, ruggedly adorable with Ferris running circles around his feet, does nothing to break my resolve. I tell myself: *You're here to work. Nothing more, nothing less.*

"Hey, Rylee." He grins, pushing up his sleeves. "You're right in time to hold the leaf bag."

I don't have time to respond before a happy splash of black fur races past us, yipping and barking. I laugh, and Carson shakes his head, smiling as well.

"Ferris loves chasing leaves," Carson says.

Ferris circles us. Running in the autumn wind, his mouth is full of fluttering colors and twigs.

I contemplate Carson's leaf bag. "The hardest part is always getting in the first few handfuls of leaves. Did you know they have these cardboard insert thingies that keep the bag open?"

Carson holds his rake with one hand. "Oh, yeah?"

"Yeah. My dad was excited when he discovered them at the hardware store. It used to be our thing, my dad and I, bagging leaves together."

"Oh." Carson's mouth goes slack, and his eyes pool with sympathy. It's like he backed over a bunny rabbit by accident. "Sorry. I didn't mean to bring up old memories."

I wave off the awkwardness as if I'm shooing away bugs. "No worries. It won't break me to hold the bag open, and I'll even push down the leaves as you put them in." My words come out in a rush. "Where should I put my computer?"

"I'll put it inside. Do you also want me to take your purse?"

"Sure, thanks." I hand him both.

He takes them through his front door as a gust of wind threatens to upend Carson's carefully constructed leaf pile. I snatch up the rake, ready for battle. "You won't escape me, bitches!" I yell at the flying leaves.

I look over to see Carson on his front stoop, watching my wild efforts like I'm a vaudeville spectacle he can't quite believe. Embarrassed, I kick at the ground. "I didn't want all your hard work ruined."

His expression is serious. "Have you tried positive reinforcement? I've found that fallen leaves don't respond well to punitive measures."

"Right," I reply, "because they have nothing to lose. Their fate is inside a garbage bag or being trapped by an uncaring tire. Snow will cover the lucky ones until after the thaw." I run the rake through the grass at my feet. "Then they'll get scooped up—along with all the dog poop and candy wrappers the trick-or-treaters leave behind."

Using his index finger to rub his chin, Carson considers this. "Trick-or-treaters leave behind dog poop?"

"Some of the angry ones do."

He laughs—and darn if he isn't cute when he smiles—before saying, "Guess I'd better buy good candy this year."

"No black licorice or breath mints." I let out a low groan. "But the worst are those peanut butter-flavored taffies wrapped in orange or black wrappers."

"Those *are* the worst. I never ate them."

"Me neither."

I hold open the bag, and Carson bends down, scoops up the leaves, and stands very close as he shoves them inside. I'm painfully aware of how his Levis-clad butt looks oh-so-good when he bends over. After the bag is full, he glances up at his tree and down at his yard, thanking me for my help. Then he sort of stands there, gazing at me, and I can't help but ask. "What?"

"Nothing. Sorry. You'd lose all respect for me if I told you," he mumbles.

"Now you have to tell me."

He brushes a leaf from his sleeve. "No, really," he stammers, "it's ridiculous."

I nudge his ankle with my sneaker's rubber toe. "Try me."

Rolling his eyes skyward, he asks, "Did you ever read *The Majestic Seven*? That fantasy about the seven heroes who must save their kingdom?"

"No," I reply. "But I've heard of it. Why?"

Carson's cheeks turn the slightest bit pink. "I was

thinking how you're like Lady Seraphina."

My hands fly to either side of my face. "It's because of my pointy ears, right?"

"What? No." He blinks in confusion. "Why would you make that connection?"

"Because I saw the trailer for the movie adaptation, and the only female character is an elf. The tips of her ears are like razors."

"No!" Carson swallows a laugh. "God, no, that's not what I meant."

I look him up and down. "Well, what did you mean?"

His voice sounds like a worn vinyl record, smooth in the center but scratched at the edges. "You're the type of girl who could save the world."

"You mean 'woman' and not 'girl,' right?"

"Of course. Sorry." He releases a self-conscious chuckle. "You're the kind of *woman* who could save the world. One hundred percent."

"Thank you." Then, feeling that magnetic pull, I drop my gaze to the ground.

He hits his forehead. "God. I'm such an idiot. I promised I'd be professional today, and I've already blown it, haven't I?"

I search for a response. Thankfully, Ferris runs up to me, and I busy myself with petting him. "It's fine. But I don't understand. Why would I lose all respect for you?"

"Because you'll realize I like fantasy novels."

Kneeling down, I let Ferris nuzzle my shoulder. "Please. As if I didn't already know? Remember how in high school, you'd check out *The Prince of Saturn* and slide it into your backpack before anyone could see?"

Carson raises an eyebrow. "Except for you."

I notice a renegade leaf on my shoulder and brush it off. "That's right. Because I was also always in the media center after lunch, most likely checking out some gothic romance, which is way more looked down upon than science fiction or fantasy."

"Yeah, but you weren't on the hockey team." He smirks. "If the other players knew about my reading habits, they'd have kicked my ass."

"So, you tried to pretend you weren't smart? How'd that work out for you, college boy?"

He opens his mouth to respond but laughs instead. "Hey, you mentioned gothic romance, and that reminds me. I dug your story. A contemporary Charlotte Brontë! It was so original. I don't have very many revision notes for you, because the story flowed. And I'm worried that if you rework it a lot, you'll lose that."

"Thanks, I'm glad you liked it. I liked your story too, and not just because you liked mine." Shifting my weight, I say, "Should we go inside and get to work?"

He nods. "Yeah. Let's do that. Follow me."

At this moment, I'd be happy to follow him anywhere.

****

Several minutes later, we're trying to unpack "Team Building Day," analyzing symbols and deciphering themes, while Carson taps his pencil like a metronome. Focus eludes us, and Carson's pencil tapping and knee bouncing don't help. I push my chair away from the table, pressing my forehead into my hands.

"Are you okay?" Carson's soft concern slices through me. Why does he have to be so likable and attractive?

"Sorry. I'm having a hard time concentrating."

Carson's face falls. "No, I'm sorry. This is my fault."

"Wait. *What's* your fault?"

He grabs a breath. "I should be better at ignoring my attraction to you."

Inside me, fourteen-year-old Rylee beams with happiness, but twenty-four-year-old me remains skeptical. "Okay." I shift in my seat, nervous we're treading into dangerous territory. "Because of Dana?"

Carson's attention snaps into focus. "Dana? No. But...why do you ask?"

"She said you two were trying to get back together, for Eddie's sake."

His staccato chuckle is like a dry cough in a vacant hall. "No way. Even if she wanted to, we're never getting back together."

"Oh." I study his face, but he's difficult to read in the dim light. "Are you sure?"

"Absolutely. Ever since I walked in on her with another guy in our bed, there's zero chance for a joyful reunion." He runs a hand through his hair. "We share a son; that's all."

"I...I don't know what to say."

Carson hears my careful tone and sees me worrying my bottom lip. "It's okay. You don't need to say anything. But if I want to see Eddie, I've got to keep her happy. Plus, she's got a jealous streak a mile wide. If she thought you and I were an item, your life at work would be over. And you need your job, right? To help with Brandon's medical bills?"

"Yeah."

Carson leans forward, his intensity focused on me. "So, that's a huge reason we should keep our distance.

But it's not because I don't want to…" He rubs his chin, as if finishing his trailing thought.

A cool, autumnal breeze blows in from an open window, and somehow my nerve endings are even more awakened. I relax and come alive all at once. No businesslike demeanor this time—just Carson's warmth and the golden skin of his arms extending out from rolled-up sleeves. There's his mouth and his hips and my desire for him to be on top of me, pinning me in place, slowing my mind and heightening my senses, so that everything—Brandon's brain tumor, the broken back door, not going to USC but sleeping in my childhood bed underneath a midnight blue comforter meant to warm two bodies instead of one—it all blurs around the edges. The only thing left vivid is him.

"Please don't explain," I plead. "It's fine."

"No," Carson counters. "Not to me. It's not 'fine.' I *can't* be involved with anyone right now, but I also can't stop feeling like this."

"Feeling like what?"

His eyes bore into mine, and they're hooded with desire. "Like it hurts not to touch you. Like it *really* hurts not to kiss you. Like it really, really, *really* hurts not to take you to bed."

When the idea hits me, I hesitate. But just for a second. "We wouldn't have to tell anyone. It could be like a side project. We could, well, take care of our physical longing and then get right back to studying. That way, our grades won't be affected."

Carson straightens his glasses. "A 'side project'? You'd be okay with that?"

I shrug. "Sure. I mean, it's not like I'm head-over-feet in love with you. I have a long-distance relationship on the back burner, and hopefully, I'm moving to California soon. But I enjoy hanging out with you, so yeah, let's be writing partners who have sex."

Worried that I've been too blunt, I cringe.

His brown eyes bore into mine. "You make it sound so transactional."

"Well, maybe it is." I tilt up my chin. "We'll agree that when the class is done, we're done, and we'll keep it on the DL."

Several seconds go by, and it's like Carson's frozen in time, his gaze pinned on me. He leans back in the chair, processing my words. "In that case," Carson finally begins, words catching in his throat, "we should establish some ground rules."

"Like?"

"No couple behavior in public."

"Got it. Because we're not—we won't be a couple." My voice breaks at the end, betraying a sudden pang of doubt. I push through. "And if either of us develops romantic feelings toward the other, we need to fess up right away and nip it in the bud."

Carson smiles. "This is a bud-nipping situation?"

"Indeed." I scoot my chair up to his table and open a new document.

"What are you doing?"

I give him a subtle eye roll. "There's no point in creating rules if we don't type them up. Do you want me to share the document with you?"

Carson rubs his face and squeezes his nose like he's considering a profound question. "I guess. But make the settings private."

I tap on my keyboard. "Done. Okay, our first rule has to be that we keep this a secret."

Carson gives his silent agreement, but as we come up with more rules, there's more back and forth. Eventually, we settle on this list:

> 1. We tell no one about our side project.
> 2. If either of us develops romantic feelings for the other, we say so, and the side project will end.
> 3. We aren't a couple, and we're only allowed to act like one or hookup on Sunday afternoons/evenings.
> 4. Our side project will end when our class ends.
> 5. No emotional intimacy. But we can be friends.

"How will that work?" I ask, worried that rule number five is vague. "Aren't friends emotionally intimate?"

But Carson says, "This will fall apart if we're not friends."

Embarrassed to press the point (I still don't get how we can be friends who have sex and *not* be intimate), I extend my hand so we can shake on it. "Okay. Deal?"

Carson takes my hand, but rather than shaking it, he draws me in. He tilts his head down to kiss me, slow and deep. The kiss grows in passion and warmth, and eventually he pulls away, winded. "There's a better way to seal the deal than with a handshake."

His gaze grows heavy-lidded as he reaches for me, his fingers tugging at my clothing and dragging us closer to the bed. Carson lowers me onto the mattress and hovers above me, one hand propped against the wall. His other hand trails along my face, neck, and slowly down my body. I arch into him, my hands grasping and exploring every muscle and tendon in his taut skin.

We lock eyes, and I swear there are sparks between us.

"I've been wanting you all week," he murmurs. "And I hope you're not offended that I bought condoms."

My laughter escapes like a happy sigh. "If your buying condoms offends me, we've got a serious problem."

He presses himself closer as he grins. "Let's say it's been a while since I purchased any—I almost forgot how to go about it."

Pushing up to kiss him again, my lips meet his lips in a deep embrace. "Don't be modest; I bet you're a natural at this sort of thing."

Carson is firm against me, and he presses himself deeper into the softness between my legs. "So…are we good to go?"

My slight moan is all the answer he needs. Everything but this moment slips away faster than a dropped bar of soap in the shower. It's him and me together, accompanied by nothing but the beating of our hearts.

Afterwards, we spoon, my head nestled underneath his chin, his blue flannel sheets pulled up and keeping us warm, but what's really keeping me warm is him.

We both drift off, but then Ferris comes up to the bed and whimpers.

"It's feeding time," Carson says. "Sorry." He gets up, pulls on some clothes, and walks toward his kitchen, Ferris at his heels.

After finding my shirt and underwear, I put them on and follow man and dog to the kitchen. "I hate to mention it," I call, "but we didn't write any rules about snuggling."

Carson stops, and I almost crash into him. He turns around. "True. Is snuggling okay?"

Unsure how to respond, I sputter. "I have nothing against it. But only people in relationships do that."

He steps closer and sweeps his fingertips against my cheek, and my calloused heart softens a tiny bit.

"If you're not comfortable with it, I understand," he says, pulling away. "But cuddling with you is a privilege and not an obligation, okay?"

I take his hand and squeeze. "Thank you. But we should get to work, Carson. This is important to me."

"Then it's important to me as well." He steps away, purposefully creating distance between the two of us. Ferris grows impatient, and as Carson fills his food dish, he asks, "Should I make coffee? Or juice?"

"You can make juice? I'd like to see that."

He grins, gives Ferris his kibble, and goes back toward the bedroom to find his jeans. "I have juice, which I could pour into glasses." Pulling on his pants, he says, "Would you prefer orange or apple?"

"Apple would be great. Thank you."

I'm mesmerized as I watch him pour apple juice into two glasses. But it's time to get serious because the electricity in the air threatens to consume me.

Focus, Rylee.

Focus.

Chapter 15

Carson

Monday. I struggle to get through class with Rylee so close. It's almost like we're both in a play that neither of us auditioned for. Not that I ever did drama club in high school. I was busy cramming in other activities like hockey, student council, and National Honor Society. Other than writing my sci-fi book in the silence of my living room, taking this fiction class—and working with Rylee—is the first time I've ever embraced my creative side.

When class ends, I want to sidle up to Rylee and drape my arm over her shoulders. It would be great to grab coffee from the little station at the student union and find two cushy chairs that stare out the window at Lake Bemidji. We could talk or just exist together for a few minutes before parting ways again.

But I don't suggest any of that. I can't—and not only because I have to get to school.

I approach Rylee as she's packing up and say, "Send me your story by Thursday, and I'll do the same."

She nods. "Sounds good, Carson. And congratulations."

"Huh? Congratulations for what?"

There's something about her, the way she stands before me in her oversized flannel shirt, her expression earnest from behind her cat eyeglasses. It makes me want to freeze time and space so I can extend this moment with her.

She smirks. "You had a drama-free class today. No heroic acts or spilled coffee. You did a stellar job at flying under the radar!"

"Smartass," I murmur, and when she responds with a sexy, guttural laugh, it brings back a flood of memories: Tangled in bed sheets. Her skin pressed against mine. Doing things to her and her doing things to me...

"See ya." I hurry out before anyone can see how much I want her.

Rushing through campus, I get to my car. I have thirteen minutes to drive to the high school before it's time to teach third-hour General Bio, my least favorite class. None of the kids want to be there or are interested in life's building blocks. Instead, they snicker every time I say "organism" because it's close to saying "orgasm," and they're all desperate to know what it's like, having an orgasm in the presence of another living organism.

It's fucking awesome, I want to tell them. And I mean that literally.

Then I remind myself: Don't get attached. It's one thing to have no-strings sex with Rylee, but it's another to flirt and fantasize about her. That can't lead anywhere good. Still, when I pull into the school parking lot, I'm in a great mood, despite the prospect of General Bio, which starts in four minutes. I shut my car door, open the trunk, and retrieve my laptop and the stack of quizzes I graded over the weekend. I'm making my way toward the outside door closest to my classroom when I hear a male voice call out.

"Mr. Meyers!"

Internally, I groan. That voice belongs to the principal, Dwayne Thatcher. "Hello, Dwayne." I refuse to call my colleagues by anything other than their first names, and I hate the affectation of educators calling other educators by Mr. or Ms., especially when there aren't kids around.

"Why are you getting to school so late?" Dwayne asks.

"I have my grad class on Monday mornings, remember? Why are *you* leaving here so early?" I joke.

Dwayne's nostrils flare, and I realize I've stepped in it. He's my boss, and I don't have a teasing relationship with him.

"Not that it's any of your business, but I have a meeting at the district center."

"Of course, sorry. Well, have a good day."

"Hold on." Dwayne never seems cognizant of the bell schedule, that the teachers are required to be in class by a certain time, like the students are. He steps toward me as if he wants a heart-to-heart.

"We need to talk. I saw the AP Bio test scores from last spring. Did you think I wouldn't notice?"

"Umm, I'm not sure how to answer that." My chest constricts. "I mean, I do my best, but a lot of these students begin with a disadvantage."

Dwayne grimaces. "Your solution is to start some program where you're away from the students while getting licensed in English? It makes no sense. Why would I let you teach both subjects?"

"Dwayne, I hadn't thought that far. I just wanted to explore. You can understand that, right?"

"Actually, no." He breathes, nostrils flaring. "If you ask me, you should 'explore' becoming a more effective biology teacher. These kids need you, and you're off being flaky. It's unacceptable."

Without meaning to, I clench my jaw, which is better than opening my mouth and losing my temper. "Class is about to start," I state. "Perhaps we could continue this conversation some other time?"

Dwayne throws me a look of contempt, one that says he still remembers ten years ago when I was the arrogant, outspoken student council president who riled up the student body, getting them to question the policies of the vice principal, who, at the time, was Dwayne. They even protested Dwayne's suspension policy once I pointed out that Black and Native American students were three times more likely to be suspended than White ones. It resulted in a lot of bad press for Dwayne, and for a while it looked like he might resign.

But Dwayne persisted. He was still vice principal when they hired me, and again three years later, when I received tenure. But not now. Since Dwayne has ascended to the top spot on the high school's hierarchy, he's made two things very clear: one, he holds a grudge, and two, I should watch my back.

Now, I'm hyper aware that I'm turning my back on Dwayne, but what choice do I have? I need to get to class.

Chapter 16

Rylee

"I need you to talk to Mom for me."

Brandon barges into my room without a preamble, startling me out of my trance. I'd been writing a romantic scene between Vivien and Anton, and Carson's kiss, his touch, our clandestine dalliance—it all swirled around inside me until I felt like a character in one of my own stories. Sad as it is, our secret, forbidden love affair is the most exciting thing that's ever happened in my boring little existence.

Except, it's not a *love* affair. I need to get that L-word out of my own personal dictionary. It's fine for Vivien and Anton, but love doesn't apply to Carson and me.

Anyway, Brandon brings me crashing down to earth. Fingers flying, I minimize my typing screen and shoot him a dirty look. "Ever heard of knocking?"

"What difference does it make? You're sitting here, writing." Brandon makes a sweeping gesture toward my cluttered desk. "That's all you ever do."

"Hey, that's not true, but even if it was, I respect your privacy, so you should respect mine."

My little brother gives me a scornful look, and his tone matches his expression. "Puh-lease. You do not respect my privacy. I hear you and Mom talking about the effects of radiation, and whether surgery altered my emotional capacity, and if my hormones and sexual development and my goddam fertility will be affected. Don't get all high and mighty when I enter your room without knocking."

Okay. Brandon's angry. He has a right, for sure. Confronting your own mortality before you've turned eighteen and dealing with the effects of brain surgery and radiation—it's been a rough road. I hate that Brandon overheard Summer and me talking about him. But that's what she and I do together; we obsess over Brandon's health and healing progress.

"I'm sorry, Brandon. You're right. I promise we won't talk about you like that anymore." It's a lie, but at the very least, Summer and I will keep our mouths shut when he might be within earshot.

I spin in my chair, my eyes meeting Brandon's. He's got his gray hoodie pulled up, but I can still make out the fuzzy head underneath, tilting like he's trying to relieve the tension in his neck.

"Awesome," he says, his face blank. "And…you'll convince Mom to let me take someone to homecoming."

"Like…on a date?"

Brandon shoves his hands into his hoodie's front pocket. "Yeah, of course. That's what people do in high school. They take dates to homecoming."

I glance away from him as he stands over me. "You asked Summer, and she said no?"

He takes on a funny voice, mimicking her. "It's risky, Brandon. All those kids dancing close, like they're in a germ factory. And what if you pass out again? I'm sorry, buddy, but it's not a good idea." His normal voice returns. "I haven't passed out since a week after my last radiation treatment, and I told her I'd be careful and not stand in a tight crowd, but she doesn't trust me."

I sympathize with Brandon's plight but still understand Summer's fear: he had fainting spells during and shortly after radiation, and they were terrifying. Even now, his immune system is weak, but of course, Brandon will want to get close if he brings a date—and if he has the chance to get to second base or beyond, he'll take it.

"Brandon…" I choose my words like I'm walking a tightrope. "You understand the risk and how important it is that you stay healthy, right?"

"Yes, but I'm done with being careful. The last few months have taught me to seize the day. Before, I was afraid to ask Joni out, but not now. Carpe diem, right?"

"Wait, who's Joni?"

Brandon's face softens. "She's from Minneapolis, and we met in band. We connected over feeling out of place, and then we started texting. I figured she was way out of my league, and I'd get friend-zoned, but I asked her out anyway—and she said yes! Now Mom's being a beast about it, and I need you to talk her down."

My throat knots. Brandon's health is key, but so is his happiness. "I'll try convincing her, but I make no promises."

"Do your best, Rye." He twists his mouth into a hybrid of resignation and acknowledgment. "I need this."

****

On Thursday, I meet Mel for lunch at the cafe in Itasca State Park. There's a great outdoor seating area, surrounded by trees and only several hundred feet from the Mississippi River headwaters. It's a weekday and not super crowded, so we find a table in a sunny spot, making a midday meal out of lattes and slices of fresh-baked cherry pie.

"What's on your mind?" Mel asks. She can always tell when something is bothering me.

I sip my coffee, careful not to get a steamed milk mustache. "Brandon wants to take a girl to the homecoming dance."

"But that's great," Mel says. "His energy is back. Sounds like he's embracing life."

My anxiety bubbles up, so I calm it with a forced laugh. "You're right; it's awesome. But somehow, it's my job to convince Summer, and I'm not sure I can. I want him to be a regular, carefree kid, but he's not, and we're still in a risky zone."

Mel stabs a cherry with her fork, a tiny piece of buttery crust joining it in her mouth. She chews and swallows. "So what are you going to do?"

I start to answer, but she holds up her hand. "Wait, don't tell me."

"Why not?"

"Because you'll always do whatever makes Brandon happy."

I tilt my head from side to side. "That's true, but this time it means convincing Summer. That may not be possible."

"I realize it's hard." Mel reaches over and squeezes my knee. "Do you want me to talk to her for you?"

My stomach flips. "What would you say?"

She spears another cherry and dips it into a forgotten dab of meringue. "That Brandon needs some freedom before he totally rebels, and that you have a life and can't always take care of them both."

God love my BFF. Her loyalty is unwavering, even

if she sometimes gets things wrong. "Okay, Summer understands all that, and neither she nor Brandon ever asked me to take care of them. It was my choice."

"True," Mel says. "But you're over-responsible. When Summer doesn't take charge, you pick up the pieces."

"Still, you're being unfair."

But is she? I became a second mom to Brandon early on. I attended his parent-teacher conferences when Summer was too busy or exhausted to go. I made sure he had the right school supplies every fall, snow boots that fit every winter, and I always enrolled him in music and science summer camp as soon as registration opened. And when he got that nasty brain cancer, I read every article about germinoma tumors I could find and took it upon myself to food shop and prepare meals that would supposedly help him heal.

Mel sips her latte and turns her focus to the distance, toward the hiking trails. "I want you to be happy, Rye. And you're so worried about their happiness that you neglect your own."

"Not always." It's tempting to tell Mel about my side project with Carson, to confess that I'm being selfish, reckless even. Then again, if she knew, she might be furious. Mel arches her back and stretches in her seat. "I have twenty more minutes. Should we walk a little?"

"Yeah."

We get up, throw away our garbage, put the utensils in the trays to be washed, and walk toward the trail leading to the headwaters. Rays of sunlight shoot through trees covered in red and orange leaves, and the sky is a perfect cobalt blue.

"What a gorgeous day. It makes me grateful to still

live here."

Mel walks while wrapping her arms around her chest. "Do you remember that time in eleventh grade when we planned a trip to Galapagos? We spent weeks researching it, figuring out the best way to get there, the trails we'd hike, and where we'd stay. We were going to sign up for scuba lessons."

"I remember. We thought the trip could be our graduation present."

"Yeah."

Mel and I stroll in unison down the dirt path, leaves crunching under our feet. We approach the site of the headwaters, where there are rocks and bridges so you can stand directly over the origin of Old Man River. Here, the Mississippi is tiny compared to the massive body of water it becomes several miles down.

"But of course," Mel continues, "we never asked our parents. Summer needed you to babysit because she was always working crazy hours at her store, and that trip was never gonna happen."

"I'm sorry, Mel."

She stops walking and turns toward me. "You don't need to be sorry. I'm not asking for an apology."

"Okay…" I pause, sensing an unusual vibe from her. "What are you asking for?"

"Forgiveness."

Her voice was low just now, and perhaps the wind made me mishear her. "I don't understand. Forgiveness for what?"

"For leaving." Mel's eyes alight with both joy and desperation. "The National Park system has an opening, and I'm starting in Smoky Mountain. Then I can internally apply for other parks, like the Everglades, during winter. It's my chance to travel and experience the best of the United States."

A heavy rock drops into my stomach, and I struggle to hide my emotions. "Mel, that's amazing! You thought I'd be mad?"

Without a word, she pulls me into a hug. We hold each other for a moment before she sniffles and pulls away. "I knew you'd be happy for me, but I remember what you said when you weren't going to California."

I furrow my brow. "What did I say?"

"You said you'd be okay staying as long as I stayed too." She eyes me like I'm written in a code she needs to crack. "I've been happy here, with you and my family and working at Itasca, but when this opportunity came up, I couldn't turn it down. It's like the Holy Grail for any naturalist's career."

My smile spreads even as my heart aches. "That's so great, Mel. When do you leave?"

"Two weeks."

"Wow. What does your family say?"

We link arms and keep walking. Mel gives me a sideways hug. "Mom and Dad are happy for me, of course."

"What about Carson?"

Mel shrugs. "When I told him about my job, he barely said anything. I'm not even sure he heard me. Or that he'll notice when I'm gone."

"Maybe you should talk to him about that."

"Nah."

As we walk, I try to align my feelings about Carson with what Mel just told me. I also attempt to hide my crushing disappointment. I love her, and I'd never want to burden her, but on the inside, I'm crying.

Don't leave me behind!

When I drive away from Itasca, I don't go home. Instead, I steer toward downtown Bemidji to Summer's salon/store. It sells artisan soaps and incense, hand-crafted leather bags, tasteful Bemidji tourist paraphernalia, and hand-knit scarves. In an adjacent room, there are salon chairs for hair styling, facials, and mani/pedis. The whole place always smells like cinnamon and suede. A bell over the door tinkles when I walk in.

A handful of customers occupy the store, and the adjacent salon has one customer, attended to by one of Summer's employees. Summer sits at the front, near the cash register, across from Leo. They each sip from a mug—presumably tea—and it's like I've walked into an ad for Nordic Cruises. Summer, with her caramel-colored hair, nose stud, and creamy complexion, and Leo, with his shiny bald head that houses a toothpaste-commercial smile. They gaze at each other, enjoying some inside joke and looking like they should be surrounded by teal-crested waves and empires of the Mediterranean. Instead, they're in a dimly lit room as a jazzy blues song—some female with a husky voice—plays through the store's speakers. Summer spots me and grins.

"Rylee, what a nice surprise."

"Hi. How's business today?"

"Not bad. The lavender beeswax cosmetics are selling like wildfire."

Leo stands. My goodness, he's tall. And broad. "Hello, Rylee. I was just on my way out."

"Hey, Leo. How are you?"

"Good. You?"

"I'm okay. I hear you're super busy?"

"I suppose." He grabs his phone, wallet, and keys, which were stored away on a low desk shelf meant for staff.

"Well, if you have a chance, could you fix our back screen door? It's barely hanging on to its hinges."

"Yeah, of course. I'll come over ASAP."

He turns toward Summer, and she holds out her hands in a, *what can you do?* sort of gesture.

"Take care, Summer. I'll call you about that screen door."

"Thanks, Leo."

He exits the store, and I run my fingers over a rack of chunky infinity scarves knit from lamb's wool. "I bet these will sell out. Forty bucks is low for hand-knit."

"She can make them quick, since the stitches are loose."

"Hmm." I study the scarves, contemplating if I should buy one in midnight blue.

"Rylee?"

I turn toward my mother. "Yeah?"

"Did you come here to talk about scarves, or is there something on your mind?"

Summer's expression is open and unblinking. I've always envied her nearly chestnut-colored eyes and straight, silky hair to match, and her height. At five-six, she has a good two inches on me, and my hair, which is a dull brown (before it's dyed black), curls sideways every time there's an ounce of humidity in the air.

"Yeah," I say. "It's about Brandon."

My mom and brother resemble each other, and their connection is like steel wire, twisted but unbreakable. Who am I to be an intermediary between them? And yet,

Brandon asked me to talk to her, and so here we are.

"He asked me to convince you to let him go to homecoming with that girl he likes."

Summer squeezes her eyes shut for a moment before meeting my gaze. "You're endorsing this idea?"

I shrug. "Maybe? It's not like the thought of him exerting himself at a dance and getting close to some girl isn't terrifying. But he's been through a lot, and Brandon is usually so stoic. How can we say no?"

"*We* wouldn't say no. I'm the decider. You understand, right?"

"Of course."

She tosses her shoulders back as her focus skims away from me. "He used to tell me everything. When I'd drive him to the hospital for his radiation appointments, we really bonded. But something's happened in the last few months. A shift. He's pulling away."

"Well, he's eighteen. He should be about to leave the nest, but he might not be able to. I'm sure that's all complicated for him."

"I suppose." Summer flicks some imaginary lint from the sleeve of her sweater. "I'll talk to him about the dance. But I'm not sure it's a good idea."

An invisible barrier is erected in the space between Summer and me, and I consider apologizing. But I won't. "Please think about it. It's important he has a good time."

"His health and safety are more important," she snaps. "But you wouldn't understand."

Anger spirals behind my eyes. "How can you say that? Of course, I understand. Everything I do lately, it's with Brandon's health and safety in mind."

A song plays through the speakers, reaching its emotional climax. *Release the past, baby fly free / Raise your lovely voice, baby dance with me.*

Summer opens her mouth to respond but thinks better of it and presses her lips shut.

"What if I volunteered to chaperone the dance?" I ask. "If Brandon knew I was there, watching him, he'd stay safe. He'd have to."

"Wouldn't Brandon hate that?"

"Of course, he would. But he'd accept it if it was the only way he gets to go."

"Fine." Summer rubs that spot between her neck and the base of her skull, where tension is stored. "But you're the one telling him."

"Got it."

I look around as if, amongst all the store's sundries, I'll find something more to say.

Nope.

"Bye, Summer."

She waves goodbye.

I leave the store anxious, like I'm walking on uneven ground.

****

Later, I'm wrapping up my busiest shift yet at Reynolds Resort. After I blow out the votive candles and put them on a tray, I spot Dana sitting at the bar, a glass of white wine in one hand and an e-reader in the other.

"Is that Key & Quill's newest model?" I ask, startling her.

"Yeah, it's great," she replies. "I love my Parchment IV."

"Me too," I say. "You can get books that aren't available anywhere else, especially if you like romance."

Her eyebrows shoot up. "You read romance? I always took for you a literary classics sort of gal."

Self-conscious, I laugh. What a surprise that Dana ever gave a moment's thought to my reading habits.

Dana sips her wine. "Hey, take a load off and have a drink."

I almost look over my shoulder to make sure she isn't talking to someone behind me. But that would be pathetic. Still standing, I ask, "What book are you reading?"

Dana places her e-reader down so it lies flat against the bar. She runs her fingertips over the case like it's precious.

"Don't judge, okay?"

"Why would I judge? I told you I like romance."

"Sure, but you're in school to become a novelist, and you have that brainy vibe..." Dana waves off the thought. "Whatever. Sit down and join me." Dana pats the stool beside her. "I'll tell you all about the novel I'm reading. It's called *A Confirmed Scoundrel,* and it's so much like *Manor House Chronicles* that I'm in heaven."

I grab the edges of my barstool, so I don't tumble right off. "*A Confirmed Scoundrel*? Is it by Shelby Simmons?"

"Yeah," she says, eyes narrowing. "Have you read it?"

"I..." My mouth goes dry. "Umm...I wrote it. Shelby Simmons is my pen name."

Dana gapes, slapping the bar in surprise. "No way! You're Shelby Simmons! Get out!"

She squeals, and I shush her before anyone overhears. "Dana, Dana, shh... You are literally the only person who knows. I've told no one I'm Shelby Simmons—not until now."

She lowers her voice to a dramatic whisper. "I have

to keep it a secret?"

"Yes."

"But why? Your books are good!"

"Thank you."

Dana squeezes my knee. "I mean it. You're one of my favorite authors, especially because of the *Manor House Chronicles* connection. *A Confirmed Scoundrel* is like Izzy Fitzgerald and Max." She drops her tone and intensifies her gaze. "But if you give them the same tragic ending, I will have to kill you."

I reel back. "Okay, wait. I didn't realize *A Confirmed Scoundrel* was like *Manor House Chronicles.* I've never watched it."

Dana drops her mouth open in mock horror. "Now, that's not right. You have to watch *Manor House Chronicles*. It's addictive, and your books are a lot like it."

Wow. Just when I thought I'd figured stuff out, life throws me a curveball. My biggest high school nemesis is now my first legit fan.

Kiki, the bartender, pauses while taking down the bar and asks me, "Do you want something to drink?"

"You should try this pinot," Dana says. "Do you like white wine?"

"Sure. Thank you."

Kiki pours me a glass and then returns to wiping down surfaces and straightening up. I sip my wine. "Yeah, this is superb."

"We ordered a case from a new wine guy who came in. He was very convincing. Not bad looking, either. And I didn't see a ring on his finger." Dana smiles like we're sharing a secret.

"Was he hitting on you?"

"No. Flirting maybe, but even if I wanted to date right now, which I don't, he'd take off once he realized I have a kid." She traces the rim of her wineglass with her index finger. "But what about you, Rylee? Do you have a boyfriend?"

My stomach clenches as I prepare to lie. But wait—her estranged husband is not my boyfriend.

We're merely sleeping together.

"No. I mean, I was in a relationship, but he's out in California, and long-distance was hard."

"Why don't you join him?"

"Family troubles. Money issues. It's been a rough couple of years, and I'm still trying to regain my sense of direction."

Dana cocks her head, her auburn hair catching the glow of the dim ceiling lights. "I was going to leave, once upon a time, and become a hotel manager in some fancy resort town. But Bemidji sucks you in."

"Oh yeah?"

"Totally." Dana grows wistful. "Do you ever feel stuck?"

How much wine has she had? And how do I respond to this kinder, gentler version of Dana?

"Only all the time," I tell her. "I catch myself wishing and dreaming that I could go."

"I'm with you there." Dana holds up her glass. "To wishing and dreaming, and one day getting out."

I clink my glass to hers.

"But back to *Manor House Chronicles.*" Dana reaches over and grabs my wrist. "There's the love affair between Marilee Fitzgerald and Thomas, and the incredible clothes and all the sarcastic humor! When can you come over to watch season one?"

Chapter 17

Rylee

I raise my hand to knock, but before I can, the door swings open. Carson stands there, smiling in his sexy way. And when I step inside, and he pulls me close, so our lips meet. No hello, just a soul-deep kiss that turns off my brain and melts my limbs.

"Is it against the rules to say that I've been missing you?" he murmurs between kisses. "That I've been counting down the hours until you're here?"

I pull away enough to brush my fingers across his smooth cheek—freshly shaved for me?—and take in his tea-tree-scented hair. He looks hot in his khaki green Oxford shirt and brown corduroy pants—totally appropriate for teaching, but enough to make any straight female student at Bemidji High have a crush on sexy Mr. Meyers.

My heart thumps in my chest. "Umm...I suppose saying that is okay. But—"

He cuts off my response with another kiss, and I give in to it. But after a moment, I step back and grasp his hand. "I need to talk to you."

His amazing eyebrows pinch together. "What's wrong?"

I glance around his living room where Ferris lies sprawled out on the sagging couch, his teddy bear nearby. With a deep breath and a subtle nod toward the couch, I sit beside Ferris while Carson settles on a chair across from us. "Nothing, not exactly. But I've had a busy week, and I need to fill you in on a few things."

"Sure." Carson tosses me a casual, unbothered smile. Why am I nervous?

"Okay, there are three things I need to tell you. One is about Mel, one's about Brandon, and the last is about Dana. Which do you want first?"

"Dana. Definitely Dana." He says this with resolve. Does he fear hearing about her the most? Or perhaps Carson is the type who'd rather jab himself in the eye than wait to get punched.

I arch my back against the armrest. Ferris scoots toward me and rests his head in my lap; his black fur is soft and warm as I pet him. "Dana invited me over to watch *Manor House Chronicles*. And I said yes."

Carson laughs. "Are you serious?"

"Yeah. She was telling me about how much she loves that show, and it sounded like fun, watching it together." Ferris licks my hand like he's reminding me not to be defensive.

As he leans back in his chair, Carson's deep brown eyes reflect light from a nearby table lamp. "But...I didn't think you and Dana got along?"

I wait for him to say more, but he leaves it at that. "Is that a question?"

His chest heaves up and down. "Okay. You told me not to talk about that time, back in high school when— you know, when Dana said something to make you cry, and—"

"And I tried to kiss you in the stairwell?" I construct an emotional barrier reinforced by my kick-ass attitude. "Dana doesn't remember that day."

"But you do," Carson says. "I mean, I don't know what went down before I got there, but—"

"Oh, come on, Carson. Yes, you do. Even if you didn't hear, you can guess. It was a long time ago, and I've moved past it. Same for Dana, or she wouldn't invite me over. So, can we please *not* talk about that day?" I stroke Ferris's ears, looking down at him instead of across at Carson. Then I tip my gaze and meet his eyes. "I hope you're not mad."

He runs a hand through his hair, making it stick up a little. "I'm not mad." His mouth contorts like it can't decide which emotion it wants to express. "Now, keep going. What else do you need to tell me?"

Anxious, I rub my nose. "You heard Mel is moving away?"

"Yeah, of course."

"Well, she thinks you don't care that she's leaving. It's not my place, except I love Mel like a sister. I'd do anything for her." I stall and scratch behind Ferris's ear before imploring, "Please, Carson. Tell her you care."

Carson's mouth falls open. "I...I told Mel I'd miss her. Did she mention that?" His voice adopts a hard edge.

"No. She didn't. According to Mel, you barely heard her."

"What?!" Carson shifts, rubbing his forehead in frustration.

"Look, I'm an older sibling, okay? I understand trying your best and still getting blamed for whatever goes wrong. But I thought you should know how Mel feels, in case you want to make some...grand gesture before she leaves."

"Grand gesture?"

"Like, take her out for lunch. Tell her you'll miss

her. Just don't mention that I told you to do it."

He drops his chin. "Of course not."

We both look down, silent for a moment. "*Now* are you mad at me?" I ask.

"No." His response is quick and loud, like he's turned the volume up a notch.

"It's okay if you are."

"If I was mad, I'd tell you. But I'm not mad."

"Fine. But you seem mad."

"I'm not mad."

He scratches the back of his neck, and the way the fabric of his shirt sleeves strains against his arm is really sexy. "Let's move on," he says. "What were you going to say about Brandon? Whatever it is, it's gotta be easier than the Dana and Mel news."

My laugh is feeble. "Maybe? But I'm asking for a favor, so maybe not?"

Carson doesn't flinch. "What kind of favor?" Leaning toward me, his muscles ripple beneath his shirt as if begging to be touched.

A tug of desire distracts me, but I manage to say, "Nothing huge. Just, please get me in as a chaperone for the homecoming dance?"

"What? Why?"

I explain the whole Brandon situation, and to his credit, Carson really listens.

"I'll see what I can do," Carson tells me, "but I can't promise you anything. In this day and age, even volunteers need to pass a background check before they're allowed on school grounds. And since the dance is next week, that might not be enough time."

"Okay. I understand. But could you sneak me in?"

Carson rubs his temples like he has a headache. "I

could, except I wasn't planning to chaperone the dance. It will be hard to sneak you in if I'm not there myself."

I lift Ferris's chin from my lap, stand, and approach Carson. "Well, maybe you could plan to chaperone? And I could be your guest."

Carson leans back, longing in his eyes as he sizes me up from head to toe. "It doesn't work that way."

"But it could, right? It could work that way?" Before Carson can answer, I press my finger against his lips. "Please, Carson? I'll make it worth your while."

My eyelashes tickle the crook of his shoulder as I lean in and plant baby kisses along his neck, sitting in his lap as I do. His earlobe between my teeth, I whisper, "Please?" I rub his chest, surprising myself at my brazenness.

He melts in my arms. "You're shameless. And you're using me."

"No," I say through our kiss. "I'm only using you if I'm not enjoying myself. But I am enjoying it. A lot." Straddling him in the chair, we're face-to-face, and our kiss deepens until he pulls away and gasps.

"I'll do whatever you want, Rylee."

His mouth crashes into mine again as he presses me into his chest.

Our kisses become full-tilt passionate as my fingers explore his body and his hands explore mine. His breath grows heavy against my cheek as I murmur in his ear, "This is what I want, Carson." But then, we don't need words to express ourselves; we communicate everything by how we move together.

As our kissing intensifies, Carson lifts me like I weigh nothing. He spins us around, so I'm leaning against the arm of the chair while he stands between my legs. His touch is electric as his hands explore my body, traveling down my arms and across my chest, inflaming my desire. He drops to his knees, still kissing my mouth and moving down until he reaches the sensitive spot below my collarbone.

"Don't stop," I command. Every single part of me is alive, and nothing else matters.

Carson removes his shirt and pants but keeps his gaze locked on me.

"You're beautiful," I tell him. And he is, with skin glowing in the fading afternoon light, and his chest, arms, and torso toned like he still plays hockey every day.

His deep, throaty laugh vibrates through the room. "Thanks, but I've got nothing on you."

The air crackles with energy. We're like two magnets being pulled together. We don't make it to the bedroom, and I hope our wild abandon doesn't traumatize poor Ferris.

But at long last, the passion that I've read and written about becomes a tangible reality. It's everything, yet more than I imagined.

Chapter 18

Rylee

It's two a.m. when I stumble home, my cells still abuzz after being with Carson. We got some classwork done, but just barely. This could become an issue. Maybe we need to meet earlier in the day, to give us more work time?

I'm lost in thought as I walk through the back—the screen door is magically fixed—and into our darkened living room, which is on the way to my bedroom. It freaks me out when a voice from nowhere says, "Nice night?"

I jump in my skin. Once I land, I see my mother sitting in an armchair by the window, looking out. "Summer. What are you still doing up?"

"Couldn't sleep. You?"

My brain must be fried because her words don't compute. "Huh?"

She speaks with precision. "Why did your study session go until two a.m.? Keep in mind, I'm not asking as your mother but as someone who recognizes the signs."

"The signs of what?"

Now that my eyes have adjusted to the darkness of the room, I can see her squint and cock her head. "The signs of mind-blowing sex, of course."

"Hey!"

She laughs. "Come on Rylee. I was once young and in love."

"I'm not in love," I retort. "It's not like that."

"Oh yeah." Summer holds out her hands in a placating gesture. "I forgot that you're anti-romance."

I bristle. "You're one to talk. Have you dated anyone since Dad died?"

Summer flinches, and then I feel like shower drain scum. "Sorry," I tell her, "I meant that we're the same. We both value our independence."

"That's okay." In the dim light, she tosses me a breezy smile. "So, who's this guy that you're not in love with?"

I collapse onto the couch across from where she sits. "Promise you won't overreact or judge me?"

"Fine. I promise." Summer widens her eyes, waiting for me to spill the tea.

"Okay. You remember Mel's brother, Carson?"

"Of course." Summer draws her legs up into the chair and crosses them, as if preparing for juicy gossip. A note of suspicion drops into her tone. "Didn't he get married young?"

I gasp. "Two seconds ago, you promised that you wouldn't judge—"

"Sorry! No judgment, I swear." She makes the cross mark over her chest, like the good Catholic girl her parents raised her to be (though Summer hasn't been to Mass in over two decades). "Anyway," she says, "Mel's brother Carson is in your grad program?"

"Yes, and by the way, he and Dana split up."

"Dana?" Summer does a double take. "Isn't she your boss at the restaurant?"

"Yeah." I peer at her in the dark. "But that's a story

for another day. Don't you want to hear about Carson?"

My mother lets out a deep, velvety chuckle. She must love that this is not her drama, but mine.

"Yes, Rylee. I *really* want to hear about Carson."

I wish she wasn't enjoying this so much. "Well," I say, willing my shoulders to relax, "Carson and I have been working together, and I guess you could say there's a mutual attraction that we both gave in to. But we're clear that it's not a relationship. It's a no-strings-for-now sort of deal. And we've agreed to keep it a secret for a lot of reasons."

"Like?"

"Like, he's Mel's brother, and she wouldn't approve. And the divorce isn't official yet. And he's Brandon's teacher. It's complicated."

"Right." Summer's reply is solemn. However, in an exaggerated whisper, she adds, "But you like him?"

My heart hiccups. "Yeah, I do. But that's not what it's about."

"So, it's about…sex?"

Never have Summer and I had such a frank, adult conversation. I hesitate, but I may as well be honest. "Partly," I confess. "I'd be lying if I said I wasn't enjoying myself. We also work well together, like with classwork and writing. But it has no future. He has a son he adores, so he can't leave Bemidji. And I still plan on moving to California."

"To be with Jack," Summer says. "Right?"

"Yes. No." I scratch my arms. "Maybe."

"Sounds definitive."

"It's all about circumstance." I cross my arms over my chest, trying to project resolve. "It is how it is, and Summer, you can't tell anyone. Swear that you won't."

"I swear. But Rylee…" She releases a supple exhale. "You're glowing. It's obvious, sitting here in the dark."

I lock eyes with her, trying my best to read her mind. "What's your point?"

She softens her voice and adopts a maternal tone. "Protect yourself, that's all. It's easy to say that you're just having fun, but it's much harder not to fall for someone attractive and out of reach."

I have no response for that. Instead, I say, "The back screen door is fixed."

"Mmm hmm. Leo came over before dinner and took care of it."

"Thank God. That door was likely to kill someone."

"Jeez, Rye. Don't be so dramatic."

****

In class the next day, I want to sit next to Carson. I want to press my face into his flannel-clad chest and revel in his fabric-softener scent. But I can't.

Yet, when class ends, he approaches me and says, "Want to grab` a coffee?"

"Don't you have to get going?"

He shakes his head. "Today's an in-service for Indigenous Peoples Day."

I should have remembered that. Brandon doesn't have school. "Don't you have teacher meetings?"

"A keynote speaker takes up the entire morning." Carson smiles like he's getting away with something. "As long as I get back for the breakout sessions after lunch, I'm good."

I shrug. "Okay. Let's get coffee."

We go to the upper level of the student union, to the Terrace Room, where a coffee stand and tables look directly out the windows and onto Lake Bemidji. "What do you want?" Carson asks. "It's my treat."

"No, it is not!" He reels back at my vehemence. I give him a playful punch, the way a friend would. "If you buy me coffee, it's like a date. We don't do that, remember?"

"It's not 'like a date.' We're hanging out after class. Okay, lamebrain?"

"Excuse me?"

He grins, and his eyes glint with mischief. "I called you that to prove a point."

"Which is?"

"That I'm not trying to impress you. If we were on a date, I'd never insult you like that."

"Oh, I'm not insulted. I'm embarrassed for you. You couldn't come up with a better dig than 'lamebrain'?"

Carson laughs. "I know you are, but what am I?"

I push him in the chest. "What, are we in middle school? Next, you'll be telling me fart jokes."

"Yes. I'm gonna let 'em rip."

Laughter fizzes out of me, and to my horror, I snort.

Carson's spectacular eyebrows raise into two perfect, upside down Vs. "Did you just snort?"

I cover my nose as if I could take the snort back. "It happens sometimes, when I don't expect to laugh."

He holds up his hands in mock defeat. "Okay, you win. You're paying for your own coffee."

We each get our own coffee, and we sit on side-by-side stools, looking out at the misty morning and the fog settling over the lake.

Carson sips his coffee. "Sometimes, I forget how beautiful it is here. If it wasn't so cold, I bet Bemidji would be like another Seattle."

"Sure, it would—but don't forget that lake breeze."

"Exactly! You go to Paul Bunyan Park, and the wind freezes your eyeballs on the spot."

Paul Bunyan Park is a Bemidji tourist hot spot with Statue of Liberty-sized statues of the lumberjack and his ox, a lake walk, and the gateway to Bemidji's kitschy downtown. But it's so windy and so, so cold.

"I bet the weather in Bemidji isn't much different from Siberia. Or Antarctica," I say. "That's one reason why I want to move to California."

"Yeah, that makes total sense."

I peer sideways at Carson, my curiosity piqued. But I must tread carefully. "So, once you're divorced, any chance you'll move away?"

Carson shakes his head several times, back and forth. "Nope."

Expected. He's a devoted father. Yet it must be difficult to abandon his dreams. "I suppose you can stand the weather," I tell him. "It's a shame you can't study medical research at Bemidji State."

He turns to me with such intensity that I almost flinch. "Medical research? What made you say that?"

The moment the words enter my mind, they exit my lips. "It was in your high school yearbook, under your senior picture. Your future goal: to cure cancer." I nudge my shoulder into his shoulder. "That's quite ambitious."

Carson surrenders a sad chuckle. "Yeah, I was pretty arrogant back then. Thought it would be no big deal to cure cancer."

He's still looking out the window. I tap his wrist so he'll look at me instead. "I don't think you were arrogant. Even though cancer is a ruthless bitch. Taking her down would be a tremendous deal, but I bet you could do it."

He turns in his seat, placing his hand on my

shoulder. "I appreciate your faith in me. But I can't leave."

"Because of Eddie." I state it as fact, not as a question.

"Yes."

"But…" I bite my bottom lip, unsure how to ask. "Would Dana ever let you have Eddie part-time some place not far away? Like Rochester? You could study at the Mayo Clinic."

"No!" Carson's shoulders tense. "I can't. Dana would never go for that, and I need to do what's best for Eddie. Every single day, I must protect him, so I'll always be his dad."

My heart breaks a little, seeing Carson so upset. "Of course, you'll always be his dad. Take it from someone who lost her father at a young age—if the bond is already strong, nothing can break it. Not even death." Placing my palm over his fisted hand, I squeeze. "But I'm sorry, Carson."

He waits like he can't quite process what I have said. In a near-whisper he asks, "Why are you sorry?"

"Because you worry you could lose Eddie. That's not right."

Carson's forehead wrinkles. For a moment, I wonder if he'll dive deep into his emotions. But his whole body relaxes like he's made peace with whatever's whirling inside his brain. "I'm breaking the rules again, aren't I?"

"Huh?"

"That one about emotional intimacy?"

"I wouldn't say—"

"Never mind." He shakes off the heaviness. "Hey, how about I throw Mel a going-away party? To show her how much I care. What do you think?"

"That's a great idea."

Carson holds my gaze, his hot cocoa eyes peering into mine. They seem as deep as Lake Bemidji, and as warm as that water is cold.

Chapter 19

Carson

WTF!? I almost told Rylee. For years, I've guarded this secret, and no one, not my parents, not my sister, not any of my friends, and especially not Eddie or Dana, knows. It hasn't been easy. Sometimes I thought the weight might break me. That my sanity will snap if I don't find a set of ears to absorb this terrible truth, to share the load. But telling Rylee? My sister's best friend, Dana's employee, and now, I guess, her buddy? Superbad choice. Besides, we came up with all those rules for our side project, which my subconscious seems hell-bent on breaking.

Last night, when Rylee laid into me with everything about Dana, Mel, and chaperoning the dance, I wasn't lying when I said I wasn't mad. But I was a little freaked out. We were having a heart-to-heart like she was my girlfriend. Wait, no. She was baring her heart to me, telling me exactly what she thought and exactly what she wanted. I sat there and listened, which is what good boyfriends do.

But I'm not Rylee's boyfriend, and I don't want to be.

Why the hell did I almost make myself vulnerable to her? I am not good at this.

I walk to my car, drizzle hitting my cheeks on this damp, hazy morning. Rylee mentioned a long-distance relationship that she's trying to figure out. Please, God, don't let her still be in love with the guy. Not that I care—but I don't want to see her hurt.

I drive to school and then go to the office and sign up to chaperone the homecoming dance. "Are we allowed to bring guests?" I ask Eileen, the activities secretary.

"Guests? You mean, like a date?"

I laugh like she's just told the funniest joke ever. "No! Not like a date. Like a friend. Like a student's overprotective sister. That's all."

Eileen stares at me, her face still, her eyes unmoving. I'm starting to freak out, worried I didn't say that last part out loud. *Is it my turn to speak?*

"I'd have to check," she says.

I smile, waving a dismissive hand and feigning nonchalance. But I can feel sweat beading on my forehead. "Don't worry about it."

"Are you sure?"

I am sure—sure that I don't want to pursue this any further. The less I know, the easier to feign ignorance if I get caught sneaking Rylee in.

****

Later that day, I roll up outside the school, and Eddie sprints over. Ferris does a doggy dance, joyful barks echoing as his favorite person approaches. Maybe I should tell Ferris my secret. He wouldn't judge, he definitely won't tell, and he's as protective of our boy as I am. If Eddie wasn't about to climb in, the poor dog would be my confessor.

But it will have to wait.

I open the door and hop out. The second Eddie is within reach, he flies into my arms with a hug. "Hi,

Dad," he says, his voice vibrating through me. When will the hugs get fewer? When will it no longer be cool to be so affectionate?

For now, I savor his embrace and let it fill in the pieces of me that are jagged and broken. Rylee said something about how if a father's bond with their child is strong enough, nothing—not even death—can break it. The thought threatens to bring tears to my eyes.

Once we pull apart, Eddie piles into the backseat, surrounded by an excited dog. I turn on the ignition and steal one last glance before steering us down the street. "How was your release day?"

"It was great," Eddie says. "At the science center, we learned about dinosaurs and why they went extinct."

"Oh yeah? What did you find out?" I turn the steering wheel and drive towards Paul Bunyan Park, which reminds me of my conversation with Rylee from earlier today. Rylee... It would be easy to indulge, to fantasize about her. But now is neither the time nor the place.

"Well..." Eddie adopts his young professor's tone. "It could be because of volcanoes, or an asteroid, or maybe climate change." Through the rearview mirror, I see Eddie fiddle with his jacket's zipper. "But don't they have to say that?"

My focus switches back to the road, and I press the brakes, stopping at a red light. "What do you mean, Eddie?"

"Because there's climate change now. And if the dinosaurs died from it, that means humans could die too."

For the umpteenth time, I marvel at Eddie's precocious wisdom. And yet, being smart is both a blessing and a curse. "Possibly," I answer. "But we're safe, Eddie. I promise."

He takes a moment to accept this. "Okay." Then Ferris licks his face, and Eddie dissolves into a fit of giggles.

When we arrive at the park, the sun begins to set, and the sky's painted in shades of orange and pink. Ferris pulls us both along the path that circles the lake.

"I still think it was global warming," Eddie says, as if there'd been no break in our conversation from before. "I mean, the earth was getting warmer, and those dinosaurs couldn't handle it."

"That makes sense." As we walk, the lake reflects the colors of the sunset in its rippling waters. Eddie tugs on Ferris's leash, and I try to take a mental photograph to capture and remember the beauty. I give Eddie's shoulders a gentle squeeze.

"You're a smart kid."

Eddie grins at me in response.

We continue our walk around the park, talking about dinosaurs and possible causes of their extinction. By the time we return to the Jeep, the sun has set. Driving home, I glance back at Eddie in the passenger seat, his head pillowed against the window, clearly growing sleepy. Ferris sits next to him, watching Eddie with an eagle eye, ready to pounce on any predator that might threaten his boy.

"Good dog," I tell Ferris. "We're in this together."

Chapter 20

Rylee

On Tuesday evening, both Dana and I have the night off, so I go to her place to watch *Manor House Chronicles*. Eddie answers when I knock on their cabin door. And when I say cabin, I don't mean the rustic, log variety surrounded by brush, guarded by guys in overalls who sport shotguns and scraggly beards. Dana's cabin is modern, cushy, and part of her parents' resort.

"Hello," Eddie says, like he's a cute little butler. "You can come in."

I walk in through the sliding glass door, which leads directly to a generic-looking living room with a tan couch and wild geese paintings hanging on the walls. "Thanks, Eddie. How are you?"

He grins, showing off a front missing tooth. "Okay. How are you?"

"I'm good. Did you lose a tooth?"

"Yeah. And I got two bucks for it!"

"Congratulations!" I look around, not seeing Dana anywhere. "Where's your mom?"

He points to a closed door. "In her bedroom, arguing with my dad. They think I won't hear, but I do."

Anticipation blooms in my chest, accompanied by the urge to run. Carson is a mere few feet away and will come out into the living room at any moment. Even though my body is desperate to see him, a chance encounter with Dana nearby will be awkward. Awkward, like when you think someone is waving at you, so you wave back, but it turns out they were waving at someone behind you.

"Hey, Eddie? I left something in my car. I'll be back in a sec."

I'm about to make a break for it, but it's too late. The bedroom door swings open, and Dana and Carson shuffle out, each wearing a tense expression. "You ready to go, buddy?" When Carson sees me, a flush creeps up his neck.

"Hello, Rylee," Dana interjects, oblivious to any strange vibes. "Sorry, Carson and I had stuff to discuss." She turns to her ex. "Don't be rude, Carson. Say hi to Rylee."

Carson clears his throat, "Hello, Rylee." His eyes avoid mine, darting away after a second of brief contact. "How are you?"

"I'm fine. *Say something casual, so it doesn't seem weird.* "I'd be better if I could make heads or tails out of 'Blood Moon over the Bayou.' "

Carson laughs, but it's like someone prompted him. "I'm with you."

Dana scowls. "What are you talking about?"

"Sorry," I say, unsure what I'm apologizing for. " 'Blood Moon Over the Bayou' is this strange short story our professor assigned this week, and it ends with a violent death scene."

"Oh." She speaks to Carson. "I still don't get why you're wasting your time and money on a class like that." Dana glances toward me. "It's not a waste for you, Rylee, since you're already an author."

I gulp. Will Dana reveal that I'm a self-published

romance writer? Carson rubs the back of his neck, looking confused. But then Dana adds, "But what's the point of that class for a science teacher?"

"Maybe I want to be something other than a science teacher," Carson says. "Maybe I'm still discovering who I am."

"You gave up the right to self-discovery when you became a parent," Dana retorts. "Or at least, I did. And if it's true for a woman, it should also be true for a man. Right, Rylee?"

"Umm…"

"Way to put her on the spot, Dana," Carson says. When he looks at me, for the first time this evening, I recognize the Carson I know. "Don't answer that."

It's a nice gesture, but does Carson realize my uncomfortable position?

"Dad, can we go, please?" Eddie tugs on his father's arm.

Even if it was unintentional, I could kiss the kid for creating the diversion.

"Yeah, sorry, buddy."

"Give me a kiss goodbye." Dana kneels and opens her arms, an invitation for Eddie to come closer. He obliges, wrapping his strong little arms around her and kissing her cheek.

While they're distracted, Carson steps next to me. My body buzzes in unison with his touch on my waist— like lighting a spark. Our eyes lock, and his crooked smile, thick brows, and stubble-covered cheeks are puzzle pieces with an unexpected fit. I'm dumbstruck by the unique beauty of his face. But time dissolves as if nothing happened, and Carson ushers Eddie out the door without saying goodbye.

Dana sags with relief once they're gone. "I'm sorry about that. He brings out the worst in me."

I must hide that I'm reeling. However, the moment that just passed will require major processing once I'm alone, in my bedroom, where I can replay the footage inside my mind.

"No worries. Is everything okay?"

"Yeah, it's fine. We weren't even fighting. He needed to ask me a favor." She walks toward the kitchen and bends to one of the lower shelves, retrieving a frying pan. "Here, I thought he was about to ask for a second chance. Nope." She opens the refrigerator and takes out a loaf of thick-sliced white bread, a stick of butter, and a package of sliced cheese. "I was stupid to get my hopes up. When I realized his 'favor' had nothing to do with him and me getting back together, I got mad and acted bitchy. Which, I swear, is the last thing I wanted." She puts the frying pan on the stove and turns on the burner. Then she slices two tablespoons of butter into the pan and lets them melt. "Hey, I probably should have mentioned this sooner. I'm making us grilled cheese sandwiches. Is that okay? *Manor House Chronicles* nights are when I allow myself cheese and carbs."

"Yeah, of course. Thanks!"

She makes herself busy assembling the sandwiches.

"Can I help?"

"No, you're good."

After building the sandwiches, Dana uses tongs to place the sandwiches into the hot pan, making sure they are arranged so they aren't touching. The scent of toasted bread, melting butter, and sharp cheddar makes my mouth water.

"Anyway," she continues. "I promise to be in a

better mood from now on."

I'm dying to discover what the favor was that Carson asked of Dana. Maybe I'll tease it out of Carson later.

"Okay," I tell her. "You need to give me the lowdown on *Manor House Chronicles*. Who's the best character?"

Dana shoots me some side-eye before turning back to the stove. "It's not about who's best, and I can't say much without messing up your personality test."

"My—personality test?" I stammer.

Laughing, she shakes her head. "Marilee Fitzgerald, Izzy Fitzgerald, or Eunice Fitzgerald? Or a staff member like Sarah Pierce or Hannah? We have a problem if you are Mrs. O'Reilly—I won't have any of her chain-smoking bitchiness."

"Oh," I murmur, scanning the kitchen for a place to sit. Two chairs huddle around a small table by the window. As I settle into one, I ask, "Which character are you?"

Dana glances at me, her expression softening. "Marilee—she's put together on the outside but lost and insecure inside...innocent about sex and love." She shoots me another look. "Yeah, I connected with her right away."

"Sure." I try to keep the shock out of my voice (because Dana Reynolds admitted to being vulnerable!) I ask, "Which character will I be?"

Dana grabs a spatula and scowls at me. "Eunice? No. She's independent, but she's also a dud. Hannah? Bright and brave, but to the point of martyrdom—no way." She uses the spatula to poke at the sandwiches. "How about I get you some wine, and you can tell me about your long-distance relationship instead?"

She moves to the pantry, where a bottle of wine waits. She uncorks it, and seconds later, I'm holding a glass of pinot noir. Dana returns to flipping sandwiches while I sip and try to describe Jack. "Well, when we first got together, he was the TA for my advanced fiction seminar. Now, he's finishing his PhD at USC and about to be published. He's a brilliant writer. Circumstances have kept us apart, but I still harbor hope for us."

"Other than being a brilliant writer," Dana says between spatula strokes. "What's he like?"

I twist a lock of hair around my finger. "He's an idealist. Jack's all about beauty and truth, even if it is built on lies." I laugh. "God, sorry. That sounds pretentious, doesn't it?"

"A little," Dana answers.

"I appreciate your honesty."

"I'm nothing, if not honest." A beat passes. "Does he love you, or does he only love his work and himself?"

Her perceptive question creates a hitch in my chest. "I don't know if he loves me. But we're not really about love."

"How can you not be about love? You're having sex, right?"

"Yeah. Well, we were. But he's in California, and I'm here. That makes sex difficult."

"You could have Zoom sex."

"That's not very romantic."

"Who cares about romance? I mean, the two of you are 'not about love,' right?" Dana turns down the burner, pivots, goes to her cabinets, and brings down two plates. She sets them near the stove, each plate ready to hold a grilled cheese.

I grasp for a response and come up short. Dana takes pity on me, and says, "I understand. You and Jack are about sharing ideas and stuff, right?"

"Yeah, I suppose."

"Is he intimidated by how successful your books are?"

"God, no. He doesn't know that I self-publish romance novels."

Dana takes the chair across from me. "Are you hiding them from him?"

"Well, yeah, but that's because—"

She thrusts out her hand, cutting me off. "Take it from someone who's been there—once the avalanche of secrets begins, it's near impossible to climb out."

"Oh." That's dark. I can't help but wonder—does she remember how she ripped apart my emotions ten years ago? "Do you want to talk about it?"

Dana uses both index fingers to rub each of her knuckles. "I won't burden you with my baggage."

"It's not a burden."

"Perhaps, but if you heard the twisted story of Carson and me, I bet you'd change your mind." She takes her wineglass and stands. "Let's forget our twenty-first-century American man troubles and watch some swoon-worthy Brits instead."

Suddenly, a weight is lifted. "Perfect."

Ninety minutes later, we're enjoying the second episode, each drinking our third glass of wine, and our grilled cheese sandwiches have become nothing but bread crust corners, abandoned on our plates.

My phone buzzes, and I look at its screen. "Oh my God," I say.

Dana grabs the remote and presses pause. "What?"

"It's Jack. What should I do?"

"Are you kidding me? Answer it!" Her eyes widen into two intense blue orbs. "But sound casual. And say you're busy."

"Okay." Faltering, I swipe to answer the call and press my cell to my ear. "Jack?" Please don't be another butt dial. That would be embarrassing.

"Hey, Rye Bread. What are you up to?"

As I scan my brain for a decent response, Dana mouths, *Say you're busy,* like she's trying to coach me through a minefield.

"Oh, not much. Visiting a friend. Can I call you later?"

There's a stretched-out moment before Jack answers. "Yeah, of course. I just needed to hear your voice."

"Are you okay?"

"Sure. A bit of writer's block is all."

How should I respond: sympathetic and concerned, or breezy, like his writer's block is trivial and will soon go away?

Then he adds, "I miss you, Rye Bread. I wish you were here like we'd planned."

My heart leaps into my throat at his confession. Wasn't he the one who decided we needed space? Wasn't he the one who wanted to focus on his writing?

"I miss you too, Jack."

"Yeah? Hey—how about you move out here next semester?"

"Next semester?" Dana tilts her head in comical confusion, and I shrug. "I mean," I say to Jack, "I just started my MFA program. I doubt I can transfer in the middle of the year. Plus, Brandon still needs me."

"Yeah, but I also need you, Rye Bread."

"Umm, you never told me that before—that you need me."

My eyes lock with Dana as I speak to Jack. Dana drags her finger across her neck, making the universal "cut" gesture.

Get off now, she mouths.

"But," I spit out, "I can't talk right now. Okay if I call you later?"

"Yeah, of course. Thanks, Rye."

"For what?"

"For being you."

"You're welcome." It comes out in a lilt, and my cheeks burn because what a ridiculous response. "Talk soon."

We hang up, and I almost gasp for air. "I'm in shock," I say to Dana. "That came out of nowhere. I wonder if he was seeing someone else, and it went bad."

Dana combs her elegant fingers through her shiny hair, contemplating. "Maybe. But that would be okay if the result is he appreciates you more. You two aren't exclusive, right?"

"No."

I look away, not wanting to reveal anything about how nonexclusive Jack and I have been.

"Do you want to pursue something more serious with Jack?"

I rotate one of my thin bracelets around my wrist, weighing my thoughts. "Maybe." I stretch into my seat. "I should text him tomorrow, yeah? Sometime midday?"

"Absolutely not!" Dana sits up straight as an arrow. "If you text him at all, it should be like, 'Oops—got super busy. We'll talk soon.' Put a heart emoji in there—

but not the red heart—blue or purple only. And no matter what, DO NOT apologize."

"But why go through the rigmarole when I just blew him off?"

Dana regards me like I'm a small child who can't comprehend. "Oh, Rylee. If you think that was blowing Jack off"—she waves her finger at me—"you have much to learn."

"Wait a sec—you said an hour ago that I shouldn't keep secrets from Jack, and now you're suggesting I play games?"

Her gaze cuts right through me. "Playing games will make him realize he values your relationship. That's when you spill all your secrets."

Dana exudes such confidence it makes my head spin. "Are you some sort of diabolical mastermind?"

"Yes." Her tone's like satin but coiled around steel. "And I'm taking you under my wing."

Chapter 21

Rylee

Dana lays out a simple plan for getting Jack to commit.

Because, of course, I want to be with Jack.

I've had this dream of Jack and me in California for so long it's like a tattoo. Removing that dream would be difficult, painful, and not quite worth it. But that's not the reason I'm still holding on. Jack is brilliant, and he brings out the best in me.

I take notes as Dana lays out five basic rules.

"How do you know all this?" I ask. "I mean, no offense, but you were still a teenager when you got married."

She shrugs. "Okay. Mozart was born with this innate musical genius, right? That's like me, but with dating."

Who am I to doubt her?

Later, I type Dana's rules up in a doc. And no, the irony is not lost on me that this doc is very similar to the list of rules I created with Carson, except it's also very different, like seltzer and tonic water. (I'd always thought they were the same, but one has sugar and artificial flavoring, and one is just fizzy water.)

Dana's Five Rules for Male Commitment:

1. Don't be desperate.

2. Encourage him to succeed while pursuing your own success outside the relationship.

3. Create a safe space for him to be vulnerable, but NEVER, EVER cry around him, unless a loved one has just died. Even then, be careful.

4. Make him work for it: Don't call him back right away, apologize, or be too available.

5. Show him you're his equal. Never assume that he knows more than you do. Challenge him.

It shouldn't be difficult to follow these rules, at least for the next few days. But that's partly because I will be very busy with homecoming this weekend.

First comes the football game. Lots of people I know will be there, including Mel. "You have to come!" Mel tells me on Friday afternoon. "Since I'm leaving town in a little over a week, you are required to do whatever makes me happy."

"Of course, I'll be there." I'm in my closet, figuring out what to wear for the game. There's my favorite gray belted cardigan, but I wore that on the night I first went over to Carson's.

Wait. I shouldn't reject something just because Carson has already seen me in it. "I'll meet you there, by the entrance to the football field, okay? Seven p.m.?"

"Great," Mel answers. "See you soon!"

I offer to give Brandon a ride to the game and swear I'll pretend not to know him once we arrive. "That wouldn't be necessary," he says. "Except that you're going to my dance tomorrow. That's why I can't associate with you."

"No worries. And I don't want to be dragged down by my kid brother tonight. I am ready to par-day with my peeps!"

He shakes his head in disgust as we pull into the parking lot. "You are the oldest twenty-four-year-old

I've ever met."

"Ha! If that's true, why am I still living at home? Huh? Answer me that!"

"Rye, if still living at home is your only defense, you're in worse shape than I thought."

He gets out of the car, closing the door with more force than necessary. I almost call after him, "How many times have I told you not to slam the door?!" But I bite my tongue because that's what an old person would say.

Brandon is already several yards away as I get out of the car and lock it. I straighten my stocking cap and scarf, both of which are dark blue and white, with *Bemidji Lumberjacks* stitched in. I'm wearing them to show my school spirit, and I'm wearing my gray belted cardigan to prove that I don't care about impressing Carson. Walking to the football field entrance, I spot Mel, dressed in her Bemidji High hoodie, waiting for me.

"Hey, you!" She looks at me. "What's wrong?"

"How can you always tell when something is wrong?"

"I can see it in your eyes."

"Oh." I blink in rapid succession, as if that could erase my hurt feelings. "Brandon said that I act like an old lady. Is that true?"

"Don't worry about what Brandon thinks." She throws her arm over my shoulder and leads me toward the gate. "All younger siblings see their older siblings that way."

"They do? How do you know?"

"Personal experience. Speaking of which, Carson is saving us a seat."

"Wait, what?" I stop dead in my tracks. "You want to sit with Carson? Why?"

"He's been super sweet lately. He's even throwing me a going-away party!" Mel's almost giddy. "I said we should sit next to each other at the game."

"Did you tell him I was coming along?"

Mel puts her hands on her hips. "I don't remember. Why does it matter? You're not still fixated on him, are you?"

"I never fixated on Carson."

"Whatever, Rye. Haven't we been over this already?" She presses one finger into my shoulder. "Besides, remember freshman year, when I was, like, the last person to find out about your crush? I still haven't forgiven you for that."

She's kind of joking, but kind of not. "Mel, you need to let that go."

"I can if you can."

"I already have."

We squint at each other in a semi-serious standoff. Mel blinks first. "Great. Let's go, then."

Mel tugs on my arm, and we move towards the bleachers. She scans the crowd, sweeping her arm in a wide gesture as she spots Carson. "There he is." Carson waves in response, and I see him register my presence. He jerks a little, like someone hit him on the back.

Does that mean he doesn't want to see me?

We climb up into the stands and step over people's feet and knees to get to Carson. "Hi!" Mel exclaims once we reach him. "Thanks for saving us a spot."

"No problem," Carson says. "But I wasn't aware I should save two spots instead of just one."

"That's okay. We can squeeze in together." Mel plops down next to her brother and scooches close to him. She pats the empty patch of bleacher next to her, which is about half the width of my butt.

"I'm not gonna fit there, Mel."

"Do you want to sit on my lap?" Mel's offer is genuine, and she may be the slightest bit taller and larger than me, but not by much. It wouldn't be comfortable for either of us if I sat on her.

"No way will I fit on your lap."

"Okay. Sit on Carson's lap."

For a moment, I'm rendered mute. Carson also says nothing, so Mel jumps back in. "I'd do it, but that would be weird, to sit on my brother's lap. People would talk."

"People will talk if I sit on his lap, too. Carson's a teacher here. He can't let a random woman sit on his lap."

"You're hardly random," Mel says. "I'd say you're pretty well acquainted by now."

How much does Mel know? What did Carson tell her? For the first time today, I look right into his eyes, but they betray nothing. "Carson, you don't want me sitting on you, do you?"

At a snail's pace, he opens his mouth to answer, but Mel breaks in. "I've got it! Rest one butt cheek on my knee and one on Carson's. If you're sitting on both of our laps, then you're not really sitting in either of them. Right, Carson?"

Carson scrunches up his forehead the way I've seen him do when he's studying a passage from a story, trying to analyze it. "I suppose?"

"Lady, come on! Can you please sit down already?" The person sitting behind Carson and Mel yells over the noise of the crowd and the game. "I can't see my son play, and he's the running back."

"Sorry," I mumble. Shuffling and turning, I try to sit

so I'm mostly on top of Mel, but it's inevitable—some of my ass meets Carson's thigh, and his inside arm hesitates, letting his hand touch the small of my back and floundering so that it isn't. I put both hands in my lap, but that's uncomfortable because I can't quite lean back.

Then there's the warmth of Carson's body as our legs touch, heat radiating between us. His mouth is close to the base of my neck, but I can sense his hesitation. "It's ok," he murmurs. "You can relax against me."

I exhale and slump into the curve of his chest. I'm aware of the rise and fall of Carson's ribcage as his hand finds the edge of my cardigan and grips it. A flashback to when he took that sweater off me floods my thoughts.

Turning, wrapping both my arms around his neck, and pressing my lips to his is all I want right now, but I force myself to watch the football game Mel is so passionate about. Except, I do not understand the rules or why she keeps shouting, "Go Jacks!"

"You're going to break my eardrum, Mel."

She huffs and gives my knee a playful shove. "And you wonder why Brandon called you an old lady?"

"That's mean," I complain, but I punctuate it with a laugh.

"Sorry," she apologizes in her good-natured way, then kisses me on the cheek before standing up. "I'm going for a hotdog. Either of you want anything?"

"No thanks," we say in unison.

"Great." She makes her way down the bleachers.

I take her place on the bleachers beside Carson. He leans in and whispers, "It's taking every ounce of my self-control to not tear that sweater off you." He grazes my shoulder with his fingers, which makes me tingle with pleasure. "Did you wear this tonight for me?"

My pulse speeds like a race car. "No comment."

The crowd erupts as the Lumberjacks score a touchdown or whatever. I join in, though I'm not sure why I'm cheering. At least it gives me something to focus on, other than Carson.

My phone vibrates in my pocket, and Jack's text screams at me: *Where are you? Can we talk?* With a wave of guilt, I remember I promised Jack I'd call him tonight.

Carson notices my distraction. "Everything okay?"

I nod, then shake my head. "Actually, no."

The words escape my mouth before I can stop them. "Remember that long-distance relationship I told you about?"

"Yeah." Carson waits for me to continue.

"He called me the other day, and I promised to get back to him, but I forgot. Now he's texting."

"This is the guy who ghosted you?" Carson's voice has an unfamiliar edge.

My heart drops like a stone. "I wouldn't call it ghosting. Jack's been busy finishing his doctorate; he already has a publishing contract for his thesis, so he's kind of hot in literary circles right now." An embarrassed heat creeps across my cheeks. "I should be thrilled that he's still in touch."

Carson's single raised eyebrow speaks volumes. "You should be thrilled?"

I nudge him in the shoulder. "What, are you jealous or something?"

He looks at me, and the sunset's golden light bounces off Carson's brown eyes. For a moment, I'm paralyzed by their shimmer.

"Not jealous." His response is a bit too quick, and a

bit too devastating. I rearrange my scarf to hide how gutted I am.

"Got it." I force out a laugh.

In a gentle tone, he suggests, "Maybe you should call Jack right now."

"Now? But what about the noise?"

Carson lifts his shoulder in a lazy shrug, and his shirt stretches against the muscles beneath, outlining his strong frame. "Find somewhere quiet, like the parking lot."

"You think so?"

He faces me, highlighted by the setting sun, turning him into a golden shadow. "Definitely."

I pivot, stalling. An abandoned cup of popcorn sits a few feet away, and I debate grabbing it before someone kicks it over, but the idea of carrying someone else's trash makes me wince.

"Is Mel ever coming back?" I curl my fingers tighter around my phone. "I don't want to leave you here alone."

His gaze flits to a group of people about our age on the other several rows down. "I'm not sure, but a lot of my teacher friends are over there, so I should go sit with them. Otherwise, it would be rude."

Carson sounds almost dismissive. Does he want me gone?

Ignoring the heat rising in my chest, I stand. "Okay. See you tomorrow at 6:55 outside door seven?"

He nods. "Yes. I'll come down and let you in."

"To be clear: I can't come in through the main door?"

"It's easier this way." Carson blinks three times before continuing. "And maybe wear something to blend in?"

"Blend in how?"

"Like you could be a student."

I put my hands on my hips. "You're not serious?"

"Don't worry about it," Carson says, waving me off. "Go call Jack and trust me. Everything will be fine."

I'd argue the point, but the same person, who grumbled about me standing before, is making noise again. I concede defeat, for now.

"See you tomorrow, 6:55 at door seven."

Carson gives me the thumbs-up.

I head out to the parking lot, texting Mel as I go. *Be back in a few. Need to make a call. When I return, let's sit somewhere else.*

Chapter 22

Carson

The homecoming dance starts soon, and I'm alone in my classroom, which is dark and unnaturally quiet on a Saturday night. I spin in my office chair and check my watch for the hundredth time in the span of a few minutes. It will take approximately forty-five seconds to walk from my classroom to door seven. Should I be a bit early, just in case?

I don't want to seem overeager. Perhaps I should be right on time?

But Rylee might decide I'm this precise guy with a stick up his butt. Hmm… I could be the slightest bit late, but what if someone sees Rylee standing and waiting outside the door, shivering in her party dress? That would call attention to her rather than blending in at the dance.

My plan is that once she's here, I'll find a dark corner of the gym where she can stand and watch over Brandon, and everyone will assume that she's a student who got jilted by her date and that she's moping, away from the crowd.

At 7:54, I travel down to door seven. I can't help it; precision is in my blood. Plus, I'm eager to see Rylee, and I wonder if she'll be late, early, or right on time. There are no windows surrounding door seven, only a bunch of concrete walls on the school's lowest level. I'll have to prop the door open with my foot and peek out, watching for her.

My stomach is in knots, and I'm not sure why. Well, no. I'm not *exactly* sure why. Of course, I fear getting caught sneaking Rylee into the dance. But it's not just that. Being with Rylee at the game yesterday was this odd mix of awkward and tantalizing. Like I could have died, having her on my lap with my teacher friends, students, and my little sister, all so close to me. Surely, they could hear my blood rushing, and they all knew how much I wanted Rylee. And yet, if I had died right then, it would have been a happy death because her hair smelled like cherry almond shampoo. It's like what I imagine heaven would smell like if, in heaven, people have amazing sex.

But Rylee got the phone call from that prick out in California. How dare this dude make her feel like she should be grateful for his attention! Rylee asked if I was jealous, and I was sort of honest when I said no. It was more like I was pissed. Like, I wanted to fly to California and beat the crap out of this guy.

Because I am protective by nature. That's all it is.

Hands shaking, I open the door at seven. Rylee is right there, so close I almost smack her with the door.

"Oh. Hi." I hold the door open so she can step inside. "You're punctual."

"So are you."

"Yeah." God. Where's my clever response? But I'm looking at Rylee, dressed in a short skirt, heels, and a jacket covering whatever's on top. Her hair is slicked back, and her lipstick is bright red, and I am filled with sudden, sharp longing.

"What?" Rylee wilts under my gaze. "Did I get my

outfit wrong? I figured you meant I should look like a student, but did I overdo it?"

"Yes."

"Yes?" Her hands shoot to her face like she's trying to hide.

"I mean, you look way too good to be a high school student."

"Oh." Her smile is timid. "I hope it doesn't sound lame when I say that you also look great. You clean up nice."

I grow warm all over. Tonight, when I chose what to wear, it was with Rylee in mind. Wanting to impress her, I put on my nicest shirt and tie. I'd even put a bit of gel in my hair, fantasizing that her eyes would light up when she saw me.

"Thank you," I say, my voice a bit choked.

What follows, I later decide, could only be described as a moment of true insanity triggered by years of frustration, betrayal, lies, and unfulfilled dreams. Because I don't consider the consequences. I act on impulse. Rylee stands before me, and I want her, and that's all I can process.

It's like our first kiss all over again. One minute, I'm looking at Rylee, wishing my arms were around her, that my lips met her lips. Then, I am kissing her, and it happens the same way that highway hypnosis does. I'm unaware of the logistics, but we reach our destination and each other. My mouth covers Rylee's mouth with such hunger you'd think I inhaled her whole. Instead, it's like I can breathe again.

"Mr. Meyers!"

I nearly jump out of my skin when my name is called. We break apart, but it's too late. The damage is done.

Dwayne Thatcher, esteemed principal of Bemidji High, caught me kissing Rylee. Rylee, who looks like a student because I told her to dress like one.

Sonofabitch.

Chapter 23

Rylee

I wasn't aware a person's face could turn so red. Carson's cheeks are the same color as the bricks that line the sidewalks of downtown Bemidji.

He's also speechless.

"Mr. Thatcher?" I recognize him from my school days, back when he was the type of vice principal who took particular joy in telling girls that their blouses were revealing, or that their skirts were too high. What a prick.

"Wow! You still work here! It's me, Rylee Lynch. I graduated six years ago. How are you?"

Other than throwing an angry scowl in my direction, Mr. Thatcher ignores me and speaks instead to Carson. "I'd ask for an explanation, but there's no way to explain this."

Carson parts his lips like he's a mime trying to find words. I step in, hoping he doesn't mind being rescued by a woman. "It's my fault. Carson volunteered his time to chaperone the dance, which meant we couldn't have our normal Saturday night date. I'm the jealous, clingy type, and I stopped by the school to say hello. But I got carried away and threw myself at him, and that's when you walked in."

Mr. Thatcher huffs and puffs, but again, he ignores me and speaks to Carson. "This is very inappropriate. What if a student saw you?"

I could point out that any student caught down in this part of the building would violate the rules. Besides, it's not a big deal. They'd see a teacher kiss his girlfriend—that would be the assumption, right? Nobody's privy to the true nature of our relationship except Carson and me.

"I apologize, Mr. Thatcher," Carson answers. "You have every right to reprimand me."

"Don't tell me what I can do."

Wow. Mr. Thatcher is even more of an asshat now than he was back when I was in high school. It must be a genetic thing, a recessive gene that causes tyranny and compels a person to become a high school administrator. Carson has studied genetics; I make a mental note to ask him to explain it later.

"Of course, sir."

Carson's complexion has gone from deep red to a sickly white. I clench my fists, angry on his behalf. "Hey! My boyfriend is chaperoning the dance out of the goodness of his heart. He cares about his students. Cut him some slack."

As a writer, I dislike cliches. But the only way to describe Mr. Thatcher's expression is that he's staring daggers. First at me, and then at Carson.

Oops. I made things worse.

"Rylee was just leaving," Carson says.

"Yes. Yes, I was." I give Carson a quick, dry kiss on the cheek, and he reaches for my fingers, giving them a tight squeeze. But he instantly lets go.

"Mr. Thatcher, it was great seeing you again." I extend my hand to shake. "And please, let me say how much I appreciate the role you played in my education. I am a very lucky girl to have had such a stellar high school experience."

There's a brief, auspicious moment when Mr. Thatcher might shake hands with me, followed by a slower, painful realization that he won't. I lower my hand to my thigh, and raise it again to give a feeble wave. "Good night."

Neither of them wishes me the same in return.

I exit back out through door seven. The October air is as cold as it's been since late March; a damp, cutting wind whips around me.

Crap. I made a mess of things. I'm pretty sure it was me who lunged for Carson first. It was me who couldn't control herself and who had to kiss this incredibly attractive guy I can't resist. He must hate me now. I wouldn't blame him.

Also, I referred to Carson as my boyfriend. What if he doesn't realize I did that for the optics? I figured Mr. Thatcher would have an easier time if Carson was kissing someone he's in a relationship with, as opposed to his piece on the side.

I want to bang my head against the cold, stone structure that is the high school. Instead, I look at my watch. It's 7:10. The dance doesn't end for nearly three hours. I can't go home. Summer would be furious that I am not here, keeping a watchful eye on Brandon. Considering my options, I decide the best course of action is to drive to Reynolds Resort. Maybe they can use my help tonight, and I can pick up a shift. If not, I'll drown my sorrows at the bar and keep company with the only other woman in the world who understands being desired by Carson Meyers, and then put on his bad list.

Not that I can talk to Dana about what happened. Still, perhaps I can ask subtle questions and get her to spill details about what went down between the two of them. I'd love to hear her side of the story.

As I drive to Reynold's Resort, it's dark, and the rural streets aren't well lit. I travel winding roads as loneliness and regret settle over me like a nasty hangover. If I was a character in a novel, this journey would portend something bad, the unlit, curvy streets a sign that my life path is dark and difficult to navigate. I grip the steering wheel and decrease my speed, fearful that a deer will run in front of my car, causing a life-ending ordeal for one or both of us. The last thing I need on my karmic footprint is a dead animal. Just look at how well that works out for literary characters. Whether it's a white whale, a skunk, a rabbit, or a rabid dog, dead animals *never* bode well.

I make it to Reynolds Resort without incident. My anxiety dissolves as I get out of the car and walk the rocky path to the restaurant. Lake Bemidji is a massive, inky hole, a background to the restaurant and hotel. Close to the water's edge, the wind hurts. I'm not dressed for this weather. My ankles wobble in my high heels as I hurry down the uneven path.

Inside, the warmth, the low hum of dinner conversation, and the candlelit atmosphere soothes me.

"What are you doing here?" Dana spots me from behind the hostess stand. "I thought you needed this weekend off."

"My plans fell through. Need an extra set of hands?"

"Are you kidding? We are slammed tonight. You're a lifesaver, Rylee." Dana comes up to me, and even though we've sort of become friends, I'm stunned when she kisses me on the cheek. "Thank you! I'll let you take over as hostess, okay?"

"Of course."

I squeeze her shoulder and step behind the stand, seeing there's a waiting list plus a full roster of reservations. Immediately, I am consumed with seating customers, doing my part to make Reynolds restaurant a well-oiled machine.

A little after nine, there's a lull, and Dana comes over to where I am. She's effortlessly sophisticated in her black wrap dress with a delicate gold chain and small opal sparkling at the base of her throat. I worry I look cheap in my short skirt and tight satin top.

"Does it have to do with Jack?"

Confused, I cock my head. "Huh?"

"Your plans falling through—did they have to do with Jack?"

"Oh." When I asked Dana for Saturday night off, I couldn't tell her it was so I could chaperone the dance, because if she pressed me, I'd have to admit that Carson was getting me in. That's why I left it vague. "Kind of," I tell her. "I let guy problems disrupt my life."

"That happens to me all the time."

"You? But you seem so in control."

Dana shudders. "It's all an act. I'm not in control. Maybe I could be, but I can't stop loving Carson."

My heart twists—a visceral reaction to Dana's words. I must have a stricken look on my face, because Dana grips my wrist. "What's wrong?" Her cool, dry fingers press into my skin. "Has Carson been flirting with someone in your writing class? Are they hooking up?"

"No!" The lie tumbles out of my mouth. "He keeps his head down. Besides, I can't imagine him interested in anyone there."

Dana nods and exhales in relief. "Good. Thanks, Rylee." She releases my wrist and pats my hand. "I won't pester you about this again. You're a good friend, and you'll tell me if there's something I should know."

"Yes, of course."

I am the biggest bitch, the conniving antagonist who's betraying Dana, and she's the clear protagonist in this scenario. And yet, I understand what Dana's saying.

I must stop loving Carson before I start.

Chapter 24

Rylee

Sunday morning, I text Carson. *Hope you're not in trouble after last night. Am I still invited over today?*

Carson answers with a simple and enigmatic *Yes.*

Hopefully, he's saying that yes, I am still invited over, and not yes, he's in trouble. Figuring we'll sort it out when I get to his place, I reply: *4 Four p.m.?*

Twelve agonizing minutes pass, and as I pace, I tell myself it doesn't matter. I'm going to end our side project today, because it's dangerous. We stand to hurt our careers, our friendships, and in my case (though I won't say it), ourselves.

Carson's response arrives. *Come at three? Something I want to talk to you about.*

Standing in my childhood bedroom, which has become my purgatory, I clutch my phone and gaze at my bookshelves without seeing them. They're filled with classics from my dad's collection, like a leather-bound copy of *Anna Karenina,* and an early edition of *Ulyssess,* which Dad found at a famous used bookstore in San Francisco. Those books sit amongst my favorite Regency romance novels, and I wonder how many hours of my life I've spent reading them all.

I walk up to my shelves, running my finger along the titles' spines. It rests on something more magazine than book: a literary journal, pages bent from being read over and over again.

I pull it out and think back to the day Jack and I strolled through campus. We went down the winding path, over mossy stones, and between Native American sculptures, past the firepit where a totem pole stood strong with carved animal heads. Jack held my hand in a steady grip.

"How old were you when you decided to be a writer?" he asked, once we'd arrived at the shores of Lake Bemidji.

I glanced up at his bearded face. "I had a vague idea sometime around kindergarten." The damp spring breeze cooled my skin, and I shivered. "But a few months after my father died, I found this old literary journal with one of his stories published inside. It was about this mysterious figure living in the forest, invisible to everyone who lied. Of course, the point was that *everyone* lies, so no one could see this guy. Reading that story was like having part of my dad back. A secret side he'd never shown me. That's when I knew for sure I wanted to be a writer."

Jack removed his scarf and draped it around my shoulders. His scent surrounded me—coffee and cedarwood—and I was immune to the stiff wind.

"Thank you." I squeezed his hand, and we resumed our walk.

Blinking back tears, I return the journal to my shelves and wonder how much longer will I stay here, in this room? Long enough for the seasons to change multiple times. Long enough for the next solar eclipse. Long enough for a Twinkie to go bad.

Yes. I can come at three.

I send Carson a thumbs-up emoji. Then I take a

shower. If I'm going to subject myself to humiliation, I'll at least be well groomed while it happens.

****

"We need to stop." I say this the moment Carson opens his front door, before I'm even inside. It's how I can dump him before he dumps me.

Carson's wide, lovely grin falls from his face. "Stop...?" His lower lip juts out a bit. "Do you want to come in?"

"Yes, of course." I walk around him and Ferris, who sniffs me like we're old friends. Once I'm inside, Carson closes the door, and I take off my coat and bring myself and my laptop over to his folding table and chairs. Sitting, I tent my hands in front of me, trying for composure. But there's this damn stirring inside that happens every time I'm within inches of Carson Meyers.

Forcing myself not to blurt out more words I will instantly regret, I stare into his gleaming eyes.

"Sorry about last night. It was all my fault. I jeopardized your career, and that's unforgivable."

Carson tilts his head, considering this. He has on jeans and the same flannel from two weeks ago, but he's clean shaven. I want to kiss his cheeks and find out if they're as soft as they look. "Are you saying we should stop—"

"Our side project," I say this as a joke, but it falls flat.

"I don't understand why we need to call it quits just because Dwayne Thatcher caught us kissing," Carson says, sitting across from me. "That guy is a complete dick, but he's not a gossip."

"Aren't you in trouble?"

"In trouble?" Carson's mouth twitches into a smile.

"I might get a slap on the wrist or a letter in my file, but I'm tenured, so it's worth the risk. And I'm grateful you stood up for me." He reaches out and takes my hand. "I appreciate it."

My heart edges up into my throat. "I said you were my boyfriend to—"

"I know." His fingers skate across mine. "You wanted to make things right. And it was hot."

Hot? Me? I push out a laugh. "It was?"

"Oh yeah." His voice grows husky. "You know what was even hotter?"

A thrill runs through me. "What?"

"That outfit you wore last night—that skirt and those heels and your hair? Damn, Rylee." Carson uses his free hand to fan himself before tightening his grasp on my fingers and pulling me closer. "But hottest of all? You, on my lap at the football game."

I stand in front of him before I have time to comprehend what happened.

"Please, Rylee, say you'll reconsider. Because I kind of have to have you, like, right now."

I settle into his lap and whisper, "Reconsider?" My mind is a jumble of longing and confusion; all sensation, no thought.

"About ending our side project. I say we keep going."

I don't even have time to agree before his lips are on mine, devouring me with an urgency that erases all my doubts. Clinging to him, I revel in the heat from his skin as he stands and carries me to bed in one swift motion.

Lust drives me to rip off each piece of my clothing like it's aflame—Carson follows suit. When I see him standing before me, throbbing with desire, drawing a breath is impossible. I inch closer to the edge of the bed and take him into my mouth; his moan sets my body alight.

"Oh God, Rylee," he says, nudging my head back. "Stop or I'm gonna come."

"That's alright," I manage.

"No, not yet," he commands and drops between my legs.

I arch up into him with pleasure, ready for more but wanting him inside me as well. "No, not yet," I mimic, before demanding what we both crave. "Get inside me now."

Carson retrieves a condom from his nightstand, puts it on, and slides into me with one thrust. Our eyes meet, and our hands grip together. The outside world is replaced by a heat beginning in our entwined bodies and spreading outwards. We kiss, and I wrap my legs around him—with every movement, pleasure shoots through my veins like fireworks until nothing can exist except for this moment between us, until we both reach the point of dissolution.

Afterwards, I lie with my cheek against his chest; its rise and fall lulls me as his steady heart beats. He strokes my hair with one hand and caresses my arm with the other. I almost drift off, but then a thought that alerts me to consciousness. "Hey. You asked me to get here early. What did you want to talk about?"

"Oh yeah." He chuckles. "I was drunk when I texted you that."

"Seriously?"

"No." His response lingers in the air. "But I may as well have been. It's a dumb idea."

I sit up, making eye contact but not bothering to tug

the sheet up with me. Carson is the first person I've ever felt immodest around, like I want him to see me naked. "What's a dumb idea?"

IIis hcad is proppcd against thc pillow, making him look a little bit vulnerable, and a whole lot seductive. "I'll tell you, but promise not to laugh."

Right now, I'd promise him anything. "Okay, sure."

He sits up and runs a hand through his hair. "Okay, pretty soon we'll need to register for next semester?"

"Yeah."

"Well, maybe it would be cool if we signed up for another class together."

It could be more than cool. The thought of separating next semester and ending our side project panics me, but if I stay this weak-willed around him, it might be my only option. What if Carson is fine continuing on like this forever? I stroke his shoulder as a million thoughts spin through my mind. "Okay. There must be more, otherwise, you wouldn't claim that taking another class together is dumb."

He uses his index finger to trace the length of my thigh down to my knee. "What if we signed up for the novel writing class?"

The idea hangs in the air between us like an invisible thread. I've studied that course description so many times, I have it memorized. Yet, it never occurred to me that Carson would want to enroll.

"Are you even allowed to take that class with your program track? I thought they limited English Education students with their choices."

"No, I'm allowed to take whatever, as long as I don't exceed eighteen credits total in Creative Writing."

"Huh." I see my clothes, flung down in a pile by the

edge of the bed. I reach for them and start getting dressed.

"Never mind though," Carson says. He gets up, retrieves his shirt and jeans from the floor, and puts them on.

"Why?"

Carson steps into his jeans. "What do you mean, why? I was stupid to bring it up, especially after you tried to break things off a few minutes ago." He pulls his shirt over his head, the fabric rustling as he slides his arms through its sleeves. "Do you still want to stop?"

Pulling my shirt on, I emit a muffled groan.

"Rylee?" His voice is gentle but probing.

I tug on my sleeves and look into his eyes. "I never wanted to stop. But maybe we should. There's a lot of potential for something to go wrong."

Carson sits on the edge of the bed, looking like I've told him the sky is falling. "Are you worried about Jack finding out?"

I nod, my stomach in knots at the passive deception. Telling Carson my concerns about Dana would backfire. "Yeah, a little. And there's Brandon. I'm pretty sure it's wrong to hook up with one of his teachers. And even though Mel is leaving, I hate lying to her."

"I see." Carson drops his chin and stares at his flannel sheets. "That reminds me of two things I was going to tell you."

"Are they bad things?"

"It depends on how you look at it."

"Ouch." With a plummeting heart, I say, "Okay, hit me with 'em."

Carson's gaze bounces between the bed and me. "The first is about Brandon. I kept an eye on him last night. He kinda just stood by himself. I asked him what was up, and he said his date ditched him to hang out with her girlfriends."

"Oh no."

"Yeah. Poor guy."

"When I asked how his night went, he said it was great. He lied to me." I press my fingertips into my temples, stress creeping in to replace the bliss from three minutes ago. "Did you say anything to him about it?"

"I would have, but no words came to mind. Besides, Mr. Thatcher was glaring at me all night. I figured I shouldn't overdo talking to Brandon in case he makes the connection that you're his sister."

"Right." My eyes sting with tears. I want to take whatever hurt Brandon is feeling and absorb it myself.

Carson stands and holds out his hands. "Come on," he says.

"Where are we going?"

"To the living room."

I allow him to take my hands and pull me up from the bed. Murky darkness drapes the day, casting his living room in a grayish-blue tone. Carson moves to the table, his phone beaming as he swipes it open. An indie pop song, "Heartless Bird," with its soaring violins, swirls around us.

I was a bird who couldn't sing/ Heartsick without a wing/ I was the sky without a star/ The cracked lid of a broken jar.

"Dance with me," he pleads.

"What? Why?"

"We need to erase the bad karma from the homecoming dance, and we can, if you'll let me hold you."

"You believe in karma? I thought you were a scientist."

"They're not mutually exclusive." His arms slide around my waist as I wrap mine over his shoulders, our bodies swaying to the languid melody. *I was a firework without a glow/A fear that began to grow/But you lit up my ink black sky/the missing piece, the reason why.*

His chin rests on my head as he murmurs into my hair. "Did you ever enjoy high school?"

I almost laugh—and snort. "No," I tell him after a beat. "I couldn't wait to be done."

"You had no good times?"

Memories of sleepovers and marathon study sessions turned into gabfests, huddling in the lunchroom and scouting our crushes while we ate cafeteria tater tots…all the plans Mel and I made, all the inside jokes we shared. They flash before me like a silent movie reel.

Pressing my cheek against his shoulder, I say, "I had a good time when I was with your sister. What about you? Student council president, honor society member, hockey player—your experience must have been pretty okay."

Carson shakes his head. "There was a lot of stress. Like one wrong step, and it'd all fall apart. Turns out I was right." His fingers slide around mine, spinning me out as his arm wraps around my waist, and he pulls me close. "No one in high school has it all figured out. But Brandon will be alright."

We're back to swaying in each other's arms. I let my hands slide from the back of his neck to along his chest. "You should tell him that. He wouldn't buy it, coming from me."

"Okay. I'll talk to him."

172

"You're not worried about Mr. Thatcher and crossing boundaries?"

Carson shrugs. "I suppose I am. But you and Brandon are more important."

I stand on my tiptoes and plant a soft kiss on his lips. "Thank you. I owe you one."

"Want to know how you can repay me?" He grins like he's won a contest.

My doubts melt away. "Of course I do."

Carson pushes his forehead against mine and murmurs, "Order us a pizza, thin square-cut crust, no pepperoni."

"No pepperoni? What kind of deviant are you?"

"The type that prefers sausage, mushrooms, and onions on his pizza." He plants a satiny, fervent kiss on my lips that leaves me breathless. But then, pulling away, he says, "Seriously, let's order pizza. I am so hungry."

We let go of each other. Carson turns the lights on in his living room, and I call Mario's and order a large, thin crust with sausage, onions, and mushrooms. We sit at his card table and get to work on our assignments.

Two hours later, the pizza box sits on the edge of the table. Our napkins are crumpled and pushed aside, our glasses of wine empty vessels, and Carson talks as he types.

"The sibling dynamic between Evie and Zephyr is reversed," he muses. "Yes, Zephyr's able to save his sister in some ways, but Evie's more cynical, and more hedonistic, don't you think?"

"Yeah." I rub my forehead. "Speaking of siblings— wasn't there something else you wanted to tell me? About Mel?"

Carson slides his glasses up his nose while he talks,

quick blinks behind them. "Oh yeah. This one's not a big deal…hopefully."

I sit cross-legged in the folding chair. "What is it?"

"I took your advice. I'm throwing Mel a going-away party."

"She mentioned that," I say. "That's great."

"It would be, except for one thing: I can't have it here—it's too small. Everywhere else I contacted was booked. So, I talked to Dana, and we're having it at Reynold's Resort instead."

"Oh." A heavy pause follows my words. "That's not so great."

"Yeah." Carson taps his fingers against the table. "I mean, Dana will be there, but now that the two of you are friends, it should be cool, right? She won't suspect anything if she hasn't already."

I swallow hard, keeping my eyes trained on his. "You make it sound so simple."

He leans forward and reaches for my hands. "Because it is. We'll pretend one more time that nothing is going on, and then we'll never be in the same situation ever again."

Like a fool, I believe him.

Chapter 25

Carson

It's Tuesday, and my AP Bio students are in the middle of an agar cube/indicator experiment. A sour, spoiled-milk scent lingers in the air. My tongue's dry, but I'm not thirsty. And I can't focus; I won't see Rylee for another three days, and that's like a brick in my stomach.

What's worse—once Friday arrives, there will be no kissing her hello, no holding her close, no laughing over some inside joke. No sly caresses, no stolen moments during Mel's going-away party.

I watch as the class, wearing rubber gloves, fill their Petri dishes with pink liquid. "Mr. Meyers? Are we doing this right?"

I stroll over to the student asking for help, give some suggestions, and work to be engaged. It's difficult because Rylee is on my mind. She assumes our side project is risky, that it only brings pain for fleeting pleasure. Rylee wants to go to California, reunite with that California guy, and find a fresh start while I'm stuck here, tied to Eddie, and haunted by my past.

Plus, Rylee might call it quits again, and next time I doubt I can convince her otherwise. The way she frowned when I suggested taking the novel writing course together... Well, I understand how Brandon felt after his date ditched him at the homecoming dance.

Now I am a few feet away from Brandon as he works on today's lab. Earlier, I'd explained about cell structure and function. And I stayed at school late last night, making agar cubes with an indicator of different sizes. The agar binds together to form a gel-like substance that is easy to manipulate yet strong enough to retain its shape when exposed to a variety of conditions. "This change provides a fascinating visual representation of what happens when cells are exposed to an acidic environment!" Brandon's eyes lit up when I announced this before starting the lab. He alone was eager for the agar cube experiment.

Which makes him and me the only true biology geeks in the room.

I watch Brandon, meticulous as he inserts his next cube into the jar filled with vinegar solution. I note how he studies each one before moving on to the next cube. For the final task, we will perform surface area and volume-related calculations to determine what happens to the surface-area-to-volume ratio as a cell gets larger.

I stroll up and down the classroom, checking in on everyone at each lab station to see if they have questions. Brandon and his lab partner, Perry, are already cleaning up. "Are you two done?"

"Yeah. It was easy," Brandon says. "Especially since you gave away the secret."

"The secret?"

"That the cells get bigger when the surface-area-to-volume ratio gets smaller."

"Oh." I fiddle with my glasses. "Sorry. I didn't mean to spoil it."

"I don't mind," Perry says. "I thought it was challenging. I'd still be figuring it out if it wasn't for this guy." He uses his thumb to point back at his lab partner.

Brandon holds up his lab report. "Want to see our written work?"

"Please." Brandon hands me the sheet of paper with their hard work scribbled in teenage-boy handwriting. I skim it, realizing it's 100% correct. Like all of Brandon's other assignments so far this semester. "This is excellent," I say to them both. "Brandon, can I have a word with you?" I tilt my head toward my desk, indicating we should step out earshot from the rest of the class. Brandon follows me up to the front of the classroom.

"Am I in trouble?" Brandon asks.

"No, of course not. It's the opposite. I have a question for you."

"What?"

Hesitating, I press my lips together. I need to make sure this comes out right, that I don't offend Brandon or set him off. "Okay. First, I need to explain something. You sort of remind me of myself, back when I was in high school, when I decided to study genetics at Harvard and find a cure for cancer." I look at Rylee's brother; his eyes are ocean-blue, just like hers. "But that has nothing to do with the fact that you've had cancer. I mean, not that you're a cancer survivor is irrelevant or anything—"

"What are you getting at, Mr. Meyers?" Brandon's face is guileless.

"I never made it to Harvard, and I have no clue how to cure cancer. It was presumptuous of me to have that goal. But I'm planning a research project, and I want you as my assistant. If we're successful, we could apply for grants, or you could use them to get into college or for scholarships. What do you think? Have you decided which colleges you're applying to?"

Brandon's gaze strays toward the ceiling, and he shifts his weight. "Don't laugh, okay?"

"Sure."

"You mentioned Harvard? They're supposed to have the best biology program, and it's my dream school. I haven't told anyone, not even my mom or my sister. Isn't it pretty much impossible to get in?"

"I got in," I state. "So, no. It's not impossible. Would you like me to help you with your application?"

"You'd do that?"

"Sure. And you could use our research project as the subject of your essay. It will be perfect."

Fingers crossed, Brandon won't ask me for a bunch of details right now because I don't have any. I literally just came up with this idea. But I promised Rylee I'd look after Brandon. This would give me an excuse to work with him after school and guide him a little. And maybe it will also be emotionally healing for Brandon to research a topic so close to home. Plus, it might help get him into Harvard.

"What would we research?"

I swallow, buying time before I respond. "Well, I'm curious if brain tumors are connected to familial cancer predisposition syndromes."

Brandon squints and seems to mull over the idea. "Why are you curious about that, Mr. Meyers? What's your basis?"

I clear my throat, nervous about proving myself to this precocious kid. "Some research has found that those with a family history of any type of cancer may have double the risk for developing brain tumors—even if there is not a known genetic mutation associated with the familial cancer predisposition syndrome. However, it's not definitive, and it's unclear how this connection works and what else might factor in."

"Oh." Brandon rubs the top of his head. Near the spot where the tumor was removed? "So, we'd research if my brain tumor was genetic?"

"Not your tumor, specifically—"

"It would have to be my tumor, though." Brandon straightens his posture and tilts his chin. "Otherwise, we couldn't do any primary research. It's not like we have a medical lab. But we could get my and my family's medical records and do outside research to see if we can make a connection."

"You...you'd be okay with that?"

"Yeah!" Brandon's eyes light up. "I really would. It would be great to find an answer for why this happened to me." He steps closer and lowers his voice. "Both my grandmothers had cancer—one got breast cancer and the other pancreatic. I mean, maybe there's a link."

The students pack up. I look at the clock. It's time for them to go to lunch. I'm disorientated, unsure if I did something wonderful, or if I've made a colossal mistake. "Okay," I say to Brandon.

"Great! See you later, Mr. Meyers!"

Brandon's happier than he's been all year.

Here's hoping Rylee realizes that too.

Chapter 26

Rylee

The patio at Reynold's Resort has a large fire pit by the shore of Lake Bemidji. It's the setting for Mel's going-away party, and people sit in chairs and at tables scattered around the patio/fire pit area. Mel flits about, talking to her friends and family, hugging her sweater around her on this cool night.

"Where's Carson?" Summer asks. "Have you said hello to him yet?"

Since Mel was pretty much a permanent fixture at our house while I grew up, Summer sees her as family. There was no way she wasn't coming to Mel's party. I understand that, and yet, I wish she wasn't here. Not because I begrudge her the chance to wish my best friend well, but because Summer is the only one, other than Carson and me, who's in on the secret of our "side project." And discretion isn't always Summer's strong suit.

"I'm not sure where he is. But remember, you're not saying anything. Right?"

"Don't worry. I can keep a secret."

But can she?

I release a frustrated breath and make my way over to the table with all the hors d'oeuvres. I'm carrying a tray of phyllo dough-wrapped sausages, annoyed to be working this party instead of enjoying it. Not to mention,

I'll have little time to talk to Mel. Meanwhile, Dana has taken the night off so she can be a guest instead of a host.

"I'm sorry I couldn't give you the night off, too," Dana said earlier. "But since you had two nights off for homecoming…"

"Except I ended up working Saturday," I reminded her.

"True, and that was very kind of you. Even so, I gave you two nights off—that's generous according to Reynolds Resort policy."

It is generous…but with my best friend leaving town, nothing is enough.

"Oh wow, fancy pigs in a blanket!" Mel appears at my side right as I put down the tray, and she's already reaching for a sausage. "Carson must have ordered the deluxe catering package. Did you put him up to it?"

Confounded by her question, I take a few seconds to answer. "What? Why would you ask me that? I mean, it's not like Carson and I ever talk, and if we did, we wouldn't talk about you. We'd talk about classwork because we have nothing in common, and I'm not sure that I even like Carson, so of course not."

Mel squints as she processes my awkward response and I flounder for words to make this better. But there's nothing that won't make it worse.

"You're coming with me." She grabs my wrist and leads me over to a darkened spot, away from the party and the fire.

"Mel, I'm working. I can't just walk off."

"This won't take long."

We're away from the heat of the bonfire and closer to the lake, where the evening breeze is quite icy. I shiver as Mel faces me down.

"Tell me what's going on between you and Carson, and this time, don't lie."

I sling my shoulders back in a last gasp of bravado. "Why are you so sure something is going on?"

"Because, Rylee, my BS detector is razor sharp. So don't pretend nothing's going on when obviously something is. I saw how you both acted when you sat on his lap at the football game."

"I had to sit on his lap. You gave me no choice!"

"That's right!" She points her finger at my chest, dangerously close to jabbing it. "I was testing you two! And guess what? You failed."

"Keep your voice down." Using a forced whisper, I plead. "It's not what you think, okay?"

"What do I think?"

"That we're secretly dating."

"Ha! You're both bad at secrets. As for the dating part…" She shakes her head. "That's not what I'd call it."

"Fine." My shoulders sag with the weight of my confession. "Carson and I are sleeping together. Are you satisfied?"

Mel lets out a cynical laugh. "It's not me who stands to be satisfied here."

It's like I'm swallowing sand. "What's that supposed to mean?"

"Rylee, ten years ago, you lied to me about him. And now you're lying about him all over again."

"Look, I never meant to—"

"Don't! Over the last few weeks, you could have come clean, but you didn't. Why? I don't understand—I thought we told each other everything."

Okay. I gotta fix this. "Mel, I'm sorry, but after you

warned me against him, I knew you'd be mad if Carson and I started hooking up. Which is why I lied."

Mel narrows her eyes; I can see the hurt there. "And you thought lying to me was better? Rylee, you know I hate dishonesty."

"Yes," I admit, trying to keep from trembling.

My vision has adjusted to the dark, and I can read Mel's expression, which is full of betrayal. I can't let her leave town angry at me.

"I should have listened when you warned me against him," I tell her, "and I shouldn't have lied. If it's weird for you that I'm hooking up with Carson, I'll stop. Okay?"

Mel sighs. "I warned you against him because he'll break your heart. Admit it, Rye. For all your tough talk, you're a romantic. Part of you is still that sad fourteen-year-old girl, looking for someone to keep you safe and thrill you all at once. You thought Carson was your answer before, and now you do again. If he didn't have a ton of crap to sort through, I'd say you were perfect for each other. But he does, and you'll be the one who gets hurt."

I shiver, telling myself it's because of the evening's chill and not Mel's prophecy. Then I say what she wants to hear. "You're wrong. I'm physically attracted to him, sure, but that's all." Squaring my shoulders, I plunge headfirst into a lie. "The emotion just isn't there, not with Carson." Searching her eyes, I see she's not convinced. So, I take it a step further. "But you're right. I am a romantic, and I'm in love with Jack, okay? Carson is keeping his place warm until Jack and I can be together."

Mel's biting her lip, looking over my shoulder. My stomach plunges.

"Carson's right behind me, isn't he?"

"Yup," says Mel.

I turn around, ignoring the sound of blood rushing through my ears. It takes all my effort to appear casual and breezy, but I give it my best shot. "Hey, Carson. How much of that did you hear?"

Carson stands there, his expression unreadable. His eyes bore into mine, their normal dusky hue now almost black. "Umm, let's see. I'm a non-emotion evoking place-warmer for Jack, who you're in love with. But you're attracted to me, which is cool, I guess."

I force out a laugh. "Of course, it's cool. After all, you feel the same way."

Carson's mouth sets into a grim line. "I absolutely am not in love with Jack." He smiles, which changes the entire geography of his face. "Lighten up, Rylee. It's okay." He gives me a reassuring pat, his touch lingering just long enough to unnerve me. Turning to Mel, he says, "Come on. Everyone's wondering where you are."

Slinging his arm over his sister's shoulders, he leads her away, leaving me alone in the cold and dark.

"There you are," Dana says, her voice kind, once I've returned to the action of the party. "Can you run to the kitchen and see if the sliders are ready to come out?"

"Yeah, of course. Sorry."

"For what?"

"You're not even officially working tonight. I should be more on top of things, so you don't have to worry."

Dana smooths her hair, which is draped perfectly over one shoulder. "It's fine. You and Mel are very close. This has to be hard for you."

"Thanks," I mutter. I move past her, but Dana stops

me by placing her hand on my forearm. "Hey, are you okay?"

"Yeah." Tears gather in my throat. "But I think I'm about to lose my best friend."

"She'll still be your best friend. And this may be a poor consolation, but I'm around if you need someone to hang with. I mean, we have many more episodes of *Manor House Chronicles* to get through!"

I stifle a laugh. Ten years ago, if someone told me that Dana Reynolds would become my new, substitute bestie, I'd have called them a heartless liar. But here we are, standing in the night air, talking about sliders, friendship, and *Manor House Chronicles*. "Thanks, Dana."

"Of course." Then, swear to God, she winks at me. "Okay, you go get those sliders, and I'm going to talk to Carson. I think tonight might be the night."

"The night for what?"

"That we'll get back on track. Maybe if I talk to him and joke around like how we used to do, he'll warm up. I know he still loves me."

"You do?"

Dana nods. Her gaze is on Carson as he stands around the fire, laughing at a joke that Mel told. "Yeah. There's no way my feelings for him could be so strong without some reciprocation on his end. Besides, we'll always be connected. We have Eddie."

I squeeze her shoulder. "Good luck."

As I head toward the kitchen and away from the party, I wish I could fly away and not return.

The party winds down after a couple of hours, and Mel states she should go, as she plans to take off early tomorrow morning. The remaining guests hover around and give goodbye hugs. Carson stands off to the side, alone.

Summer is next to me. "Where's Dana?"

"She had to go. Her babysitter could only stay until ten."

"Oh." Summer packs a lot of emphasis into her one-syllable response.

"What?"

"Nothing." She pauses, jutting out her bottom lip. "Maybe you can explain something to me?"

"I can try."

"Didn't you say that Carson and Dana are divorced?"

"Yeah. Well, they're getting a divorce. Technically, they're still married?"

Summer smirks at the lilt in my voice. "But you aren't sure?"

I open my mouth but flounder for words.

"Because," she continues, "looking at the two of them tonight, how they acted with each other, they seem like this beautiful couple."

She's right. I noticed how happy they were in each other's company, laughing at each other's jokes and flirting like they did in high school. I shrug, feigning nonchalance. "Dana wants to get back together with Carson."

"What does Carson want?"

I hug my chest, hating my reply before the words even escape my mouth. "That's a little unclear."

"Shouldn't you find out?"

I'm about to form an indignant response, but suddenly I'm tackled, caught in a fierce hug by Mel. She squeezes me so tight I may as well be an almost empty tube of toothpaste. And to be sure, my insides are getting wrung out. "I'll miss you, Rye."

The relief that she doesn't hold a grudge mixes with the heartache of losing her. This is goodbye. "And I'll miss you. Promise that we'll still talk often, okay?"

Mel's chin quivers, and she gives me a teary-eyed grin. "I promise. As long as you promise to tell me everything that's going on with you. And I mean *everything*."

"Okay." I swallow my tears, but more instantly appear. "I hate seeing you go, but I'm so happy for you and proud to call you my best friend."

Mel sniffs and wipes her eyes with the back of her hand. "Me too."

We cling to each other, but I let go first. "You should go. You don't want to be exhausted tomorrow. It's going to be a big day."

We say goodbye a couple more times while wiping away tears, and Mel gives Summer a farewell hug. Carson walks Mel to her car. My heart breaks open a little as I watch them go.

"Are you okay, sweetie?" Summer asks.

"Yeah, thanks. I'm going to the bathroom, and then we'll head out. Okay?"

"Sure. Take your time."

Once I make it to the ladies' room, I splash cold water on my face, dry my eyes, and take several deep, steadying breaths. "You're going to be okay," I tell my reflection, but the girl who stares back at me isn't so sure. She's red-eyed, sagging with despair. And she looks lost and confused.

"Whatever," I say to myself, and I exit through the swinging door.

Carson stands on the other side, waiting for me. He wears his dark, wool peacoat, his hands shoved in his pockets. Then, his arms drop to his sides like he's shedding a heavy burden.

"Oh," I falter. "Hi."

He strides toward me and cups my cheek, pressing his forehead to mine. It's warm against my skin. "I'm sorry."

"I, uh… What are you sorry for?"

"For how tonight went. It was messed up."

My heart swells at the apology, but I can't move on. Not yet.

"Are you mad? Because—"

"Rylee." He exhales my name like it's an enchantment. "I'm not mad. I can be a place-warmer, okay?"

I want to melt into him and forget about everything but this moment. "Umm…" I tilt my chin up, and our lips collide. We kiss until every emotion from the night has been forgotten, and heat burns under my skin with each passing second. It's dangerous, though. Dana's co-workers might see us. I pull away. "We shouldn't do this here."

His eyes sparkle with longing. "You're right. Come over."

"To your place? Tonight?" My mind races with possibilities—and reservations—of what might happen if I go to Carson's house.

"Yes, and yes." His intensity stops my heart for a second.

I'm about to refuse, but something takes over, daring me to follow my heart. "I suppose." Outwardly, I'm hesitant, but inside I'm jumping up and down at the opportunity for bonus alone time with Carson. "I need to drop my mom off, but then I'll come over."

"Good," he says, and it's like a promise passes between us. "Please hurry."

****

I find my mother, and we leave the party, me at the wheel because she hates to drive at night. Summer fiddles with the radio, trying to find a good song, but it's mostly commercials. We're both silent the entire way home, lost in thought.

When we pull up to our house, I turn off the ignition and say to her. "I'm just dropping you off."

"You're going out again?"

"Yeah, and I'm not sure how late I'll be, so don't worry and don't wait up."

Summer lifts a hand to smooth back my hair like she did when I was little. "You're going over to Carson's?"

"Yes." My muscles tense, and my nerves are on edge. "But please, don't say whatever you're thinking. I've already heard enough tonight."

"Not from me." She pauses, and the air surrounding us grows melancholy. "Listen for a few minutes, Rylee. It won't take long." She squares her shoulders before continuing. "When I was young—younger than you are now—I naively thought bad stuff happened to other people, not me. Even after my dad left and my mother got sick." A solitary tear slides down her cheek, but she wipes it away. "I never would have imagined that my husband would die so tragically or my son would get brain cancer." Her body trembles with a silent sob or perhaps silent laughter? "But here I am, counting my blessings and trying to live my best life."

She takes a deep breath. "Rylee, you are my number

189

one blessing. You're healthy, strong, and alive. And for that, I'm grateful. I love you, babe."

"I love you too." I lean in and kiss Summer on the cheek. Turning the ignition back on, I give her the cue to leave.

"But Rye, there's something I need to tell you..."

A lump forms in my throat, anticipating her words of warning. "Summer, we don't have to do this—"

She holds up a hand to cut me off. "I'm almost done." Her eyes stare into mine, silently commanding me to turn the ignition back off.

I comply and pretend to study my hands. My chest is heavy as I wait for Summer to say her piece.

And then, finally, "Carson is gorgeous. Honey, I get it. You can feel his energy when he's around. It's like all he has to do is say your name, and you become the center of his world. That's how your father was with me. He had this power that was hard to resist." Summer shakes her head. "Be careful, Rylee, okay? Just be careful."

My fingers glide over the steering wheel. "I realize bad things don't only happen to other people. You don't have to worry. Because you're right, I am strong. And Carson won't hurt me because there's no way I'll let him."

"Okay," she croaks. Summer leans forwards and presses a gentle kiss on my cheek. "I'm glad we had this talk." She moves to exit but turns back around. "One more thing?"

"Yeah, Summer. What?"

"Promise me he's wearing a condom."

Chapter 27

Carson

Rylee.

Our lips meet, her tongue coaxing me to do more. The salty taste of sweat, the soft skin of her shoulder.

A steady rhythm: our breathing, our beating hearts. Our whispers in the dark.

My face pressed against her back, her black hair sweeping her neck and tickling mine. Before bed, the mint of mouthwash and toothpaste on her tongue.

We spoon all night. In the morning, the coffee maker gurgles as she approaches. "You're making coffee?" she murmurs into my ear. "What a great host!" Then she pulls away and smiles.

"Hey, this is a full-service operation. I'm also making toast."

Rylee wraps her arms around me. "I'm giving you the best Yelp review ever."

"Does that mean you'll stay for a bit? Eddie isn't coming over for a few hours."

"Sure."

After taking Ferris for his morning walk, we cuddle on my couch. With each stroke of my fingertips against her toes, I'm more content than ever before—until she says something to burst my bubble.

"We still have time to discuss last night and what it means."

My happy, peaceful state flies out the window. I must swallow this conversation like a bitter pill without a glass of water.

I hope it won't lodge in my throat.

"Okay."

My right hand is out of Rylee's line of vision, so I grip the lumpy throw pillow by my side.

Please, don't bring up what you said to Mel.

Once was enough for those words to sink in. Their acidic power spread through me last night, making me want to hurl. Convincing Rylee to come over and taking her to bed soothed my wounded ego. But if we have to *talk* about it all now, that will be like experiencing that awful moment again, only worse. Yet, what can I do? Tell her, no, we *can't* talk about things? Rylee's not the type to respond well to that.

"We need to revise the list of rules for our side project."

"Wha…what now?"

Rylee straightens her already pristine posture. "We've violated most of the original rules we laid out. Either we break things off now, or we revise our list. I can't do this if I don't understand the parameters."

I rub my eyes. "Sure. But you were the one who typed them up. Maybe we should wait until Sunday when you've brought over your laptop?"

"You mean you don't remember our rules?" Rylee squints at me, disbelieving. "I thought the whole point of making rules was that we'd remember and follow them."

"I do remember them, but you said we should revise them, which implies we need a document. That's all."

"Okay." She gives my chest a playful push, in the spot where underneath flesh and bones lies my heart.

"What are they?"

My entire life, people have praised me for my quick mind and nearly photographic memory. Too bad being around Rylee turns my brain to mush.

I release a prolonged exhale. "Okay. The first rule was that we weren't supposed to tell anyone about our side project. But you," I point out with pretend anger, "violated that one."

She scowls. "I violated nothing. My mom and Mel figured it out. That's not my fault. As for Mr. Thatcher, I'd say we're both to blame."

I try to form an argument but come up blank. "Fine."

It must look like I'm pouting because Rylee says, "Come on, don't be like that." Then she squeezes my knee. "Keep going."

"We're only allowed to hook up on Sundays." I pause, tilting my head back and forth, playing out hot scenarios in my mind. "Okay—breaking that one is on me."

Her mouth turns down, but she makes this little squeaking sound that's almost like a laugh. "Continue."

This is worse than my most difficult oral examinations in college. "If either of us wants to date someone else, we need to say so, and that'll be that. Are-are we there?" My heart does a few quick fire rounds between hope and dread. Will she bring up Jack?

The seconds stretch like chewy taffy before Rylee answers with a simple, "No."

I relax a little and rub my hand over my nape, but I'm pretty sure I'm missing two rules.

"Do you need me to tell you the rest?" Her tone is sanctimonious, which ought to annoy me, but instead makes me want to press her against the wall and kiss her until she's putty in my hands.

Bad idea.

"No." I hold up a finger as if to say, give me a sec. Like a miracle, I remember. "No emotional intimacy, but we can be friends."

There's a heavy moment when that sinks in. "Okay," I concede. "With that, I've sort of crossed a line. But there's a ton of messed up stuff I haven't told you about. That should count for something, right?"

Rylee grasps my wrist, putting my hand in her lap. "Sure. No problem. And I've barely told you anything about all my issues." She frowns. "I have a lot."

"Okay. I mean, you can tell me about them, if you want?"

Her gaze drops to our intertwined hands. There's a split second of silence. "Maybe someday. For now, let's just enjoy our dysfunctional, twisted little world." Looking back into my eyes, Rylee emits a liquid laugh. "Okay. There's one left—the most important rule. Do you remember?"

Shit.

My mind is blank. I search the recesses of my brain but come up empty. "Uh…" I stammer, and a rush of heat descends on my face. "No."

Letting go of my hand, Rylee implores, "Tell me you're joking."

"I remembered them all except one. Isn't that pretty good?"

She twists a wavy black lock of hair around her finger, considering. "It's the one you can't remember that most needs revising."

"Okay, tell me what it is, and we'll talk through it."

"Hey, never mind." She picks at a coffee stain that

came with the used couch. "If you can't remember that one, it's a sign we shouldn't worry about it right now."

"Are you sure?"

"Totally." Rylee does a funny little couch leap, inserting herself into my arms. "Do we have time for a quickie before you have to go?"

I concede. Because why wouldn't I?

Hours later, after spending the day with Eddie, after playing soccer in the park and fetch with Ferris, and then going to Target to pick out new little toy cars and setting up a course made from sheet pans and ramps built on books, after a microwaved dinner of canned spaghetti and a cartoon movie marathon, after giving Eddie a bath and putting him to bed, and after lying on my couch, envisioning Rylee—her beautiful eyes, her satiny skin, and her unrelenting mind that I want to unlock—do I remember the last rule.

If either of us starts to develop romantic feelings for the other, we must say so, and our side project will end.

The next day, Dana calls. "Can you keep Eddie until three?"

I hesitate. Two extra hours with Eddie! Normally I'd be thrilled, but Rylee is supposed to come over.

My friends and family might say I'm good at thinking on my feet, yet I'm a terrible liar, and now I can't conjure a single reason Dana can't pick Eddie up at three. I text Rylee, telling her to arrive at three thirty, and then I pass the day, letting Eddie play computer games while I grade lab reports and plan lessons for next week. With Ferris napping at our feet, we work side by side. Eddie is focused on multiplication games with rockets, satellites, and exploding planets.

"Do the planets explode when you get an equation

right or when you get it wrong?" I ask.

"Jeez, Dad, isn't it obvious?"

"No, not really."

"They explode when you get it right. Duh."

"Yeah, okay." I look sideways at Eddie, over his shoulder, as he selects the correct response for six times five. "But isn't the point to save the planet? Like, you want to get all the multiplication problems right so that the planet *doesn't* explode?"

Eddie presses his finger into his chin. "Maybe it's an evil planet? But Dad, come on. Everyone loves an explosion."

My son has a point.

Dana doesn't come to pick up Eddie until three fifteen. Then she breezes in, unapologetic. "Thanks for being flexible!"

She smiles, looking radiant in what must be newly highlighted hair and a suede jacket I've never seen before. Ferris runs up and greets her with a flurry of wagging tail and excited barks. Dana and I freeze in place, unsure of what to do or say. After a few moments of awkward silence, Dana kneels down and gives Ferris a pat.

"Hi, Ferris."

Eddie beams. "He likes you, Mom!"

Ferris seems as surprised by this revelation as anyone, and he runs around in circles before settling at Dana's feet.

Relieved that her interaction with the dog is over, Dana turns to Eddie, crouches down, and extends her arms for an embrace.

"Hi, buddy!"

Eddie, ever the mama's boy, rushes toward her.

They hug, and I know that while Dana hurt me, she is an excellent mother to our son.

"We were both very productive," I tell Dana. "I finished grading and lesson planning, and Eddie practiced his timetables."

"I blew up five planets!" Eddie declares, extending his hand, fingers spread, in a display of pride.

"Cool!" Dana stands up straight. "Thanks, Carson. I've had, like, zero time to myself lately, so I appreciate it."

"No problem." I look at the clock. It's 3:22.

Man. The explosion that would happen were Rylee to show up right now... "Eddie's bag is packed." I hand it to Dana. "Here you go!"

She takes it from me. "I had a great time the other night. I mean, I'm sorry Mel is leaving. But it was fun, nonetheless. The bonfire, and getting to hang out like we used to."

"Yeah," I reply, hoping no nervous beads of sweat materialize on my brow. "It was fun."

"Maybe we could do it again sometime? Maybe you, me, and Eddie—we could go bowling?"

"Yes! Bowling! Please, Dad?!" Sweet, innocent Eddie beams up at me.

I have no reasonable choice. It's how I get them to leave and ensure that Eddie doesn't break out in tears.

"Sure. Bowling. Let's do it."

Eddie jumps up and down in joy. Dana grasps my bicep in this territorial sort of way, pressing her fingertips into muscle and letting go with a slight caress, like how she used to when we were a couple. "Great," she says. "How about Tuesday?"

"Yeah. That should work." It's now 3:25. "I'll text

you to hammer out the details."

"Great." Dana heads towards my door. But, oh God, please no, she stops. "One other thing."

"What's that?" I relax my breathing, so my desperation won't show.

"Can you take Eddie on Friday night? I have plans."

Plans? Whatever. "Sure, of course."

"Great." She leans in and gives me a chaste kiss on the cheek. "Thanks, Carson."

They move towards the car, and my heart races with relief that Dana will leave before Rylee arrives. The thought of the two of them colliding is like rolling thunder during an electrical storm.

The ensuing explosion would be a disaster.

Chapter 28

Rylee

When I turn onto Carson's street, I see Dana and Eddie coming out, walking toward their car.

Crap.

It's impossible to turn around without calling attention to myself, and if I drive by and continue down this gravel road, they'll for sure notice me.

My one option is to pull into someone's driveway, turn the ignition off, scrunch down into my seat, and plead to Heaven that I'm not busted. Looking straight ahead, I see curtains crack open. A woman peeks out, likely wondering why a stranger parked right outside her house.

I lunge in the passenger seat for my purse and take out my phone. Idling on a stranger's driveway is always suspicious, but it's a bit less suspicious if you're talking on your cell phone.

Guess I'll have a pretend conversation with a nonexistent person until Dana and Eddie drive away. With one eye looking out my rearview mirror and the other on the home I face, I press my phone to my ear. I'm almost startled to death when my phone comes to life, ringing and vibrating in my hand, demanding to be answered. A quick glance down, and I see that it's Jack.

Without much hesitation, I swipe to accept the call.

"Hey," I say. "What's up?"

"The worst case of writer's block I've ever experienced. Rye Bread, I need your help."

"You do?"

Through my rearview mirror, I see Eddie disappear into the backseat of Dana's car. Dana and Carson stand at the curb, and Dana puts her hands on Carson's chest and tilts up her chin, expecting a kiss. Carson leans in. But is he kissing her on the lips or on the forehead? I can't tell because my field of vision is blocked.

"Yeah," Jack says. "Remember, I told you about the scene where Anna is trying to decide if she should leave her husband or just have an affair?"

"Uh-huh."

"I can't get past her walking into the living room and seeing the scarf her husband's mistress left behind. No matter what I do, Anna is stuck in her living room holding a quilted scarf that reeks of patchouli. Can you please read through it for me? I could use your feedback."

I'm flattered that Jack wants my help, but his timing is bad. This morning, I read Max Olson's short story "Crashing into Fate" for my fiction class. With unassuming prose, the story is a desolate yet passionate account of a fatal car crash, describing the smoky clouds, the acrid smell of gasoline and burnt rubber, and how the driver drooled blood like he'd regurgitated tomato soup. The theme? In tragedy, no one can tell what's real or imagined.

Okay. *Maybe* that's the theme—the story hit too close to home, and I didn't complete my assignment. Meanwhile, Jack loves Max Olson's writing so much he says he is a genius.

I'm not in the right headspace today to help Jack

with his novel. But I can try.

"Okay, Jack…does Anna have to either leave him or have her own affair? Maybe they could go to therapy, work through their issues, and find a happy ending."

There's several seconds where Jack is silent. And the lady whose driveway I've invaded glares at me. I give a little wave and point to my cell phone as if to say, *Sorry, on the phone, I'll only be a moment or two.*

She drops the curtains, and I no longer see her. Jack punctures the silence with a cynical laugh. "You're joking, right?"

"Umm…"

"Rylee, I'm not writing a crappy romance novel where the happily ever after is all tied up with a pretty bow."

"Sure, of course." I spy Dana climbing into her driver's seat, but not before giving Carson's shoulder an affectionate squeeze. Carson stands on the curb, watching them go and waving goodbye. "I'm saying there are more than two options—"

The lady who lives here bangs on my car window, almost startling me to death. "Excuse me!" she yells. "This is not a parking lot."

"Ryy-lee." Jack lowers his voice and draws out my name. "Babe—my work isn't a reflection of my personal life. Don't worry. There's every possibility that you and I can have our happy ending."

"Sorry," I say to the lady, but Jack assumes I'm speaking to him.

"Don't apologize, sweetie."

"I'm not," I say to Jack. "But I can't talk right now. Can I call you later?"

"Yeah, great. And I'll email you the scene. Rye

Bread, if you can fix it for me, you're a genius, and I'll love you forever."

Huh. He used the "L" word, and that sort of registers, but I'm too distracted to dissect it. "Bye." I end the call and turn on the ignition, putting the car in reverse. Dana and Eddie have turned off Carson's street. He remains standing at his curb, his eyes focused on me.

Minutes later, I step into Carson's home. He pulls me in for a hug. The familiarity of his embrace gushes through me like a river. Despite my better judgment, I want to pull him toward the bedroom while peeling off his clothes. But I remember I'm a home-wrecker, and guilt drowns my desire. "Let's get down to work," I tell him.

"Sure," Carson replies.

If he's taken aback by my tone, he doesn't show it.

I sit at the folding table and get out my laptop. "I read both your story and your analysis of 'Crashing Into Fate.' You did a great job."

Carson arches an eyebrow and sits across from me. "Thanks. But how come you never sent me anything? Was there some mix-up?"

"No. I procrastinated and didn't read the story until this morning, and…nothing gelled."

He tents his fingers like a mediator attempting diplomacy. "Oh. You're skipping this week's assignment?"

"Sorry." I stand up and stretch, trying to diffuse the tension between us. "I tried. But I was blocked."

"Okay." Carson gets up and walks a few feet into the kitchen to fill a glass of water. Tension radiates off his shoulders as he stands at the sink, back turned to me.

"*Is* it okay?" I ask.

"Of course." He turns off the faucet, gulps down his water, and then he faces me. "It happens, right? Everyone gets blocked from time to time."

"Sure." Something inside my stomach twists, and I can't accept his kindness. "Except, how will you get full points for this week's assignment if I don't give you anything to critique?"

Carson takes one last swig of water. "I don't know."

Suddenly, I'm itchy, like I'm breaking out in hives. But that's absurd. That happens to me in situations far more stressful than this one.

"You're angry at me."

He shifts his weight. "No, I'm not."

"Don't lie. The idea of receiving partial points for an assignment sends you into a panic. Am I right?"

Carson's face is blank, like he refuses to settle on an emotion. "Let's move on, okay? We can discuss your reaction to my work and leave it at that."

Scratching at my arms, I pace his living room to put some distance between him and me. "Fine."

"Are you alright?" Carson approaches, his arms raised like he's moving in to touch me.

Stepping back as if cornered, I realize I sort of am. I'm stuck between the wall with his TV shelf and a crate full of video games and DVDs. "Of course. But I don't understand why you won't admit you're angry."

I scoot past him and sit at Carson's table. He follows suit.

"I've never been one for conflict," Carson says. "I prefer smoothing things over."

Leaning back in my chair, I cross my arms over my chest. "Do you?"

Carson's mouth falls open, his expression wounded.

"Did I do something to annoy you?"

I want to shout at him, to accuse him of messing with my heart while stringing Dana along. But that would totally break our rules, so I lash out, aware I'm being 100% unreasonable.

"No. But I wish you'd say what's on your mind."

"I—"

Cutting him off again, I pitch myself forward in my chair, pointing at him. "You feel sorry for me. That's why you won't admit that you're pissed—because of what happened to my dad. You assume I still can't cope. But that's not it!" I slap the table. "Okay!"

"Rylee." His voice is soft and warm, like a blanket pulled out of the dryer. I want to bury myself in the safety of his presence and be soothed.

But I can't. I won't. "I'm sorry." I bolt up from my chair and start gathering my stuff. "I should go."

"What? Why?" He stands and comes around to me like he will block my path to the door. "Rylee, come on. Tell me what I did wrong, and I'll fix it." When I don't answer, he continues, "Okay. Yes, this week's story made me worry about you, what with the graphic descriptions and the part about 'ruling your own tragedy.' Anyone who'd lost a loved one that way would have a hard time reading it. But I'm confused because you walked in here like you were mad at *me*."

It's like my anger is a foggy window that he's trying to wipe clean. But the air is too dense for him to succeed.

I say nothing.

Carson shifts his weight back and forth. "Are you just upset in general, or did I do something wrong?"

I jut out my chin. "Can't it be both?"

"It can. But please don't leave without telling me

what I did."

"Fine." The words are painful, catching in my throat. "I saw you kiss Dana goodbye."

Defiant, Carson expands his chest. "That's not what happened."

"Whatever." I glance away. "She's befriended me, and she's my boss, and she wants you back. This is wrong, Carson. You're stringing her along, and I'm letting you. I mean…" I let out a sad little chortle. "Are you still married?"

"Technically."

I shake my head. "This is as much my fault as yours. But it's got to stop."

He adopts a thoughtful expression, his warm brown eyes blinking and widening at the same time. In a silken tone, he says, "I hear what you're saying, but I disagree. What if, instead of stopping, we don't stop? Because I don't want to stop."

I bury my annoyance. "Me trying to end things—it's become funny, right? That's why you're not taking me seriously." I glide past him.

"Wait." He takes me by the shoulders, but not so hard that I can't escape his grasp. "Rylee, it's not funny, and I am taking you seriously, but let me explain." He peers into my eyes. When I don't protest, he continues. "First, none of it is your fault. I have to stay on Dana's good side until the divorce papers are signed and we've agreed on joint custody." He swallows like he has a sore throat. "I can't lose Eddie, Rylee. But I don't want to lose you either."

He stands a little straighter, releasing my shoulders. I smell his spicy scent and swear I hear his heartbeat, and my mind scrambles for words. All I manage is, "I don't know what to say."

"Say you'll stay," he pleads.

But how? "We've broken almost all the rules we made."

"I don't care." Carson rubs the back of his neck and whispers, "Let's forget the rules." He takes my hands in his. "Last night, I remembered the one about no romantic feelings. But I broke that rule before we even wrote it. You consume my thoughts, Rylee."

I step closer, seeking comfort from him. His fingers thread through my hair, and the foundation of my inner walls weakens.

"Rylee…" His deep voice reverberates against my skin. "If you stay, I could help you finish your assignment. Not because I care about getting full points, but because you might feel better if you work through…" He trails off, perhaps nervous to complete his thought. "Or, I could make us dinner. And if you wanted, we could talk about your dad. I'm a good listener."

I flatten my forehead against his chest. "Can I tell you something?"

"Yeah, of course."

"What I said about you panicking over not receiving full points? That's me. I *hate* the idea of getting a zero. But…" I sniff back tears. "I couldn't write anything."

Carson hugs me tight. My cheek is pressed against his chest when he says, "I understand. And I want to help. Okay?"

"Okay," I murmur. "That sounds good."

We sit back at his table.

Carson becomes industrious. "Alright. For your response, we can take what I wrote, reword it, and shuffle it around. Or, I can come up with new, different literary analysis, and you can type it up."

"Isn't that cheating?"

Carson shrugs. "Victimless crime. But for your story, what if you write a flash piece about a psychic who knows the world is about to end?" His smile is self-deprecating. "That was my first idea since the narrator is supposed to be psychic, telling the story of his apocalypse before it happens. But you could write about something unrelated to car accidents, like a plague or nuclear war."

I laugh. "Which are both way more cheery than a car accident." It's a joke, but it's also the truth, at least for me. "Thank you, Carson. I appreciate it."

"Don't thank me yet."

"Fine. I'll thank you later."

We spend hours working together, writing my story and literary analysis of "Crashing Into Fate." As he explains his ideas, Carson's earnest grin and reddening cheeks are adorable. After a while, I'm desperate for a break. "Let's move this study session to the next room."

I rise, go to him, and clutch his shirt in both hands, pulling him up.

He doesn't resist. Together, we walk to his bedroom, where the only light comes down the hall from his laptop, which still displays the last line of my story. *There was always going to be an apocalypse. But we can still find a happy ending.*

"The story turned out great," he murmurs, between kisses.

"You're great," I answer.

"So are you."

I pull off his shirt. We come together, and I forget all my problems and hangups. There's just us, bathed in the pale, flickering laptop light, lost in the rhythm of our beating hearts.

Chapter 29

Rylee

"You're taking the novel writing course next term, right?"

Jack's face stares up at me from the bottom of my computer screen. We were going over a scene from his novel where Anna, torn between divorce and adultery, holds a patchouli-scented scarf. We go back and forth until it's believable that she'd stay with Stu—self-destructive cycle or not. I jot down some dialogue for Jack, so he can give her an authentic female voice.

Now, we've moved on to small talk. "I'm not sure," I say. "Isn't it better to wait until my second year before I take that class?"

"Not at all," Jack states, as he strokes his beard. "You could practically teach that class yourself." His eyes meet mine, and for a moment we're not separated by two thousand miles or two time zones. He's right here, understanding me in a way no one else does. "You're ready, Rye. And besides," he adds, with a flicker of a grin, "you'll be out here in California next year, right? Tell me you're still planning to transfer. You're way too talented to stay at Bemidji State."

"What do you mean? You got your MFA from Bemidji State."

"Yeah, because I got a full ride and a TA position, and Blue Loon Press expressed an interest in my first novel. But I always intended to transfer to USC. Their program is unparalleled."

How nice for him. Jack forgets that I was only ever wait-listed at USC. Now if anything, my chances of getting in there have diminished. Unless he wants to pulls some strings. I could never ask him to do that, but I often wonder if he'll offer.

"Well," I deflect, "I'm impressed so far with Bemidji's program. Professor Aldrich is amazing. And she gave me an A on my Brontë story."

"We've been over this, Rylee. Updating Austen and Brontë is so overdone, and you're way better than that."

An ember of annoyance burns in my stomach. "What if I'm not? What if I like writing romance?"

His mouth drops open. "Rylee, come on. Would you rather write the next *Sylvia's Lovers* or the next *Sons and Lovers*?"

I clench a fist. "Neither. They're both obscure novels written over 100 years ago. I want to write something new."

"Then forget about Regency romance tropes, and get your ass out to California so you can become the next Grace Palardy."

I never wanted to be Grace Palardy, I almost blurt out. *I like Ava Barlow's writing better, even if her style is more feminine.* Jack forgets this. And it never bothered me until now. I remind myself that two months ago, I would have given anything to hear Jack say I'm talented and that he wants me with him in California. But a lot has changed.

"Okay, maybe, but, Jack, it depends on stuff that is out of my control."

"Brandon will be fine, Rye."

There's a pang in my chest. Jack realizes Brandon will always be my top concern, and yet, he's so dismissive. Which confuses me like hell. Jack knows me, and he gets me. But does he care about anyone but himself?

"I hope you're right, but I can't make any promises right now."

Jack lowers his eyelids and speaks in a playful tone. "I miss you, okay? And I admit I have selfish reasons for wanting you out here."

I smile. "Oh yeah? And what are they?"

He leans toward his camera so that his face takes up most of the screen. I can see up his nose, but I decide to overlook that and enjoy the romantic moment. "Remember the night we went camping?"

"Of course."

Jack and I had pitched a tent at Itasca State Park. We sat around the campfire, snuggling, drinking from a flask, and retiring to his tent, where we made each other come a handful of times. Even though Jack came more than I did, it was the most passionate night of my life.

Now the unwelcome thought barges in.

With Carson, it's always at least twice as good.

No, I argue with myself. *But even if that's true, it doesn't matter.*

"I think about that night all the time," Jack says to me. "If you were out here in California, we could go camping at Angeles National Forest or beach camping at Leo Carillo. Baby, I'd pitch my tent for you any time."

"Ha." I try to be genuine as I laugh at Jack's juvenile joke. And I appreciate the sentiment. "I'd love to go beach camping with you."

"Good. I'm holding you to that. So, here's the deal:

you'll plan on transferring next year, which means taking the most worthwhile courses at Bemidji next semester. You haven't registered yet, have you?"

"No. Registration is on Monday."

"Okay. You'll sign up for the novel writing course?"

I scratch my arms even though they don't itch. Carson and I haven't discussed taking that course since the one time he brought it up. If I sign up for the course, I'll have to tell him. But do I tell him before or after I register?

"I promise I'll think about it," I tell Jack.

The back door slams, and I hear Brandon's trademark stomping.

"I have to go. Brandon's home."

"Do you need to bring him milk and graham crackers?"

My scowl is full of switchblades.

He holds up both hands, palms out. "Sorry. But you hover over him, Rye. I've been a seventeen-year-old boy, and I'm saying—give him space."

"Fine. But he's home late, and I want to know why."

"Okay."

We say goodbye, Jack smooching the air, and me hitting the "end session" button before he hits "leave call."

I go out to the kitchen, where Brandon leans against the counter, eating from a bag of nacho tortilla chips.

"Hey, how was your day?" I ask.

"Good!" Brandon grins as he chews.

"Why are you late?"

He rolls his eyes. "I already told you, Rye. But you weren't listening."

I doubt that's true, but I'll play along. "Okay, tell me

again."

"We're doing scientific research to get published and help me get into Harvard."

"Huh?"

"I'm *sure* I told you about this." He wipes orange chip powder from his upper lip. "We're researching my medical history to see if a genetic pattern may have caused my brain tumor. Mom even released our family's medical records and Dad's records too! Then, we're going to write a research essay and try to get it published in a scientific journal. I can also make it the topic of my application essay for Harvard."

"Slow down," I say. "Who's 'we'?"

Brandon does a double take like he can't believe my obtuseness. "Mr. Meyers and me, of course."

I try to hide my shock. Yes—Carson is kind, but this is way beyond what I could've expected, even when he said he'd "keep an eye out for Brandon."

"How did you get him to help you with this research project?"

"It was his idea! He said I remind him of himself when he was my age, and since he got into Harvard, maybe I can too. We have lots of data from my medical records, so we're using that to look for patterns in the genetic connection with cancer. And we'll analyze a lot of medical journals and talk to some specialists."

I stare at him in amazement. "That's incredible! Do you need any help?"

Brandon chuckles and shakes his head. "No offense, Rye, but what do you know about genetics?"

"Nothing," I admit. "But I could sharpen your pencils, or conduct web searches—"

"Thanks," Brandon interjects. "But it'll be easier

just with Mr. Meyers and me—plus he can get us access to great academic resources." He takes another crunchy bite from his chip bag before continuing, "He really cares about getting results, and suppose we find something meaningful in all this data. We might make a real difference in understanding cancer better."

I ask more questions, and Brandon must be amped up about this project because he's quite forthcoming. "We're going to use the university library for research, and maybe we'll even use their labs. And Mr. Meyers will teach me to write scientific research articles!"

It sounds super cool. And yet, while I am grateful to Carson, I'm also miffed. Why did he never mention it?

Oh well. If we were in a legit relationship where we tell each other everything, I still couldn't be annoyed, so I can't be annoyed now. But while some things are more confusing than ever, others have become more clear.

Like, I need to sign up for the novel writing class, and I don't need to worry about telling Carson.

Chapter 30

Carson

Mid-October in Bemidji can be glorious, with sunshine highlighting the red and gold-hued trees and the ripples on the lake. It can all be bone-ass cold. However, Tuesday afternoon is in the high fifties, with a mild wind. So, I suggest to Dana that we enjoy the nice day and meet at the corn maze instead of bowling.

Eddie runs ahead, holding his map and marking off clues as he finds them on the scavenger hunt. In his other hand, he holds the end of Ferris's leash. "This is the fourth clue!" Eddie cries. "We need to turn left."

"We're following you, buddy," I call. Eddie charges forward, with Ferris keeping pace. Dana and I meet eyes and enjoy the wonder of our boy.

"He'll run the world one day," I say.

"Yeah, he's his father's son," Dana responds.

Splat. My bubble burst. *And just who is Eddie's father?* But I hold my tongue.

Dana must sense my 180 mood shift because she does what she used to do, back when we were together, and I'd grow testy. She changes the subject.

"What's the important project you're working on?"

Earlier, I told Dana I couldn't go to the corn maze until late afternoon, because I had to work on an important project after school. Now, we stroll along the dirt path, surrounded by giant stalks of corn, following

Eddie as he disappears around the bend. It's a bonus that Ferris could come along, and Dana even seems to like the dog.

"I'm doing some research with a student of mine," I tell her. "He's still recovering from a brain tumor, and we're trying to find out if there's a genetic connection to getting cancer."

"That sounds complicated. How do you even start a project like that?"

Dana gazes at me, and a ray of sunlight catches on her burnished gold hair. Her open face with its soft smile is a bittersweet reminder of when I couldn't stop looking at her, couldn't stop thinking about her, couldn't stop touching her.

But that was so long ago.

"Carson?"

I brush off my nostalgia, roll my shoulders back, and stare ahead, keeping my eyes on Eddie and not on Dana. "We'll read through other people's findings, but Brandon got his mom to release his medical records, and his family's. We hope to publish our findings, so Brandon can use it to get into Harvard."

"That's cool, Carson. And so generous that you're helping him."

"Thanks. But he's a great kid, and very talented. Plus, I have this connection with him. I still remember when he was just a kid, and he and Rylee stayed at our house the night their dad died."

Stopping in her tracks, Dana grasps my arm, making me halt as well. "Wait. Brandon is Rylee's little brother. He has a brain tumor?"

Dana looks like she ate something putrid that she might barf up. Despite myself, I feel bad for her. "Well, he *had* a brain tumor. He's in remission, but yeah. I thought you knew. Haven't you and Rylee been hanging out?"

Dana gives me a squinty-eyed look, and for a moment, I panic. Then, it comes to me. "Rylee was over at your place when I came to pick up Eddie that one time. You were about to have a girl's night."

She huffs. "I hate that term. It's dismissive."

We resume walking, but Dana uses her index fingers to massage the knuckles of both thumbs. That's what she does when something's bothering her. I figure I may as well ask now, and do damage control.

"Are you okay?"

"Yeah, I'm fine, but shocked about Rylee's brother. And I'd forgotten about her dad."

"It happened almost ten years ago. You didn't even know her then."

"Yes, you and I had just started dating, and I remember you telling me about what happened—how sad it was. Wasn't it his fault? He was drunk driving, right?"

Rylee's tearful frustration pops into my mind. Her pain when she couldn't do the assignment for that car crash story. How she'd trembled when she croaked out, *I couldn't write anything.*

"No! Christ, Dana! It wasn't their father's fault."

She sucks in a breath, and I regret my vehemence like it's a burn, scalding and instantaneous. "Sorry. That drunk driving thing was a terrible rumor. According to Mel, Rylee and Brandon's parents were coming home from a party, and he'd had a lot to drink, so their mom drove. Another car slid on the ice and barreled into them."

"Okaaaay." Dana draws out the second syllable while rubbing her knuckles. "You didn't have to snap at me."

"Again, I'm sorry." We walk in silence for a moment, as Eddie, who stopped to pet Ferris, comes into view. "I'm protective of Brandon. He's had a rough time, and I don't want to make it worse."

"I understand." She uncoils her hands, and her features relax.

Eddie runs up to us. "I can't find the fifth clue. I thought we were headed in the right direction, but we're going in circles." He shoves the map into my hands. "Dad, can you figure it out?"

I take the map and study it, aware that Dana's scrutinizing me. What's going on in her mind? "Let's try that way." I point towards a corn corridor to the right.

"Fine. But don't blame me if we get lost again," Eddie says.

He takes off.

I laugh. "God, he can be such a little adult."

Dana smiles like she used to, but there's an edge of sadness. "Well, he's had to grow up fast. Like we both did."

Her comment hits me in the solar plexus. The very last thing I want is for Eddie to follow our path, to shoulder a burden too heavy for his young shoulders.

I'll fix it. I'll do better. I'll sacrifice more. The corpse of my youth has already grown cold, but Eddie's youth is still alive and kicking. I won't let it go on life support; I won't let it pass away.

Chapter 31

Rylee

This morning, I have an appointment with Professor Aldrich. Registration for next semester starts tomorrow. She's my advisor, and I need to ask about which courses to take. When I get to her office, the door is wide open. I step inside its frame and clear my throat. Professor Aldrich, sitting at her desk, looks up from her work. She's wearing dangly earrings again. This time they're a bunch of seed beads sewn together into a peacock ombre effect.

"Rylee, hello! Come in and have a seat."

Her office sort of reminds me of my dad's shed, with its braided rug and overflowing bookshelves, and a vibe as friendly as she is. I sit in a wooden armchair across from her desk. "Thank you. How are you today?"

"I'm doing well," she answers. "How are you? And how's the program going for you so far?"

"It's good!" Shifting in my seat, I tug on the sleeves of my dad's old flannel shirt. "I never intended to stay in Bemidji for undergrad, let alone grad school. But there's a silver lining, and I don't mean the huge tuition break I get because of my dad." My eyes lock on the *Pride and Prejudice* framed poster on her wall. "I've come to understand what he was working towards here. My father had such a passion for writing and literature, and I'm proud that he contributed to this remote, underrated program that's also first class."

My statement must paralyze her. Professor Aldrich's mouth falls open before she says, "You're Gordon Lynch's daughter?"

"Yes."

She leans forward. "Oh my gosh, I'm sorry I didn't make the connection before. I worked with your father. He was exceptional."

Something catches in my throat. "Thank you."

"I hope you don't mind me saying this, but I imagine he'd be very proud seeing you thrive here, following in his footsteps."

I look down at her multicolored braided rug. "Why would I mind? It's one of the best compliments I've ever received."

Professor Aldrich taps a pearly pink fingernail against her desk. "I remember one time, not long after I first started teaching here. A literary journal featured a short story I wrote. It was a romance, so I'd had a hard time finding a publisher, and I was thrilled. When I told your father, he decided to throw me a 'published party.' " Her fingers bend into knuckles, which rub across her lower lip. "I told him it wasn't necessary, but he insisted. On the day of my story's release, he ordered a cake with my story's title written in icing, and he invited everyone in the Creative Writing Club to eat cake while I read my story aloud—" Choked up, she cuts herself off to sniff. "He even brought champagne and a bunch of those plastic champagne glasses…" Blinking back tears, her gaze moves toward the ceiling. "I'll never forget his toast: 'We must celebrate and share our passion for words. May we never stop reaching readers with stories of love.' " She laughs a little and wipes her eyes with the back of her hand. "He was so supportive and generous, your father. It's been years, but I still miss him."

"Thank you." I'm sniffing back tears of my own. "Hearing that memory of my dad means a lot."

I want to ask, *Were you at that party? The one where he got drunk because he'd been dropped by his agent? The one where he never made it home?*

But she reaches for my hand, skimming it with her fingers as light bounces off her pretty pink nails. "He'd be proud. I know because he talked about you all the time! And that story you wrote about Charlotte Brontë? He'd love it. Have you pursued publication?"

"Not yet."

"Well, I can help you, if you'd like. In the meantime, have you thought about your thesis? Perhaps you should consider something that explores romantic tropes. As a fellow romance writer, I'd love to work with you."

I gasp. "That sounds fantastic. But how did you know I write romance?"

Professor Aldrich smiles, her dimples peeking. "Call it a hunch. A hybrid of literary and romantic fiction can be magical, and you have the skill to bring that about."

My heart swells at her words. "Thank you."

The professor nods and leans back in her chair, steepling her fingers.

"Of course. Now let's look at your course options for next semester—have you considered the novel-writing class?"

****

On Wednesday night, when we're about to close, Dana approaches me. "Want to have a drink?"

"Sure!"

After the last customers leave and Dana and I clean up, we sit at the bar and enjoy a glass of wine.

"I figured out which *Manor House Chronicles* character you are," Dana says.

"Oh yeah? Who?"

Dana smiles like a game show hostess revealing the prize hidden behind door number two. "You're Beatrice!"

It takes me a minute to place her. "You mean, I'm the mom?"

"Yes!" Dana reaches over and squeezes my hand. "Everyone says she's a hottie with a spine of steel hidden beneath compassion and warmth. That's you!"

Truth? I'm a little flattered. But I laugh it off. "At least I'm not Grammy Elle."

Dana grins. "You could be so lucky. She's a badass, and her quips are the best part of the show."

"You're right," I reply, laughing. "Hey. I've been meaning to tell you. Jack has been calling a lot, saying I should move to California. And the other day, I looked over those rules you gave me." With an embarrassed shrug, I admit, "I'd typed them into a document. Anyway, without realizing it, I've been following them all, and now he seems ready to commit."

"That's great! Will you go to California?"

I sip from my merlot. "It's too soon to say."

Dana reaches her hand out toward me but stops short of contact. "Are you worried about Brandon?"

"Well, yeah. That's part of it." Looking away, I try to remember if I ever mentioned Brandon's health to Dana.

She must sense my confusion. "I hope you don't mind me asking. Carson told me about his brain tumor, and the research he and Brandon are conducting."

"Oh." I smooth back my hair. Why is Carson telling Dana about his research project with Brandon when he won't tell me? "Yeah. Brandon is thrilled to have Carson as a teacher."

Dana drinks from her pinot grigio. "Everyone loves Carson. He's a great teacher, and his students are crazy about him. But sometimes I…" She trails off, then waves her hand as if to clear any negative energy she released. "Never mind. We went to the corn maze with Eddie yesterday, and it was fun. I don't want to get my hopes up, but maybe Carson and I have a second chance."

"That's great." I'd better change the subject before my guilty conscience blurts out something I'll regret. "Hey, I have a question for you. You know how I'm getting my master's in creative writing?"

"Yeah." She winks. "But that's not the question, is it?"

"No." I laugh. "No. I need to figure out my thesis. And I want to do something using Regency romance themes and tropes, but in a modern context. As a romance fan, I'm wondering what you think?"

"I love it!" Dana's claps like she's applauding me. "It could be like *Manor House Chronicles* meets *Pride and Prejudice*, but set today. Can I help you brainstorm ideas?"

Her enthusiasm is infectious. "You already are!"

****

It's pouring when I leave the restaurant, and I run to my car. Once I'm inside, rain pounding on my windshield, my phone vibrates with a text before I turn on the ignition.

Wanna come over?

Carson.

I text back. *Is this a booty call?*

He responds right away. *No! It's a booty text.*
Ha ha.

The ellipses move back and forth, stopping and resuming twice. *Remember when I said you consume my thoughts?*

Yes, I text back. *That was three days ago.*

Right. Still true. Miss you. Please?

Why does his text make my heart burn with such need? Dammit.

On my way.

My windshield wipers are at their fastest speed. Barely able to see two feet in front of me, I grip the steering wheel, nervous I'll meet some tragic end before I get to Carson's house. And when I die, everyone will be like, *why was she driving* that *route and not toward her house?* Dana will put two and two together, and she'll curse my memory.

Dana.

I deserve to be cursed by her now.

When I arrive at Carson's house, his door swings open the moment I pull up. He comes running out, holding a garbage bag over his head.

As soon as I open the driver's side door, he's by my side. "Sorry, I don't have an umbrella. But I thought this would be better than nothing."

He shelters me, but also uses his upper body to protect me from the rain. I turn towards him, wrapping my arms around his shoulders and bringing my face to his.

The rain beats down as we kiss, but nothing can make me stop now. We're both drenched, and I don't care. I want more—more of him, more of this.

"Let's go inside," he murmurs. His arm moves to my waist, dipping low enough to lift me. He almost carries me inside, his lips joined with mine, my toes grazing the ground. Somehow, he opens his door, pulls us both inside, and closes and locks it, all while still kissing me.

"Shower," he grunts.

"Umm hmm."

Locked together, we stumble toward his bathroom, where we have to break apart so he can turn the water on. Fingers fumbling, we take off all our wet clothes and then step underneath the hot spray to come together again.

I kiss him but look down long enough to see he's already rock hard. I grab him, and he groans.

Now he really does lift me, and I wrap my legs around his waist. Carson presses my back against his shower wall and enters me, making me moan. We stop kissing so we can catch our breath. "You have no idea what you do to me," he says as he thrusts inside me.

Waves crash over me. His eyes sear into mine as he slams and thrusts until I grab his hair and dig my nails into his back. "Don't—ever—stop!"

But never stopping is not how sex works, and thank God for that. Later, Carson and I lay on his bed, our limbs entwined.

"Bliss," Carson murmurs.

"Who'd have thought we'd find it here, in Bemidji, Minnesota?"

Carson's chest rises and falls as he chuckles. "Not me."

I run my fingers down his arm, loving how his smooth skin is taut over his biceps. "If you could go anywhere and do anything, and Eddie would be there with you, safe and happy, what would you do?"

"Hmm." He sighs. "I have no idea."

I study his face. It's become familiar, and yet also endlessly fascinating. "I'm not sure I believe you."

"No, really. I used to have goals, dreams, and ambition, but now it's… What I'd love is time and space to figure out what I want."

"So, you want freedom?"

"I guess you could call it that. But it's never going to happen."

I stroke his cheek. "Maybe it will."

His brown eyes meet my blues, and they're filled with desire, but not for me. It's a desire for opportunities or the chance to be reckless. I see the exact same thing every time I look in the mirror.

"Hey," I say. "Brandon came home the other day all hyped about the research project you two are doing."

Carson grins. "Your brother is very talented."

"Why didn't you ever mention it to me?"

"That Brandon is talented? I figured you already knew."

"No." I swat his arm. "Why didn't you mention the project and that you're helping him apply to Harvard?"

"It's hard to explain." He props himself up, elbow against his pillow. "I guess I was worried you'd think I was using him."

"What?! Why?"

"Because I kind of am."

I tilt my head back, giving him an *explain please,* sort of look.

"It's nothing bad," Carson continues. "Brandon researched his own medical history. I would never take advantage of that."

"Okay. But…"

"But—and this is going to sound arrogant, so forgive me—Brandon reminds me of myself at his age. Except I never had to face his challenges. But the potential and the drive… I like to think that was me ten years ago. And now, the best I can do is live vicariously and help Brandon answer questions about himself. In the process, maybe he'll get into Harvard on a scholarship."

"I wouldn't call that 'using him.' "

"What would you call it?"

"I'd call it amazing." I lean in to kiss him. "You're amazing."

We kiss some more, and it turns into an embrace while our tongues dance. But when I hear a familiar, distant melody coming from the other room, I pull away. "Is that my cell phone?"

Carson doesn't answer, but he doesn't have to. Unless we have the same ringtone, someone is calling me.

I pull a blanket from his bed, drape it over my shoulders, and run into the living room, trying to find where I'd dropped my purse. It's by the front door. But by the time I've figured that out, the ringing stops.

Before I can see who the missed call is from, my phone goes off again.

It's my mom.

"Hi, Summer." Guilt crawls through me. "Sorry, I forgot to call. I'm at Carson's."

She makes an angry grunt. "What the hell, Rylee? Didn't you see all my texts?"

Knowing I deserve this, I cringe. "No. Again, I'm sorry." I brace myself for what she'll say next.

"Rylee, I don't care if you're having the most mind-blowing sex ever—this is not okay! It's pouring down rain, you are hours late, and I pictured you dead in a ditch! Like your dad." She pauses, and her silence scares me. "I called and texted you several times, and I called your work, and Dana said you'd left already, and then I called the hospital—"

My gut drops. "You talked to Dana?"

"Yes, that's what I said."

My heart races as desperation rises within me. "Did you mention Carson?"

"Seriously?! That's what you're worried about?" Her question is laced with disappointment and rage.

"Summer, I'm sorry. It won't happen again, and I promise to make it up to you." Sniffling, my voice wavers. The raindrops pelting against the window punctuate my desperation. "Please say you didn't mention anything about Carson to Dana?"

"I'm not stupid, Rylee," she snaps. "And I'm not inconsiderate—not like you. Perhaps you should ask yourself if this is the person you want to be."

The answer terrifies me, so I stay silent.

"Goodnight." The single word stabs me like an icepick, and before I can respond, the line goes dead.

Carson wanders into the living room, wearing sweatpants and a white V-neck T-shirt. "Is everything okay?"

I can't stop staring at my phone like it might light up and bring back a nicer, more forgiving version of my mom.

"Rylee?"

I drop my phone back into my purse. Underneath this thin blanket, I'm naked and rather cold. "Do you have anything I can put on? My clothes are still wet."

"Yeah, of course."

I follow him back into the bedroom, and he gives me a T-shirt with *Bemidji High Lumberjacks* written across the chest and long underwear that I roll up at the waist.

"That was your mom on the phone?" Carson sits on the edge of his bed, watching as I dress. "You call her by her first name?"

"Yeah." I rub my eyes. "Ever since the accident. She was driving the night that my dad…" I cut myself off by swallowing down tears. "I should have called her. Of course, she'll always assume the worst. How could I be so selfish?"

"Are you okay?"

"Not really."

He opens his arms so I can step into them. "Come here."

I walk into his embrace and press my cheek against his shoulder.

"You're not selfish, Rylee."

"You don't know that."

"Of course I do." His words come out breathy and rushed like he feels my pain. "That night—when your mom was banged up, unconscious in the hospital and your dad…"

"Yeah…" I'm not sure how to stop him from finishing that thought.

Carson understands. "Mel, me, and my parents—none of us knew what to say. But I tried to make you feel safe and comfortable."

"I remember."

He rubs my back. "You were so strong, Rylee. There I was, almost an adult, thinking I was ready to take on the world, but I had nothing on you. You'd just lost your dad, but you insisted on sleeping in the same room as Brandon in case he needed you."

I wipe my nose with the back of my hand. "You would have done the same for Mel. Look how you came through for Dana and Eddie."

Carson's laugh is cynical. "That's up for debate. Besides, Mel mentioned how you let your mom lean on you through the years."

"She did?"

"Yeah."

I lift my head so we can look at each other. "Well, my mom's had a hard time. Her dad left, and her mom died. At my age, she'd already gotten married and had me. She lost her husband, and then her son got sick. Anyone would need someone to lean on."

"Yeah, but you needed someone to lean on too."

"I had Mel. Except, now she's gone."

Carson rubs the back of my neck. "She's only a phone call away. And you also have me."

Hugging him, I ignore the twisting in my chest. It's great that Carson wants me to lean on him. But I know what happens when you lean against someone or something that gets snatched away.

You fall.

Chapter 32

Rylee

Carson and I find a rhythm. We're both super busy—me with a full course load, hostessing, helping Jack with his novel, and finishing *A Viscount for Vivien.* Carson with teaching, grad school, spending time with Eddie, and now the research project he's doing with Brandon. And yet, we often spend at least one night a week together, besides our Sundays. But we don't talk about what will happen next semester after our fiction class ends.

We don't talk about the future at all.

In mid-December, a week before finals, I go over to Carson's house after work. On my drive there, I notice a tickle in my throat but tell myself I'm imagining it.

That night, Carson is sniffly, and I keep coughing.

"I bet it's nothing," I say.

But the headlines about how this year's flu strain is both bad and resistant to the shot runs like a chyron inside my mind.

The next morning, Carson makes coffee with one hand and holds a Kleenex in the other. Every other second, he's wiping or blowing his nose. Dressed in sweatpants and a T-shirt, he's also wrapped in a blanket. I didn't realize Carson ever got cold, but now he's shivering.

"How are you doing?" I ask. "You sound pretty

stuffed up."

I punctuate my statement with a cough.

"Honestly? I'm kind of achy. And I don't know. Just…off."

"Yeah, me too."

We meet eyes. Carson clutches his coffee mug with both hands like he needs to warm his fingers. A chill travels through me, and I long to dive back into Carson's bed and cocoon myself under his comforter.

Carson places down his mug and wanders toward his bathroom. In a few seconds, he's back with a thermometer. Coming right up to me, he says, "Lift your tongue."

I comply, he sticks the thermometer into my mouth, I close my lips, and seconds pass like minutes until the thing starts beeping. He takes it out, squints, and says, "101.2."

"That's not good," I state.

He raises his eyebrows as the corners of his mouth pull down. "Now do me."

I run the thermometer under the sink, wipe it with a paper towel, and stick it in his mouth. After it beeps, I look at it and tell him, "100.9."

Carson shivers. "We should get tested for whatever this might be. Make sure we don't need antibiotics or a prescription. Do you want to go to Urgent Care?"

"God no." A cough erupts from my chest. "But we have to."

"Okay. I'll drive." He rubs his forehead and scans the room like he's confused. "Where's my phone? I should call in for a sub before we go."

It takes longer than it should for Carson to realize his phone is in its charger, and I wonder if he's too dazed to drive us to the clinic. But I don't want to drive, and it would be rude to call an Uber, since we are both contagious.

Carson gets us to Urgent Care, and then we have a long wait before we're each seen individually. When the doctor gives me a rapid flu test, my eyes won't leave my test card. It's like my pregnancy scare during my junior year of college. I never told Jack. Instead, I bought a drugstore test and peed on a stick. Pants around my ankles, I sat on the toilet and prayed. When just one line turned pink, I thanked a God I wasn't sure I believed in.

But this time is different. Strong purple lines form in both the "t" and "c" windows. The doctor is unsurprised but sympathetic. "Lots of people are getting the flu, since this year's shots aren't as effective as we would have liked. Make sure to drink lots of fluids and get lots of rest. You'll need at least a few days to fully recover."

I emerge out in the lobby, where Carson sits waiting for me. "It's positive. I have the flu." My knees buckle, and I collapse onto the chair beside him.

He reaches for me and gives my knee a half-hearted pat. "Yeah, me too. Let's get out of here. I want to go home and sleep."

I say nothing and make no move to leave. Carson peers at me. "Are you okay?" he asks. "You look like you're about to pass out."

"Well, I have the flu. So no, I'm not okay."

"Yeah, but it's like you're on the verge of a heart attack."

"I might be. What if I gave it to Brandon? He's still not back to normal after radiation and his brain surgeries. For him, the flu could be quite serious."

Carson starts to answer but presses his lips together instead.

I comb my fingers through my hair. "Okay. We should make a troubleshooting list. People we need to call, obligations to get out of, and I need to figure out logistics."

"I…" Carson seems like he can't keep up. "What do you mean, logistics?"

"Like, if my mom and Brandon aren't sick yet, I should go to a hotel." I scratch my arms and wish I could erase this reality. "I better call and warn her."

I search my bag for my phone.

"You can stay with me," Carson says. I don't answer, as I dig past my wallet, keys, a comb, and three separate tubes of lip balm. "Rylee, did you hear me? You don't need to call a hotel."

Finally, I clutch my phone, ready to dial the Days Inn to book a room. "I can't stay with you," I tell Carson.

"Why not?"

"Because people will put it together that we're both sick, and then we'll be busted."

Carson's still slumped in his chair, but he straightens his posture a bit. "By that logic, we're busted anyway. And if you stay at a hotel, you'll spend several hundred dollars minimum. Besides, what if you get really sick? You can't be all alone."

"Why not?"

"Because." He attempts to breathe through his stuffed-up nose. "It's not safe. Have you ever been alone and sick before?"

Truth is, I've never been alone. As for being sick, that's not something I do. I'm the healthy one whose shoulders are always squared, who doesn't get lost because it's her job to find everyone else.

"No." I hug my chest. "But I'll have my cell phone. Besides, you're as sick as me. How are we supposed to take care of each other when we need to take care of ourselves?"

He looks like it hurts to think, hurts to breathe, hurts to be.

"I guess that's the essential question in every relationship."

"This isn't a high school lesson plan, and we're not in a relationship, Carson."

"But we're not nothing, either." Squeezing his eyes shut, Carson tilts his head back. "Call me crazy, but we should take care of each other. It's better than being alone."

Through the fog in my brain, something occurs to me. "Are you afraid to be by yourself?"

Carson's bottom lip trembles. "No."

"Liar." I can tell he's terrified. "You want me to stay with you?"

He squeaks his answer. "It's the practical solution."

I stand in front of him, take his hands in mine, and pull him from his chair. Wrapping my arms around his neck, I give him a hug. Carson's arms circle my waist. "Okay," I murmur. "We'll look after each other."

Chapter 33

Carson

Thank God neither Brandon nor Rylee's mom are sick. "I'm staying with Carson," Rylee explains on the phone, once we're back at my place. "I won't be alone. Summer, I'll be fine. Promise."

At least they're not arguing. I can tell from Rylee's soft tone that she's responding to her mom's genuine concern.

But the people in my life? Their concern is for themselves and not for me.

The school's HR lady asks how long I'll be out. "We'll need a doctor's note," she says.

"Okay," I concede.

Then, I call Dana. But she doesn't freak out the way I expect. Instead, it's like she's lost a boxing match. "Figures," she says. "Everyone is getting sick at the same time. You're the third person today telling me they have the flu."

"Oh. Who else has it?"

"People at the restaurant."

I meet eyes with Rylee, who's curled up on my couch. "Two people at the restaurant have the flu?"

Rylee's mouth drops open. "Who?" she mouths.

"Are they waiters or cooks?" I ask Dana.

"One of each," Dana responds.

For Rylee's benefit, I ask, "So a waiter and a cook?"

Dana's response drags over the line. "Yeah..." she says, and I can almost see her shaking her head, exasperated. "If more people call in, we might have to close for a while. You can't run a restaurant if you're short-staffed."

"Do you have any symptoms?"

"No," Dana answers. "You know me. I never get sick."

I roll my eyes—Dana's always sure of herself. After a beat, Eddie's muffled voice filters down the line, and Dana clicks her tongue. "What's that?" Pause. "Yes, Dad has the flu. What? Okay." Eddie is talking again, and Dana tries not to laugh. "Eddie said to hold on while he does an internet search."

Another beat passes before I realize it's my turn to speak. "What's he searching up?"

"Hold on." Her voice is muted as she murmurs "Uh-huh," and, "Okay." Then speaks again into the receiver. "Eddie says that dogs can get the flu from humans. You should be careful...wash your hands before giving him his food and water and don't kiss him."

It's like my chest won't expand. My words come out strangled. "Tell Eddie that I'll be super careful with Ferris."

"Sure," Dana answers. "I should go. Call me later and let me know how you're doing, okay?"

"Yeah." I'm hit with a wave of sadness. When will I get to see Eddie again? "Of course, and I'll talk to Eddie and explain why I can't see him for a while."

A heavy silence reverberates between us before Dana breaks it: "Right... Bye, Carson."

The line goes dead.

"Well, at least she didn't freak out," Rylee says.

"True." I scoot toward Rylee so we can snuggle. She curls into me, and together, we lay back, my head on the couch cushion, her head on my chest. Thump, thump, thump, goes her heartbeat. Slow and steady.

"My mom texted," Rylee says. "She's gonna pick us up some groceries and leave them on your front step. We need to send her a list."

"That's nice of her." My breathing slows, and I wish we could stay like this. Rylee in my arms. "I should call my mom. Hopefully, she hasn't already heard through the high school grapevine."

"Wouldn't she have called you by now?"

"Depends on how busy her morning's been. And how many sophomores need help with their research papers."

"Oh." Rylee nestles closer. "Speaking of busy mornings, we should email Professor Aldrich and let her know we'll miss finals week. I'll email my other professors too. And you'll work on sub plans, right?"

"Yeah." I shut my eyes for a moment. "I'm still responsible for creating lessons and grading assignments while I'm out sick."

"That's awful."

"That's public education." I should get up, but I'm tired. Plus, this couch is quite comfortable. Because Rylee's here with me. "Maybe we should nap before we do all that stuff?"

"Okay. A short one."

My thoughts swirl as I drift off, but then they snap into clarity. "Hey—who was that author you like? The one who started the romance genre?"

Rylee stirs against me, her response a groan. "Babette Highland. Why?"

"What if we do a book exchange? I'll read one of hers, and you read one by Anton Ireland."

"Yeah, okay." She yawns and looks up at me. "Anton Ireland's your favorite? What did he write?"

"Umm, the best science fiction ever. Have you read *Robot Man*?"

"Can't say that I have."

I take her hand in mine. "Now you will. I've got a copy you can borrow—and when you send your mom a list of groceries, ask her to bring one of your Babette Highland books."

"Good idea." Rylee lifts her head and kisses my cheek before nestling back into my chest and falling asleep.

A surge of tenderness wells inside me. I touch her cheek with the back of my hand. Rylee and I have a lot of sex, and it's even better than I knew sex could be. Like, before, I was a fan of sex, but now, with Rylee, I'm a sex superfan. If sex with Rylee was a sport, I'd paint my chest and face with my team's colors and attend each game with undying devotion.

And yet, this moment is platonic. But we're more intimate than we've ever been before.

Chapter 34

Rylee

The universe shrinks. Carson, Ferris, and I are the only ones who exist. Okay—others exist but in a fabricated parallel reality. Sure, there's life outside of Carson's humble ranch-style home, but I can't be bothered about that.

It's like we're on an island as we write/study/grade from the relative comfort of Carson's couch, in our sweatpants, long underwear, or pajamas. We snuggle, take lots of naps, hand each other Kleenex, give each other cough medicine and Tylenol, remember to drink lots of fluids, and watch episode after episode of some true crime documentary. Also, several times a day, we take Ferris for a walk, crossing the street whenever we're in danger of sharing oxygen with a fellow pedestrian.

And we have our own private book club.

"I'm into *Robot Man*," I tell Carson as I rub his feet in my lap. We're both reading on his couch, me with my back against the cushion and him with his shoulders against the armrest.

"Of course you are." He uses his foot to nudge me in the belly.

"Don't sound so sure," I retort, amused. "It was just as likely I'd hate it."

He snorts out a laugh, but he's congested and it comes out like a snuffle. "No way. Not when Ireland's protagonist is a woman!"

"Right. Because I'll always enjoy a female main character, even if she's written by a man."

Carson's cheeks turn pink, and God, he's charming. "But aren't you impressed? Ireland was ahead of his time."

"Of course. My favorite part is the rules of robot and human interaction." Paraphrasing, I list them off on my fingers. " 'One: Robots must admit to being robots; Two: robots must report any subversive act made by man or robot; and Three: if a robot develops feelings for a human, it must self-destruct.' Why weren't our side project rules that clean and simple?"

Carson lifts his glasses to rub his eyes. "Because their rules were for robots, and not for messy humans, like you and me." He waves his copy of *The Regency Rogue,* its pages fluttering. "And not like the characters in this. What a tangled web."

"I know, right?"

"So, is Nicholas an asshole, or is he secretly in love with Natasha?"

"You'll have to read and find out."

Carson raises an eyebrow and smirks. Then he starts paging through the novel and skipping ahead. "Hey!" I try to snatch the novel from him, but he holds it out of reach. "Carson, no cheating!"

We both laugh, but the laughter turns to coughs, and soon we're both keeled over, gasping for air.

Carson manages to breathe well enough to speak first. "I'm enjoying the book. Don't take this the wrong way, but you should write something like it."

Between punctuated little coughs, I ask, "Are you suggesting I write a Regency romance?"

"Yeah. I mean, if you enjoy reading them, why wouldn't you enjoy writing them? I bet you could come up with something great and get it published."

I take a sloppy inhale through my stuffed-up nose. "Why would I take that the wrong way?"

Removing his feet from my lap, he sits up and shrugs. "Because you're in the MFA program to write literature." Carson uses air quotes when he says literature. "I'm sure that the novel you wrote was literary fiction, right? Explain it to me. Why aren't Regency romances considered literature? Is it because they're entertaining?"

"No. It's because they use certain, specific tropes, like they'll always have a happy ending."

"Oh." He fingers a lock of my hair. "And what's wrong with happy endings?"

As I try to craft an evasive reply, something stirs inside me. Is it exhaustion? Maybe I'm tired of pretending. Or perhaps Carson makes me want to scoop out my heart and hand it to him in a neatly wrapped gift box.

"Can I show you something?"

"Sure," he quips. "As long as it's not you naked. Not that it wouldn't be nice, but with all these cold meds I'm on…well, expectations should be low."

I ease up from the sofa while he speaks, and by the time he's done, I've retrieved my laptop from the nearby chair. "Don't worry," I assure him. "Keepin' my clothes on." I hand him my laptop and nod towards the open Quill & Key page. "This is what I wanted to show you."

Carson takes deliberate hold of my computer and focuses on the screen. "Who's Shelby Simmons?"

"That's me," I tell him. "Shelby Simmons is my pen

name."

An awed smile spreads across his face. "No way."

I slide next to him and peep over his shoulder. "These three books are mine—self-published under a pseudonym—and there's another one coming out soon."

He scrolls farther down, eyes flipping through the text. "Wow," he exclaims. "This one has over 300 five-star reviews!"

"Yeah…"

He shifts to make eye contact, his gaze curious. "But why use a pen name? Are your stories some big secret?"

"I suppose they are."

"Why?" he asks. "I don't get it."

"I guess it comes down to my own insecurities. I mean, there are many top notch, successful self-published romance authors whose work I admire, but at the same time, I'm afraid I'll be considered a literary lightweight. That's why I haven't told anyone, not even Mel, my mom, or Brandon."

"What about Jack?"

Hearing Carson say Jack's name is like acid reflux, unnatural yet inevitable. "Jack's a snob when it comes to publishing and literature."

"Oh." Carson shifts, leaning away from me. "Does he look down on happy endings?"

"Yeah. Jack says literature should reflect real life, and in real life, there's always messiness and heartache."

"*Always*?" Carson asks. "I mean, call me an optimist, but there's got to be room for hope, or for the chance that love can win."

My chest tightens, and I'm ready to argue, but it hits me like a ton of bricks—hope drives us, doesn't it? Every day, we risk it all for a chance at happily-ever-after, even when the odds are near impossible. "Yeah, you're right." Pausing, I tug at my sweatshirt's frayed cuff. "Messiness, heartache, and happy endings don't have to be mutually exclusive."

Carson's smile is like a confession. "I don't know about all that, Rylee. But if anyone deserves to be happy, it's you." He coughs, covering his mouth. "And nothing against Jack, I'm sure he's a great writer, but you're a great writer too; if your novels have happily-ever-afters, that doesn't make them less valuable than his."

"Thank you," I whisper.

He studies the computer screen, which is still on my Quill & Key page. "Where do they list the paperback version?"

"They don't. It's only available for e-readers."

"Oh." He hands me back my laptop and gets up and goes to his own computer, which is on his table. He sits down and starts typing and clicking. "Okay, which kind of e-reader should I buy?"

"You're not serious? You don't have to buy a e-reader just to read my books, Carson."

He shakes his head like I spoke in Latin. "Isn't that the only way to read them?"

"Yeah, but it's okay. You don't have to read them."

"But I *want* to read your books, Rylee. I mean…" He looks back at his computer. "You've been holding out on me. I *can't wait* to read your books. I hope they do overnight delivery for e-readers."

He keeps typing, clicking, and scrolling until he settles on what type of e-reader to buy. "Okay, I'm getting The Parchment IV." Tap, click, tap. "Done! It will be here in a few days." Smiling, Carson meets my eyes. But when he sees my expression, he frowns.

"What's wrong?"

I sniff back tears. "Nothing."

"Then why are you crying? Should I have—"

I cut him off with a kiss. It would be more passionate if we both weren't so congested, but oh well. He pulls me into his lap, so we both sit in his chair and go from kissing to hugging. "You're a nice guy," I say.

He chuckles into my hair, the rumble vibrating through me. "Oh God. That's the kiss of death."

"Not in my book."

"Oh yeah?" I nod, and he laughs again. "Now I really can't wait to read it."

Later, we're in the kitchen, Carson by the stove heating up canned soup and me preparing cheese toast. Out of the blue, he says, "I also wrote a novel."

My heart stops as his words sink in. He's mentioned it before but never gave any further details. "What's it about?"

"It's science fiction, and it's not great," he admits. "But it's dystopian, about a world where everyone must be genetically engineered—except one guy who wasn't, and he's facing certain death in a few months, so he starts a revolution."

My hand freezes in a mid-sprinkle of cheese over the buttered bread. "That sounds cool."

Carson shrugs. "I mean, I wouldn't say it's Pulitzer-worthy. It's probably not up to your standards."

Heat rushes to my cheeks. "You're a good writer, Carson—and I'm not a snob."

His eyes meet mine. "But you can be intimidating. It's like you were born with a pen in your hand."

I place the slices onto a tray small enough for Carson's toaster oven. "Well, my dad was a writer, head of the English department at Bemidji State. He read to me when I was little and gave me my love for books."

His spoon keeps rotating in slow circles while he stirs his soup. "That must have been very special."

"Yes." Hoping he doesn't notice my mood shift, I use one hand to sweep any errant pieces of grated cheese into my other hand. "Anyway…" I grasp for what to say next. "When are you going to let me read your novel?"

Carson grins. "Slow down, lady. I just worked up the courage to tell you about it. You're going to have to give me some time."

I abandon my toast, walk to him, and wrap my arms around his waist, pressing my cheek against his shoulder blades. "You have all the time you need."

I mean it. Yet, I wonder. What other parts of himself does Carson keep hidden? And will I know the real him before our side project comes to its inevitable conclusion?

Chapter 35

Carson

I jolt awake, feeling as if something is missing. A few seconds pass before coherent thought takes over, and I realize that something—no, someone—*is* missing. The clock reads 4:08 a.m., and I am alone in bed.

Where is Rylee?

I shuffle through the darkness, letting instinct guide me to the living room, until I find light and a soft hum emanating from the couch. My brow furrows as I see Rylee there, eyes glued to her laptop. Ferris snuggles close to her side, paws tucked against his chest. His ears flutter to and fro, brushing against her arm like a wispy caress.

I move closer, voice gentle in the stillness. "Rylee?"

She startles when our gazes meet. "Sorry. I tried to keep the volume low. Did it wake you?"

"No. You not being in bed woke me."

Her shoulders sag with guilt. "Oh. Sorry."

"That's okay... What are you doing? Why aren't you asleep?"

She pulls up the blanket that's around her: brown, green, and purple zigzags that my grandmother knitted ages ago. "I woke up with the worst headache ever." She gestures to the back of her skull, making an up-and-down movement. "There was this pulsating pain like something was alive back there. I wonder if that even approaches what Brandon went through with his tumor."

"Yeah, I don't know."

"You haven't gotten a headache like this yet?"

It's a statement posed as a question. "No. I guess we have different symptoms."

"You're lucky. Anyway, I couldn't sleep, so I came out here to take Tylenol and watch a movie to distract myself."

"What are you watching?"

"Blonde Academia."

I start laughing.

"What?" Rylee demands. "I needed something easy to follow. In middle school, Mel and I watched this movie together on constant repeat."

"Yeah, I remember that." I sit next to her on the couch. Ferris grunts when forced to shift over.

"You don't have to sit here with me," Rylee says. "Wouldn't you rather be asleep right now?"

Good question. I've never thought of myself as clingy or needy, but maybe I am. Maybe that's what I've become. Over the last few days, I've gotten used to having Rylee nearby, and this tiny bit of separation has thrown me for a loop. What will I do when we're both better and she leaves?

I look back at the movie. "Doesn't the main character go to Harvard?"

"Oh no." Rylee nudges my shoulder with hers. "Does this movie reopen old wounds?"

"No."

"Are you sure?"

"Yeah. Harvard isn't an open wound. It's more like a 'what if?'" I slouch down so our faces are parallel and close. "What if I'd never made the decision *not* to go?

What if I never disappointed my parents? What if Dana never lied? What if I'm living a parallel life where I'm a completely different person?"

Rylee's eyes search mine. "What did Dana lie about? That she cheated, or is there something else?"

"There's something else," I whisper, tracing her cheekbone with my finger. "I'm not sure I should tell you. Because once I tell you, there's no going back. And I wish I could go back."

She leans in closer, giving me a soft, warm kiss on the lips. "I can handle it, but only if you want to tell me."

My chest heaves with a tremendous longing to unburden myself.

"Eddie isn't my biological son."

It's the first time I've spoken those words out loud. Saying them takes the wind out of me. I have to pivot away from Rylee and switch my focus to the wall, to the construction paper collage Eddie gave me six months ago for Father's Day. "I'm not his dad."

Rylee places her palm against my back. "But in every way that matters—you are."

I breathe in and out, trying to collect myself. "Thank you."

"How did you find out?"

I squeeze my eyes shut and relive for the millionth time what happened that day. But now, I'm sharing it with someone else…

Eddie had RSV, and I wanted to trade places with him, to be the one with the scary-high fever and wheezing cough. But I couldn't, and his cries echoed through the hospital hall, his red face contorted in pain. Dana wrung her hands and muttered prayers while I fought with myself, trying to stay strong. At twenty-one, I still wasn't sure how to be a man, let alone a father. The doctor had a difficult time inserting the IV needle into Eddie's tiny hand, and with each failed attempt, Eddie's cries grew louder, his piercing eyes full of betrayal at Dana and me.

Dana had to step into the hallway, and I wished I could follow her.

Instead, I asked the intern caring for Eddie, "Can I see his chart?"

I wasn't trying to be pretentious or prove that I knew how to read a medical chart. I needed something to concentrate on, something other than my son's congested tears or my wife's powerless fear.

The nurse handed me Eddie's chart, and my focus snagged on something up top.

Blood type: B

My heart stopped as I remembered that high school biology lab where we had to prick each other, put a drop of blood on a special card, and determine our blood type by using a little dropper and identifier. Dana had squeezed her eyes shut and hid her head in her arm. When it was time for her to prick me, she couldn't do it. I'd had to prick myself.

But we'd gotten through the lab and determined that I had blood type O positive, the most common type, and Dana had blood type A positive, which is the second most common.

But Eddie was type B positive. He had to be either type A or O. He couldn't be B. Unless…unless I wasn't actually Eddie's father.

No. That couldn't be right.

Dana had insisted he was mine when she got pregnant at eighteen.

And I'd never questioned it until then.

Once the intern finally inserted the IV, Eddie's crying calmed down, and Dana came back to the hospital room.

"How's he doing?"

I shoved Eddie's chart back to its place at the foot of his bed, where there was a hook it could hang from.

I tried to say something like, "I need coffee," but my words sounded jumbled to my own ears. And I thought I grabbed my wallet as I rushed out of the room.

But when I got to the coffee machine, I realized I didn't grab my wallet but instead grabbed the paperback romance that Dana had been reading.

How could I be so blind?

I thwacked the book against the coffee machine.

I stayed in Bemidji. I gave up Harvard to marry Dana, so we could have the baby she said was mine.

I thwacked the book again.

Eddie would always be my boy; I would always put him first.

This changed nothing. This changed nothing.

When I've finished my story, Rylee leans over and captures me in a tight hug. "I'm so sorry, Carson."

I hug her back but pull away to see her face. "You're the only one who knows. And you can't tell anyone. Not Mel, and definitely Dana."

There's been a headache behind Rylee's eyes, but now there's confusion there as well. And concern. "My lips are sealed, I promise. But Carson, how have you gone for so many years, never saying anything to Dana? Didn't that drive you crazy?"

"Of course it did. But the alternative—confronting her—was much worse. Dana can be ruthless."

Rylee furrows her brow. "Yeah, but she must want

you to be Eddie's dad. Why would she ever try to keep him from you?"

I shrug. "Maybe she wouldn't. But she's threatened me before—the first time was when she told me she was pregnant. I don't always understand how her mind works, but Dana has this power over me. She could keep me away from Eddie...I can't rock the boat."

"Okay." She reaches out and strokes my cheek. "What can I do?"

All at once, I'm exhausted. But I doubt I'd be able to sleep. "I have an idea," I tell her. "Why don't you close your laptop, and we can stream *Blonde Academia* from my TV?"

"Oh. Okay."

A couple of minutes later, we're snuggling, ankles resting against ankles, my arm over Rylee's shoulder, her arms circling my waist.

My eyelids grow heavy, and somehow, I drift off to sleep. But as I do, the thought occurs to me. This thing with Rylee?

It's *way* more than a side project.

****

Two days later, I'm taking a shower when there's a rush of cool air. My pulse quickens when Rylee steps inside, her eyes on me as she strips off her clothes.

"Mind if I join you?" Her voice is thick with desire. I don't answer but instead pull her into the shower with me. I kiss her like it's been months since we last touched each other, our tongues dancing together in desperation under the running water.

I'm so greedy that I make love to her a second time on my bed, and a third time, also on my bed, but in a different spot. Afterwards, we're laying there, panting, and Rylee says, "I suppose this means we're better?"

My brain isn't quite functioning after that third orgasm, so I grunt in reply.

Rylee sits up and gazes at me, pulling on the sheets and covering her nakedness. "I suppose I should go home; it's time to get back to my real life."

I put on a smile like it's a shield, but her words go straight to my heart. "Sure. I understand. Let me get dressed, and then I'll help you pack up."

"You mean we can't stay naked?" she jokes.

"Rylee, you're always welcome to be naked around me."

"Except for when you have the flu," she retorts. "There you go—more proof that we're all better."

"Uh-huh."

She gets up, retrieves her clothes, and puts them on. "This place could use a good cleaning. Get rid of all the residual germs."

"Yeah, you're right."

"Of course I'm right. I'm *always* right. Haven't you learned that by now?"

There's a seismic shift inside my chest. "Of course I have," I tell her.

And I mean it.

As she finishes putting on her clothes, I take a moment to watch her. The way she pulls her hair back into a ponytail with such ease, the effortless grace she carries in every movement. It's mesmerizing.

"Come on," she says. "Where are your cleaning supplies?"

We get to work. Rylee strips my sheets off the bed. I scrub every surface of my bathroom, kitchen, and living room like I'm a plague doctor from centuries past. But despite all my hard work and antibacterial efforts, I still can't fight the dread that she's leaving soon.

After Rylee finishes wiping down the living room, she says, "That should do it."

She calls her mom, sharing the good news that she'll be home tonight. Then she starts to pack, and my heart sinks like an anchor.

"Carson, I can't thank you enough for letting me stay. I owe you one."

She owes me one? Like we're colleagues or neighbors? Like I shoveled her sidewalk after it snowed, so she'll shovel my sidewalk next time? "You don't owe me anything."

Rylee looks up from cramming a shirt into her bag. She takes in my tone and my sad smile. "Well, I'll find a way to thank you, nonetheless."

"You already did a great job thanking me this morning." I arch an eyebrow, trying to be playful. "Three times. Not bad."

I can tell by Rylee's face that I missed my mark. My little joke sounded pervy.

"Yeah." She shifts her weight and zips up her suitcase. "Walk me out?"

"Do you have everything?"

"I think so."

We go out through my front door right as a Quill & Key delivery guy drops off a small package and drives away.

"Ooh, is it your e-reader?" Rylee asks.

"It must be!"

Suddenly, the mood between us shifts, and Rylee places her bags down and throws her arms around me.

"I'll miss you," Rylee says. "Is that weird?"

"No. I'll miss you too." We kiss like one of us is leaving on a dangerous mission where we won't have cell reception. I tighten my arms around her, wishing I never had to let go.

Rylee pulls away first. "We'll see each other soon, right?"

"Yeah. You know where to find me."

Then, we look away from each other and towards Rylee's car, which is parked by the curb. But with the noise and bustle of the Quill & Key driver coming and going, we missed another car approaching and stopping outside of my house.

Because standing right in front of us is Dana.

Chapter 36

Rylee

Carson bolts back like he's been shocked. "Dana. Hi. What are you doing here?"

Dana doesn't answer right away, and we wilt under her intense stare. I'm aware of how I must look. Washed out with no makeup on, my hair flat from using Carson's shampoo and conditioner combo instead of my own styling products. Wearing the same sweatpants and shapeless sweater I've worn over and over for the last week. Meanwhile, Dana is stunning in skinny jeans, high black boots, and a fitted puffy parka. Its shade of teal makes her eyes look like aquamarines. Her hair, in a perfect messy bun on top of her head, glows like burnished gold.

She presses her glossy pink lips together before speaking to Carson. "It's been almost a week since you got sick. I figured you must be running out of food. I brought you this." She holds up a cardboard takeout container. "It's your favorite—chicken fried rice."

"Wow, that's so nice of—"

Dana cuts him off by speaking to me. "Hi." The single syllable comes out fast and forceful, like a bullet.

"Hi, Dana. I was just on my way home."

Her gaze scans down to my suitcase, which is still at my feet. She gapes at me, with a restrained, simmering wrath. "Is that right?"

"It's not how it looks," Carson says to her.

"Oh yeah?" Dana speaks to him but doesn't take her eyes off me. "Tell me. How does it look?"

"Like we're a couple," Carson answers. "But we're not. We've been spending time together, and when—"

"You mean, you've been fucking. Right?" Her voice is this eerie calm before an epic storm.

"Dana—"

She turns to him. "It's fine, Carson. You're allowed to fuck whomever you want. But I wish you'd told me because I feel like an idiot."

"But there was nothing to tell. We mean nothing to each other. It was just sex. Right, Rylee?" Carson gapes at me, raising eyebrows that, until this moment, I've always loved. Now, his nonchalant expression pours salt into my wound.

We mean nothing to each other. It was just sex.

"Right," I say, struggling to play it cool. "It was just sex, but then we both got the flu, and I needed a place to stay for a while…"

Dana morphs back into the mean girl she was in high school. Her laughter turns my ears raw. "I get it, Rylee. I do."

I have no strength left. I can't resist asking, "What do you mean?"

"For Carson, it was just sex, but you've been in love with him for years, haven't you? Did you think I'd forgotten?"

I pick up my suitcase and mumble, "It's not like that." Bags hanging heavy from my shoulders, I walk around them both. Carson and Dana are as still as statues. "Bye," I state, before moving towards my car. Neither answers me. Instead, Carson says to Dana, "Come in, and we'll talk."

"Fine," Dana answers.

Before I reach my car, I hear Carson's front door slam behind me.

On my ride home, I listen to the radio, which refuses to play anything but breakup songs, no matter which station I tune to.

"Screw it," I mutter and switch off the radio. "I don't need this."

Tears build inside me, but I won't be that girl who believed the guy when he said he cared, and once she realized the truth, mourns a love that didn't exist. I'll be the pragmatic girl who packs up her emotional baggage and moves on.

I pull up to my house, with its tan paint job, green shutters, natural wood picket fence, and twin birch trees—one on either side of our front yard. It's the perfect little bungalow within walking distance from campus. I park in our driveway and take a deep breath before climbing out of my car.

I'm home. Thank God.

When I walk inside, I'm greeted by Brandon and his saxophone. He starts playing a peppy fight song. Summer stands there, holding a helium balloon with *Congratulations!* written in swirly, colorful letters.

"What's all this?"

Summer hands me the balloon and captures me in a hug. "Congrats on surviving the flu."

Brandon puts down his saxophone and embraces us both.

"Thanks, guys, but was there ever any doubt I'd survive? I mean, I got my flu shot, and I'm not at risk."

"Sure," Brandon says. "But we still worried. That's

what families do."

We squeeze each other again before making the silent, mutual decision to break apart.

"Okay." Summer smooths out her hair and straightens her sweater. "I made your favorite lemon chicken for dinner."

"And we're going to play Scrabble," Brandon says. "Mom and I both promise not to give you a hard time for being super-competitive."

"Sounds perfect," I say.

Two hours later, I'm exhausted after Summer's delicious lemon chicken and some skilled word-forming on my part. Even though it's only eight thirty, I'm ready for bed. The flu may have left my body, but the fatigue still lingers.

I strip off my clothes, leaving them in a pile on the bathroom floor. The shower water is so hot it nearly burns the skin off my body, but I like it that way. It seems unreal that Carson and I were in his shower this morning. I rub my scalp, willing my mind to go blank under a haze of heat and steam, so I can feel human again.

After my shower, I move toward the bedroom. I left my phone on my nightstand before spending the evening with my mom and Brandon. That way, I wouldn't be tempted to see if Carson texted. It was hard enough not to picture him and Dana having passionate makeup sex. I didn't need my phone and its ability to mock me with silence.

My stomach turns over when I check it. I'm not sure if I'm hoping that he did text or that he didn't.

He did. Over an hour ago. One word.

Hi.

Equal parts exasperated and confused, I switch off my phone and dive into bed.

Chapter 37

Carson

I messed everything up. It was out of panic. I hated the words *just sex,* and *we mean nothing to each other*, the moment they'd left my mouth.

Dana came inside and yelled, "Man whore! Liar! Cheat!"

The injustice stung more than the accusations did. "You cheated on me first! And we're getting a divorce, remember?"

Worse than her anger, came Dana's tears. "I thought there was hope for us, that maybe we were getting back together. But this whole time, you were sleeping with Rylee?" She clenched her fists, rubbing both thumb knuckles with her index fingers. "You must have had a great laugh at my expense."

"It wasn't like that."

"Ha! Whatever, Carson. She's been fooling us both. Not me, not anymore. But you—are you in love with Rylee?"

"That's none of your business."

Dana's cheeks turned pink, which with her was either a sign of passion or extreme anger.

Yeah. I could for sure rule out passion.

"It's none of my business?" Dana's voice ventured into screeches. "We're still married, Carson, so it *is* my business. If my husband, if the father of my son, is in love with someone else, I deserve to know!"

The father of my son.

That jolted me back to reality. "I'm sorry." But I wasn't remorseful. Dana was right about one thing, anyway.

I am a liar.

"Look, can we calm down and call a truce? Let's table this and talk about it later, okay?"

"Fine." She let out a hard laugh. "As long as you agree not to see Rylee anymore."

"You can't dictate that."

"Oh?" Dana's mouth dropped open, and she seemed to compose some curt response. But then she started in on a series of short, shallow breaths. I went to her, but she waved her hand around as if pushing me away. Disoriented, Dana turned, like she was looking for the couch but couldn't find it. "I need to sit."

Putting both my hands on her shoulders, I guided her into the living room. She plopped down on the couch's edge and put her head in between her knees.

Sitting next to her, I placed my hand on her back. "Dana. This is crazy."

"Don't call me crazy."

"I didn't. I said—"

"You have no idea. If you knew what I've been through…" Her watery gaze met mine as she sat up, facing me. "If you ever loved me, and if you have any respect for me now, you'll stop seeing Rylee. At least until we're divorced, and we've figured out how we'll co-parent Eddie."

How could I refuse?

Now, I'm desperate to talk to Rylee and explain. I've almost called her a dozen times but couldn't find the courage to dial her number. And she didn't answer my lame text last night. There was so much to say that I couldn't settle on any combination of words. I resorted to *hi* out of default.

She must be mad. And I can't blame her. I'm mad too, but only at myself.

All day, I've been fighting fatigue and wishing I was home, cuddling with Rylee on the couch. Instead, here I am at school, faced with a million questions from students who didn't understand my assignments from when I was gone.

"I'm so glad you're back," Mom tells me when I stop by during lunch to say hello. "How are you feeling, sweetie?"

Most of the time, I avoid interacting with my mom at school because she'll call me "sweetie" and I must remind her she can't do that, not if I want my students to respect me. But she forgets, and it's easier for me to stay away from the media center.

Today, I make an exception, partly because she was worried and partly because I sort of need my mother right now.

"I'm fine, Mom."

She lifts her arms and steps toward me, like she wants to hug me but is worried I'll refuse. I erase the space between us and hug her first.

Tell me what to do, Mom.

I wish I could ask her advice, but it's not the time or place.

"Come for dinner tonight?"

Our hug ends, and I see her open face, posing the invitation. "I'll have Eddie."

"Perfect! Bring him along. I can make spaghetti. Six

p.m.?"

"We'll be there, Mom."

Walking back to my classroom, I silently berate myself. It's been way too long since Eddie and my parents have seen each other, and we all feel deprived. But both Mom and Dad have IQs in the triple digits. They are capable of looking at my brown eyes and at Eddie's green and putting two and two together. Besides, they were furious when, ten years ago, I told them I wasn't going to Harvard because Dana was pregnant.

My father had yelled, "Do you even know that baby is yours?"

It took me years to forgive my father for saying it, about as long as before I realized he was right. Now I fear they'll figure it out and what it will mean when they do.

I have an energy drink to make it through the day, wishing I was home napping with Rylee. Instead, I settle for being awake and hanging with Rylee's brother.

This morning, Brandon asked if he could come after school so we could work on our research project. I had to say yes. We lost a lot of time while I was out sick. Brandon's Harvard application is due soon, as well as his applications to his backup schools. If he wants to boast about this research project, then we need to get going.

"There are several medical journals we can try to get published in," I tell Brandon later, once school is out and we're working together in my room.

"Would a medical journal publish us? Aren't those for actual doctors?"

"Yeah, but lots of universities have medical journals, and they sometimes publish promising student work. We'll pose the question about a familial, genetic connection with the genesis of germinoma brain tumors, and argue that based on our research, more research should be done."

Brandon takes off his hat and scratches his fuzzy head. "Yeah, but our research is inconclusive."

"Of course it is. It was always going to be. But that's great! All the questions we've uncovered validates our thesis."

"So, we'll finish our report and submit it?"

"Yes." I'm on my computer, and I go to my favorite's bar, where I've saved links to several university medical journals. "We'll do U of MN, of course, since we have that in-state connection. Otherwise, our best bets are the University of Michigan, Ann Arbor, and the University of Wisconsin, Madison. Both have great medical research programs. And aren't you applying to those schools?"

"Yes. But Mr. Meyers?"

"Yeah."

"Can I ask you something without you getting mad?"

I look away from my screen and over at Brandon. "Of course."

"Did Rylee put you up to this?"

"What? No, of course not. Why would you say that?"

His laugh is silent. "Because I know my sister, and that the two of you are…" Brandon gestures with his hands, as if reaching for something invisible and impossible to grasp. "My mom let it slip that Rylee stayed with you while she had the flu."

My gut does a nosedive. "Oh, fuck no." Realizing I swore in front of a student, I hit my forehead. "Sorry."

Brandon waves off my apology. "I didn't tell Rylee anything. My mom made me promise not to. She was so freaked out, and I was like, Mom, come on. They both had the flu at the same time, and Rylee is staying with some mysterious guy she's been 'seeing,' and you"— Brandon points to me—"are her best friend's brother, so yeah, I kind of figured it out on my own."

Rylee would hate that Brandon knows. But I can't turn back time. "Okay. I'll tell you the truth. At the beginning of the school year, your sister asked me to keep an eye out for you, and I promised I would. Then Rylee and I started spending time together because we're writing partners for this class, and, well…" I shrug. "We're not in a serious relationship, but I'm still crazy about her. That has nothing to do with our research project. I've been impressed with your work ethic, and with your talent. Maybe Rylee put you on my radar, but that's where the connection ends."

"Well, that's better than the alternative."

"What's the alternative?"

"That you're sorry for me because my dad is dead, and I had a brain tumor." This time, when Brandon laughs, it's out loud. "I mean, who has luck like mine? I refuse to feel sorry for myself, but if I was someone else, I'd pity that kid."

"Brandon, I don't know what to say."

"It's cool, Mr. Meyers. You have done nothing wrong. I mean, yeah, you're boinking my sister, and that's the reason why you're 'keeping an eye out for me,' but you still have done nothing wrong."

Wow. I hadn't realized how much I needed to hear someone—anyone—say that. *You have done nothing wrong.* The fact the words come from this amazing kid reinforces their healing power. I laugh in relief.

But then, I turn and see a lurking presence in the doorway of my classroom.

Mr. Thatcher.

One look at his expression, and it's clear.

He's heard my entire conversation with Brandon.

Chapter 38

Rylee
Just checking in. Hope you're okay. Miss you! Did you get the stuff I sent? Got a delivery notice but haven't heard from you.

The text is from Jack.

"Summer!" I rush to her bedroom and knock on its door. "Summer! Was anything delivered for me in the last few days?"

It's six thirty a.m. here in Bemidji, so it's three thirty a.m. in California. Jack's text woke me. I bet he's been up all night writing. My mother must still be asleep.

"Summer?! Did you hear me?"

Her bedroom door creeps open. "Rylee..." My bleary-eyed mom blinks against the hallway light. "What's going on?"

"Did a package come for me while I was at Carson's?"

She tosses off sleep. "Oh yeah. I forgot to tell you. Sorry."

"Where is it?"

"I put it in the hall closet."

I bolt over there and pull out a large box. It's not heavy, but bulky, and I carry it to the kitchen. I need scissors to cut through the tape.

After opening the box, I peel back layers of tissue paper. Inside are three gift baskets—one a collection of soup mixes with gourmet crackers, another with lemon ginger tea and a mug, and the last one is the "Cozy Bundle Gift Set" with an impossibly soft blanket and flowered mugs in midnight blue (my favorite color), and a koala tea infuser (koalas are my favorite animal). The card reads, *Rye Bread—Get well soon. Wish I could nurse you back to health. Love, your boyfriend Jack.*

Jack has never called himself my boyfriend before. Have I entered some alternative reality?

Brandon stumbles into the kitchen. "Good morning." He takes one look at the gifts and asks, "What's all this?"

"A get-well present from Jack."

"Jack? That hipster guy?" Brandon creases his brow. "I thought he moved to California."

"He did. We're trying long distance."

My brother gasps in disbelief. "What?! Does Mr. Meyers know?"

It's like I've been doused in ice water. "Excuse me?!"

"Give it up, Rylee! You were out with the flu at the same time Mr. Meyers was absent from school." Never one to suffer fools, Brandon scowls. "Not to mention those nights you didn't come home."

My cheeks burn at his accusation, but I say nothing, meeting his speculative gaze with stony silence. He's trying to get a reaction, and I won't give him one.

Shaking his head, Brandon seems repulsed. "Besides, Mr. Meyers was always so content on the days after your sleepovers. It didn't take a genius to figure out that the two of you were—"

"Enough," I state. "I get it. But even if it had taken a genius, you would have caught on, right? Because technically, you *are* a genius."

Brandon smirks, neither confirming nor denying his genius-hood.

"Well," I continue, "you're way smarter than me. But I'm still older and wiser, okay? And whatever you think is going on between me and Carson Meyers, you don't see the whole picture."

"Thank God for that," Brandon grunts. "But he's a good guy. And he's crazy about you."

"You *don't* know that, Brandon."

"Yeah, I do. He's one of the few people who's treated me like I'm a normal human and not the brain tumor kid. Plus, he *told* me he's crazy about you, and why would he say that if he didn't feel that way? You'd better not hurt him, Rylee."

"The two of you talked about me?"

"Yes, because I brought you up."

"Fine. I get that you are friends, and he's like…a mentor—"

"You asked him to look out for me. What did you expect?"

God, kill me. It's not even seven a.m., and already my day is spiraling out of control. "Look, here's the thing…" I grasp for more. What *is* the thing? Oh yeah. Carson is still married, and when confronted with his estranged wife's wrath, he threw me under the bus. But I can't say that to Brandon. Better to let him regard his favorite teacher/friend/mentor as a hero and believe his sister is the villain.

Brandon looks at me with two raised eyebrows, waiting for my response. "The thing is, I'm too screwed up to appreciate Carson Meyers. It's a case of right guy, wrong time. I don't expect you to understand, but maybe you will one day."

"Whatever, Rylee." He squints and flicks his wrist. "You make everything so complicated." Stalking off, he disappears down the hallway. I am left alone with my thoughts, and it's not a good place to be.

Minutes later, I dial Jack's number.

"Rylee." As he exhales my name, it's tinged with affection and defeat.

"I'm sorry." My words tumble out. "My mom signed for the package and chucked everything in a closet without telling me. Thank you! I love the mugs and koala tea infuser and blanket—it was so thoughtful of—"

"Are you feeling better?" he interrupts.

"Yes, it's taking longer than I'd hoped, but yeah, I'm getting back to normal."

A relieved sigh from him. "Thank God. I need you."

My heart skips a beat at that. "You do? That's so…"

"Listen, I'm sending my pages over now. Make whatever changes are necessary. I tried to channel your voice, but it didn't work… Will you help with rewrites?"

Time slows as he awaits my answer. His card said "boyfriend"—is he nervous? My mind races as I decide how to respond. "Of course," I reply. "I'm always happy to help you, Jack."

****

Tonight at work, I wonder which version of Dana to expect. Will it be the invulnerable high school version, the one with all her smarts and beauty who could flatten me with a single tweet? Or the vulnerable, insecure Dana, who, for a fleeting moment, exposed her fragility? No matter—she won't even look my way. Dana keeps herself in the kitchen, back office, or bar—anywhere that isn't near me.

At the close of the night, she sits at a four-top editing tomorrow's specials.

I approach her table, afraid to sit down. "Dana, can we talk?"

Without glancing up from the paper in front of her, she says, "Rylee, if we were fully staffed, I'd fire you for dishonesty. As it stands, stay away and only speak to me about business."

I step closer. "I want to explain."

Dana slaps the table and stares at me with the heat of an inferno. "Do. Not. Talk. To. Me." Her nostrils flare. "I'm trying here, but if you keep testing me, I swear to God I'll explode, and you'll regret it."

I manage a nod before dropping my eyes onto the floor's dark green swirl-patterned carpet.

"Got it."

Heart pounding, I move towards the exit. As I reach the door, she calls out.

"And Rylee?" I stop but don't turn around. "You better hope Carson Meyers is worth it."

When I get home, all I want is to collapse into bed. But my phone vibrates with a text from Carson.

On ch. twelve of The Duke's Descent. *God. I miss you.*

Chapter twelve is *The Duke's Descent*'s sexiest Chapter. I try to limit my steamy scenes because I believe less is more. But readers don't always agree, and sex sells. Carson texting me about that scene shows he meant what he said.

We mean nothing to each other. It was just sex.

Even still, part of me is thrilled he's reading my book and missing me. But I can't type a response. My fingers lock up, refusing to tell my brain what to say.

Another text from Carson comes in.

I promised Dana I wouldn't see you until the divorce goes through.

Okay. He's breaking up with me via text.

How was I so stupid to fall for Carson Meyers twice? Here I thought our connection meant more than our no-strings side project. Hot tears sting my eyes, and I want to call him, yell at him, and even throw my shoe at him.

Suddenly, my texting writer's block is cured.

No worries. Now that Brandon knows, it's time to take a break.

He responds right away.

I'm sorry.

It's okay, I text. *Not your fault.*

That is a lie. I'm not okay.

The dots move up and down for a while, stop, and move up and down again. Did he type some long reply, change his mind, and delete it? After way too long, his text comes through. *Please check your email.*

I do as requested.

Rylee—If I can't see you, I'm glad I can at least read your books. It's almost like you're here with me. In case you're interested, I've attached my novel w/some new revisions. It's terrifying, showing it to you. If you don't have time, I understand.

I miss you. All the time.

-Carson

My anger bubbles up. He's asking me to read his novel while breaking up with me! Carson thinks he can dupe me into feeling special while establishing his own importance. That I'll connect with him on an emotional level... I pound my fist against my desk, incensed that he expects me to be close while he pushes me away. It doesn't matter how much I miss him, I won't fall into the Carson Meyers trap again.

Taking a deep breath, I resolve to forget him and our stupid side project.

Chapter 39

Rylee

Christmas comes and goes, the semester ends, and there's no word from Carson. That's fine because I do a fabulous job of banishing him from my brain. Sure, every now and then a memory will stab me, like when I see aviator-style prescription eyeglasses, or Henley's, or charcuterie boards, or black-and-white dogs, or Brandon's AP Bio textbook, or anything by Anton Ireland, or cups of takeout coffee that might get spilled. But that's it. Except, when I see a woman wearing dangly earrings with a scarf, I think of Carson. But come on. I bet that's the same for everyone in our writing class.

Dana is still glacially cold towards me, and one day the ice vapor is thick enough for me to see my breath. She strides past as I stand at the hostess stand, and the restaurant is quiet. Before I can stop myself, I blurt out, "I guess you remember what you did back in high school? Because you were super mean."

She pivots toward me and stares hard. "Excuse me?"

Straightening my spine, I imagine it's made of steel. "Weeks ago, when you caught me kissing Carson, you said I used to be in love with him. That means you remember humiliating me, and kicking me while I was down, mourning my father's death. There was no reason to do that."

An emotion I can't identify flickers behind her eyes.

"That's true."

"So why?"

Dana tilts her chin. "It was high school. I was immature. But you were an adult when you slept with my husband. You knew I wanted him back."

I flinch, feeling the sting of her words and wishing I could redo the last few months. "Things started with Carson and me before you and I became friends."

"That doesn't matter," she snaps. "You could've ended it any time." There's venom in her glare.

"I tried. I know it's no excuse, but Carson always convinced me to stay. And he said you cheated on him first. I know what happened, Dana. I know…" My voice wavers. "I know a lot."

Her mouth twitches. "You know nothing, Rylee."

My throat closes up, and I'm sure I'm the villain in this story. "Okay," I rasp. "Tell me. Let's talk about it now?"

"Oh, absolutely," she responds, her icy tone cutting the air. "You want to talk? Let's talk." She folds her arms across her chest, her gaze unwavering. "We'll have a heart-to-heart here in public, surrounded by customers and restaurant staff."

"Alright." I shrug. "When?"

She glances away. "You can come over later."

It's a risk to go to her home turf and let her lay into me. And yet, I'm intimidated enough to comply. "Sounds good."

Two hours later, we sit in her living room. Dana reclines on the armchair across from me. "You've only heard Carson's spin on what happened. It's time to hear my side. Maybe you'll understand the damage you caused."

My throat aches from fear and tension. "Is Eddie with Carson tonight?"

The bitterness plastered across her face is breathtaking. "You don't have his schedule memorized?"

"I haven't talked to Carson in weeks." I shift, and the overstuffed couch rebels against my lower body.

"You expect me to believe that?"

I look at Dana, her auburn hair and aqua eyes mocking me with their perfection. She's got the body of a runway model while I'm stuck rocking my average curves. Frustration chases away the guilt that's consumed me for weeks.

"Why would I lie?"

"That's a good question, Rylee," she snaps. "But all you've done is lie, so forgive me for saying you're full of shit."

"Okay, stop." My hard voice surprises even me. "You cheated on Carson—not the other way around. Sure, there's a history I'm not privy to, but I'm sick of all the games. Enough is enough."

The pink in her cheeks deepens to a furious red as she looks away from me, her gaze landing on a framed painting of geese flying above a lake.

"You don't understand. And neither does Carson," she says after a long pause.

"Maybe if you explained, we would."

Dana's jaw clenches. "I don't owe you an explanation." Her words are hard and accusatory. "But I will explain—give me a minute. This isn't easy for me...there are some things you keep hidden because the truth is unbearable."

As a single tear slides down her cheek, I see

vulnerability behind her icy facade.

"Dana," I offer, "if you can talk about it, I can listen without judgment."

She wipes the tear with a trembling hand and, studying me, says, "Do you promise not to tell Carson what I tell you?"

My throat is oddly thick. What am I getting myself into? But how can I deny her?

Tilting up my chin, I say, "I promise."

It's like Dana grows an inch as she sits up straighter. New determination is written across her face. "Okay. I'll start at the beginning."

****

Dana had just turned eighteen and couldn't wait for the rest of her life to begin. She and Carson agreed to go their separate ways for college but would reunite when he was in medical school, and then they'd figure out the long-term plan. Maybe she could convince him to move back to Bemidji one day, though she hadn't mentioned the idea. Not yet.

Sure, Carson had all this promise, with his desire to cure cancer, but Dana was no slouch. She planned to be her family's savior. She would study hotel management and discover new ways to keep Reynold's Resort relevant. Her spring break internship in Florida was the first step.

The program was a dream come true. A week learning the hotel business at a luxury resort on the beach. She'd do a bit of everything: work the reservation system, set up for events, greet guests, even do some marketing. But once she arrived, it wasn't what she'd expected. Throughout her life, Dana had been a big fish in a small pond; she was always the prettiest and the smartest girl in the room, always the one who stood out. Here, all the other teens in the program looked like characters from a soapy teen drama, and they all acted like that too.

There was pettiness and undermining. One girl spread rumors about Dana, saying she'd gone down on Josh, the thirty-eight-year-old program director, on the very first day. Josh had a nice face, with eyes that crinkled when he smiled, and the body of someone who used to be hot but now, probably due to aging and less gym time, had a beer belly. Otherwise, he was still attractive, but Josh was married with three young kids, and no way would Dana go down on a married dude twice her age—especially not one she worked for.

The rumors started because as soon as she arrived, Dana was struck with a bout of homesickness. It happened after hitting the beach. The sand and humidity stuck to her like jelly dripped from a PB&J, and the college kids were this beer-soaked mass, yelling obscenities and gyrating in public. When one guy grabbed her and insisted she "dance" with him, Dana felt trapped and, to her horror, began to cry.

Josh saw and came to her rescue, pulling her away from the guy and the crowd. He rubbed her back as she wept—Dana hated that she couldn't stop her tears. She'd never been more embarrassed, and that made it worse.

Her peers in the program witnessed it all and made her life miserable for the rest of the week. Only Josh was nice to her, and their friendship fed the rumors.

The last night of vacation wrapped up with a party that Dana skipped. She wanted to be home and was packing her bags when there was a knock on the door. Josh had come for her—he needed someone to make him feel young again. To make him feel alive. And Dana was the perfect candidate—beautiful and fragile beneath his drunken advances.

His clammy hand muffled her screams as she fought, trying to push him away with every inch of strength she could muster. But it was no use—he was strong and twice her size. Shaking in fear, she allowed her limbs to go limp, praying it would end soon.

Four weeks later, Dana discovered she was pregnant.

Dana had always been confident and always trusted her instincts. Now, she second-guessed herself at every turn. But she knew one thing with certainty: she'd never feel safe unless she stayed in Bemidji and had her baby with Carson. Dana told herself that it had to be his, from that one time when the condom slipped. God wasn't cruel enough for it to be otherwise. She tried to be a good person, and she was adamantly pro-life. Having this baby was the right thing to do. God would reward her by making Carson the dad.

Dana prayed that's what would happen.

But then, Eddie had green eyes, like Josh.

Still, she refused to acknowledge the truth because she couldn't wrap her mind around something so awful. Dana's guilt consumed her; she'd trapped Carson into this life, and watching him turn away from her was an agonizing reality. He no longer called her "babe," his arm no longer draped over her shoulders when they walked, and he never kissed her hair anymore. She tried to retrigger their intimacy, but it was a terrifying chore. Longing for what once was but could never be again, Dana felt a dismal void.

Eddie's well-being became Dana's priority; she

wanted nothing less than Carson as Eddie's dad—Carson, who was good in every way. So she did what any mother would do; she provided the best for her child. But years dragged on, and Dana and Carson's interactions dwindled down to two roommates who met out of obligation. Until Dana grew close to a waiter at Reynold's Resort who said all the things Carson had failed to utter. Being close to him was like drinking water after a ten-mile hike through the desert. His touch made her body respond. It was a miracle.

Then the economy tanked, and the restaurant had to lay off its newest employees first. The waiter moved away, and Dana had nothing.

So she clung to the hope of winning Carson back.

****

I use my sleeve to wipe away tears that won't stop falling. "Oh, Dana, I'm so sorry. Have you ever told anyone about this?"

"Who would I tell?" she pleads. "Not Carson—he'd be devastated that Eddie isn't his. My parents would be heartbroken, and my dad would have tried to kill Josh or at least press charges and prosecute. I needed to put it behind me and forget it ever happened."

"What about a girlfriend?" I ask.

She shakes her head. "I don't have female friends like that. It's my fault. I was sixteen when Carson and I became a couple, and I ignored my girlfriends and canceled plans with them so I could hang out with him. I couldn't blame them for not being around."

If it wasn't so sad, I'd laugh at the absurdity of how both Dana and Carson trusted me with their most sacred secrets. And yet, my heart twists for her. "Are you saying that I am the only person you've ever told?"

Dana studies her feet, ashamed. "No," she whispers. "I told Brent."

"Is Brent—"

"He's the waiter I slept with," she blurts through her sobs. "I shouldn't refer to him as just a waiter. Brent's an artist, and he uses stuff from nature in his work. That's why he moved up here. We'd hike together on the trails near the resort, we talked about all sorts of things, and one thing led to another. It was only three times, but it felt significant. When we had to lay people off, he moved down to the Twin Cities because his uncle could give him a job."

I long to reach for her, perhaps to squeeze her hand. But we're not there yet. "Are you still in touch with him?"

"No. I broke things off when I decided to get Carson back. Nothing is more important than us becoming a family again." Her bright eyes narrow like a hawk. "I mean it, Rylee. You can't tell Carson. He can't ever find out that he's not Eddie's biological dad, it would kill him, and I can't even imagine what Eddie would—"

Maybe it's because Dana seems bereft and guileless. Maybe it's because I believe that both she and Carson already understand the truth deep down. Or maybe I'm sick of all the secrets. Nevertheless, before I can stop them, the words are out there.

"But…Carson already knows."

Chapter 40

Carson

My first day back after Christmas break was rough like sandpaper. The long weeks of winter stretched before me, with no relief until March. Dark days, cold nights, and nothing to look forward to, not now that it was a new semester at Bemidji State. I signed up for the novel writing course, but I assume Rylee did not. There will be no guarantee of seeing her, and she hasn't texted or called.

In fact, I haven't heard a peep from Rylee since I hit send on an email with my novel attached, complete with a brand-new scene crafted just for her. In the scene, the protagonist and his love interest meet in an abandoned hallway, and when the Rylee-inspired character moves to kiss him, I give them a happy ending, penning all the words I wished I'd said and every action I never took. Either she hasn't read it yet—or she has, but she's horrified by both the sentiment and the execution.

How could I have been so stupid to send Rylee my book?

I should give up writing. It's not like I have time for it anyway, not with everything else that's going on. And as if I needed a further sign from the universe, there was the conversation with Principal Thatcher. This afternoon, I was summoned to his office.

I tried to make nice, asking, "How was your

holiday?"

Principal Thatcher scowled. "Are you still working with Brandon Lynch on the research project?"

"Yes, sir. It's very exciting. The research is promising, and Brandon will have all sorts of opportunities open up—"

"Why didn't you clear it with me first?"

I stopped short, glancing down at a family photo of Principal Thatcher with his wife and kid. He looked like a happy, normal guy, posing in a canoe, wearing a baseball hat and lifejacket, one arm around his wife, the other around their son. This man was reachable. We were both human, after all.

"I'm sorry, I should have. Brandon and I came up with the idea together, and then we were excited to get started. I didn't think about consulting you."

"Do you realize the position it puts me in, Mr. Meyers?"

Was it a trick question? "Umm…no. Sorry."

Thatcher puffed air out through his nose. "What if parents find out that we offered a privileged student an opportunity while we denied other students from different backgrounds?"

"I wouldn't say that Brandon is privileged. His father died several years ago. And Brandon had cancer. The research project is about cancer. Other parents would understand."

"Mmm." Principal Thatcher glared at me over his reading glasses. "He doesn't qualify for free or reduced lunch, so at this school, he's privileged. More importantly, you're sleeping with his sister. That's nepotism, and I can't imagine it wouldn't upset the parents of little Johnny or Judy, who needs a scholarship to go to college." Thatcher lowered his voice and adopted a dramatic tone. "But you're not screwing Johnny and Judy's older sister, so Johnny and Judy are out of luck." My boss raised an eyebrow. "I hear that Rylee Lynch gets around. I mean, the way she dressed and behaved on the night of homecoming..." He chuckled. "I'd be careful, Mr. Meyers. Trashy girls like her aren't worth the trouble."

My rage erupted like a long-dormant volcano. I slammed my fist down on his desk, rattling Thatcher's pencil holder and turning over his stapler. "Listen, you sonofabitch. Insult me all you want, but say another word about Rylee, and you'll regret it."

Thatcher smiled like he'd gotten the result he wanted. "Is that a threat?"

Realizing I'd taken his bait, I flexed my fingers to uncoil my fists. I couldn't beat the crap out of the guy, not if I wanted to keep my job and my life intact. I had to collect myself.

"Please forgive my outburst. But Rylee is a good person, and she and Brandon have been through a lot. They both deserve respect and admiration for their resourcefulness. If you need to discipline me, okay. But please leave their names out of it." I turned to go.

"Mr. Meyers!"

I was reaching for the doorknob, wanting nothing more than to flee his office. It took all my strength to turn back toward Principal Thatcher.

He rolled up his sleeves, as if preparing for a fist fight. "Are you still enrolled in that graduate English program?"

"Yes," I replied, stopping short of puffing out my chest.

"I can't dictate your coursework, but I can say that you will never teach English at this high school. At the rate you're going, you won't hold on to your advanced biology courses either. Watch yourself, Mr. Meyers, or you'll be relegated to remedial earth science for the rest of your career."

My body shaking with anger, I imagined hitting Principal Thatcher in his smug, flushed face. But no. Instead, I offered a simple salute. "Yes, sir!"

Perhaps that was over the top. Oh well.

After leaving school, I needed to blow off steam, so I drove to the ice rink and skated about a million laps with a single thought: shoot some imaginary puck into some imaginary goal, and erase all my inner turmoil. I circled the rink until I was exhausted, wishing that physical exertion would be enough to banish my inner demons forever.

When I finally trudge home, Ferris greets me at the door. He needs a long walk, so I keep my coat on and grab the leash. In the sub-zero winter wonderland, my troubles come flooding back. The icy air penetrates through my layers of clothing, and thoughts of Rylee filter back. Ferris whines, troubled by the frozen sidewalk against his paws. "I guess we're both having a tough time," I say to my dog.

We head home.

Returning to the warmth of my kitchen, I contemplate an egg for dinner and a beer for company, but the only solace I'll find tonight is re-reading one of Rylee's books on my Parchment IV.

Urgh. I should grow a pair and call her…but there's a knock on my door. My heart races as I rush to open it, praying it's Rylee standing in front of me ready to talk things through. Yet, instead, Dana looks back at me with a determined gaze.

"Where's Eddie?" I ask.

"With my parents." Her tone is severe as she steps past me, not waiting for permission. "We need to talk."

I watch as she wraps her arms around herself and leans against the couch. "Rylee and I talked last night," she begins, hesitating as if her words are a physical burden. "I get that you and I are broken up. You had every right to sleep with her. And I appreciate that you've cut things off for now. But why did you confide in her about something that affects Eddie and me? And why did you shut us out?"

Even though my stomach is empty, I think I might throw up. No. *No.* This can't mean what I think it means. "Dana, what are you talking about?"

"Don't play dumb, Carson!" She straightens herself, widening her stance, with her hands on her hips. "Rylee told me. You've known for *years* that you're not Eddie's real dad! And yet, you kept that from me as some twisted form of punishment."

"Wait. I wasn't punishing you! Did Rylee say that? Tell me exactly what she said, word for word."

Okay. That was the wrong thing to say. I've never seen Dana so angry. It's like lasers shoot out from her eyes. She takes the deepest of breaths. "I come to you with this long overdue conversation that will determine the fate of our marriage. Yet, you're worried about what Rylee said, or what she didn't say? Go to hell!"

She starts to storm off, but I jump in front of her, blocking her path. "You won't keep Eddie from me. I am his father in every way that counts, and if you dare—"

She tries to get around me. "I'll decide that on my

own, thank you very much."

"Dana, please."

"Get out of my way!"

I dig in my heels.

"I said get out of my way!" Dana rails her fists against my chest. "You bastard. If you don't let me go right now, you'll never see Eddie again!"

Those words, those chest punches, they may as well have been a knife stabbing my heart. I move to the side, and Dana rushes out.

Chapter 41

Rylee

Last night, I tried calling Carson. No answer. Perhaps Dana confronted him after our conversation? I'd figured it was pointless to tell Dana, "Don't let Carson know you know that he knows." It was juvenile, and the stakes were high.

Besides, neither of them could go on like this. Maybe it wasn't my place to interfere, but then again, maybe it was. I hope he calls me before tomorrow's novel writing class. I'm not sure if he signed up for it, but it's best to tell him I'll be there just in case.

Meanwhile, I haven't given him any feedback on his novel. Every time I tried reading it, my heart grew heavy, and I longed for him to say he hadn't meant to hurt me. Steeling myself, I push Carson as far away from my thoughts as possible. He must think I'm being a bitch.

I walk to the campus bookstore, and it's so cold my bones ache. Even once I'm inside, I'm still cold. I leave my parka hood up, partially unzip, and drift over the shelves searching for *Thornton Smith's Requisite Guide to Novel Writing.*

I'm scrunched up with no peripheral vision, looking for the book, when finally, I see there's one left on the shelf. I reach for it, but someone else reaches for it at the exact same time, and our hands knock into each other.

"Excuse me," I say.

Neither of us is successful in grabbing the book, and I don't try again because a familiar voice says, "Rylee?"

I lower my hood and turn to him. "Carson. Hello."

His face changes when I say his name. Something that was open slams shut. "Hi." His single, angry syllable comes out like a missile ready to detonate.

"I called you last night."

He doesn't respond but glares at me instead. I can almost see the wheels spinning in his brain; there are things he wants to say, but he's holding back.

"You're taking the novel-writing course?" I gesture to the lone textbook. We both want it, but only one of us will get it.

"Yeah."

"Me too."

"Nice."

But his tone implies that it's anything but nice. His tone implies that he's beyond pissed.

I wait a beat, hoping that all his bad vibes will disintegrate, but they don't. "That's one reason I called last night, to tell you I'm signed up for novel writing. I didn't decide until after I met with Professor Aldrich. She thought I would benefit from it—"

"When did you meet with her? When did you decide to sign up? Why didn't you mention it before?"

I open my mouth to respond, but he cuts me off.

"It doesn't matter," Carson states. "I don't want to know."

"Okay…" I gulp down my anxiety. A shopper steps around us and walks up and down, searching the tan metal shelving underneath the fluorescent lights.

"You're angry. Should we go somewhere and talk? I'd like to explain."

"You can't be serious, Rylee."

Carson's eyes are wild beneath his furrowed brow. His hair stands straight up in waves. He leans into me, and I smell cinnamon; it's like he's breathing fire. He pulls back and points an accusing finger at me. "*You're* the root of all my problems. *You* broke the one promise I asked you to make. *You* ruined my life."

His sharp words reverberate between us, making me speechless for a moment. "Umm, well…I'm guessing Dana talked—"

"Yeah. You had no right to tell her anything!"

"I'm sorry." My chest aches with guilt. "Carson—"

"I don't care," he says through gritted teeth. "The damage is done. Stay away from me." His gaze lands on the last copy of *Requisite Guide to Novel Writing,* and he grabs it. "I'm taking this," he says, as if I need a declaration of his intent.

"Hold on!" I jump in front of him, my pulse twitchy and uneven. "You don't get to blame me *and* walk away with the last textbook. Because here's the thing, Carson. At least half of everything that happened is on you! It's high time that you stop feeling sorry for yourself and stop playing with people's hearts—including mine."

"Wha—what?" he sputters.

"You heard me!" I look him dead in the eye. "Carson, you avoid taking responsibility. And you're so afraid of conflict that you fly around like an airplane in a holding pattern, too scared to face the storm."

His nostrils flare, and his cheeks puff out. "God! You and your stupid similes! What do you know about airplanes? You've never been anywhere!" He steps close enough that I can feel his heat.

My pulse pounds in my ears. "Sure. Insult me if it

makes you feel better. But at the end of the day, the only person who can clean up your mess—" I take a step forward, invading his space even further. "—is you!" I snatch the textbook from his hand before he can blink an eye. His defeat is so clear that he doesn't even attempt to stop me.

"One more thing," I add, power coursing through me. "My similes aren't stupid."

Turning my back on him, I make my way to the counter, riding high on the fumes of victory. Only after I pay for the book, exit the store, and peer back through its windows to see Carson still standing there stunned, does a hard lump form in my stomach and spread up into my throat.

What have I done?

****

That night, sleep is elusive. I almost call Carson a dozen times but my courage fails me. I compose a bunch of texts which all begin with, "I'm sorry," but as soon as I remember how he blamed me for everything that's wrong with his life *and* insulted my similes, I delete the text and throw my phone on the bed.

Even if I wanted to rekindle things with Carson, I can't, not after what Dana told me. And even if Carson wanted to rekindle things with me, I'd still need to step aside so he can put his family back together. It's better to let him hate me.

The next day, I wake to a text. My mutinous heart lurches with hope that it's from Carson, but no.

Hi, beautiful. Surprise! I'm in town. Meet me at the coffee cart in the student union. Eight thirty a.m. There's much I need to tell you.

The text is from Jack. He's in town? WTF?

I text back that I'll meet him, hoping that if I sound excited, I'll feel excited.

I get dressed, wishing I had done laundry the night before. It's another cold day, and the classrooms are drafty, so I need to wear something warm. But my one clean sweater is that gray cardigan—the one that Carson wanted to pull off of me. Twice.

What if, when I sit across from him in class, he sees me wearing this sweater and thinks it's a message, like, *Yes, Carson. I'm desperate, and I want you back in the worst way.*

But what if I am desperate, and what if I do want him back in the worst way?

Screw it. It's my only clean sweater, and I refuse to overthink this. I put it on, style my hair, and apply mascara. And it's not because I'm trying to look good for Carson. Jack, the man who sent me an incredible gift basket with a note signed "Love, your boyfriend," who's called almost every day and relied on my help with finishing his novel, who says that he needs me, is here in town! This jittery sensation is excitement because I get to see Jack and not despair because I messed up everything with Carson.

And that sensation of a knife is twisting in my heart? I bet it's something I ate.

At 8:35 sharp, I stroll up to the coffee stand, and Jack spots me from a mile away. His bearded face bursts into a goofy dad grin. He blurts out, "Rye Bread!" In an instant, he's bear-hugging me and twirling me around as if we're in some demented rom-com.

"Jack."

I laugh as he twirls me, and when he sets me back down, I open my mouth to ask him what he's doing here.

But Jack takes my open mouth as an opportunity to slide his tongue between my lips. Then he's clutching me so close that I get this acidic reflux sensation, almost like bile rising in my throat.

Because I wasn't expecting the kiss. That's got to be why.

I press against his chest with my hands to create space between us. "Jack, why are you here?"

He puts both hands on my shoulders and leans in like he's speaking to a toddler. "It's the most fantastic news ever, Rye Bread. I'm back at Bemidji State for the semester! USC didn't have any teaching positions available, but by some stroke of luck or fate, BSU needed a published author to teach their novel writing course. Isn't it perfect?! I'm going to be your instructor."

I stumble over my words, trying to be coherent. "But...why—why didn't the course catalog list you?" Another professor I'd had in undergrad was listed.

"Because," Jack explains, "Cal Anderson had to take medical leave, and BSU wasn't sure if he'd be okay after his surgery. They asked me to be ready to drop everything just in case. That's why I didn't mention it sooner—it was still up in the air until days ago."

I plaster on a smile.

"Oh! That's great. Not about Cal Anderson's health, of course, but because you're here!" Attempting to show affection, I squeeze his shoulder. "Won't it mess up your book release?"

Jack laughs, white teeth twinkling underneath the overhead lights. "That reminds me.... More great news! My editors approved the last set of changes for *Family Casualties,* and it will be out in five months!"

"Five months!" I exclaim. "That's fast!" Jack seems

pleased with himself, so I hastily add, "Congratulations! It's all wonderful, and I'm happy you're here. Do you have a place to stay?"

As Jack describes his new apartment, we get in line for coffee. My mind races with a million questions, but just one truly matters.

What will Carson do when he finds out Jack is our instructor?

Chapter 42

Carson

After my confrontation with Rylee, I spend the evening in a daze. Rylee called me out, and somehow her words had the power to turn my entire world upside down. It's like pieces of my life scattered everywhere, some too far gone to gather back up. And now everything's exposed in the light, forcing me to take a hard look at myself. Did I make all the wrong choices? Am I really an entitled coward, careless with people's hearts?

When three a.m. rolls around, I'm in bed alone, staring at the water-stained ceiling, and all the thoughts rolling around in my mind come together in one lightning-bolt realization.

I fucked up. No one else.

Just me.

With bleary eyes and an unsettled stomach, I decide that the best way to fix this is by using the scientific method. I'll ask a question. I'll do research, form a hypothesis, conduct an experiment, analyze the results, and then I'll communicate—if only with myself.

Okay.

The question is, do I love Rylee?

No, that question is easy. Even though I've tried hard not to, I'm head over heels. The real question is, does she love me back?

I plan to figure that out.

After a lot of brainstorming, I have an inspired idea. Since it's the first day of class, I'll bring Rylee a cup of coffee, like I did the morning after we almost hooked up. Like before, this will be a peace offering. With any luck, she'll find it cute, and we can talk things through. Then I'll ask her if she loves me.

No, wait. That might make me seem needy or, worse, arrogant. Perhaps I should tell her I love her first. Truth is, I've wanted to say those words to Rylee for a while now.

I leave early for class, and when I get to campus, I go straight for the student union, to the coffee stand.

However, I see something that makes my scientific method stutter to a halt. Rylee is kissing some guy and stroking his bearded cheek. Those ocean-blue eyes gaze at him with affection.

It's like how she used to look at me.

I spin around, wanting to sprint toward the exit like I'm a superhero. Like getting outside is the one way I can save the world. But my heart is this huge, heavy boil weighing me down. It might burst apart from the pain. My brain takes over, and as I walk away, I rationalize.

Well, that was the quickest research process/experiment ever.

Does Rylee love me?

Nope.

Not a chance.

Chapter 43

Rylee

Jack is still talking as we carry our coffee cups to class. But before we turn at the bend in the hallway leading to our classroom, I pause and put my hand on his arm.

"Wait. We shouldn't walk in together. If we're obvious about being a couple, it will set a weird tone."

The way he looks at me, it's like I professed some wisdom for the ages.

"Of course. You're right, Rye Bread. You wait here, and I'll go ahead. As the instructor, I shouldn't be late."

"Okay."

He kisses me on the cheek and strides off. I wait five minutes, scrolling through my phone but not seeing anything, except Carson's wounded face in my mind's eye. Is there any chance he won't put two and two together? That he won't figure out that Jack is *my* Jack?

I realize that I'm roasting. Putting down my coffee and my bag, I take off my coat, tuck it underneath my arm, and gather everything back up. With a deep breath, I walk toward class. When I get there, right away, I spot Carson. He's become unhinged; I can hear it in his voice and see it in his eyes.

Plus, he stands quite close to Jack—it's like he's never heard of personal bubbles.

"California, huh? Bemidji's weather must be a huge

shock to your system." Carson's smile is wide and deranged.

Jack sips his overpriced cappuccino, ordered with two honey ginger flavor shots. "It's fine. I grew up in Minneapolis, and I got my MFA here in Bemidji. So I'm used to it."

"You went to school here!" Carson says this way too loud. As if he can sense my presence, he turns around. "Rylee!" he almost shouts. "Guess what! Our instructor, Jack, got his MFA from Bemidji State, and now he's back! It's like kismet! Any chance the two of you crossed paths?"

My mouth drops open, and I flounder for a response. Carson cocks his head as if he doesn't know the answer.

I clear my throat. "Jack was a TA for a couple of my classes."

Then, I find a seat in the rectangle of tables that compose the classroom.

Carson's laugh borders on hysterical.

"Of course. The two of you were a couple, right? You dated your TA. Isn't that what you told me?"

My jaw sets, and I glance down, aware that as other students file in, they're all looking at me.

"No, wait," Carson continues. "Didn't you say the two of you are *still* a couple?"

It's like I've swallowed hot coal, so of course, steam comes out.

"Stop."

I meet Carson's eyes, and the heat of my command catches him off guard.

But not enough to make him cower. Instead, he squints at me and scowls. Like we're in a staring contest, a face-off. Who will break first?

Turns out, it's Jack.

"Okay, let's get started," he says. "Welcome to *Advanced Fiction Writing; the Novel.*"

Chapter 44

Carson

I don't want to be an asshole. I had half a mind to leave, to walk off campus after seeing Rylee kiss bearded-turtleneck-wearing-douchebag-Jack. But I remember Rylee's simile about me as a plane in a holding pattern, and I mutter, "Let's see who can face a storm."

I walk to class and wait for Rylee to get there, but bearded-turtleneck-wearing-douchebag-Jack gets there first. Turns out, Rylee's California boyfriend is the instructor for our novel writing class.

Okay. *He's* the guy I've been a non-emotion-evoking-place warmer for? This bearded, turtleneck-wearing-douchebag is the one Rylee loves? More importantly, how long has Rylee known that he's teaching our class, and why didn't she say something sooner?

I play it cool, expertly hiding my inner turmoil and hurt, and carry on a vigorous conversation with bearded-turtleneck-wearing-douchebag-Jack. However, inside me, there's a locomotive speeding toward the edge of a cliff, and unless I commit 100% to being fine, it will crash.

Then Rylee enters wearing her goddam gray cardigan sweater. That's *our* sweater, it has significance, or so I thought. I bet she wore it to hurt me.

Bearded-turtleneck-wearing-douchebag-Jack starts class, everyone takes a seat, and Rylee sits near him.

"We must be truthful in literature," Jack says, tugging on his beard and adjusting his turtleneck. "Life is messy, and good literature reflects that." He cites his own novel about a loveless marriage and an artist whose husband destroys all her paintings. "Without them, she becomes lost in the world. But through it all," Jack says, "we see realistically portrayed moments of joy mixed with overwhelming sadness and frustration as our heroine struggles to cope with what has happened to her art, and ultimately to herself."

His words are like quinoa mixed with kale and prepared with almond butter—a bit pretentious for my taste buds. I can't bear another moment.

I groan.

Jack turns to me, lips poised to argue. "Do you have a question, Carson?"

"Yes." I wait a beat, letting the tense silence bolster me. "When will you stop talking about yourself and start teaching us how to write novels?"

The long tables at which we sit form a rectangle around bearded-turtleneck-wearing-douchebag-Jack, and he shifts his weight. Meanwhile, Rylee clenches her hands into fists like she's dying to scratch her arms.

Jack smirks. "I'm teaching you how to write novels by example. You should learn from me, Carson, if you want to be a great writer." He addresses the rest of the students. "My point isn't that my work defines the only way to write literature—it's to remind you that truth matters when creating art. That's what brings stories alive. Don't be afraid to show your readers something real and raw, even if it makes them uncomfortable."

I tap my pencil against the table. "So what you're saying is, you want us to write like you?"

"No," he says, calm with certainty. "I'm saying everyone has their own truth, which they should expose through their writing."

I glare at him. "Oh, I get it now." My voice drips with sarcasm, but I don't care. "I need to find my truth." *Too bad,* I almost add, *that's lost forever.* I lean toward Rylee. "What about you?"

It's a vague question, but Rylee understands. After an uncomfortable silence, she says, "I agree with Jack. A novel's primary goal is to reflect real life in some fundamental way."

Well, shoot. Her answer isn't what I was hoping for. I want to tell her, "Don't let bearded-turtleneck-wearing-douchebag-Jack define you or your work."

But that would make her angry.

However, she already sounds angry. Clipping her syllables, she continues. "Truth in fiction is way better than a feel-good lie. If a story promises that everything will be fine when in the end it won't, that's a disservice to readers. And romantic tropes insult their intelligence."

I stare at her. "Which romantic tropes do you mean, Rylee?"

"Any of them." She crosses her arms. "The brooding, misunderstood hero. The damsel in distress. The contrived plot twists. All of them are pointless if they don't reveal something about the human condition."

It's very tempting to mention Shelby Simmons, *The Duke's Descent,* and Rylee's secret literary life. Now I understand why she never told him about it herself. This guy is a pretentious snob. And while it would bring me a fleeting moment of satisfaction, I could never embarrass

Rylee like that.

I'm not above challenging her though. "What about happy endings?" I stand and enter the middle of the table rectangle. Rylee has to look at me.

Which she does, but her gaze is as cold as her voice. "Especially happy endings. They're trite cliches."

"Isn't it redundant to call something a trite cliche?"

"You're redundant!" Rylee squares her shoulders and tilts her chin. "Anyway, happy endings belong in fairy tales, sure, but that's it. Smart readers realize that happy endings just aren't real."

Chapter 45

Rylee

"Happy endings just aren't real?" he implores. "Do you mean that?"

Carson stands in the middle of the class like he's drowning underneath the soft ceiling tiles. His gaze almost screams, *How could you betray me after what we shared?* I have the urge to reach out. To save him, to be his life raft. But I can't.

"That's what I said, and I stand by it."

"You're such a hypocrite."

For a second, I'm terrified that Carson will unmask me as Shelby Simmons, and I almost wouldn't blame him for it. Instead, he moves out from the center of the tables and gathers his coat, bag, and laptop. "This isn't the class for me. I'll withdraw right now."

Carson slams the door on his way out, and the entire class, plus Jack, let their mouths hang open over the drama of it all.

"That was interesting," Jack states. "I'm sorry he left. He would have provided lots of comic relief."

I stand. "What's that supposed to mean?" Jack's mouth flaps open, but I preemptively cut him off. "Never mind. I'll be right back."

Hurrying out, I rush to catch up with Carson and see his receding form, clad in a black wool overcoat, his head of wavy hair sticking up and out. He's far enough away that I need to yell. "Carson!" He stops like he's been shot. "Wait."

Carson doesn't turn around, but he also doesn't resume walking. I move toward and then past him. We stand face-to-face.

Has he been crying? Carson's eyes are red and rheumy. My desire to kiss away his pain waylays any anger inside me.

But no. I can't.

"I have nothing to say to you, Rylee."

"Fine. I'll make this quick." It's like there's a crucible around my heart. "Did Dana tell you about Eddie's biological dad?"

"No." Carson's response is hard and flat. His pale cheeks turn crimson, and his eyes are still wet. "And I don't want to know."

I take a step closer and lower my voice. "But you need to hear her out, and you need to be kind. Carson, it's important to really listen. Because if you don't get defensive, and if you practice forgiveness—I promise you won't lose Eddie." Stepping toward him, I stand on my tiptoes and kiss him on the cheek. He stays frozen and silent. "And if you *can* be kind and forgiving, I hope you'll extend that to me as well. Because I am so sorry."

He blinks a few times as his lips part and dammit. Every cell in my traitorous body wants him right now. "I have to go."

Then, I walk away from Carson Meyers, which hurts like…it hurts like a…jeez. It hurts so much I can't even come up with a decent simile to describe the pain.

Chapter 46

Carson

There's no time to mull over what Rylee told me or to lick my pummeled heart's wounds. I must return to rationality.

First, I will change my course enrollment. Sure enough, there's a line, so while I wait, I page through the course catalog and find the perfect substitution for the novel writing course. When it's my turn, I step up to the harried young woman behind the counter, her computer off to the side, so she can pivot back and forth between it and whoever stands in front of her. "I have to drop Eng 5208. I want to take Bio 5362 instead."

The admissions lady types something into her computer and cocks her head in confusion. *"Developmental and Tumor Biology?"*

"Yes, that's the one."

She gives me a skeptical eye roll. "But the Biology department offers that class. You're enrolled in the English Education program."

"Right. But for undergrad, I majored in biology, and I teach AP Bio at the local high school, and Harvard once accepted me as a pre-med student. I guarantee you, I'm qualified to take Bio 5362."

"I don't doubt that you are." The woman has to be exhausted, with dark circles under her eyes, and frizzy, unkempt hair. It's got to be a busy time for her; she must not have much time for sleep or grooming. "But," she continues, "before I can enroll you in this course, you need to have been accepted into the graduate program in Biology."

"Understood." I try to come off as kind and forgiving, like Rylee suggested. "What if we called the head of the bio department? He had me as a student, and we're still in touch. If he okays me taking the course, can you enroll me?"

She seems deep in thought as she inhales and fiddles with her name tag. I take it as a sign of encouragement.

"Please?" I read that name tag. "Please, Beth? Because, I'm having one of the very worst weeks of my life and something good needs to happen. I would deeply, deeply appreciate it if you could make the call and ask." I lace my fingers like I'm praying. "Please?"

****

When I get to the high school, it's earlier than it would be if I'd stayed for the entire novel-writing class. *Kindness and forgiveness, kindness and forgiveness, kindness and forgiveness*...it's my mantra as I approach Principal Thatcher's office.

Miraculously, Thatcher is there, not in a meeting or on the phone. I knock but don't wait for an invitation to come in.

"About our last conversation," I state, "there are things I need to say."

Thatcher looks at me with skepticism. "Oh yeah? Because if you berate or threaten me again, you're out on your ass before you can blink."

"No threats today. I come in peace." Raising my hands in surrender, I try to smile. Thatcher won't make this easy, but that's no surprise. "First, I ended my relationship with Rylee, so there's no conflict of interest, doing research with Brandon Lynch."

"Well, that's good," Thatcher says. "You figured out that she's playing you, huh? I knew she was bad news."

Clenching my fists, I shove both hands into my pockets. I want to shake the man until his teeth rattle, but I won't play into his trap. "Rylee is out of my league. She's intelligent, kind, and driven, while I'm all over the place. However, Brandon and I *will* complete our research project."

Thatcher stretches his mouth into an odd expression, a combo of friendliness and dominance, while drumming his fingers against his desk. "How nice. But there's still a conflict of interest."

"No, there isn't. No one with an ounce of humanity would begrudge Brandon the chance to research a disease he's been inflicted with." I pause and let my words sink in.

Leaning back in his chair, Thatcher folds his arms over his chest and waits to hear more.

"Also," I continue, "I'm done taking English courses. Instead, I enrolled in *Developmental and Tumor Biology*. When Brandon Lynch and I discover the cure for cancer, it will be great for Bemidji High. You can take all the credit, okay?"

With a scowl, Thatcher says, "You don't really believe that you'll find the cure for cancer?"

I shrug. "Not if we don't look."

Later, after sharing the good news with Brandon, after teaching the rest of the day, and after grading and lesson planning, I call Dana. "Can we talk? I promise to listen."

She agrees. I drive to Reynolds Resort while Eddie is at his after-school program and she has a break from the restaurant. We sit in her living room, me on the couch, her in a chair.

"I need to understand what happened." My words are icy hot, sticking in my throat. "Can you tell me about Eddie's real dad?"

Dana looks small, shrunken down in her seat. "It's like you said, Carson. You're Eddie's dad in every way that counts. And you always will be."

"Okay. That's good to hear, but…you know what I mean."

She nods. "I'm sorry. I thought I was doing the right thing for our son. I lived in denial, and then once I couldn't lie to myself anymore, I was so ashamed."

Dana's crying. I grab a tissue from the box on the end table. She takes it and wipes her eyes. When she lifts her gaze, it's like she's doubled her strength. "I'll tell you everything. But you have to let me finish before you ask any questions, okay?"

"Sure," I say, bracing myself. *Warning! Pain is imminent!*

"First, we both agree—you are the only dad Eddie will ever know. And second, I never meant to hurt you. But here's what happened…"

Chapter 47

Rylee

A Viscount for Vivien is a huge success. I published it in mid-February for a Valentine's Day release, and a month later, both the sales and reviews are even better than I'd hoped for. I want to share this news with someone, but who? Not Dana. She and I keep a polite distance at work, calling a truce that stops short of friendliness.

And I haven't talked to Carson for weeks, not since the day he stormed out of class.

Yet, Brandon gives almost daily updates about the research he's doing with Carson.

"Mr. Meyers shares all the reading and assignments for his tumor class with me," Brandon explains as we drive towards the hospital for his routine MRI.

It's a check-in to make sure the cancer hasn't come back, but we're not expecting anything to light up on his scan. Brandon's energy and spirits have increased, and he's talking about going to college out of state, confident that his health will be fine. We're keeping our fingers crossed about Harvard.

"What, so you're doing his homework for him?" I ask.

"Of course not, Rye. Mr. Meyers gives me the latest assignment as soon as it's been graded. It's like he's both a student and an instructor. Last week was about carcinogens, but this week we're doing genetics of the cancer wheel. I can't wait!"

Summer smiles as she keeps her eyes on the road. "If every cancer survivor had your determination, there'd be a cure by now. I'm so proud of you."

"Thanks, Mom, but it's all because of Mr. Meyers."

I press my palm against the car window.

"Rylee," Brandon says. "You're okay if I invite him to my grad party, right?"

I turn toward him. "What grad party? It's only March. Isn't it a little soon to start planning?"

"I'm graduating in less than three months. You need to come to terms with that."

True. But I need to come to terms with a lot of things.

Brandon hates getting MRIs, and Summer and I find it incredibly nerve-wracking. So we've made a tradition of doing something celebratory afterwards. Today, we're going out to eat and to see the latest comic book movie.

Brandon gets through the MRI just fine, but this time, instead of the radiologist saying that she'll send a report to Brandon's primary physician, she tells us to sit tight. Brandon gets dressed, and the radiologist, Dr. Esper, enters, elegant even in scrubs, her shiny black hair slicked back into a tight bun, her brown skin glowing despite Bemidji's late winter climate.

"Is something wrong?" Summer asks.

Dr. Esper clutches a file of Brandon's most recent brain images. "There may be an issue," Dr. Esper says. "Or, perhaps, it's a false alarm."

"What might be a false alarm?" I ask.

"Sometimes, very rarely, we get irregular results from MRIs. False positives."

She mounts images from Brandon's MRI against the backlit wall. The scans of his brain show several spots lit up.

"The lighted spots are tumors?" Brandon asks.

Summer reaches for my hand and grips it like she's hanging from a cliff, and I'm her only lifeline.

"That's possible," Dr. Esper says. "But we won't know unless we do another MRI. The, umm…" Dr. Esper taps her finger against the biggest lit up spot. "The MRI indicates that Brandon's tumor has resurfaced with significant spread. While that might be the case, Brandon's asymptomatic state—he's not experiencing blurred vision, headaches, confusion, or dizziness—suggests there may be a discrepancy."

"You mean, like, a glitch in the MRI?" Brandon asks.

"Yes," Dr. Esper responds. "There could be a glitch. MRIs are powerful imaging tools, and we have a great deal of faith in their accuracy, but they're far from perfect. They can give false positives from time to time. But, if the results are real, Brandon's brain tumor is more serious than before."

We all take a collective breath, and it's like I'm gasping for air.

"I understand this is difficult," Dr. Esper says. "But I will personally monitor these results until we can get another MRI done. It's my job to help your family get through this tough time."

I'm the first to find my voice, and I'm surprised I can muster such a powerful tone. "Okay. You'll perform a second MRI. *Today*. Now. And we'll need to see the results right away."

Dr. Esper looks like she's about to deny my

command, but all she says is, "Of course."

Brandon groans. "Not again," he says. "I hate MRIs."

As Brandon is prepped for his second MRI, Summer and I sit in the waiting room, fidgeting and festering fear. My phone vibrates with a text from Jack.

Coming over tonight?

In the last few weeks, I've spent a lot of time with Jack. I was floored a few days ago, when he took my hand and said, "Let's follow our dreams together. You can transfer your credits to USC. I'll help you get in."

It's like part of me had been holding my breath for months, waiting for Jack to make that offer.

Even when I was on the waitlist, my chances of getting into USC were next to zero. They only accept half a dozen Creative Writing grad students a year. But with Jack's help, it could happen. And the connections I'd form, the opportunities to become a serious, literary writer—it's everything I ever wanted. Plus, we'd be together. And yet sometimes, when I think about being with Jack long-term, I get this combo sensation of indigestion and fever chills.

I run my thumb across my phone screen, returning his text.

Not tonight. Something came up with Brandon's MRI. Long story. I'll tell you more later.

He takes a few minutes to respond. *Hope everything is okay. Sending love! Also, look in your tote bag. I left you a surprise.*

Curiosity piqued, I dig through my bag, finding an ARC (advance review copy) of Jack's novel. A wave of pride washes over me. His novel is a legitimate object that I can hold and smell and run my hands over.

"What's that?" Summer asks.

"Jack's book."

She eyes the cover before losing interest and looking away. Her concern for Brandon has taken her over, like it has for me. But I'm desperate for a distraction, so I flip through the book's pages. At any other time, this would be exhilarating, after the effort Jack and I put into getting his female characters right. He even relied on me to write segments on my own.

First, I read the book's foreword. He talks about his inspiration for the novel and thanks his mentors at Bemidji State, USC, and his editor and agent.

That's nice.

Then I turn to the back where the acknowledgments are. He thanks a bunch of people, like his parents, his high school friends, his past roommates, and some coffee shop baristas. In the middle of the list, there I am. *Thank you, Rye Bread. You rock!*

Stunned, I page through his novel. Entire passages are written by me! I wasn't exactly expecting a by-line, but perhaps an acknowledgement of my contribution. Yet he doesn't even list me by name.

It doesn't matter, I tell myself. *Jack's getting you into USC, and he wants to be with you. For real.*

My chest tightens, and my arms itch like crazy. But if I double over and scratch away, that would freak out Summer. Why am I upset? Jack's book means nothing compared to my brother's health. Yet this dread in my chest is both crushing and all-consuming.

Without meaning to, I let out a low, rumbling moan.

"What's wrong?" Summer asks.

"I need coffee." I'm already out of my seat and walking away. "Do you want anything?"

"Sure, bring me a cup."

I stumble to the coffee machine, realizing I don't have my wallet. All I have is Jack's ARC, a perfect reminder of how messed up my life is—nothing I do matters, not really.

My fury and frustration is so intense that I raise the book high in the air and bring it down hard against the machine's metal rim. The ensuing thwack puts everything in perspective.

Brandon is all that's important.

I hit the book over and over, each slap a release of tension, each thud my pledge that he *will not* go through this again. I *will not* fail my baby brother a second time.

It wasn't supposed to happen.

Thwack!

Not now.

Thwack!

Not ever.

Thwack!

"Rylee."

A quiet voice cuts through my violent trance.

I whirl around, and there he is—Carson, like a mirage in this miserable landscape. Is he really here? Or is he a figment of my exhausted imagination conjured up out of sheer desperation?

Cautious, I reach out and touch his arm—solid flesh, not an apparition.

"Carson." His name lingers in the space between us, laden with everything we haven't said since he stormed out of the novel writing course. I want to freaking fling myself into his arms. I want to trace his perfect face with my fingers and utter a thousand apologies. I want to tell him how much I miss him.

But all I say is, "What are you doing here?"

Hands in his overcoat pockets, he shrugs. "Brandon called, saying he might have important research for our project. I read through the lines and realized he was worried about some MRI results. And that maybe he needs support." Carson's like I remember him on our good days—combed hair, freshly shaved, wearing a clean sweater over a crisp Oxford shirt. Comfort and strength personified.

"Are you okay?"

I let my gaze roll toward the ceiling, releasing a sigh that sounds like a wounded animal.

"My brother might have multiple, life-threatening brain tumors." Tears stream down my cheeks. "So no," I gasp. "I'm not okay. Not even close." I wipe furiously at my eyes. "Soon, I'll sit in the waiting room with Brandon and Summer and wait for the radiologist to read his MRI—but I can't be strong this time." I shake my head. "It's always been an act. I've never been strong. I faked it when Brandon was diagnosed and also when Dad died…" Fear pools in my stomach. "I'm exhausted and scared." Tears fall faster than ever before. "I can't do this anymore."

I'm almost inaudible from my hyperventilating.

Carson pulls me into his arms, and his strong, safe embrace is like an impenetrable shield. His hand moves to my hair, stroking it and soothing me.

"Shh," he breathes into my ear. "It's okay."

"You don't know that," I mumble against his chest.

He pauses for a moment before admitting, "No, you're right, I don't. But I do know this. You don't have to be strong right now. I can be strong for you. Okay, Rylee?" He grazes my jawline with his fingertips, lifting my chin until our eyes meet. "We'll sit in the waiting room together. I'll make conversation, tell jokes to distract your family, and I'll hold your hand when the radiologist comes in."

My heart swells and—for now—I allow myself to lean on him.

"Okay," I whisper, grateful for all he's offering. When I remember everything, my chin starts to quiver. "But why would you do that for me when I ruined your life?"

He winces like I pinched him. "You didn't ruin anything."

My chest heaves as emotion rises in my throat. "Carson, I'm so sorry."

He tightens his grip around me so that my cheek presses against his shoulder. "Don't worry. I'm fine. And Brandon will be fine too. I have a good feeling about this."

"You do? Because I am terrified."

"Of course you are," he says. "But we'll get through this together. Okay?"

"Okay." I look down at the paperback still clutched in my hand.

"What's this?" Carson asks.

It takes me a moment to remember Jack's book, and when I do, I can't comprehend how it ever mattered, even for a second.

"It's nothing," I say, curling it in my fist and hiding it from view. Carson takes my free hand, and we walk off together, him giving me strength.

Chapter 48

Carson

I sit in the radiologist's office with Rylee, Summer, and Brandon, as they wait for his second MRI results. The air is dense with anxiety, and I try my best to dilute it. Whatever pops into my brain comes out of my mouth, whether it's funny stories about Eddie, or how Brandon's classmate spilled frog guts in AP Bio, or my guess about when Bemidji's weather might turn spring-like. Now I remember why I chose not to become a doctor. There's no way I could give families earth-shattering news every day.

Yet, maybe at some point, I'll do medical research. Once Eddie is in college, I'll have the freedom to move and go back to school. By then, I'll be thirty-seven, which is not too old to start a second career.

Finally, Dr. Esper arrives. I've been holding Rylee's hand this whole time, and I worry she might break my metacarpal bones—that's how tight her grip is.

"Good news. It was a false alarm. Brandon, your MRI scan is clean."

Both Rylee and Summer start happy-crying, hugging Brandon and each other. Brandon, who'd been putting up a brave front, lets his guard down, his relief manifesting into an unsteady laugh. He runs a hand through his tousled brown hair; in the last few weeks it's grown enough that he no longer needs a baseball cap.

"You scared us," Summer says, playful as she uses one hand to jab him in the ribs and the other to wipe her face.

"I scared myself!"

"Congratulations, Brandon." I slap him on the back.

"Thanks for being here, Mr. Meyers."

"Yes, thank you," Rylee says.

She's wiping away tears, a shaky smile playing on her lips. I shift closer and pull her in for a hug. Her body relaxes against mine, sending a pang through my chest, and a rush of desire that I stifle right away.

The three of them have a ton of questions, and Dr. Esper settles into her office chair, ready to answer each one.

"Hey, I should get going." I grab my coat. "Brandon, thanks for calling me. I'm glad everything worked out, and I'll see you tomorrow at school, okay?"

"Sounds good. Thanks again."

"No, wait," Summer says. "Come celebrate with us. We missed the movie, but we can still go out for dinner. It will be my treat."

"I wish I could, but I have grading to do tonight."

Rylee stands. "I'll walk you out."

I was afraid she would say that. "You don't need to. I can find my way."

"Yeah, but I'll walk you out, anyway." She turns to her mom. "I'll be back in a couple minutes."

Silently, we exit Dr. Esper's office. After reaching the door adjacent to where I parked, we emerge into the cool evening air. "I can't thank you enough, Carson."

"You don't need to thank me at all. I didn't do anything."

"That's not true." Rylee reaches out a hand and

places it on my shoulder. "You were there for me when I needed you. That's everything." She raises up onto her tiptoes, tilts her chin, and leans in for a kiss.

I have to turn away from Rylee's stunning face and step back so she no longer touches me.

"I was there for Brandon." My words rush out like a river flowing downstream. "He's a great kid, and I'd do anything to help him. That's all." I'm lying through my teeth—at least about the "that's all" part—and like a coward, I can't meet Rylee's eyes.

Rylee's laugh is sharp and brittle. "Oh my God. This is just like high school. Remember? It's The B.A.I., Part Two!"

"Umm…" I tug at my collar. "Huh?"

Laughing some more, she shakes her head. "The B.A.I.—The Big Awful Incident? That's what I named the first time I tried to kiss you, and you rejected me."

"Oh," I say, not understanding why any of this is funny. Is she just making light of her hurt feelings? Or perhaps, after tonight's emotional roller coaster, humor is her best defense. I'm torn between wanting to hold her close and running away. "Rylee, this wasn't a rejection. My life is complicated right now. Do you understand?"

She doesn't respond. Now I can sense the pain radiating from her body.

"Rylee." I stop and gather my thoughts. "I should thank you. You told me to practice kindness and forgiveness, and that's the best advice anyone ever gave me. You see, Dana and I talked, and we're trying to start fresh and fix our marriage."

Rylee doesn't say anything but gives a small nod as she scratches her arms.

"That's great," she murmurs.

"Yeah," I reply, a heavy ache building in my chest. "And you and Jack are together, right? Wasn't that his book you were holding? You must be so proud."

"I am proud." Yet she sounds deflated. "You and I are both getting what we wanted all along." Something inside her shifts into gear, and she brightens. "Well, we can at least be friends."

But I know better. And as terrible as it is telling her no, lying would be worse. In one swift motion, I wrap her in my arms and hold her tight—tighter than either of us expected. "Rylee, I'm sorry, but that would never work."

I release her and take a step back.

"But—" she protests, and her voice splinters against the air between us.

"We can't be friends." I look away. "It's—the two of us—we have to be all or nothing."

"Oh." Her eyes find mine, and they hold a silent plea. "Then, we're nothing?"

"I'm sorry."

"Don't be." Her words are jagged, her gaze even more so. She shrugs off my apology like it's too heavy and cumbersome to bother with. "Do you remember what you said after the first B.A.I.?"

I swallow hard. "No."

"You said, 'It will be okay. You'll get through this.' And you're right." Her voice turns husky, and her chin lifts like she's ready for battle. "I will be okay, and I will get through this. I always am and I always do." She takes a deep breath. "Goodbye, Carson."

She leaves me standing there, and something she said just now echoes in my ears—*You and I are both getting what we wanted all along*. I can't speak to that,

but one thing is clear.
    The destruction of our side project is complete.

Chapter 49

Rylee

We go out for pizza, and Brandon and Summer are so happy they don't seem to notice my devastation. To be fair, I put on a good front, going through the motions of a sister celebrating her baby brother's clean MRI.

And, of course, I'm over the moon that Brandon is okay. But at the same time, on the inside I'm like roadkill, splayed out on the highway, vile and decaying.

Hours later, I'm curled up on my bed, tears streaming down my cheeks and onto my pillow. I've convinced myself that Brandon and Summer are fast asleep after our tumultuous evening, that they're unaware of my meltdown. Then comes a soft knock at my door.

"Rylee?"

Summer peeks inside. "What's wrong, honey?"

Her sympathy almost cracks me open. It's futile pretending everything is okay, that I'm not falling apart. "Mom." My chest heaves. "I don't know what to do."

It's the first time I've called her *Mom* since my father died, and the word floats like a cloud above us.

She inhales as if absorbing my pain. Rushing to sit by my side, she pulls me close.

"Oh no. What happened? Is it Carson?"

I nod between hiccups before speaking through sobs. "I lost him. He doesn't even want to be friends. He told me that we're *nothing*."

My mother considers this, stroking my hair with such tenderness that I almost forget Carson's rejection.

"Did he tell you why?"

I take a huge sniff. "He and Dana are trying to work things out, so he says it wouldn't work for him and me to be friends." A new wave of pain hits me in my stomach. "I mean, that's crazy, right?"

"Perhaps it isn't, sweetheart," she says, shrugging. "I mean, not if you're in love."

I reel back. "But I don't even believe in love!" Like a wounded animal, I curl up into a ball and rest my cheek against her lap. "God. How could I be so stupid?"

"Oh, Rylee." She says my name, and it's like I'm little again and she's singing me a lullaby. "You weren't being stupid—you were being brave."

"But you told me to be careful and not lose my heart to him."

"Right," she admits. "I said that…but I was wrong. It's okay to let yourself love someone." Summer pauses, still running her hand through my hair. "Carson seems very special…and he obviously loves you."

Incredulous at this last remark, my head snaps up. "How is it obvious?"

Her eyes fill with empathy. For a second, I'm a young girl again—one who ran into her mother's arms every time she fell off her bike or lost her favorite doll. One who believed in fairy tales and happy endings.

"He wouldn't insist on separating himself if he didn't have strong feelings for you. We tend to protect those we love while hurting them in the process." Summer offers a faint smile. "Plus, there's the way he looks at you. And the way he held your hand tonight. He was there when you needed him."

"He was there for Brandon, not me."

"Maybe that's what he said, but it isn't the truth."

I consider this while wiping my eyes. "Well, even if you're right, it makes no difference. He's trying to make things work with Dana, and I can't break up a family. I know what it's like, to not have your father around, and I couldn't live with myself if I made Eddie go through what I've—"

"Rylee, don't do that!" Her words hit like lightning, and her intense gaze pierces me even in the dark of my bedroom.

"Don't do what?"

"Don't take responsibility for other people's happiness," she says. "You shoulder enough—Brandon, me—and now you have to take on Eddie and Dana? If Carson wants to be with you, it doesn't mean he'll abandon Eddie. And this situation will never equate with how your father died."

My mother's statement soaks in like a falling, early-spring snow. Then I shiver and pull blankets up around my knees. "How *did* Dad die, Mom?"

Her mouth drops open. "What are you talking about? You know how he died."

"I know it was a car accident, that a truck slammed into you when you were coming home from a party. And I know he'd had a lot to drink because his agent had dumped him, which was why you were the one driving. But what I don't know is…" I pause before uttering what I'm afraid to ask. "Did he want it to happen?"

"Oh, Rye." Her head drifts towards the hallway, the one source of light in my darkened room. "Of course not. Why would you ask me that?"

"Because I overheard you once; you said you'd never forgive him for giving up."

She buries her head in her hands for a moment. When she returns her gaze to me, her eyes mirror the confusion and pain I've hidden for years. She takes my hands in hers.

"You've heard of the seven stages of grief?"

"Sure."

"Well, after the accident, after my shock and denial wore off, anger set in. Your father knew I don't like driving at night, that I didn't even want to go to that party in the first place. Then he drank, and I had to drive us home. So, instead of blaming myself, I blamed him."

My body deflates, and I let go of her hands to trace the stitching on my comforter. "I used to worry that his death was my fault."

She cups my shoulders. "Your fault? How could it ever have been your fault?"

"If I hadn't come along," I stammer, still tracing the comforter design. "He could have followed his dreams and moved to California. But instead, we settled here. He became busy and burdened and couldn't focus on his writing, and his agent dropped him." Tears lodge in my throat, making it difficult to say the next part. "If that hadn't happened, he wouldn't have gone to that party and had too much to drink..." I'm unable to go on.

A tear drops onto my comforter, and then another. But they're not my tears; they belong to Summer. "Oh, Rye, you've been carrying around this burden without saying a word. And here I thought you blamed me. I figured that's why you stopped calling me *Mom.*"

Guilt washes over me. "That was never it." Afraid to look at her, I speak while crying. "It's...when he died, and you were in the hospital, I was terrified you would die too. And I figured I had to grow up and not need you anymore because even if it turned out you were alright, *someday* you would die, and there was no way I could go through that kind of pain again." I scrub my eyes. "Not for you, not for anyone."

"Oh, my sweet Rylee. I am so sorry." Summer wraps her arms around me, her grip strong and intense. The dam of unspoken sorrow breaks, and we cry *together* for the first time since Dad's death.

After our tears dry out, she releases me and says, "I should have seen what you were going through. I should have told you that protecting yourself from love doesn't work." She brushes a lock of hair from my face, tucking it behind my ear with such affection that my tears threaten to restart. "I speak from experience."

"What do you mean?"

"Okay, don't take this the wrong way, but when I told your father I was pregnant, he had to convince me we should get married and start a family. He couldn't wait to be a father, and he loved you so much. *You* were his dream come true."

"Do you mean it?"

"Yes. I was the one who wasn't sure. I was quite young, and it scared me—how much I loved him. But I wouldn't change anything if I could go back and do it all again. And he wouldn't have either. You and Brandon were—are—the best things that ever happened to either of us."

"Really?" I croak. "Because I'm sorry for all the times I've been mean or unforgiving."

"Baby," she whispers. "You're my girl. My pride and joy. I love you so much."

"I love you, Mom."

She places her hand, palm flat, over her heart. "I must say, I like hearing you call me that."

We capture each other in another fierce hug, and then we part and sit side by side again, relaxed in each other's company.

"So what do I do now?" I ask.

"About Carson?"

"Yes."

My mom takes a moment, her chest rising and falling in delicate waves. "You respect his wishes and hope he changes his mind."

"That's it?"

Her nod is firm. "For now. But Rye, while you're waiting, you need to stop taking care of everyone— myself included—and start looking out for you. Don't stay here in Bemidji for me or Brandon. Don't move to California for Jack. And don't do anything just to honor your dad's memory. Decide what will make you happy and do that."

I remember Carson's answer when I asked him what he'd do if he could go anywhere.

I'd love the time and space to figure out what I want.

I turn towards my mom, whose pretty face has grown contemplative.

"What about you, Mom? What would make you happy?"

She shakes her head. "It's been such a long time since I even thought about anything besides staying afloat… The one time I did…" Her voice trails off as she looks away.

"What is it?" I ask.

Mom's shoulders quiver as the truth unfolds. "It

329

happened once, on the morning of Brandon's diagnosis. I wasn't at work. I was with Leo… We were…together for the first time."

My jaw almost hits the floor. I wasn't aware there had been any "times" between them.

"Just that once," she adds, her words lingering in the room as if they've hung midair for the last year. I'm trying to come up with a polite yet probing question when she adds, "It's complicated."

"I wish I'd understood better what it's been like for you. But Mom, isn't it time to forgive Dad? Then maybe you and Leo can figure out what you mean to each other."

She pulls at the sleeves of her thin sleep shirt. "I'm not sure…"

I cup her shoulders in the same way she did mine minutes ago. "You just told me love is worth the risk. Now prove that you believe it."

Chapter 50

Rylee

Mel sits in a coffee shop near Smoky Mountain National Park, because that's where she has the bandwidth to call. She takes one look at my face, which is still puffy from last night, and asks, "What's wrong?"

I divulge the whole story. Well, not the *whole* story—I leave out Dana's private details and how Eddie isn't Carson's biological son. That's not my information to share.

"Well, I'm glad Brandon is okay. But I'm sorry about everything else. I don't understand Carson right now," Mel states.

"All I can say is, it's super complicated. I learned that the hard way." My eyes begin to sting, but I blink it away. "The week I stayed with him when we both had the flu, we grew close. Taking care of each other, spending every moment together...I told him stuff I haven't even told you."

Mel furrows her brow. "Like what?"

What's the point of keeping secrets anymore? "Like, I write Regency romance novels and self-publish them under a pen name."

There's a pause. "Are you serious?"

"Dead serious. I've sold tens of thousands of copies, and I have lots of five-star reviews. The moment I told Carson, he went on Quill & Key and bought an e-reader so he could download them." My heart pangs at the memory. "It was very sweet."

"Hold up." Mel extends a finger in a *wait a sec* sort of gesture, and peers at me while squinting. "You're a best-selling romance novelist on Quill & Key, and you never thought to share?" Her eyebrows jump in disbelief, her mouth curving into a half-smile.

"Yes."

"And you didn't mention it because…"

"Because people look down on self-published romance writers."

"Not me. Rye—this is super cool." Mel's voice adopts a pained edge. "How could you think I'd judge you?"

I comb my fingers through my unwashed hair. "It wasn't like that. I didn't tell anyone because the more people who knew, the more likely it would be that—"

"—That Jack would find out?"

My chest heaves up and down. "Yeah, I suppose. But there was more to it than that."

Behind Mel, there's a line of people waiting for coffee. Some customers, after finishing their espresso and pastries, deposit ceramic cups and plates into bins not far from where she sits. Mel watches them for a moment before turning her attention back to me. "Rye…" Her head tilts in confusion. "I don't understand. Why would you go to ridiculous lengths, hiding your talent and success from your friends and family?"

"Because…" I start, clearing my throat. "Because it all means more to me than most people could understand. Or more than even I understand. My writing…it's the last connection I have to my father. But it's also my last connection to the person I was before he died. To the girl who believed in happily ever after."

"Oh, Rye." Mel reaches out like her hand could break through both screens and hold mine.

Damn. I've shed so many tears in the last twenty-four hours, it will take me months to rehydrate. I wipe my cheeks and blink hard, trying to push back the tide of emotion. "It's okay. I have to believe that everything that's happened is for the best. Carson and I were never meant to be. But Jack and I have a lot in common, and he's going to help get me into USC."

Any compassion that was in Mel's face falls away. Her mouth sets into a firm line. "Okay, Rye. *Truth Time.*"

It's like a rock sinks in my stomach. "No, really? I hate *Truth Time.*"

And yet, *Truth Time* is also sacred. It started in seventh grade, when Mel wanted to sing the latest Top 40 power ballad for the talent show, but she was so off-key, and I knew she'd get laughed at. "Truth Time," I'd told her.

She remembered it a year later when I planned to bleach my hair and cut it short, like I was some burnout ex-childhood star having a quarter-life crisis. Since then, we've made it our mission to deliver hard truths that everyone else is scared to tell us, whether it's about relationships, school, jobs, or any random delusion.

"Sorry," Mel says. "But *Truth Time* is long overdue. You've been pretty dishonest with me."

"Only about two things."

"Two super big things—I mean, what the heck?"

I sit up straighter, ready to defend myself. "I've been honest about Carson ever since your party. And I never lied to you about the books. If the subject had come up,

I would have told you."

She scowls. "Fine. I'm not mad, but someone needs to level with you. Are you ready? Because this might sting."

I roll my shoulders back. "Go ahead."

Mel leans toward the camera. "Here it is. Carson was right to reject you last night, and I'm glad he did. You're way too screwed up to be in a relationship—and not just with him, but with anyone."

It's like she hit me in the chest. "Wow. Okay."

"Meanwhile, Rye, you've been pining for Jack for what, three years now? And I don't get it. Why are you ready to ditch Bemidji for California to pursue some literary fantasy Jack cooked up, while hiding what you actually like to read and write—not to mention your astounding talent—all so you can help him write a novel that only a few people will read?"

I stare at her. "That's harsh. Everyone has different tastes. There's room in the world for popular fiction and romance as much as there is for literary fiction. And I wanted to move to California before I even met Jack. I told you this. It was my dad's dream too."

"Yeah, but why?" Mel's voice drops an octave. "What'll it get you?"

"Do I need a reason? You never gave one when you left Minnesota."

My friend's inhale is slow. "Other than my dream job, of course." She exhales before continuing and softens her tone. "Look, Rye, I adore you. I'd give anything to take away all the pain you've endured, especially your grief for your father… But I can't do this for you; you alone can make it right. And chasing Jack out West will change nothing."

****

Later, at work, Dana approaches me. I'm standing at the empty hostess stand and the dinner rush is over. "I like *A Viscount for Vivien.* It's your best yet."

It's one of the first nice things she's said since catching me with Carson. "Thank you."

She hesitates. "Have you started working on your next novel? The one for your thesis?"

"No." It's hard, remembering how Carson chose her over me. But what's worse is my guilt. I would have thrown her and Eddie under the bus if it meant being back in Carson's arms. "Rylee, I meant it when I said I'd love to brainstorm ideas with you. If I could be of any help…"

"Thanks, Dana. I appreciate that. But I've been changing my mind about my thesis. I'm not sure about writing a romance."

Dana's eyes grow wide with surprise. "But what else would you write? You're so good at romance."

I scratch my arms, trying to come up with an explanation that will sound legit, but I'm tired of evading the truth. So, I level with her.

"Jack is teaching the novel writing course that I'm taking."

Dana blinks, her expression unreadable. "Oh. I didn't realize…" She lets the sentence hang as she rubs both thumbs with her index fingers. I can see the wheels turning in her mind, connecting the dots. "That's the class Carson dropped?"

"Yeah."

"And it's the same Jack as your boyfriend from California?" I nod my reply. "No wonder Carson wanted out."

"It's not like that."

She waves me off. "No worries. But how are things going between you and Jack?"

Hope fills the blank spaces on Dana's face.

I shift my weight and press an elbow into the hostess stand. "I don't think I love him anymore. Well, I'm not sure I ever loved him. And I can't write a romance in his class."

"Why not?"

When I answer with a soft groan, she comes over and places a gentle hand against my shoulder. "Hey. Don't waste time on a guy who doesn't appreciate you. And if you change your mind about brainstorming, I'm around, okay?"

"Thanks, Dana."

She squeezes my shoulder and walks off.

My phone pings with a text from Jack. *R U coming over tonight?*

I haven't talked to Jack since Brandon's MRI scare. No way will I spend the night in his bed, not after reading the acknowledgements in his book that just had my nickname—a nickname that I hate. And certainly not after his failure to ask how Brandon's MRI went.

Can't. I need to work on my novel for your class.

I'm confident he'll buy this excuse. Sure enough, seconds later, he texts, *Cool. I expect greatness from you.*

A customer calls to make a reservation, and I grip the phone so tight, I'm surprised it doesn't dissolve. After I hang up, I abandon my post and find Dana in the pantry, taking inventory of our condiments.

"Hey," I say to her back. She startles and turns around. "Any chance we can do that brainstorming tonight?"

Chapter 51

Carson

"More wine?" Dana holds up the bottle, offering to replenish my glass.

I came for dinner and stayed, even after Eddie went to bed. Tonight, Dana's wearing her heart on her sleeve, obvious in her attempts to romance me. But try as I might, I can't let go enough to trust her.

"Dana, we need to talk."

The candlelight flickers across her face, but her expression, open and expectant, doesn't change.

"Sure. What is it?"

"Today I met with Professor Harris—the head of the Biology Department at Bemidji State."

"I remember Professor Harris."

"Right." Nervous, I fiddle with my fork. "I told him about the research project that I'm doing with Brandon, and we talked about how my classwork is going. He was very encouraging."

Dana offers a cautious smile. "That's great."

"Yeah, and I mentioned how I want to become a medical researcher one day. He said he could help make that happen."

Dana glances down at the table where her dessert sits, the remnants of pecan pie crust still spotting the small china plate that came with our wedding registry.

"Okay," she says, not looking at me.

"He says I should enroll full-time next year and take as much grad-level biology coursework as possible. And he said he could find me a TA position to cut down on tuition expenses."

She swallows. "But how would you have time to teach?"

"You mean at the high school? I wouldn't. I will resign."

Dana seems to crumple inward, her shoulders rounding. She looks back up, and her wide eyes glisten in the soft light.

"Resign? But you love teaching?"

It's not quite a question, more an affirmation of something she wishes were true. "No." I exhale my response.

"How are you going to pay your bills?" Dana's face hardens. "And how will you help support Eddie?"

"I'd take out loans for my own expenses. As for Eddie, that's something we'd figure out together."

Dana shifts in her seat, reaches for the wine bottle, and empties the rest of the merlot into her glass, filling it to the rim.

"In other words, you wouldn't be supporting him at all, right? And meanwhile, you're enrolled in a program that's a dead end. Don't you need a PhD or an MD to do medical research? An MS in bio won't get you anywhere."

It's like I'm walking on a field laden with land mines. My word choice, inflection, and delivery must be perfect, or else this truce with Dana will explode like dynamite.

"Dr. Harris mentioned the PhD program at the Mayo Clinic, down in Rochester. He has connections there, and he says if I do a year's worth of graduate-level biology coursework, I'd be a shoo-in for the program." I lean forward, urging Dana to meet my eyes. "Everyone who's accepted gets a five-year fellowship covering full tuition, a stipend, and benefits. Plus, I'd have an in at Mayo Clinic! Think of the job opportunities."

Dana takes a swig of wine. "Rochester."

I wait for her to say more, but realize that's it for now.

"It's only around five hours away. And I wouldn't leave for another year and a half."

"Right." She places her glass down and, with a sharp inhale, meets my gaze. "And when you leave, will Eddie and I come with you?"

"I guess that depends on what you want."

Her laugh is soft and sad. "No, it depends on what *you* want. I mean, if it wasn't for Eddie, would you even be here right now?"

My heart sinks as I struggle for a response.

"Don't answer that," Dana says. "We both know that if I never had Eddie, you'd have gone to Harvard, and we'd be broken up."

"Not necessarily."

"Come on, Carson. Let's be honest. You stopped loving me when you realized I'd lied about Eddie, but no matter what, we were never meant to last."

Spine straight, she regards me, beautiful as candlelight flickers across her face. And I hate how much she's suffered. "Dana, do you even still love me?"

She turns her head, and a tear spills down her cheek. "For so long, I tried to make sure that you'd always be Eddie's father and that you'd always be in his life. Everything else—like what I want and who I love—has been secondary."

For the first time in years, I look at Dana and see her for who she is. So strong and so broken. A wave of sadness rushes over me.

Her chin trembles. "I'm sorry."

"I forgive you."

"Why? I don't deserve your forgiveness, Carson."

"Don't say that." I stand up and move around the table until I'm in front of where she sits. Taking both her hands in mine, I whisper, "Of course, you deserve my forgiveness. You gave me Eddie. He's like this miracle, and you chose me to be his dad. Dana, I promise that no matter what happens, I will always be there for him."

Dana squeezes my fingers but then removes her hands from mine so she can wipe her eyes. "Someday, we'll have to tell him the truth. Like when he plans on having kids of his own."

"True, but let's take things one step at a time."

Her lips quiver as she says, "You should sign up for the program, Carson."

Kneeling down, I gather her in my arms and nestle my head against her knee. "Thank you."

Dana's slow hand rests in my hair as I look up at her. "Rochester, huh? I suppose I can deal with that… If you buy a car with good gas mileage. Because Eddie will want you to drive up here a lot."

"Sure," I say. "And maybe he can spend school breaks down there with me?"

"Maybe."

Our fingers entwine, and I place a tender kiss on her knuckles before laying my cheek back down against her leg. We stay like that, frozen in time, both of us breathing in the last intimate moment we'll ever share.

Some love stories aren't meant to last, I reflect, as a lump forms in my throat. *But that doesn't mean they can't end with "happily ever after."*

Chapter 52

Rylee

My new novel, which Dana helped me brainstorm, is about a young woman who loses her dad in a tragic accident. To ensure her family's financial stability, she's forced to marry an unkind duke who doesn't treat her well. But then, she falls for the artist hired to paint the duke's portrait. He's a young widower with two small children, dependent on the money from her husband's commission. But they just can't quit each other.

I'm rubbing my eyes after my latest attempt to nail the dialogue between the heroine, Isobel, and her asshole-duke husband, Victor. In need of a break, I check my email and discover a message for Shelby Simmons, submitted yesterday through my author website.

Dear Ms. Simmons,

My name is Violet Rice, and I'm an editor at Rendezvous Books. We specialize in historical romance novels that capture the hearts of readers everywhere. I read A Viscount for Vivien *and was enchanted! I can't even put into words how much I enjoyed it.*

I am writing because you have a brilliant talent for creating stories with captivating characters and powerful emotions. That is why we would like to offer you a book deal with our esteemed publishing house. It would be an honor to work with someone as talented as yourself, and I am certain you could create a masterpiece in no time!

We would make your novels widely available in print and electronic formats, and we offer competitive author advances and royalties. If this is something that interests you, please contact me here at Rendezvous Books so we can discuss this exciting opportunity further. I look forward to hearing from you soon!

Sincerely,

Violet Rice

Editor at Rendezvous Books

Thinking this must be a scam, I almost press delete without reading the entire message. But when I get to the part about how they offer author advances, I reconsider. I do a web search on Rendezvous Books and find this on their "About" page:

Rendezvous Books is an independent publisher of Historical Romance stories created by and for women. Our acclaimed romance novels are multiple award-winners, New York Times Bestsellers, and Quill & Key's number one eBook publisher of Historic Romance! Margaret Du Bois founded Rendezvous Books with the mission to help authors find readers, grow their fanbase, and make a living from writing. We don't charge money to publish books like a vanity press—we provide quality products at reasonable prices. In fact, we invest more in marketing than many small presses. If you're looking for your next read in Historical Romance, be sure to check out Rendezvous Books. We work hard every day to empower women writers! You can trust that Rendezvous Books stands for excellence.

Another quick search, this time on Quill & Key, confirms Rendezvous Books's claims. They do indeed publish several bestsellers.

Figuring I've got nothing to lose, I grab my phone and dial the number that Violet Rice left at the bottom of her message.

"This is Violet."

"Hello. This is Rylee Lynch—but I publish under the pen name Shelby Simmons." I almost trip over my tongue. "I got your message on my website?" Hearing the question in my tone, I square my shoulders. No need to sound insecure.

"Ah, yes! You wrote *A Viscount for Vivien*. Such a grand work." Violet's voice is fresh and lyrical. "So, Rylee is your real name?"

It's sort of hard to speak like a normal person, but I pull myself together. "That's right."

"Spectacular!" says Violet. "Well, Rylee, your work is the perfect fit for Rendezvous Books, and we'd love to give you a publishing contract. Is that something you'd be interested in?"

Sparks fly through my veins, but I keep calm. "Yes. I am definitely interested. But first, are you for real? This isn't a cruel prank where you'll ask for my checking account number or all my passwords?"

The other end of the line erupts with laughter. "No way! We love your work and want to snatch it up before someone else does. Now, do you have an agent who would handle this negotiation, or are you going solo?"

My mouth hangs open as shock sets in. This isn't a question I ever thought I'd need to answer. But what the heck.

"I'm going solo, Violet. I don't have an agent."

"That's absolutely fine, dear. We can guide you through the process. Our legal team will ensure the contract is transparent and fair. Does that sound okay?"

"Umm…yeah. It sounds better than okay. It sounds perfect."

****

Several days later, after submitting a portion of my new novel to Jack and my fellow classmates, I sit and await their feedback.

The class setup is the same as on the first day, tables arranged in a rectangle, students sitting on the sides, and Jack in the middle, standing at a podium.

"Well," he says, pushing up the sleeves of his signature black turtleneck. I happen to know that he owns six of them. On laundry day, he wears one of his two USC sweatshirts. "Let's discuss *The Betrayal of a Duke.*"

"That's a working title," I say. "I'd like to figure out one that centers more on the heroine. Perhaps to empower her?"

Jack gives me an uncertain smile. "Am I missing something here? Like, irony?"

"Why would there be irony?"

He squints at me like I just criticized literary realism. "It reads like a Regency romance novel."

"Good. Because that's what it is."

Jack's mouth falls open, and the distance between us shrinks and expands, all at once.

"Rylee, why would you write something trite when you're capable of so much more?"

"Oh, you mean like the extensive passages that *I* wrote for *your* novel—the 'truthful' ones that you bragged about on our first day of class?" I take out Jack's book, hold it up, and flip through, exposing multiple highlighted passages written by me. "These words that I wrote, and which you gave me zero credit for? I'm not sure, Jack—I guess I hoped to attract real-life readers with a pulse."

There's an audible, collective gasp from the rest of the class, and I hear someone mumble, "Dang!"

Jack raises his unremarkable eyebrows, which add neither charm nor intrigue to his smug, condescending face. He's nothing like Carson when it comes to eyebrows. But all of Jack pales in comparison to all of Carson. "Perhaps we should talk about this in private."

"No," I say, louder than necessary. "I'd like some feedback."

"Rylee," Jack uses a tone most people reserve for toddlers. "I'm trying to spare you embarrassment."

"Oh!" Extending my arms in a grand, theatrical gesture, I stoop to using sarcasm. "That's nice of you. But here's the thing. I've been self-publishing Regency romance novels for a couple of years now, and I just got offered a contract with Rendezvous Books that includes an advance and an advertising budget. And they love my ideas for *The Betrayal of the Duke.* I'm here to gain insight into what other people—not you—think of it so far."

There's a heavy pause. Jack's face is like a souffle taken out of the oven too soon, but it rises as if given an egg white injection. "Sure, Rylee. Appeal to the lowest common denominator; we can try to help you out."

My chest tightens. Even though I'm looking up at him, I stare him down with contempt. "I'm not sure what I want. But I can tell you what I *don't* want. I don't want your pretentious standards to dictate my work, I don't want to write entire passages of your novel only to suffer your pedantic advice, I don't want to move to California with you, and I *really* don't want to be called 'Rye

Bread' ever again."

He laughs like he's in pain. "Sounds good. Okay. Let's move on."

"No." The voice comes from across the rectangle. It's Marcie, aka, False-Eyelash Girl from last semester, who also enrolled in Novel Writing. Two weeks ago, she submitted her novel to the class, a genre fantasy about evil mermaids which I tried not to love, and which Jack derided. "I'm totally here for Rylee's Regency romance, and I want to discuss it." She turns toward me. "First of all, can you tell me about the dad character? Is it possible to incorporate him more into the story, like via flashbacks?"

"Maybe," I say. "Wouldn't that distract from the central love story?"

Marcie shakes her head. "No, because the heroine needs to reconcile with her grief before she can give her heart in a romantic relationship."

I open my notebook and grab my pen, ready to record her useful feedback. "Please, tell me more."

We spend the rest of class discussing my novel, and I take notes as Marcie and several of my other classmates give me a lot to consider. When the clock strikes ten thirty a.m., I gather my stuff and approach Jack, tossing his book at him. His hands flail to catch it. "I won't make a fuss about my non-credited work, and I concede that some of what you taught me—like finding your truth and your unique point of view—is valuable. But here's what I'll give you for free: lose your misogynistic attitude and learn how to write female characters. Because news flash, Jack: women read twice as many novels than men. A lot of those books are romances. Get over it."

He doesn't have time to respond—I spin on my heel

and make a beeline for Professor Aldrich's office. Lucky for me, I've caught her between meetings.

She smiles when she sees me. "Rylee, what can I do for you?"

"I need your help," I reply, catching my breath after that adrenaline rush. "Do you have ten minutes so I can explain?"

"For you?" Professor Aldrich's smile turns sly. "I've got twenty."

Chapter 53

Carson

It's lunchtime. What's taking Brandon so long? Often, he brings his tray to my room to eat while we have a working lunch, doing research side by side. Other students are welcome to sit here, but they almost never do. Brandon and I often eat alone, while continuing to explore the genetic connection with brain tumors.

But not today. When Brandon arrives, he rushes to set down his tray and states, "I got an email from Harvard. Admission decisions are in." He pauses, expecting me to respond. But my throat gets jammed with nerves. "I can find out if I've been accepted," Brandon finishes.

He's flushed with anxiety, and I've got major sympathy pains. Part of me wishes we weren't sharing this moment. What if Brandon has been rejected? I'll be terrible at consoling him, muttering stupid platitudes like "rejection is just redirection," or "everything happens for a reason." I don't believe in either of those statements, but if necessary, I'll comfort my favorite student of all time. Yet deep down, I realize rejection hurts like a bastard, and no empty words will numb the pain.

Then again, maybe Brandon's been accepted. "What are you waiting for?" My pulse quickens. "Log on and find out."

Brandon gets out his phone and starts swiping. It

seems to take forever, and the agony is almost as bad as when, years ago, I was opening my own letter from Harvard.

"Okay, I'm logged on. Let's see." He furrows his brow and murmurs, "Open letter…" Brandon taps his phone and sucks in a breath. His face freezes as he reads.

Several seconds pass, until I can't stand it any longer. "Well?"

When Brandon raises his gaze from his phone, there are tears in his eyes. "I got in. Full ride." He shoves his phone in front of me. "I mean, I'm not dreaming, right? This isn't another brain tumor making me see what I want to see? Please tell me it's real."

I take Brandon's phone and read the letter. "Dear Mr. Lynch. I am delighted to inform you that the Committee on Admissions has admitted you into Harvard University with a full scholarship. Please accept my personal congratulations for your outstanding achievements." My smile comes from the deepest section of my heart. For a moment, I'm choked up and can't speak, but I'm able to say, "It's real, Brandon. You're in. Congratulations."

Brandon lunges toward me and gives me a bear hug. "Thank you, Mr. Meyers. I could never have done it without you."

I pat his back. "That's not true."

"No, it is. Your help, plus my brain tumor got me accepted into Harvard." Brandon releases me, takes a step back, and laughs. "But I don't care. I'm in!"

His joy is infectious, and I laugh too. "They wouldn't have accepted you if you weren't exceptional, Brandon."

"But there are lots of exceptional people. I happened

to have an extra edge." Brandon shrugs. "Don't worry, it's all good. After the hell I've been through—the radiation, the surgeries, all the MRIs, and going bald at seventeen—maybe I deserve an advantage or two." His face changes when a new thought registers. "I have to call my mom. And Rylee."

Brandon calls his mother first, and Rylee after that. I can hear her shout with joy, Rylee's voice loud and clear enough to carry through Brandon's phone and into my classroom. Something inside me melts, and I want to live inside the cadence of Rylee.

When Brandon hangs up, I say, "She sounded so happy."

"Yeah." Brandon studies my expression. "You miss her, don't you?"

"I, uh…" Stupid, that I can't respond to such a simple question. "What makes you say that?"

"Seriously?" Brandon swallows a laugh. "Come on, dude."

With a sigh, I mumble, "Can you just tell me if she's doing okay?"

"She's doing great. I mean, she wasn't for a while. Whatever you said to her on the night of my MRI made her cry more than once. But now she's moved on."

It's like there's a lump of coal in my throat, and the idea of causing Rylee pain makes it burn. But what does Brandon mean by "she's moved on"?

God. I'm pathetic. No way should I pump a student for info on his sister. Good thing I'm leaving at the end of the year because now I'm crossing a line. "Does she ever ask about me?"

Brandon sits at the desk where he'd set down his lunch tray and opens his carton of milk. "No, and that's

351

for the better. Rylee's been on this self-improvement, independent kick. She dumped Jack, and she's staying in Bemidji for at least another year so she can write her next novel in the place our dad both loved and hated. Rye's always had demons when it comes to our dad. But now she's dealing with them, and she's been happy ever since she got her publishing contract."

My heart swells. "Rylee got a publishing contract?"

"Yeah. I guess she's been writing romance novels for a while, but now that she's going to get paid a lot of money, she's stopped using her pen name."

"Good for her." I lean against my desk, considering this recent development. It's all excellent news. She's staying in Bemidji, and she dumped turtleneck-wearing-douchebag-Jack. I wonder if she heard Dana and I are finalizing our divorce. Maybe—Dana told me that she and Rylee are friends again. But why would they discuss me? I bet I'm their least favorite topic of conversation.

"Rylee's going to be in a symposium at the college tomorrow afternoon," Brandon says. "As soon as her advisor found out about Rylee's publishing success, she asked her to talk to the students about it. It's open to the public."

"Should I go?"

"Maybe?" Brandon swigs his milk. "But only if you're serious about her. Rylee's in a good place now. Don't mess with her unless you mean it."

The idea of seeing Rylee makes me shaky with excitement. And yet, a voice inside scolds me, saying I should stay away. "I'll think about it. She might not want me there."

"True," Brandon says.

I have to change the subject. This isn't fair to

Brandon. He never signed up to mediate my relationship with his sister.

But God, what have I become? Before Rylee, there was space to breathe, room to live.

Now that I know her, love her, need her? She'll always occupy the empty space in my heart. Because I just can't have her—not if she's better off without me.

I shake off the thought. "Anyway," I say to Brandon, "back to Harvard. Will you live on campus?"

Chapter 54

Rylee

Mom, Brandon, Leo, and I celebrate at a bustling barbeque joint downtown. Laughing as we clink mugs of beer and root beer together, our joy resounds off the walls like an anthem: *To Boston accents and baked beans! To joining the rowing team! To the best biology program in the nation!*

"He asked me about you," Brandon says later after dinner is over, and we're walking out of the restaurant.

"Who?"

Brandon pushes me a bit too hard, unaware of how much his strength has returned. "Who?" he mocks, using a high voice. "Mr. Meyers, of course."

I tense up. "What did he say?"

"Nothing, really. Just that he thinks you don't want to hear from him. Is that true?"

Brandon's words are almost as damp and cool as this spring evening in Bemidji—and all but impossible to answer. "It's complicated," I reply.

Brandon opens the door for me, and we walk along the brick-paved sidewalk toward the car, following Mom and Leo, who stroll hand in hand. Streetlamps light up the sidewalks, giving the downtown area a warm yellow glow. The smell of passing rain wafts around us, and faint laughter comes from one of the pubs up ahead.

"I figured," Brandon says. "He seemed to feel the

same way."

Later, sitting at my computer, I realize that I never read Carson's novel. So I search my emails until I find his name. There it is. Steeling myself because this might reopen old wounds, I press enter.

Time passes as I read, but my eyes stay glued to the words on the screen. The characters come alive, and I'm entranced by his story. I keep clicking to the next Chapter, again and again, even though I should get a good night's sleep since my symposium is tomorrow.

At five a.m., bleary-eyed but content, I reach the last scene of his manuscript:

Cipher stands alone. Someone calls his name. Nova, her cheeks marked with tears, approaches.

"I thought I'd lost you." She throws her arms around him, and they hold each other. Something stirs inside Cipher—something he thought was gone forever.

Nova steps back and regards him, hesitating. He moves closer, almost kissing her, but she retreats. Then it hits him: every truth Cipher has ever known can be found in the depths of Nova's ocean-blue eyes. "You could never lose me, Nova. My heart belongs to you."

Cipher prays that she returns his feelings. And when she reaches to kiss him, he meets her halfway, clinging to this moment that promises forever.

Wiping away my tears, I wonder if I'm crazy or delusional. Is Nova me and is Cipher Carson? Did he write that scene to tell me how he feels? No. It's a novel. It's fiction. And I've been wrong about Carson's feelings for me before.

Twice.

Nevertheless, I write him an email.

Dear Carson,

I read your novel. Sorry, it took me so long. But it's really, really good. I mean it.

Also, thank you for helping Brandon get into Harvard. (That sounds so lame. A million thank-yous could never express my gratitude.)

I hope it's okay that I'm emailing you. You said we had to be all or nothing, and I assume you are still in the "nothing" camp. At first, I was devastated. But now I realize it's for the best. I've been working on myself, at long last dealing with my grief and learning how to be okay on my own.

But I have no regrets about our side project—except for when you overheard me at Mel's going-away party. That was pure bravado. Carson, you never were just a place warmer. Ever since you comforted me after my father died, it's always been you. But after The B.A.I.— once, then twice—I forced myself to move on. Months ago, you asked how I feel about happily ever after. I'm still not sure they exist.

Yet, I dream that they do. Maybe one day we'll each find our way back to each other, but we both need time and freedom, right? And if we'll always be "nothing" to each other, that's okay. Just know that when I picture happily ever after, I see your face.

Love Always,

Rylee.

After sending the email, I experience a strange sort of release. I fall into bed and, for a few hours, sleep without dreaming. But soon, I must rise and prepare for my symposium.

Panic and a legit case of imposter syndrome hit me during my walk to campus. Once I'm inside the lecture hall, Professor Aldrich greets me, and her Zen attitude calms my nerves. Before long, a sizable audience has gathered. Professor Aldrich introduces me. I read from my novels, including the work-in-progress I intend to use as my thesis, which will also be published by Rendezvous Books. The audience has questions, and I talk about self-publishing, romance writing, and how I scored my publishing contract.

The whole thing goes by in a blur, and soon, I've been reading and answering questions for over an hour. "I was so shocked to get that email, and I'm still pinching myself. But now, I want to draw from my experiences and create three-dimensional characters. Yet I also plan to follow the romance tropes that readers love and expect."

"Excellent. Thank you, Rylee." Professor Aldrich beams. "That just about does it unless there are any more questions from the audience?"

"I have two questions."

My heart plunges and vaults inside my chest. I'd recognize that voice anywhere, but it comes from the back row, hidden from view. Carson stands and strides down the aisle until he's standing a few feet away from me. His wild hair is tamed, and a brown crew-neck sweater stretches over his broad chest and toned arms.

Looking at him brings vivid memories flooding back. My breath hitches, and my pulse quickens. "Okay," I choke out. I can almost smell his skin and feel his lips pressed against mine.

"First of all, congratulations on your success," Carson says. "It's well-deserved—all of your novels are amazing."

"Thank you." Do I want to laugh or cry? Is he here to congratulate me before leaving my life forever?

"What's your first question?"

Carson clears his throat. "It's about romantic tropes. Where do you stand on grand gestures?"

I hesitate for a second, confused. "I…I'm not sure what you mean."

"You once suggested I make one, though in a different context. How do you feel about grand gestures on a personal level?"

Carson and I lock gazes, neither of us moving. We used to look at each other like this—stretched out in bed together, our hearts slowing after we'd exhausted ourselves with passion.

I can't speak.

"Alright," Carson says, his voice soft like the way his touch used to be. "Let me give you an example. Say there's a man—a flawed one who made all kinds of bad choices and was a weak coward when he should've been strong. But he loves the heroine with all he has and wants to win her back." Carson smiles, but then I notice his hands tremble with nerves. "Keep in mind, he's not an enigmatic billionaire with mysterious depths or anything fancy like that. He just… He's been so afraid of storms that he didn't realize it was time to land."

"Nice metaphor."

"Thank you." Carson's eyes never leave mine. "What if I said I'd take on any storm for you? What if I pushed past my fear of conflict, tried to kiss you in front of everyone here, and gave you the chance to turn me down flat? What if I told you I love you, Rylee Lynch? Because I do. Would that be enough to secure our story's happy ending?"

"No."

Carson's face falls, but before he turns around in

defeat, I stand.

"If our story is about real, true love, it doesn't have an ending. It keeps going."

He grins in that lopsided way I know well. "Oh."

He seems stumped for words, and yet I'm sure we both have a lot more to say. "So…you've already asked me way more than two questions. But is there anything else?"

Carson's gaze scans the room, like *now* he's self-conscious that we have an audience. "Did you honestly like my novel, or were you just being nice?"

My mouth curves into a small smile. "Come on. You know I'm never 'just being nice,' not when it comes to writing. Of course I liked it. But I do have some notes that I'm happy to share—that is if you want me to be your writing partner again."

His chest rises and falls, and I can almost feel the steady beat of his heart. "Rylee, I'll be whatever kind of partner you want."

I leap off the stage, and we rush toward each other. And suddenly, finally, I am in his arms. He lifts me up, and we lock eyes before our mouths come together in a kiss.

The audience cheers, and after a moment, we pull away, laughing with joy. "I love you, Rylee."

"I love you too."

From the stage, Professor Aldrich speaks. "I can't imagine a better ending to this evening's event. I've always believed that writing fiction is akin to any romantic relationship: take chances, courageously commit, and anything is possible."

People clap some more, and then they start to file out. Carson cups my cheek in his hand. "Thank you for your email." He peers at me with the intensity of a pressure cooker.

"You're welcome." I place my hand against the warm skin of his neck. "Why are you looking at me like that?"

"So I can remember this moment."

"Our happy ending?" I tease.

He shakes his head. "No. It's like you said. Our story is just beginning, but now everything has fallen into place."

"Right."

My heart dances as I stand on my toes and lean in for a kiss, half expecting him to step away again. But no. Carson envelopes me in his strong arms and pulls me close; his soft, eager lips meet mine. Time seems to stop, and all the missed opportunities of our past bleed into one unforgettable moment.

Our happily ever after has arrived.

A word about the author...

Laurel Osterkamp is from Minneapolis, where she teaches and writes like it's going out of style. Her short fiction has been published in numerous online literary journals, and her recent novels include Just Like the Brontë Sisters, Favorite Daughters, and Beautiful Little Furies. When she's not writing, you can find her visiting MN state parks with her husband and two disgruntled teenagers, petting her cats, or going for runs while listening to audiobooks. The Side Project is her first romance and her first novel with Wild Rose Press.

www.laurellit.com

Acknowledgements:

Many thanks to all my Beta Readers, including Shauna Slade, Lynn Osterkamp, Allan Press, Pamela Stine, Penny O'Shea, Pamela Stine, Gail Olmsted, Shari Presnell, Dawn Wilmouth-Wilson, Elaine Casey, Melissa Steadman, Karen, Amanda Waters, Sue Dawson, Marlys Frisby, Gillian Simpson, and Angie Kuhnle. Your guidance and feedback was invaluable.

Many thanks to The Wild Rose Press and Ally Robertson for believing in and publishing *The Side Project*. Most especially, thanks to my editor, Najla Mahis, for her amazing guidance, encouragement, and for helping me grow as a writer.

Thank you for purchasing
this publication of The Wild Rose Press, Inc.

For questions or more information
contact us at
info@thewildrosepress.com.

The Wild Rose Press, Inc.
www.thewildrosepress.com

Printed in the USA
CPSIA information can be obtained
at www.ICGtesting.com
JSHW011053181024
71745JS00001B/2

9 781509 257751